Jayhawk

For Jolene —
Much happiness!
Dorothy Keddington

Jayhawk

Dorothy M. Keddington

SKYBIRD PUBLISHERS

9025 Chablis Circle • Sandy, Utah 84092 • (801) 571-4599 • (801) 572-0028

ISBN: 0-913420-80-8
Library of Congress Catalog Number:
78-13429

TO MY
HUSBAND

Foreword

The sharp bang of a screen door rattled the early morning stillness and roused Jason from a sound sleep. Who would be up this early? he wondered. Raising himself on one elbow in the bed, he could barely make out the hands of the alarm clock which stood on a small bureau. Four o'clock. It wouldn't be time to feed the stock and do the milking for over an hour. He turned over with a weary sigh and pulled the blankets up around his chin. A short time later, the hollow clop of a horse's hooves moving over hard ground tripped into the peaceful pattern of his early sleep. Jason's young, muscular body grew tense as he listened. Someone was not only up and around, but apparently going for a ride. Now what could be so fascinating at four o'clock in the morning?

Jason eased himself over to the side of the bed, then slid off slowly so the springs wouldn't squeak too much and awaken his wife. Even so, the old bed groaned disgustingly with the change of weight. Jason glanced swiftly at his wife. The dark eyes were closed and her soft breathing undisturbed. He studied her sleeping form with pleasure. Masses of blue-black hair framed her small face. Hair like ravens' wings shining in the sun, he'd thought when he saw her for the first time. Then his eyes traveled down to the large swell under the blankets. Jason smiled softly. It would be a son. He felt sure of it. Maybe because she had told him so often, he believed it himself now. Her time was very near. Jason's smile faded as he realized that his son would not be born on the ranch like father and grandfather before him. But did it really matter? Whether he takes his first breath in a hospital or a wagon, my son is more important than the whole damn ranch! Jason thought fiercely, and smiled once more. Still smiling, he pulled his pants over his pajamas, pushed his bare feet into his boots and left the bunkhouse.

Outside, Jason peered at the thin gray sky and shivered. He didn't like it somehow, even though cold May mornings were commonplace in Wyoming. His deep-set eyes made a quick inspection of the grounds. No one was around the barn or corrals, and up at the big stone house all was quiet. That house was very much like the morning, he decided. Cold and gray and bitter.

He was about to go back into the bunkhouse, thinking he must have been mistaken about someone leaving, when a soft whinny ruffled the air. Turning toward the sound, Jason saw a rider and his mount making their way up the ridge trail.

"Now where in the name of heaven does he think he's going?" Jason muttered, staring through the half-light at the departing figure.

I think I'll follow along and find out what this morning ride's all about. He hasn't much lead on me and he'll probably pace his horse pretty slow 'till he gets out of earshot from the ranch, thought Jason as he went back inside.

He made an effort not to clomp with his boots as he moved across the linoleum floor of the main room to a high-backed chair hewn of rough pine. His shirt and buckskin jacket were draped across the back and his hat lay on the seat where he had tossed it the night before. They were cold to the touch.

Maybe I'd better get a fire going in the stove before I leave, he thought as he finished dressing, then reconsidered. Besides making too much noise, it would give that scoundrel too big a lead. He'd have to take care of the fire when he got back.

Jason went to the door and turned the knob soundlessly, then glanced over his left shoulder into the bedroom where his wife lay sleeping. She stirred slightly as he watched, one small, calloused hand coming round her swollen abdomen in a protective gesture.

"Take care of our little son," he whispered without really knowing why, then hurried out into the gray dawn.

Chapter 1

"somewhere I have never travelled, gladly beyond any experience . . . ."

e. e. cummings

I was the only passenger for Dusk. The driver pulled two, large brown suitcases from the storage area beneath the bus and I barely had time to check the tags, making sure they read: Angela Stewart—Ann Arbor, Michigan, before he deposited them at my feet with a nondescript grunt. I murmured a "thank you" to his back as he boarded the bus and took his place behind the wheel all in one swift movement. The bus moved on with an impatient roar.

To arrive at Dusk at dusk sounded a little absurd but whoever had given the little Wyoming town its name must have done so at such a moment. The western sky still throbbed with color, a vivid gash of gold cutting into its jagged horizon where the sun had just fallen behind purple hills. Hovering over the hot gold was a soft mantle of mauve. Before my eyes it seemed to tremble and pulsate under evening's massive blue curtain. I turned away from the glories of the sunset and looked about with excited, eager eyes.

One wide, main street ran the entire length of the town with businesses scattered at random on both sides. Most of the buildings were white-frame with one or two boasting red brick fronts. Beyond the business district, the residential area spread itself out in leisurely fashion, with many of the homes nestling beneath towering old cottonwoods and pines. To me, the town's most distinguishing feature was its contented silence.

The air was decidedly cool for the middle of June. I shivered and tried to dismiss a sudden feeling of loneliness. Soon I would be with Janet and her family; that is, I would be as soon as they learned of my arrival. I had planned to call the Bradfords directly from the bus depot, but a torn blind was pulled down over the door of the small frame building and a lop-eared sign pronounced in plain black letters: CLOSED. It was quite obvious that I would have to go elsewhere to find a telephone. But where?

The only establishment in town which appeared to be open for business was "Nick's Bar." Several cars were parked in front of the red brick building and jutting out from the roof was a garish neon sign which blinked on and off spasmodically.

I looked to my left where railroad tracks bisected the main street. Across the tracks, the road changed from asphalt to gravel and led to scattered residences. Behind any door should be someone who knew the Bradfords. There couldn't be many strangers in a town of barely five hundred people. All I had to do was gather my nerve and my suitcases and hope for a telephone and a little Western hospitality.

I stepped westward across the railroad tracks and it was then I saw the narrow gravel road for the first time. My heart thumped heavily as I gazed down the furrowed lane and every blessed chuckhole seemed suddenly familiar. I could almost hear Janet's voice saying, "The ranch isn't too far from town. You go along an old gravel road by the tracks to get to it. The road is pretty bad until you get around the first bend, but after that the way is really lovely—especially where the road follows the river."

Why should I wait in town for the Bradfords to come after me when I could easily walk out to the ranch and surprise them? I really didn't want to ask a stranger for the use of his telephone. Especially when walking out to the ranch would complete the surprise of my early arrival and save the Bradfords the trouble of driving in to Dusk to get me.

Down the gravel road, the subtle brown curve which swung away from the railroad tracks beckoned. With a smile, I answered its call.

Around the bend, the way was every bit as lovely as Janet had said. The roadside weeds of the town gave way to orderly fields of alfalfa encrusted with golden blooms of mustard. Not too far ahead, I detected the silky movement of a stream running fairly close to the road. The two traveled side by side for a short piece, then disappeared to the right behind a dense woodlot which blocked my view of what lay ahead. I shifted the weight of my luggage and walked on, hoping my first glimpse of the Triple J Ranch would be just around the next bend. I wondered if I would find the ranch as marvelous as Janet had said it was.

Everything was marvelous or wonderful to Janet Bradford. Perhaps the openness of this country was the source of her carefree spirit. As we shared a dormitory room at Michigan State University, she was always bubbling about something and took special delight in acquainting me with the life histories of her parents, grandfather and four brothers—not to mention the name and genesis of each horse and cow on the Triple J Ranch.

It wasn't long before I was completely caught up in her enthusiasm for the ranch and thoughts of spending another summer in Ann Arbor became positively morbid. When Janet invited me to spend the summer on the

Triple J, I thrilled as Wordsworth must have when he wrote: " . . . stepping westward seemed to be a kind of heavenly destiny."

Mother couldn't understand why a 20-year old girl wanted to go to some "queer place out West called 'Dust,' " when the two of us could visit Aunt Mildred in New York. How could I explain to her why a ranch I had never seen should mean so much to me when I really didn't understand it myself?

The shrill cry of a night bird flying overhead broke into my thoughts as I made a somewhat staggering approach to the brush and tree bordered curve in the road. Just now, "stepping westward" wasn't nearly as "heavenly" as Wordsworth made it out to be. But then, he probably wasn't lugging two heavy suitcases along a bumpy gravel road. With a sigh, I renewed my grip on the luggage and forced my feet on around the bend. Suddenly, my feet refused to carry me any farther. To second the motion, my hands released their hold on the luggage and both pieces dropped to the ground with a dusty thud.

There it was, a brown thread of a road stitching through endless fields of alfalfa and grazing land. Far ahead in the blue-gray twilight, it dipped secretly down into a grove of cottonwoods and was once more lost to view.

I was much too tired to cry and too disappointed to laugh at my foolishness. That Janet and I had opposing definitions of the phrase, 'not too far' was obvious, and even if I weren't so tired, I had no idea how long it would take me to walk to the ranchhouse—that is, if this really were the road to the Triple J. I swallowed hard as a little twinge of fear pricked my spine. It was too late now for thoughts like that. The only sensible thing to do was walk back into town and telephone the Bradfords—which was what I should have done in the first place. At least, there was some consolation in the fact they would never know what I had done. But thinking of the long trek back to town was almost more discouraging than not finding the ranch. I collapsed on top of the luggage and kicked off my shoes. I couldn't start back without a short rest, and since no one knew I had arrived, it certainly wouldn't matter if I remained here a few minutes more.

I'm not sure how long I sat there, watching stars appear one by one, listening to the murmuring of the stream mingled with the breathy whispers of cottonwoods and river willows. All around me, the singing sentences of crickets punctuated the air.

Then, suddenly, I was aware of a new sound interrupting the conversations of the night. As it grew louder, I recognized the gutteral grumblings of a motor coming from somewhere around the other side of the curve. Judging from the various thumps, shakes and rattles which accompanied the vehicle, it was traveling with considerable speed.

I hauled myself off the luggage, forced my feet into my shoes and glanced up—just in time to see a huge truck charge around the curve, heading straight for me like an enraged bull. The unblinking stare of its headlights was almost hypnotizing and for one terrifying moment I couldn't move. Then, flinging my arms in front of my face to cut out the angry white glare, I willed my legs into action. They stumbled back two steps—right into the luggage. I lost my balance completely and went sprawling backwards into the stream.

The driver must have seen me at the last moment because the truck made a violent swerve to the right, thundered off the road and crashed into the brush. I saw this as I struggled to my feet, sputtering and gasping for breath. I took a step toward the bank and nearly toppled over again. I heard the truck door slam. Wiping hair and water from my eyes, I looked up to see someone running toward me.

"Are you hurt?" came a voice.

"N-no. Just cold and wet."

A tall man somewhere in his mid-twenties reached the bank and stared anxiously at me through the gloom.

"You're sure you're all right?"

"Yes. Yes, I think so."

"Then would you mind telling me what the hell you were doing in the middle of the road? You might have been killed!"

Anger pumped sudden warmth into my chilled body as I glared up at the black-haired giant who had nearly run over me. Judging from my own five feet eight inches, he had to be well over six feet, and he had the neck and shoulders of a young bull.

"I was not in the middle of the road!" I flung back at him. "And if you hadn't come around the bend like a wild—achoo!—a wild Indian, this never would have happened!" My reproach was made somewhat ineffective by the sneeze, but he stiffened suddenly as if I had struck him. There was a moment's silence between us, then he said:

"If you're not hurt, why don't you come out of that stream? You must be freezing."

I wiped a strand of dripping hair out of my eyes. "I'd like to, but thanks to you, my suit is so water-logged and my knees are so shaky I can't walk!"

A smile touched his lips and he said, not ungently, "Give me your hand."

I ignored the tone and shot him another scorching look. I didn't want to stop being angry just yet. I bent down and made a fumbling attempt to wring out my skirt.

"Are you going to give me your hand or would you rather stand in that creek all night?" he said, leaning over to stretch out his arm. I gave an exasperated sigh and took his offered hand. His grip was firm and hard. The

4

bottom of the stream was soft and muddy. As a result, I stepped right out of my shoes and mud oozed over my feet past the ankles.

"Wait! I've lost my shoes!"

"Well, reach down and get them."

I thought of the crawling things that must lurk in the muddy bottom of the stream and said miserably, "I can't."

He let go my hand and before I had time to think what he might do, he was beside me in the water, calmly groping around for my shoes. He pulled one, then the other out of the mud and handed them to me. I felt so ridiculous I didn't dare look up into his face.

"You better take them before a fish bites your foot," he said dryly, and that same moment something wriggled against my legs. I gave a little scream and grabbed hold of his arm.

"Something touched me!"

"Careful, or we'll both go under!" he said with a laugh.

I looked into his eyes for the first time and felt their sooty warmth waken a like temperature in me. We could just as easily have been standing in a warm tropical pool. Then I sneezed. That one sneeze set off a chain reaction which would have resulted in another crash landing in the stream if his arms hadn't held me. The next instant I was swooped up, muddy shoes and all, and carried out of the water. Just as abruptly, he put me down and before I could utter a word, vanished into the shadows as silently as a cat. I could only assume he had gone for the truck and a moment later the throaty roar of the engine startled the crickets into silence.

As the truck emerged from its camouflage of brush, I saw that it wasn't nearly so monstrous as I had thought, meeting it head-on. A few bridles were tied to the wooden, fence-like sides and from the unmistakable aroma wafting on the air, there must have been a goodly portion of manure as well as hay strewn about in the back. The truck came part way onto the road, then the tall young man jumped down from the driver's side, leaving the motor running, and came around to where I stood.

"Before I get this thing pointed in the wrong direction, maybe you'd better tell me where you want to go," he said.

"Go? Oh, y-yes," I said, trying to keep my teeth from chattering. "Do you think you c-could take me to the Bradford's ranch?"

Even the near-darkness couldn't hide the look he gave me. "Is that where you were headed? The Triple J?"

I nodded, hugging myself to keep warm. "Isn't this the right road?"

"Yes, it's the right road, but the ranchhouse is some fifteen miles from here."

It was my turn to gape at him. "Fifteen miles! Janet told me the ranch wasn't far from town. I had no idea that meant fifteen m-miles!"

He gave me a sympathetic grin. "You must be Angela. The Bradfords weren't expecting you until tomorrow."

"Yes, I know," I sighed, then shivered.

"Look, we've got a good forty minute ride ahead of us, and that ought to be plenty long enough for introductions and explanations. Right now, you've got to get out of those wet clothes. You've got something in those suitcases you could put on, haven't you?"

"Y-yes, but—"

"You can change in the cab of the truck," he said matter-of-factly and walked over to where my suitcases lay abandoned in the dust. He brought them to the truck and set them down in the back. "Take what you need, but be quick about it. I'd hate to see you spending your summer vacation in bed with pneumonia."

I was too cold to argue and there was really no need. What he said made sense, and at this point I think I would have changed clothes in the bushes. I took my sneakers and socks and a pair of corduroy slacks out of one case, a sweater and a scarf from the other, then snapped the lids shut.

"I'll only be a minute," I told him.

He followed me around the other side of the truck and opened the door. I tried to step up to the running board, but with my arms full of clothing and wearing a skirt that was little more than a sodden dishrag, the whole attempt was sheer slapstick.

"Let me help," he said and with both hands on my waist, boosted me up to the running board. I climbed inside and he shut the door after me. "Call me when you're ready."

I peered through the gloom at his dark face and deep-set eyes. "What do I call you? I mean, you know who I am but—"

"I'm Jay—" he began, then stopped short, giving me a close look. "I'm Jay Bradford, Janet's cousin," he finished hurriedly and walked away.

Chapter 2

". . . . I did hear
The galloping of horse: who was't came by?"
William Shakespeare

Evening was moving deeply into night. We had been traveling perhaps twenty minutes and I still wasn't able to reason why Jay Bradford's name should sound so familiar to me. If Janet had been the one to mention her cousin's name I wouldn't have given the matter a second thought, but I was quite sure she hadn't. For one thing, in all her ramblings about relatives she had never even hinted that her father had a brother. But if Jay Bradford weren't Janet's cousin, how could he have known who I was and when the Bradfords were expecting me? Perhaps Janet had purposely omitted his name from our conversations. But for what reason?

I took a breath and tried to turn off my thoughts. They were getting far too complicated. Just because Janet had a tendency to rattle on where her family was concerned didn't mean she couldn't forget a few second or third cousins. If the name Jay Bradford still sounded tantalizingly familiar, there had to be some explanation for it. If I couldn't think of one now, perhaps it would come to me later.

As my thoughts cleared, my brain finally registered what my eyes were seeing—charcoal sky, ebony hills, and dusky clumps of trees. I casually shifted my position on the seat so I could see the face of the man beside me. The lights on the dashboard illuminated his slightly jutting chin and wide, full mouth. His high cheekbones were accentuated by the shadows which cut across them and blackness masked his eyes. He had the sensuous, brooding looks of a modern-day Heathcliff and I thought, one doesn't see a face like his and then forget it. Why then, was it so difficult for me to remember where I had heard his name?

"You're very quiet," Jay Bradford said suddenly, and I wondered if he had been watching me watch him.

7

"I know," I admitted. "It's one of my faults, I guess."

He smiled. "Then it's one of my faults, too. I haven't even asked you how you enjoyed your trip out West."

"Oh, it was fine. The only thing I didn't like was not being able to stop when there was something I wanted to see."

"What did you want to see?"

I looked at him and smiled faintly. "A field of wild-flowers. I suppose that sounds silly. Actually, I could see it very well from the window, but that isn't the same as getting out and walking through the field and smelling the flowers."

"I know what you mean. Driving past something and never stopping is so impersonal. When you stop and take the time to just stand there—feel the personality of a place—then it means something."

"Yes, it does," I murmured in agreement.

Neither of us made any effort at continuing the conversation but the silence between us was not uncomfortable. I watched the road expose its brown curves under the penetrating glare of the headlights, amazed that I was able to feel so at ease with a man who was little more than a stranger. Then the headlights caught the wild, confused leaps of a rabbit as it darted into the path of the truck. Jay Bradford braked sharply.

"Did we hit it?" I asked.

"No, there he goes," Jay said, pointing to a soft curve of brown fur leaping into the safety of some tall brush on the other side of the road. My breath came out in a relieved sigh.

"Headlights really throw rabbits into a panic," Jay said.

"I know just how they feel."

He looked at me and his jaw tightened. "Yes, I guess you do. I'm sorry about what happened."

"It was just an accident."

His dark brows narrowed into a frown. "An accident which never would have happened if I hadn't come around the bend like a 'wild Indian.'"

Remembering my angry words brought warmth to my cheeks. "Well, I'm none the worse for my dunking—except for my suit. It will never be the same, I'm afraid."

"A suit of clothes is one thing. A life is quite another," Jay said. "And I doubt whether Janet and her parents will be as forgiving as you. What kind of logical explanation can I give them for what happened?"

I smiled at him. "For that matter, what kind of logical explanation can Janet's idiot friend give for traipsing off on a fifteen mile hike at twilight?"

He laughed and it was wonderful how laughter changed his face. Something warm began stirring inside me. I forced my gaze back to the road.

Ahead of us, it ran straight and smooth as far as the headlights illuminated. Then, a great black clump of trees loomed into view on my right. From the core of the blackness I saw an orange sliver of light spit at the truck and heard a sharp crack. That same instant a headlight exploded and suddenly, the truck was one-eyed.

I glanced at Jay Bradford in bewilderment and he yelled roughly for me to get down. I had no time to question why. His fingers found my neck and shoved my head into his lap, then he sunk his foot into the gas pedal. The truck surged ahead as another sharp crack split the air, then lurched wildly, like an animal in pain, and knew a tire had burst.

I was pinned in Jay's lap, my head crushed against his right thigh, while he fought for control of the truck. Twice, as he wrestled with the steering wheel, his elbow stabbed into my back and I winced with pain.

Finally, the jolting and swerving stopped and the truck slowed to a limping halt. Jay cut the engine and switched off the lights. I felt his stomach muscles relax against me, even though his breathing was slightly ragged. I ducked out from under his arms and sat up, waiting for him to explain what had happened. He didn't look at me, just slowly unclenched his fingers from the steering wheel. I waited a moment more then asked, "Please! Won't you tell me what happened?"

"Shhh! Listen!" he whispered.

I held my breath and stared out into the darkness. All I could see were black fields and swaying trees. All I could hear was the sound of my own heart thudding heavily. Then I realized there was another sound, rhythmic and thudding, almost like my heart but growing more faint as I listened. I stared at Jay Bradford with eyes that were wide and tight with fear.

"He's gone," was all he said.

My mouth had gone so dry I had to swallow and moisten my lips before I could speak. "You mean—someone was shooting at us?"

"Not at us—at the truck."

"But why? Why would someone do that?"

"Angela," he said softly, "I know that I have to explain a few things, but first you've got to promise me you won't mention any of this to the Bradfords. They mustn't find out what just happened!"

My jaw would have dropped to the floor if my lap hadn't been in the way. "Not mention it?"

"I know it sounds crazy, but I have a reason for asking. Please! Just trust me."

For a full minute I could do nothing except stare at him. Of all the ridiculous clichés! Please. Just trust me. I tried to speak but my throat was too dry and constricted. Tears began welling up in my eyes, then spilled down my cheeks before I could blink them back. I lowered my head, hoping he wouldn't notice I was crying.

Jay Bradford reached over and put something in my lap. His handkerchief. I dabbed at my eyes and still the tears came. His fingers pressed my shoulder. I looked into his face but it was too dark to see anything more than a fuzzy outline.

"I don't usually cry like this—I'm sorry."

"It's all right," he said. "Feeling any better now?"

I nodded and blew my nose.

"Back there, after the shots were fired—" He paused and the warm pressure of his fingers tightened a little. "I'm afraid I hurt you."

"Well, yes—a little," I admitted, aware of the painful throb in the middle of my back. Jay slouched down in the seat and I added quickly, "But please, don't apologize for that. I'm just grateful you were able to control the truck."

"You're an amazing girl, Angela Stewart," he said in a husky tone. "I've given you one hell of a night and you ask me not to apologize."

I clutched his handkerchief a little tighter and looked down at my lap. "Why don't you want the Bradfords to know what happened?" I asked him.

He sighed and rapped his knuckles on the steering wheel. "Because what happened back there concerns me—not them!"

"But they're your family! If you're in some kind of trouble I'm sure they would want to know. Perhaps they could help."

"I'm afraid not," Jay said in a tight voice.

I knew he was worried, but more than that, I sensed he was alone—terribly alone. "You asked me to trust you," I began hesitantly, then took a quick breath. "I'm not sure why, but I do. If it will help, I promise I won't say anything to the Bradfords."

Jay straightened up slowly. Although I couldn't see his features, relief and sheer wonder were visible in his posture. "Like I said before, you're an amazing girl," he murmured. The next moment his voice was matter-of-fact. "Well, we can't sit here all night. I've got to get you to the ranch." He opened the truck door and jumped down to the ground.

"Do you have a flashlight?" I called after him. "It's so dark I don't see how you'll be able to change the tire without some kind of light."

At my words Jay stopped dead and swore under his breath.

I slid over to the driver's side and stepped down to the running board. "Is something wrong?"

"You might say that," he muttered and turned back to face me. The small light inside the cab was more than ample in revealing the anger blazing in his eyes. "I drove into town tonight because John—Janet's father—wanted the spare tire for the truck repaired. The service station was closing when I got there, but the guy took the tire anyway and said I could pick it up in the morning."

I looked at his dark face and tried a smile. "What you're trying to tell me is that we're going to have to walk the rest of the way. Right?"

"Look, if you're too tired you can wait here. I'll walk out to the ranch and get a car, then come back for you."

"How much farther is it from here to the ranchhouse?"

He looked at me closely. "About two miles."

"Then I'm coming with you. Besides, even if the ranchhouse were ten miles away, I think I'd still rather walk than wait here alone."

"Are you sure? You've already had a pretty rugged evening."

I shook my head and sat down on the running board with a nervous laugh. "You know I can't believe it. I really can't believe it!"

"Can't believe what?"

"Any of this—that it all happened! There's been so much in so short a time—" I stopped short as more tears suddenly blurred my vision. I swallowed hard and wiped my eyes with my hand.

Jay leaned one arm against the side of the truck and looked down at me. The wind had blown his dark hair across his forehead and he seemed more than ever like Brontë's stormy Heathcliff.

"If you hadn't come a day early, none of this would have happened," he said.

"It wouldn't have happened to me, but there still would have been someone waiting for you in that clump of trees."

Jay considered this in silence then turned away, saying over his shoulder, "I'll go get your luggage."

I went back inside the cab for my purse then climbed out and shut the heavy metal door behind me. Jay appeared out of the blackness, a suitcase in each hand.

"Ready?" he asked.

I gave him a nod and a tremulous smile. He made no move, just stood silently for a moment. Then he said in his quiet, husky voice: "Are you sorry you came early?"

"No," I answered truthfully. "I'm not sorry."

Then we were off, leaving the truck to sulk alone on the shoulder of the road.

Chapter 3

"He is gone on the mountain
He is lost to the forest,
Like a summer-dried fountain
When our need was the sorest."
Sir Walter Scott

As we walked the silent black road, my ears were listening for hoofbeats on every breath of wind. Janet's cousin moved forward through the darkness as if he had his own private radar while my unsure, plopping steps were almost laughable.

Thus far, Jay Bradford and I had exchanged very few words and although I was anxious to hear his explanation, I didn't want to ask for it. I had promised to trust him and somehow, I felt that included letting him be the judge of what I needed to know and when. Instead of permitting my mind to manufacture wild questions that would only heighten the fear I was already battling, I forced myself to concentrate on our surroundings. I had never been anywhere at night where there were no lights whatsoever, and I had expected total darkness out here. Instead, the mountains and hills stood stiffly against the blue-black sky like crisp cardboard cutouts and there was a sharp delineation of trees and other foliage against the wandering land.

I tilted my head back to gaze at the night sky and said, "You know, I can't ever remember seeing so many stars. Wyoming must rustle some from other states."

Jay gave a low chuckle. "You're going to get a stiff neck if you walk that way very long."

The next moment my star gazing came to an abrupt end as my left foot struck a rock. I staggered forward, arms outstretched, and Jay let a suitcase fall in order to grab my arm.

"Are you all right?" he asked with a smile in his voice.

I should be writhing with embarrassment right now, I thought. Instead, I laughed and told him, "Yes, I'm fine."

Jay's tousled black head bent closer and he said with sudden urgency, "You haven't asked me to explain anything yet. Why?"

"I was just waiting for you to tell me what you think I should know."

"Do you really trust me that much?" His voice was so full of wonder that I was suddenly too embarrassed to answer. Before I could try, he released my arm and stooped down for the fallen suitcase, saying brusquely, "Nevermind. You don't have to answer that."

We started walking again and after a few moments Jay asked casually, "Has Janet ever mentioned me to you?"

"No. Never."

"Or anything about my father?"

I shook my head. "I'm sorry. She talks about her family quite a lot, but—"

"There's nothing for you to be sorry about. Janet had her reasons for not mentioning either of us. I haven't lived at the ranch for some time—my last visit was over two years ago. As for my father, no one has seen or heard from him for twenty-six years."

I stared at Jay. "No one? Not even you?"

"I've never seen my father. He disappeared about a week before I was born." He spoke with the callousness that time brings, but I sensed the wounds had far from healed. I stretched out my hand and touched his arm lightly.

"I'm sorry. It must have been terrible for you all these years." He said nothing and I went on haltingly. "It's hard to lose one's father as a child—but to never have had the memory of him at all—that would be much worse, I think."

Jay glanced at me and I noticed his features were clearer now than they had been a few minutes before. It was as if his face were slowly coming into focus.

"Why do you think that?" he asked.

"I—well, my father died when I was four," I told him in a low voice.

He said, "Oh," in a gentle sort of way, then, "How did he die?"

"In an automobile accident. A head-on. The other driver had fallen asleep at the wheel. Of course, I didn't know all this at the time. Mother saved the clippings and I read them years later. She thought I should know how it happened."

"I admire your mother for that," Jay said. "Because you know what happened to your father, you're better able to accept such a loss and adjust to it."

"I suppose that's true. I've never thought about it in that way before." I looked down at our feet, plodding along in a steady one-two rhythm. "You make me feel a little ashamed," I said quietly.

"I do? Why?"

"Because I've never understood my mother's reasons for saving those

13

clippings until now. I just thought she was being morbidly sentimental about the whole thing. I never thought that knowing what happened was important at all."

"Not knowing—trying to live your life without the whys and the hows—is plain hell," he said, and the pain in his voice was as real as the throb of a burn.

A long stretch of road was covered in aching silence before either of us spoke again, then Jay said, "You were so young when your father died. Do you remember much about him?"

"Not too much. Just a few impressions, really. I remember his hands, how large they were, yet so gentle. And I remember that he called me 'Angel' instead of Angela."

Jay's lips parted in a wide-curved smile and I glanced away, suddenly embarrassed for having revealed so much about myself to a stranger. I rarely talked about my father, even with close friends, and now I was disclosing intimate childhood recollections to someone I barely knew.

"It's getting lighter, isn't it?" I commented, trying to throw off some of my self-consciousness.

"The moon will be up soon and it's nearing the full," Jay said. "It'll be easier walking then."

"How far are we from the ranchhouse?"

"Less than a mile, and there's still a lot you should know before we reach it."

I shot him a swift look but his dark face was intent on the road before us. "There's a gulley up ahead," he told me, "and I was thinking it might be a good place to rest for a few minutes. It's warmer down there and we'll be sheltered from the wind."

I could see the gulley now, looking like a thick black dent in the hillside. As we approached the rim Jay mumbled a brief, "Careful now." His words were hardly necessary for the road tumbled down into the hollow with an abruptness that demanded caution. At the bottom of the gulley, the road grasped the aged timbers of a narrow wooden bridge. The uneven planking showed plainly, even in the darkness, like toothless gaps in the bridge's mouth.

"Is it safe?" I asked.

"If you mean the bridge, yes," Jay answered. "It's old, but solid enough. The road on the other side is more dangerous. It goes sideways down the gulley through that line of maple trees, then makes a sudden turn onto the bridge. In times past, a few cars have landed in the creek trying to make that turn. It's especially bad in winter."

But now, the heart of the gulley was a delightful place. River birch, willows, and cottonwoods caught the chill of the sweeping night air in their

14

lofty branches and cradled it with a whispery lullaby until the breeze was only a contented sigh. Mint must have grown along the banks of the stream, for the air was kissed with its spicy aroma. The stream seemed only half-awake, muttering sleepy gurgles as it moved along.

Jay set my luggage on the edge of the road and guided me to a grassy spot adjacent to the bridge. As we seated ourselves, the moon floated over the tops of the trees with startling whiteness. Its opalescence turned the creek into milk and bleached the timbers of the old bridge. "I'm glad you suggested that we rest here," I said, taking a deep breath of the fragrant night air. "It's so lovely, and I'm more tired than I realized."

"Maybe you won't mind listening to a long story then," Jay said, looking out over the water.

My lips were open to make some reply when a sharp twinge of apprehension went through me. I couldn't help thinking that it might be safer for both of us if I were told nothing at all. There was still no reason why I should mention any of this to the Bradfords. I could just forget about the two wild shots fired at the truck tonight and stay silent—strictly on the outside.

Jay's eyes shifted from the moon-washed stream to my face, and it was almost as if he knew my thoughts. "If you'd rather not get involved any deeper, I'll understand."

Something in his lonely black eyes cut through my fear and left me with a feeling of shame instead. I had always detested people who avoided unpleasant situations because they didn't want to get involved, and now I was doing that very thing.

"I want to hear it," I told him firmly.

A small spark of a smile lit his eyes before they returned to the stream. He took a long breath and said, "The shooting incident tonight is a direct result of my father's disappearance, so I guess I'd better begin with that. I really don't know too much except, twenty-six years ago on the night of May 15, my father was here at the ranch and the next morning he was gone. All he had with him were the clothes on his back. According to the reports I've read, the sheriff organized a search party and this whole area was gone over. The search lasted for several months off and on, and was finally abandoned. Nothing was found. Not one blasted thing! As a result, people stopped thinking something happened to my father and just assumed that he deserted my mother."

My hands fell into my lap with sudden decision. "I don't think he left your mother! Especially that late in her pregnancy."

Jay's dark brows lifted. "You sound awfully sure about that. For all you know, my father could have been a drunken bum."

My spine straightened and I said defensively, "Your father could have

15

been a lot of things—good and bad. Is it so terrible to want to believe that he didn't leave your mother?"

A look of surprise caught his somber features unaware. "No, it's not terrible. I guess I don't understand why you should want to believe in him."

"I—I don't know why, exactly. It's just a feeling I have."

Jay smiled a little. "Well, I'm certainly not one to dispute a woman's feelings."

I looked down at my hands, nervously twisting a blade of grass around one index finger. "What about your mother's feelings? Did she believe your father left her?"

"No. She refused to consider desertion as even a remote possibility. Something inside her never stopped believing he would come back."

"It must be wonderful to have that kind of faith in the one you love," I said.

Jay answered me with bitterness in his voice. "Not so wonderful when nothing comes of that faith except emptiness. What good did it do her to keep on believing? She died without an answer as to why he left."

"When?" My voice caught on the word and I asked softly, "When did she die?"

"A long time ago. I was eight years old." His eyes pierced the darkness with a bleak expression and I had the strongest feeling he was seeing another time and another place.

"We used to go riding together nearly every day," Jay said quietly, as if he were talking to himself. "Mother never bothered with a saddle—said she liked the feel of the horse beneath her rather than hard leather. She could ride as well as any man—even better than most because she had a special feeling for horses."

A smile formed on my lips and faded all in the same moment as I watched Jay's face and jaw grow rigid with a kind of horror.

"One afternoon we rode farther than usual and she was worried about getting back in time to fix supper. It would have been all right if we hadn't run the horses. Hers stumbled and rolled on her. If she had been thrown it might have been better, I don't know. I wanted to go for help, but Mother begged me not to leave her. I knelt down beside her and all I could think was: 'she won't die because my father isn't here. She said he would come back, so she can't die now!' "

Jay took a breath and I thought, I shouldn't let him go on. Why is he telling me this? I've got to tell him to stop. But I didn't. Looking at the raw pain in his face, I knew he hadn't planned to tell me the details of his mother's death any more than I had planned to hear them.

"I did my best to shade her from the sun and brush away the flies," he went on, "but she was in too much pain to know what I was doing. I didn't think I could stand watching her suffer any longer when suddenly she looked at me and said, 'Don't forget your father! He didn't forget us! Promise me—you won't forget him!'

"I think I nodded. I'm not sure. I kept insisting that she couldn't die because he wasn't there. Then she smiled and looked somewhere beyond me. Her eyes lit up and she said his name. I jumped up and glanced around, half expecting to see my father come riding across the desert at full gallop—but he wasn't there. When I looked back at my mother, she was dead."

I clasped my hands tightly together and stared out over the water, not knowing what to say and wishing my throat didn't ache so. After a moment, I heard him take a deep breath and his shoulders straightened with a brisk shrug.

"Don't look so sad," he said, managing a half-hearted smile. "It happened a long time ago."

I wondered if he were trying to convince himself or me. Then I saw that some of the agony had left his face and the ache in my throat subsided.

"What happened to you after your mother died?"

"About a month after the accident, my grandfather sent for me. He was my closest relative, so I had no choice but to come to the Triple J and live with him."

"Didn't you want to come?"

Jay picked up a smooth stone and flung it at the peaceful creek. "I didn't want anything to do with my grandfather or his ranch, simply because he was my father's father. Maybe that sounds unreasonable to you, but at the time, that was more than enough reason to hate him." His husky voice deepened. "When something happens—something that hurts you down deep, you need someone to blame for it. At least, I did and my father seemed the logical one to pick. I blamed him for my mother's death and hated him with everything in me. I guess that hatred sort of spread itself out to my father's family and the Triple J Ranch."

"Grief can express itself in anger and hatred as well as tears," I said quietly.

Jay looked at me and rubbed his chin with his hand. "I suppose that's true," he conceded, "because as years passed, my feelings for the ranch did change. The Triple J was my birthplace. John and Helen were more than fair to me, and I had to admit that I felt love for them and the ranch in spite of my outward bitterness. Even so, I left the ranch when I was eighteen. Being away from Dusk made it easier to forget . . ."

I was wondering why Jay mentioned only Janet's parents and not his grandfather, when he said, "About a month ago, my past suddenly caught up with me."

17

I saw the dark glimmer of excitement in his eyes, heard the pulse of it in his voice and asked quickly, "Caught up with you? How?"

He grinned. "In the form of an old rancher named Parley Evans. He has a large ranch just south of Lander. My folks worked for him years ago. They met for the first time at his place, in fact."

My mind rushed ahead of his words with a wild hope. "Jay—did Parley Evans tell you—does he know—?"

"What happened to my father? No. That's for me to find out. But he does know what didn't happen!" Jay turned so that he faced me and our knees touched slightly. "Angela, my dad didn't leave her. For the first time in my life, I can say that and know it's true."

A shiver of excitement and gladness ran through me. "How did Mr. Evans find this out? Does he have some sort of proof?"

"There were letters."

"From your father!"

Jay smiled a little, most likely at the concern and eagerness in my voice. Somehow, I didn't mind at all.

"Yes, from my father. But I'd better explain how he and Evans met up in the first place or you won't understand how it all ties in. I'll try not to make it too long. Do you mind?"

"Of course not!"

"Well, as I mentioned before, Parley Evans has quite a spread south of Lander. He's not what you'd call a cattle baron, but he does all right for himself. Years ago, he was in Rock Springs for a horse sale and got acquainted with my father by talking over the horse flesh that was up for bid. Evans told me that Dad had come to Rock Springs to find a buyer for ten head of horses. The previous winter had been a bad one for the Triple J. They lost nearly all of their beef. Selling those horses was the only way the ranch could hope to make up for its losses."

"I don't know very much about livestock, but could the sale of just ten horses really make up for the loss of all that beef?"

"I asked Evans the same thing. According to what my father told him, those horses weren't ordinary cow ponies. There were several thorough-breds, a few choice Appaloosas, and even two or three Arabians in the bunch. I imagine their sale would have brought in a good-sized bundle of cash for the Triple J."

"Would have brought? Wasn't your father able to find a buyer?"

"Oh, he found a buyer all right. Parley came back to their hotel after the auction and overheard my father talking on the phone with someone. Dad was saying he'd found an interested buyer who was willing to pay a good price for the horses once he saw them, when the person on the other end of the line interrupted him. Parley said Dad was stone quiet for a minute, then he burst out yelling: 'What d'you mean stolen? They can't be! You're lying!' Parley thought it'd be a good idea if my dad finished the rest of the conversation in private, so he left. When he came back a while later, Dad asked him if he knew anybody who needed an extra ranchhand. I don't know if Evans really needed an extra hand or whether he just wanted to help my dad, but he hired him right then. And there was never another word said about the stolen horses or the Triple J."

I sat for a moment, mulling over what Jay had just told me, then said, "You said your parents met through this Parley Evans. When did that happen?"

Jay smiled at me. "The first day my dad got to Evans' ranch. You see, Parley's wife wasn't too strong and since ranch life demands a lot of hard work and the strength to do it, my mother was hired to help with the housework and chores. Parley insists he heard bells ringing the minute he introduced them."

I returned his smile. "It happened that quickly?"

"The realization that there was something special between them did. They had so little time together, I'm glad it wasn't wasted in uncertainty."

Something in his steady black gaze made me lower my eyes. "Were they married right away, then?"

"No. I guess my dad felt obligated to help the Triple J out of its financial difficulties before he took on the added responsibility of supporting a wife. Parley told me that Dad sent half his paycheck home to my grandfather every month for a year, and saved a good portion of the remaining half as a nest egg. My parents were married the following June, a year to the day when they'd first met."

I put my chin in my hands and gazed at the silvery current rushing under the old bridge. Images of the long ago couple drifted before my eyes. I saw Jay's father, tall and muscular, wearing the handsome face of his son. And his mother? Here, the images blurred and faded. What had she looked like? What was her name?

"My mother and father stayed at Evans' ranch until the end of summer," Jay went on. "Then Dad told Parley they were going back to the Triple J. Parley didn't hear from them again for almost nine months, so he doesn't know what happened during that time. When my father finally wrote, it was to ask for his old job back. He didn't give any reasons why, just said things hadn't worked out the way he'd hoped. Parley wrote back and told Dad there'd be a job for him any time he wanted it and just to let him know when he was coming. Not too long after, Parley received another letter. In this one, my dad thanked him for the job offer and told Parley he could expect the two of them to arrive within the week. Parley said my father was especially anxious to get my mother moved and settled before the baby came. In a post script, Dad mentioned he'd found out what happened to the horses that were stolen from the Triple J two years before. Apparently, four of the ten belonged to him."

"What happened to the horses? Did your father tell Parley Evans anything more about them?"

Jay shook his head slowly. "No. He disappeared the next day."

I felt the aching tightness return in my throat. In my mind, I saw a young wife, her body swollen with the unborn son her husband would never see. What kind of agony and heartbreak had she endured during the weeks and months and years which followed that day?

"My father's letters to Parley Evans are positive proof that he didn't desert my mother," Jay said in a tight voice. "And Mother knew it all along, in spite of the rumors and stories that spread around town. What she couldn't accept was the only other explanation for his disappearance."

"You mean, something happened to your father and he was killed?" I said slowly, not wanting to accept such a tragic explanation myself.

"No. I mean someone *caused* something to happen to my father." Jay read the question in my eyes without my asking it and added, "I don't know whether it was murder or an accident, but someone here in Dusk knows and I think that same person also knows what happened to the Triple J's horses. In fact, I can't help thinking those horses are the key to the whole thing."

"Why is that?"

"You remember I said that the Triple J suffered a tremendous cattle loss after a severe winter? Well, I think it's only logical to assume that other ranchers in the area were hard hit, too. Suppose one of them heard my dad had gone to Rock Springs to find a buyer for ten valuable horses. This person may have decided to steal the horses and sell them himself to make up for his own losses. With my dad out of town, Uncle John and my grandfather were the only ones left to run the ranch. The two of them couldn't possibly be everywhere at once. It wouldn't have been difficult for the thief to ride in to wherever the horses were kept and drive them across the range to his own spread."

I stared at Jay. "I think it would be awfully difficult to get ten horses into one truck!"

Jay's mouth split into a grin. "Sorry. I forgot you don't speak ranch language. What I meant was, this man probably rode in on horseback and herded the horses back to his own land."

"I see, and then shipped them out by truck to be sold."

"You've got the idea," Jay said. "This next bit is sheer guesswork on my part, but it makes sense to me. I'm assuming first of all, that my father must have done a little investigating on his own or else stumbled upon some vital information concerning the horses. And once he knew who had made off with them, he would still need proof before going to the law. Two years had already gone by since the time of the theft, so the chances of his getting any positive proof were probably pretty slim. I think Dad must have figured that his only real hope would be to get a confession from the thief.

"Let's say he left the ranch early on the morning of the sixteenth with the intention of confronting the horse thief with the whole thing. If the man wasn't about to admit to such a crime, the two of them could have gotten into an argument, maybe a fight. After that, well—" Jay's out-stretched hands fell into his lap.

It sounded like the plot to an old Western movie, except somehow the ending had gotten twisted around—the hero had been killed and the villain had gotten away unpunished.

I took a deep breath. "So you think the thief was forced into commit-ing a second crime in order to conceal his first one?"

Jay shrugged. "Something like that, yes. I realize my little theory could be way out in left field. The only thing I can be really certain of is that my father didn't just ride away from the Triple J that morning and fall into some hole. If he had, there wouldn't be someone right now who's so determined to stop me from finding out the truth."

"It seems fantastic to me that this man has been able to keep so much hidden for so long," I said. "I mean, all the search parties, the investigation, and everything."

"I know it's unusual," Jay conceded, "but in a small town like Dusk where everybody knows everyone else, you just don't go around suspecting your neighbor of being a killer. I'm sure people wanted to believe my dad just walked away rather than getting himself killed. It's a lot simpler that way."

"Yes, I can see that. But so much time has gone by since it happened—twenty-six years! How can you hope to find the man responsible for your father's death?"

Jay gave a short laugh. "Aren't you forgetting something? I don't have to find him. He's found me!"

Chapter 4

"His name I know . . . ."
Francis Thompson

The piercing cry of a night bird hunting its prey jarred the simple quiet of the gulley. I glanced up at the moonlit sky to see a black-winged shadow glide into some trees above us. Then I looked back at Jay Bradford with a little shiver.

"Do you really think the person who fired those shots at the truck is the one responsible for your father's death?"

"Yes, I do."

For just a moment my mind refused to accept the situation. "But you can't be sure! Maybe it was someone playing a prank."

"Busting a headlight and blowing out a tire is hardly my idea of a harmless prank."

I put a hand to my forehead. "But why has this person waited until now to start shooting at you? If you've lived at the ranch since you were eight, he must have had hundreds of opportunities. I just don't understand! Why now?"

Jay leaned forward and looked into my face with taut earnesty. "Because I wasn't a threat to him then! Don't you see! He thought he was safe! I was too busy hating my father to question all the gossip and stories. My bitterness made me perfect sucker bait. After talking to Parley Evans I felt sick! When I think how blind and stupid I've been all these years—!"

"You weren't stupid!" I blurted out, adding in a softer tone, "—only young. Besides, you never knew your father."

"You didn't know him either, and yet you believed he didn't leave my mother. I should have had more faith in him, but—" he stopped and shrugged, "the past is in the past. It's too late for me to change what has already happened. But I can find out the truth. I owe him that much!"

The fierce expression on his face frightened me a little. "I know what you're trying to do is right—I won't argue that. But Jay, this person must be desperate to do what he did tonight! You might have been killed!"

"No, I'm sure he wasn't aiming directly at me. From his position in those trees and with the lights of the truck as guide, he could have put a bullet right through the windshield if he'd really wanted to. I think he's just trying to scare me off. I have to admit though, his second try was more to the point than the first."

My eyes strained open until the lids ached. "Second try! You mean, he's done something before tonight?"

"A few days ago when I was in town talking to the sheriff, a note was left on the front seat of my car. In essence, I was warned to stop 'meddling with the past and trying to find out things that were best forgotten.' " Jay gave me a dry smile. "Pretty trite for a warning note, don't you think?"

My pent-up breath came out in an exasperated sigh. "Whether that note was trite or the work of a creative genius doesn't really matter! Whoever wrote it meant what he said! What happened tonight is proof of that. Aren't you worried about what he might try next—once he realizes you aren't going to be scared off?"

"I can take care of myself when that happens," Jay answered calmly. "It's you I'm worried about."

My heart gave a curious leap inside my chest. "Me?"

"The person waiting in those trees didn't expect me to have company along for the ride."

I looked at Jay, knowing what he was trying to tell me, yet feeling nothing. Was it because I had already experienced so much this evening that there was no room left for this new fear? Jay reached out slowly and took one of my hands in both of his. The warmth of his skin against my icy fingers made me realize that perhaps I was a little frightened after all.

"I'm sure it was too dark for him to see you," Jay said. "And if we keep quiet about this, there's a good chance word won't get back to him that I drove you out to the ranch tonight. Did you see or speak to anyone in town after you arrived?"

"No, I didn't go into town at all. I had planned to call the Bradfords from the depot but no one was there—at the depot, I mean. Then I saw the road—" My voice trailed off and I hoped he wouldn't ask me to explain why I had decided to walk alone to the ranch. He didn't. Instead, his features relaxed slightly with relief.

"Well then, I think it's safe to assume that no one saw you back in Dusk. And I want you to give the impression, if possible, that the Bradfords picked you up—not me! This is necessary for their protection as well as your own. Your involvement in this whole affair was accidental, but it's not too late to keep Janet and the rest of her family out of it."

I nodded my understanding, hoping I didn't look as frightened as I suddenly felt.

His dark eyes regarded me soberly. "Maybe I've told you too much. I only wanted to explain a few things. Somehow, I ended up telling it all."

Without knowing how it came to be there, my other hand was suddenly resting on his. "Thank you for trusting me enough to explain," I said softly. "I just hope I won't make a mistake and say something that might spoil things for you."

"You won't," he said, giving my hand a reassuring squeeze. "Just remember, as far as you're concerned, you don't know me or anything about me other than my name. I'm just Janet's cousin who's visiting at the ranch."

He made it sound fairly simple, but to follow through with such an act was something else entirely. Could I do it? Walk in tonight and face the Bradfords as if nothing had happened?

"Oh, no! What about the truck?" I reminded him. "We can't walk in this late without some kind of explanation—especially since I don't know anything about you other than your name."

He laughed and said, "You make it sound like we've had quite a promiscuous evening."

I felt myself starting to blush and quickly pulled my hand out of his. "I was referring to the broken headlight and the flat tire! We'll have to tell the Bradfords something!"

"I'll take the blame for those things," he said easily. "Our little accident will come in handy as an explanation for the damage to the truck."

"But you weren't going that fast!"

"They'll be more than happy to believe I was," Jay said with a slight edge to his voice. He got up then and pulled me to my feet. "Once we get to the ranch, you just forget about me and everything that's happened. O.K?"

"I'll try," was all I could manage.

Our steps echoed as we walked across the bridge. I followed Jay around the sharp turn in the road, then up the avenue of maples. Through their trembling leaves I had a shadowy glimpse of the stream and moonlit glen below. All was still except for a wreath of matted leaves turning idle circles on the surface of the water. At that same moment, I realized an idle question had been turning round and round in my mind.

"Jay—?"

His dark head turned in my direction and I smiled self-consciously. "I know I've asked you dozens of questions already, but I was wondering how you happened to meet Parley Evans, and how he recognized you as your father's son after so many years."

"Oh, that. I met Parley at an art show in Cheyenne," he answered offhandedly. "He was there on business and saw my name in the newspaper in connection with the show." Jay met my inquiring look and explained further. "I go by Jay, but my full name is Jason, after my father. Anyway, I was listed as Jason Bradford in the paper and that really roused the old man's curiosity, so he came to the exhibit to look me up."

A faint light of remembrance flickered in my mind for a moment, but it was extinguished by the night wind as we came up out of the gulley. The tempest assailed us with chilling force as it swept across a vast, moonlit domain of rugged rangeland and rolling hills. I ducked my head away from the bitter torrent with a shudder.

Jay immediately moved in front of me. "Here, you'd better put on my jacket."

"No, I'm all right."

He slipped off his Levi jacket and placed it over my shoulders with the soft command: "Put it on."

I shoved my arms into the sleeves and pulled the jacket around me. It was rough and warm and smelled faintly of hay. I smiled a thank you as another rush of wind swept between us. Jay looked down at me and something in his smile was strangely familiar. Before I could think what it was, he bent down for my luggage and we moved on.

Lodgepole fences walked with us on either side of the road, pointing the way to a small cluster of lights which gleamed against the black hillside. This then was the ranch. But my mind was too busy trying to grasp an elusive memory to feel elated at the long awaited sight of the Triple J. Where was it I had heard or seen Jay Bradford's name? What was it that had jogged my memory a few moments ago? Something about him meeting Parley Evans at an art show. Art show. The words seemed to roll up a gauzy shade which had been obscuring this particular memory, and as Jay and I trudged down the last length of road to the ranch, my mind wandered once again down a long hall of paintings.

Most of the frames held only blurred images of color, but one group of paintings hung just as vividly in my memory as they had on those plaster walls six months ago. The artist's style was unlike any I had seen before and his work refused to be placed in any of the usual categories. He made no use of the pallett knife and his brush strokes were light and sensitive. Combined with this almost delicate technique was a brutal use of color. Each canvas bled earthy hues—bitter browns, cruel yellows, savage reds.

I remembered a desert, lying feverish and forgotten under a sulphur-yellow sun. There was a canyon with black pines pricking a deep night sky, and lonely cliffs baring their smooth white sides to the moon. In every painting but the last, the artist was consistent in his use of stark, angry color. His final painting in the exhibit was a complete contrast in subject matter as well as technique. Instead of a wild landscape, I saw the lovely face of a

25

young Indian woman. She was wearing a simple dress of pale green which opened at the throat to reveal a pendant hanging from a silver chain. It was such an unusual piece of jewelry that I remember taking particular notice of it. There was nothing Indian in the design. Two heads were carved in profile from smooth green stone—a man's and a woman's, one overlapping the other. There was no definite background in the portrait, only soft swirls of muted color. The artist's sudden gentleness of mood might have made this painting bland in comparison with his landscapes had it not been for the woman's expression. There was something in her face that reached out and touched one's soul. I saw it most in her eyes. In them was a look of longing, expectancy and hope. But there was loneliness, too, and heartache. The feeling of this portrait was in such variance with the artist's other paintings that I felt I had to check his signature to be sure the same person had painted all five. On every one I found the name Jay Bradford.

An unexplainable feeling came over me as I stared at the tall young man walking beside me. What kind of strange coincidence had brought me over a thousand miles to become involved with someone whose work had fascinated me months before? But supposing the coincidence were in name only and Janet's cousin was not the artist Jay Bradford?

Jay saw me watching him and looked down inquiringly. I took a quick little breath and asked, "Have you ever painted the Triple J?"

His face registered more than mild surprise but he recovered himself and said evenly, "Not the ranchhouse, but some places around here."

For some reason my legs suddenly went weak.

"You never said anything before about knowing I paint," he remarked.

"I—just remembered. Your name sounded familiar, but I couldn't think why until you mentioned meeting Parley Evans at an art show."

I looked away from his absorbing glance and saw that the gravel road we had been traveling suddenly veered to the left, taking the lodgepole fencing with it. Ahead of us was a long, tree-lined driveway and in the center of the 'v' formed by the two roads was a broad expanse of lawn. The lawn moved upward in a gentle slope until it reached a large, two-story stone house. A soft amber light shone through the front windows but the first thing I noticed was the eerie effect of strong white moonlight reflecting off cold gray stone. I shivered slightly. There was something too austere about the place to be very welcoming. Once again, Janet and I had opposing ideas. Her descriptions of the ranchhouse had conjured visions in my mind of a simple, white-frame affair. And here instead, was this impressive old structure brooding in the moonlight for all the world like a western Wuthering Heights.

I cast a side-glance at Jay as we turned our footsteps up the drive, remembering how he had reminded me so strongly of Heathcliff. That was what came from having a wild imagination. The next thing I knew, I would probably be hearing the mournful baying of hounds across the moors.

As if on cue, a rousing combination of barks and yelps shattered the deep quiet of the night and two, furry black and white streaks came hurtling across the front lawn and through the trees, making straight for Janet's cousin. He let go of my luggage to return the dogs' frenzied greeting.

"A fine pair of watchdogs you are," he chided, fondling them both. As Jay ruffled the thick coat of one dog, the other sidled over to me and sniffed my hand.

"That's right, fella, introduce yourself," Jay said with a grin.

"What's his name?" I asked nervously, not quite over the surprise of their greeting.

"Marshall. And this one's Dillon."

I looked at Jay with an amused smile and visions of moors, hounds, and Wuthering Heights suddenly vanished. "Marshall and Dillon?" I repeated with a little laugh.

"That's right. Janet's two younger brothers got the dogs last fall and named them. Wait until you hear Tadd call them for supper. His voice is starting to change and that high, cracked, 'Marshall, Dillon!' is something else again."

I was laughing already. I looked at Jay and thought how much younger he looked without the lines of worry and tension marking his face. He reached down for my suitcases and we continued up the driveway which led to the back part of the house. Marshall and Dillon provided escort for a short distance but soon grew impatient with our leisurely pace and bounded off to parts unknown.

The bitter wind had softened considerably and its voice was barely a murmur in the towering old cottonwoods which grew on either side of the drive. The moonlight was like trembling silver on their leaves. A sweet, heady fragrance drifted on the cool night air and in a moment my eyes discovered a large lilac bush growing between two of the cottonwoods. I couldn't resist going to it.

"Mmmm, they're so heavenly," I breathed, bending a stalk heavy with blooms close to my face.

Jay left my luggage in the drive and crossed to where I was standing. He leaned his tall form against the trunk of a cottonwood and asked, "How did you become familiar with my work?"

I glanced up from the lilacs. "Oh, I saw several of your paintings in an exhibit at Michigan State University some months ago."

"That's right. Janet mentioned you're from Michigan. But if I remember correctly, that was quite a large exhibit. I think I only had four or five landscapes on display. What made you remember them—and my name?"

I looked deeply into the fragile cupful of blossoms I held in my hand. "When something beautiful touches you—you remember it," I said, thinking of the Indian woman's lovely, sad face. Jay was silent for so long I felt compelled to look up. When I raised my eyes, I saw with a shock that his shadowy features bore a haunting resemblance to those of the Indian woman in his painting. A strange tingle of realization ran up my spine as the title of the portrait played upon my memory: "Waiting." An Indian woman, waiting as Jay's mother had for eight long years, hoping to see a husband who never returned. I couldn't keep the tremor out of my voice as I said, "It was the portrait of your mother which moved me most. She was so lovely . . . I've never been able to forget her face."

Jay's dark form stiffened against the trunk of the tree and his voice was half-stunned. "Who told you she was my mother?"

"No one. It—was just a feeling. I wasn't completely sure until I remembered the title of the painting. Then I knew why your smile—and eyes, seemed so familiar."

Through the wavering pattern of moonlight and shadow I felt his dark eyes burning into mine.

"What was her name?" I asked weakly.

He moved close beside me and answered softly, "Wenona."

A shower of purple blossoms fell to the ground as my hand released its hold on the branch. I felt suddenly afraid—not of Jay, but the startling new emotions that warmed my blood and set my heart pounding. I turned my face away from his penetrating gaze and tried to regain some control of myself.

I heard Jay mumble, "I guess we'd better be going in," and was acutely aware that he had moved away from me and gone for my suitcases. I turned my steps toward a narrow cement walk which led to the back porch. One side of the little porch was sheltered by heavy vines clinging to a white, lattice-work trellis. I grasped a tangle of soft green vine and watched Jay Bradford as he came up the walk.

He placed my suitcases on the porch beside two empty milk cans and a pair of manure-stained work shoes, then said: "Back there on the road—when you asked me who I was—I started to tell you, but I thought that after what had just happened, it might be more reassuring for you to know that I was Janet's cousin instead of Jayhawk, a Bannock-Shoshoni Indian."

I looked up into his proud face and clung a little tighter to the supporting vine. "Especially after I had just called you a 'wild Indian,' I suppose."

"That had nothing to do with it," he said and smiled. "You were upset and I thought Jay Bradford might be able to ease your fears more than Jayhawk could."

"That may have been true then," I admitted, daring to look up into his eyes. "But I'd like to thank Jayhawk rather than Janet's cousin for bringing me here tonight."

Jay opened the door, then moved back so I could enter. "It is good that you have come," he said.

Chapter 5

"Come, come,
You'll never meet a more
sufficient man."
William Shakespeare

I stepped into the Bradford's spacious kitchen and glanced around the room, taking in the gleaming white walls and cupboards and the brick-red linoleum floor. To my immediate left was a long, oval-shaped table with a red formica top and eight chairs tucked around it. Opposite the table, a large bay window was draped in cheery red and white homespun. Looking to my right, down the length of the L-shaped kitchen, I saw a modern counter-top range with double built-in ovens and a large refrigerator-freezer strung out against one wall. Behind the open door stretched a long line of cupboards and counter space with a double sink situated in the center. An abundance of green potted plants were crowded along the window sill above the sink and a few stray vines crept down toward the faucet as if in search of an extra drink. Here, I saw a woman of medium height and build stacking a few plates and glasses into a dish drainer. She glanced toward the doorway as we entered and when she saw Jay a spark of warmth flickered in her calm brown eyes.

"Jay—I was beginning to worry a little," she said, then stared at me with an interested smile.

"I'm sorry to be so late, Aunt Helen, but I picked up a passenger along the way. Is Janet still up?"

"Janet?" she said with a puzzled look. "Yes, she's up, but—" Mrs. Bradford looked at me a second time and the sudden light of recognition dawned in her face. "My goodness, don't tell me you're Angela! We weren't expecting you until tomorrow!"

"I hope you don't mind if I'm here a little earlier than planned," I said quickly. "I thought it might be fun to surprise Janet."

"She'll be surprised, all right," her mother chuckled, wiping her hands

30

on her apron. "And why should I mind, for pity's sakes! You're welcome any time, dear!"

I smiled into her kindly brown eyes. She wasn't really a pretty woman. Her once-dark hair was streaked with gray and her eyes were smudged with shadows and looked very weary in spite of their persistent twinkle. Her complexion was almost sallow and the simple, gray cotton dress she wore accentuated her pale skin tone even more. But the gentleness in her voice and manner softened the flaws in her appearance so much, that just then she seemed quite beautiful to me.

"Call me Helen, dear," she insisted, "and Jay, why don't you take Angela into the living room and have her meet the family. Grandpa Judd and the younger boys have gone to bed," she explained to me, "but Thayne and Janet and my husband are watching a movie on the television. I think I'd better put a pot of coffee on the stove. You two look exhausted!"

"Coffee sounds wonderful!" I said with a self-conscious swipe at my windblown hair. It was completely dry now but several long strands had escaped the blue scarf which kept it tied away from my face.

Then, from behind, I felt Jay's hands upon my shoulders. "I guess you won't be needing this any more," he said, fingering his Levi jacket.

I slipped my arms hastily out of the sleeves. "No—no, of course I won't. I forgot I was still wearing it."

"So did I—almost," he said with a smile.

I looked up in time to catch the warmth of that smile and had my first real look at Janet's cousin. In the brightly lit kitchen the deep bronze tone of his skin was instantly noticeable. So was his thick, jet-colored hair. It came well below his ears and hung close to his shirt collar in the back. I also noticed that his eyes were not black as I had first supposed, but a dark, earthy brown.

I realized, too, that Jay was seeing me clearly for the first time as well, and suddenly wished there were some place for me to hide. After my fall in the stream and our windy walk, I probably looked like a pale, wide-eyed mop handle with a head of wild brown hair.

Jay took my arm and said, "Come on, it's time for your grand entrance."

He led me from the kitchen through an open doorway and into the unlighted dining room. We made our way around a massive table which stood solidly in the center of the room with what seemed like an army of high-backed chairs standing guard around it. The carpeting was thick and soft and swallowed the sound of our footsteps.

The boundaries of the dining room ended in a sweeping archway, the curve of which was nearly as high as the ceiling. I scarcely noticed the magnificent wooden banister and stairs curving upward to the second story of the house which stood to the immediate left of the archway. My eyes were focused straight ahead on the living room. The utter immensity of the place was staggering. Heavy wooden beams ran across a white plaster ceiling in what seemed like an endless brigade, and at first glance I counted three 9' x 12' rugs which came no where near touching one another. Across the expanse of floor, rugs and furniture, I saw a rough stone fireplace with a yawning black mouth that looked as if it could consume an entire woodpile in one gulp. Over the mantle, a cattle stampede was kept from rampaging through the house by its heavy wooden frame. There was a lovely old grand piano in one corner of the room and one wall to the far right was devoted entirely to shelves of books and curios. Sprawled in leisurely array about the room were a wide assortment of chairs, sofas, and lamp tables, each one looking comfortable and settled, but without the appearance of having occupied that particular spot for the past thirty years. The room was neat and clean, but not scrupulously tidy. Instead, it gave off a mellow, lived-in atmosphere combined with a masculine roughness that set it completely apart from any home I had seen back East.

One large couch was placed at an angle to the fireplace so that its occupants could view the adjacent television set, and it was here that I saw Janet's dark head resting against a bright orange sofa pillow. Beside her, postured in a near-horizontal position of relaxed manly elegance, was her older brother Thayne. In a nearby brown leather recliner, I saw a middle-aged man with wavy brown hair, who I assumed must be Janet's father. None of them had taken any notice of Jay or me—and for two very good reasons. First, their backs were partially turned toward us and second, their attention was focused on the television screen where a man and a woman were embracing one another with passionate fervor.

Jay started forward but something in me held back. He felt my hesitancy and whispered, "What's the matter?"

I looked up at him and made a helpless gesture.

"Are you worried about what they'll say?" he asked.

"No. Not too much."

"What is it then?"

A mirror-image of the immaculately groomed, carefully coiffured and white-suited Angela Stewart who had boarded the bus for Dusk flashed across my mind and I said miserably, "I wish I didn't look so awful!"

Jay smiled and smoothed a wispy strand of hair back from my forehead. "For a girl who's fallen into a stream, had a wild ride and walked over two miles tonight, I think you look great! Come on," he said softly and took my hand.

After that, I was too shaken by his touch to care how I looked. We crossed the living room as the late movie, embrace and all, was ending in a cadence of musical bliss. John Bradford left the comfort of his recliner to switch off the television set and as he turned around he saw Jay. A definite frown crossed his otherwise pleasant features. He seemed about to speak when he noticed me standing beside his nephew. Sheer surprise left him standing there with his mouth open.

"Janet, I met a friend of yours on the way back from town," Jay said.

"A friend of mine?" Janet queried, shifting position on the couch so that she could look over one shoulder at Jay and me. "Angela!" she shrieked, shooting up from the sofa like a rocket. "I can't believe it!" She flew around the couch and gave me a quick hard hug, during which time I felt Jay's hand release mine. "What on earth are you doing here?"

My nervousness dissolved in a little laugh. "I believe I was invited."

She pulled a face then laughed herself. "You know what I mean! How did you get here so soon?—" She shot a quick sideways glance at her cousin. "—and with Jay?"

"I think your friend can explain things just as well sittin' down as she can standin' up," her father said. "Probably, a lot better, by the looks of her. Why don't you just sit yourself down right over here," he suggested, offering his own chair.

I thanked him and moved my weary legs toward the inviting recliner.

"Angela, I'm sorry," Janet said. "I should have asked you to sit down. You look positively worn out. But you surprised me so, I'm forgetting everything."

"Including me," said her brother, coming forward as I was about to sit down. "I'd certainly like to get introduced to our guest," he drawled, fixing his brilliant blue gaze squarely on mine.

"I haven't forgotten you, silly," Janet said with an affectionate smile for her brother. "I was just saving the best 'till last. Angela, this is my brother Thayne."

Thayne Bradford reached out a strong brown hand and clasped mine possessively. "I've been lookin' forward to meetin' you," he said with that incredible drawl and a well-practiced smile.

I had to admit Thayne was every bit as handsome as Janet had told me. His dark brown hair was thick and wavy, and although he stood barely as tall as I, he had a tough, muscular build. A full brown mustache added a roguish bandito touch to his tanned face. Yes, he was undeniably handsome—and very much aware of his good looks.

I struggled out of his grasp and said with a general smile at nothing in particular, "I've been looking forward to meeting all of you."

Thayne retreated to the couch beside his sister and I sat down in the recliner. My entire body fairly sighed with ecstasy. Until that moment, I hadn't fully realized how tired I was.

"Where's Helen?" John Bradford asked Jay. "Has she met Angela yet?"

"Yes. She's out in the kitchen making some coffee."

John gave a satisfied nod, then pulled a straight-backed chair up near mine and regarded me with a friendly but inquisitive smile. I noticed that his eyes, from behind a pair of wire-rimmed glasses, matched Thayne's in blue brilliance.

"Did I hear right, or was Jay mistaken when he said he met you on his way back from town?"

I glanced at him, then at Jay who had just gotten himself a chair and was sitting almost directly opposite me. The inquisition had begun.

"Jay wasn't mistaken," I told Janet's father. "I suppose I must have been almost a mile and a half out of town when we—uh, ran into each other." Out of the corner of one eye I saw Jay's mouth twitch at my choice of words.

"Angela! You weren't really going to try and walk all the way out here!" Janet said, giving me an incredulous look.

"Well, I—"

"Taking off on a fifteen mile hike at night doesn't seem like the thing a young girl ought to be doing, especially when she's new to the country," John Bradford said in stern fatherly tones that made me feel like a seven-year old child who had been caught running away from home. "Why didn't you call us?"

"Well, I—I know I should have, but—"

"I'm sure Angela would never have started walking out to the ranch unless she thought she could reach it by nightfall," Jay said, breaking into the conversation for the first time. "And she certainly didn't know the ranchhouse was fifteen miles out of town. Janet told her it wasn't far from Dusk, and for someone used to city blocks and not our kind of distance, 'not far' hardly suggests fifteen miles."

Janet gave me an apologetic smile, then said to her father, "I remember now, describing the way out here to Angela. I guess I did say it wasn't too far from town."

"Here's the coffee!" Helen Bradford announced, coming into the room with a tray laden with a steaming coffee pot, cups and saucers, and a plate of doughnuts.

I slumped back into the deep brown softness of the easy chair as Mrs. Bradford poured coffee for Jay and me, then set the tray down on a small table beside the couch.

"I hope you like applesauce doughnuts, dear," she said to me. "Mrs. Stillman in town brought these out just yesterday. I minded her little ones while she went to visit her mother a few days ago. Her mother is down in the hospital in Rock Springs with a broken hip. Very painful they tell me. Especially for a woman who's past seventy. 'Course I never make doughnuts myself. Cakes an' pies are more my thing. Little fancy foods like doughnuts and cookies don't last long enough around here to be worth the trouble it takes to fix 'em. Just like throwin' em out the window, I always say. Has Jay told you yet what a fine artist he is?"

Her question, coming at the end of such a string of domestic trivia took me completely by surprise. I gulped the hot coffee and stammered, "Yes—I mean, no. That is, he didn't tell me exactly, but I've seen some of his paintings in an exhibit back East."

"Well now, what a coincidence!" Helen exclaimed, utterly delighted.

"You never told me you were familiar with Jay's work," Janet said with an interested lift in her voice.

"When I saw his paintings I had no idea Jay was your cousin," I told her, then gave Jay a quick glance over my cup of coffee, wondering if he were upset by the conversational trend. His lengthy frame was postured easily in the high-backed chair and he was taking slow, deep gulps of coffee. I could see no tenseness in his face and assumed that his painting must be a safe subject to discuss.

What time did your bus get in?" John asked me during the lull.

"About eight o'clock, I think."

A frown creased his sunburned forehead and he glanced down at his watch. "It's after eleven now," he said with a meaningful look at Jay. "I can't understand why it should take you three hours to get here."

This is it, I thought, noticing how both Janet and Thayne were leaning forward on the sofa with sudden interest. Janet's eyes sparkled with curiosity and Thayne's held almost a suspicious gleam.

Jay set his cup on the saucer and met his uncle's stern look with one that was equally rigid. "Angela had already been walking for some time before I met her, so it must have been eight-thirty or past before I came along in the truck. And, our meeting wasn't exactly what you'd call casual."

"What d'you mean by that?" Thayne demanded, all traces of that soft mellow drawl gone from his voice.

Jay's dark head didn't turn even a fraction of an inch toward his cousin. Instead, he continued speaking to his uncle. "I was driving at a fairly good speed and as I came around that sharp curve in the road where it follows the creek—"

"I know the place you mean," John grumbled. "What happened?"

"Well, I came around the bend and saw Angela in the road straight ahead of me. To avoid hitting her, I ran the truck off the road into the brush."

"You must have been driving like a damn fool!" was Thayne's muttered remark.

"Oh, Angela, I bet you were scared to death!" Janet said. "Were you hurt?"

"No, only my pride," I answered, smiling a little at Jay. "When I saw the truck coming at me I tried to jump out of the way and stumbled into my luggage. I lost my balance and then—well, I fell backwards into the stream." The incident sounded almost comical in the telling, but no one else saw any humor in the situation. Especially, Janet's father.

"This girl could have been killed or seriously hurt!" John Bradford said, turning stormy blue eyes onto Jay. "I hope you realize how serious this is!"

Something in his tone warmed my blood even more than the hot coffee. "What happened was an accident!" I blurted out. "It was nearly dark and there was no way Jay could haved seen me until the last moment. It took fast thinking for him to turn the truck so quickly—and he might have been the one to get seriously hurt! Besides, I had no business being in the middle of the road!"

I'm not sure who was more surprised at my little speech, Jay or the Bradfords. There was a potent moment of silence, during which I looked up to find Jay's eyes regarding me with an expression that made the warm drowsiness of the room seem cold by comparison. Vaguely, I heard Helen say in her sweet, concerned voice: "Well, I think it's a blessing that neither one of you was hurt. That piece of road has always been dangerous!" To which John muttered, "Not when you drive slow enough," but said no more.

I forced my eyes away from Jay's to reach for an applesauce doughnut and nearly spilled my coffee in the process.

"What about your clothes?" Janet asked me. "After falling into the stream you must have been soaked to the skin."

"Oh, I changed in the cab of the truck," I said, biting into the doughnut.

"You told me about that gorgeous knit suit your mother bought you for the trip," she went on. "If you were wearing that, it must have been ruined."

I waved my doughnut carelessly. "Oh, don't worry about it. You know how easy those 'wash and wear' things are to care for."

Jay coughed on a mouthful of doughnut and gave me an amused look.

"Even with the accident, three hours still seems like an awful long time to drive fifteen miles," John pointed out.

"We would have been here a lot sooner but one of the tires picked up something sharp when I crashed into the brush," Jay explained. "It developed a slow leak and finally went flat about two miles from the ranch-house. I could have fixed it, but I had to leave the spare in town to be repaired."

I leaned back in the recliner, marveling at the ease with which he explained the truck's flat tire. Looking at John's face, I knew he could find no fault with what Jay had told him. It appeared as if the inquisition might be over but Thayne refused to let the issue rest without one last comment. "So after nearly running Angela over and knocking her into the stream, you make her hike two miles to the ranch!" Thayne shook his head and looked at me with raised eyebrows. "Sounds like you had one swell evening!"

I responded to Thayne's sarcasm with frosty politeness. "Jay didn't knock me into the stream. I fell in. And he did offer to walk to the ranch and get a car, then come back for me, but I didn't want to be left behind. I guess it sounds silly, but I felt nervous about waiting alone in the darkness."

"It doesn't sound silly at all," Helen agreed in motherly tones, giving Thayne a warning look.

"Seems to me you'd feel a lot more nervous walkin' through strange country at night—with a stranger," Thayne said, with a side-glance at Jay.

"Oh, no. Everything was so beautiful—especially after the moon came up."

Janet's eyebrows rose significantly at this last remark. I tried to ignore her look by brushing a few crumbs off my slacks, then I set my cup and saucer on the coffee table.

"Janet, will you help me clear away these dishes?" her mother asked, rising from her chair. "The sooner we get you to bed the better," she added, smiling at me. "It's no wonder you looked so tuckered out when you came in."

"I feel much better now," I told her, "and the doughnuts were delicious."

"I'm glad you liked them, dear. I'll be sure to tell Mrs. Stillman the next time I see her."

Janet gathered our dishes and followed her mother out of the room, but not before she had given me another one of her looks, this one titled, 'I want to talk to you later.'

Across from me, Jay and his uncle were discussing plans to go out the next morning and have the truck repaired. I listened for a moment as Thayne made some grumbling remark that he couldn't help because he had the milking to do. Jay quickly offered to handle and pay for the necessary repairs and John agreed to the arrangement.

I leaned my head against the back of the recliner and soon the men's voices faded into a low, droning background for my own thoughts. I was thoroughly relieved that the Bradfords had accepted the explanations Jay and I had given them concerning the accident with the truck, but I couldn't help feeling disturbed about their attitude toward Jay. It was possible that John Bradford's anger was merely the natural result of worry and concern, but even then, he gave the impression of being less than fond of his nephew. Thayne's dislike of his cousin was blatantly obvious, and even Janet had acted distant and suspicious around him. As far as I could tell, Helen

Bradford was the only one who seemed to have any real liking for Jay. Of course, in all fairness to the Bradfords, I had to admit it was possible I was imagining their antagonism. But, whether it was real or purely imaginary, I understood now why Jay had been so insistent they not find out about the shooting incident.

I shut my eyes, feeling the last bit of tenseness drain out of me. Except for the tenderness in the center of my back it was difficult to believe those shots had been fired. I tried to remember the moment I had seen that small spark of orange fire, but the warm room, the soothing softness of the big easy chair, and the low, murmuring voices blocked all visions of that former terror. Food and lights, warmth and rest, these were tangible things. Safe things. Rifle fire in the night was only a distant dream . . . .

From far away I heard a voice calling my name and felt a hand on my shoulder. I recognized Janet's voice and my eyes struggled open.

"I'm sorry to wake you, but I know you'll be much more comfortable in my room than down here."

"What?" My head jerked away from the chair and I rubbed my eyes. "Have I been asleep? I'm sorry."

"After the night you've had, I can hardly blame you," she said.

"Where is everybody?" I asked, looking around the room and seeing Jay had gone.

"Dad's gone to bed and Mom's just finishing up in the kitchen. She'll turn out the rest of the lights down here. Thayne has taken your suitcases up to my room so you can get right into bed."

I rose stiffly from the chair. "Bed sounds heavenly, but do you think I could get a quick bath first? I feel so grubby after traveling all day and then falling into the stream."

"We've got a shower in the upstairs bathroom if you'd prefer one."

"A shower would be perfect," I sighed, moving rather doggedly across the room. "Just as long as it's scalding hot."

"Believe it or not, we do have a few new-fangled conveniences around here," Janet said with a laugh, "and hot water is one of them."

The shower was like a healing balm. I stepped out feeling warm all over with my skin atingle. Jay Bradford and his problems still existed, but I was too blissfully relaxed and tired to let them bother me now. All I wanted was a good night's sleep.

I put on my nightgown and robe and stepped into a pair of soft furry slippers, then went out into the upstairs hall. This ran almost the entire length of the house with various rooms branching off on either side. I padded along the aisle of worn floral carpeting without a sound, looking at the somber, high ceiling and massive wooden doors, and wondering as I passed each room, who the occupants were that lay sleeping within. One of the bedrooms would be Mr. and Mrs. Bradford's, and another must belong to Janet's grandfather. Then there were the three younger boys and Thayne. I knew already that Janet's room was the farthest down the hall to the left, but where did Jay sleep when he was visiting with the Bradfords? For that matter, where had he slept when he lived with them? I called a halt to my thoughts right there, wondering why he should enter them so frequently.

I was nearly to Janet's room when I lost a slipper and stopped to retrieve it. As I did so, a door to my right opened and an arc of light flooded the shadowy hall. I gasped a little in surprise, then, seeing that it was Thayne, clutched my loose robe about me more securely.

"Feeling better?" he asked softly.

"Yes, much better."

"I sure am sorry you had such a rough time gettin' here," Thayne said, and I noticed his Western drawl was back again, full and rich. He was leaning casually against the door jamb, arms folded across his tanned, muscular chest, clad only in pair of low-slung jeans. "And I want to apologize for my, uh, cousin's reckless driving."

"There's no reason you should apologize for the accident. Jay has already done so."

Thayne shrugged his shoulders and smiled disarmingly, a white flash of teeth showing beneath his mustache. "Oh, well, I just wanted you to know how I feel about your stay here gettin' off to such a bad start. I kinda feel like it's sort of my responsibility to make it up to you."

I didn't dare ask how he proposed to 'make it up' to me, and the intimacy with which his eyes traveled up and down my form was making me increasingly uncomfortable. "I'm sorry you think I've gotten off to such a bad start with everyone," I told him.

Thayne straightened up and said quickly, "Look, honey, I didn't mean it that way." I gave him a purposely blank stare. He brushed a hand over his head of thick brown hair and said with a sigh, "Oh, well. Nevermind. I'll see you in the morning."

It was all I could do to keep the relief out of my voice as I said goodnight to him and hurried to Janet's room. Once inside, I shut the door fervently behind me, wishing I could lock it.

Janet was in her pajamas and turning down the bed covers. I looked about with delight. Her room was just as sunny as her personality. Three walls were painted a light yellow and the fourth was papered with white and yellow daisies. White, airy curtains waved gently across a tall window and the floor was carpeted in a soft, moss green. The furnishings were an interesting combination of various periods. Two lamp tables, one on either side of the bed, were definitely Early American and so were the milk-glass lamps. There was a modern cedar chest in one corner and the large chest of drawers with pictures of the Bradfords crowding its top had to be an antique. The dresser and mirror were traditional, and yet somehow, all the pieces complimented one another and the total effect was charming.

"Your room is just like you and I love it," I said.

"I'm so glad. I hope you're not too disappointed at not having your own room."

"Don't be silly. I wasn't expecting one, nor do I want it." Especially if Thayne were half the Casanova he appeared to be.

"By the way," Janet said lightly, and gave me a smile that was brimming over with innocence. "I thought I heard voices in the hall. Were you talking with someone?"

It was so obvious she knew exactly who that someone was, I couldn't resist teasing her a little. I picked up my hairbrush from the dresser and said nonchalantly, "It was only Jay."

"Jay! But he's over in the bunkhouse!" Janet burst out, her brown eyes widening in surprise.

The bunkhouse. Was that where Jay always stayed or was this only a temporary arrangement? I gave my hair a few idle strokes with the brush, then turned back to face her with a smile.

"Janet, you know I was talking to Thayne."

She made a pretense of straightening the sheets and said with a foolish smile, "Well, I thought it *might* be Thayne, but you're so full of surprises tonight . . . What did he have to say?"

"Not much. He apologized to me for Jay."

"That's just like Thayne," Janet said, beaming with sisterly pride. "He's so responsible and considerate himself, it's hard for him to understand people who aren't. What did you say to him?"

"I told him Jay had already apologized and there was no need for him to do so."

"Did you have to put it quite that way?" Janet said, sounding slightly annoyed. "After all, he was just trying to be nice."

"It's the way he put it that bothered me—assuming that Jay didn't care whether he ran over me or not, when I know how bad he felt."

"Oh, do you?" she asked with an interested lift in her voice.

I put my brush down and walked around to the opposite side of the bed from her and took off my robe. "You know what I mean."

"I know you and Jay certainly defended one another tonight," she said.

"I just hated to see him get all the blame for something that was my fault, too."

"Is that really all there is to it?"

I sat down on the bed with a sigh, wishing there were some way to stop all her questions about Jay without hurting her feelings. We had always been

40

completely open and honest in our confidences and it was difficult for me to purposely withhold the truth from her. I made an effort to keep my voice light as I answered her question with another question.

"Why do you say that? What else could there be?"

She flopped down on the bed with a confused shrug. "I don't know. I honestly don't know. But when my best friend, who happens to be a very reserved and shy person, walks in with a stranger at eleven o'clock at night acting as if she's known him all her life, can you blame me if I start wondering what's been going on? Especially when the stranger happens to be my cousin who has always been 'Mr. Remote'—until tonight, that is. Don't think I didn't notice all those deep dark looks he gave you!"

I gave a shaky laugh. "Janet, really! Where was I when all those 'deep dark looks' were floating around the room?"

She looked at me and giggled in spite of herself. "Oh, all right. Maybe I am exaggerating a little—but you two still seemed awfully friendly."

I yawned and got into bed. "Is there anything wrong with being friendly? You're always telling me I shouldn't keep so much inside myself, that I should 'open up' more with people."

"I know I said that, but—"

"It's against the rules to be friendly with your cousin when I'm supposed to fall madly in love with your brother. Right?"

She made an effort to keep a straight face, but a smile kept sneaking out of the corners of her mouth. "Angela, that's not fair!"

I laughed out loud. "But it's true, isn't it? Come now, Janet, 'fess up!"

"Oh, all right. But what's so terrible about hoping you and Thayne will hit it off together? He likes you already—I can tell. And you have to admit that he is awfully good looking. Half the girls in town are crazy about him."

"Why hasn't he married one of them?"

"Oh, you know, he likes to play the field. But that's just because he hasn't met the right one yet. You're so different from the girls around here—the one's he's dated especially. I know you made quite an impression on him tonight. And think how wonderful it would be if you and Thayne did get together. Then, we'd practically be sisters!"

"Jan, you know how much your friendship means to me—but I couldn't ever marry someone I didn't love. I want to be sure, and that takes time."

"Well, you've got all summer," she replied cheerfully. "Just promise me you'll give things a chance to develop if you get the opportunity."

I sighed and nodded. There was really no point in my holding out. I would never get any sleep until Janet got her way. With a look of complete satisfaction she reached over and turned out the bedside lamp. I did the same, then snuggled down between the smooth, satin touch of clean white sheets. I felt myself fairly melting into the bed, my thoughts lying pleasantly idle until Janet's voice came out of the darkness: "You're not interested in Jay, are you?"

"Does it really matter that much?" I groaned into the pillow.

"Well, I don't know if you noticed or not, and I guess Jay wouldn't tell you, but I think you should know he's half Indian. His mother was a full-blooded Shoshoni from the reservation over in Wind River."

Her words were edged with a certain reticence that suddenly infuriated me. I counted to ten silently in the darkness before answering her. "As a matter of fact, Jay did tell me that he's Indian. His mother's portrait was one of those I saw back in Michigan. I thought she was one of the loveliest women I'd ever seen and I told him so. Oh, and Jay's Bannock-Shoshoni, not just Shoshoni. There's a difference."

Afer a moment of startled silence, a voice from the other side of the bed said, "Oh," rather vacantly.

I turned over with an amused smile. "Goodnight, Janet."

"Goodnight," answered the voice.

Chapter 6

"I know the shaggy hills about,
The meadows smooth and wide,
The plains, that, toward the southern sky
Fenced east and west by mountains lie.

A white man, gazing on the scene,
Would say a lovely spot was here . . . ."

William Cullen Bryant

When the first gray fingers of light crept into Janet's room I was completely awake. I lay for a long while listening to the dawn chorus of birds, thinking perhaps I might doze off, but sleep would not come. It may have been the newness of my surroundings that caused me to awaken so early, or possibly I had slept deeply enough to be refreshed. In either case, I knew I could not lie in bed and wait until Janet awakened; not with the morning calling and a new world outside waiting to be discovered—a world without sirens and horns and exhaust, a world without houses crushed together, a world without endless acres of asphalt and cement. What better time to see the ranch than in the early morning when no one else was about? There were times when my love of solitude simply could not be denied. This morning was such a time.

I slid out of the covers and tiptoed across the cold floor. My suitcases lay open as I had left them the night before and it took scarcely more than a minute to dress. As I stood before the dresser mirror brushing my hair, I gave myself a critical look. Maybe the Levis were a little tight, but they certainly didn't look indecent as Mother had deplored. I didn't have enough hips to suggest indecency of any sort. I deliberated a full thirty seconds as to whether my blouse looked better tucked in or hanging out and finally tucked it in.

Did I look all right? I put on a touch of pale pink lipstick and a little mascara, then gazed at my reflection with a sigh. All this concern over the way I looked was really ridiculous. I probably wouldn't see Jay or anyone else. It was only quarter after five and that was even too early for the milking to begin. At least, I hoped it was. I knew that Thayne was responsible for that particular chore, and hoped I wouldn't run into him.

I glanced over my shoulder at Janet's dark head which was barely visible

43

among the bedcovers. She wouldn't be at all pleased if she knew how little I counted on a romance developing between her brother and me. She would insist that I was making a snap judgment and not giving things "time to develop." But surely, a person shouldn't have to try to fall in love—that should be something that just happened. I thought of Jay's parents' meeting—how he said they both had realized there was something special between them from the beginning. Was I just being foolishly romantic to want something like that to happen to me? No, I was not a romantic—I was an absolute idiot! With that conclusion reached, I left the room and hurried through the silent house.

I got away from the ranchhouse without seeing another soul, smiled a good morning to three pompous magpies who were strutting about on the back lawn, and took a deep gulp of tender morning air that tasted and smelled as if it had never been breathed before.

The boundary of the back lawn was marked by a single row of lodgepole pines and I knew once I moved beyond them it would be difficult, if not impossible for anyone in the house to see me. My time for solitude was guaranteed. I walked swiftly past the pines and found the driveway which circled the back of the house. I scarcely took notice how it widened out into a huge, open courtyard. Across the driveway was a small, white-frame building with a red tarpaper roof. Parked to one side of the shanty under the spreading branches of a poplar tree, was a four-wheel drive vehicle with an out-of-state license. I knew it must be Jay's and made an effort to walk past the bunkhouse without slowing my steps or staring conspicuously.

Soon all the ranch buildings and roads were behind me and I was wading through dew-wet grasses toward sloping green hills. The sky was like a painting in chalk pastels, with soft smudges of pink, yellow and gray clouds brushing against its powdery blueness. I stood very still for a moment, then ran straight up the hillside like a six-year-old child, plunging through the tall grass, startling a meadow lark into flight and nearly tripping over a large stone. The morning breeze sent my hair streaming out behind me and filled my lungs with an exhilaration I hadn't known for years. I reached the top laughing and breathless and absurdly happy. I stood for a few seconds to catch my breath, gazing at a wide expanse of meadowland which waited in cool, green silence for the coming of the sun. Blooming in purple profusion amid the whispering grasses were thousands of slender lupines, and there was the fiery pink and orange of Indian paintbrush as well. Up from the meadow loomed the shaggy black growth of a pine forest, still cloaked in shadow with an almost unearthly silence.

I sat down upon a large, flat rock feeling a little weak-kneed, whether from the exertion of the climb or from the exquisite vastness of so much open land all around me, I wasn't completely sure. Just to be able to look and look, and look again without spidery networks of wires and poles tangling my vision fairly made my eyes ache with wonder. I turned about to face the east and saw the Triple J far below, resting comfortably on the shoulder of a broad river valley. The ranchhouse, barn and other buildings appeared miniature in size, and the horses and cattle, grazing placidly in the fields, looked as motionless and small as rubber animals placed in a child's toy farm set. My eyes found the gravel road Jay and I had traveled the night before, but I wasn't exactly sure in which direction the little town of Dusk lay. Among the pastures and trees, a river glided along its ribbony course, and far to the east I thought I detected a highway. Beyond the gray strip of road were rolling plains of furry, gray-green sagebrush. Rising abruptly from the plains were sandstone cliffs colored in earthy hues of yellow, red, and fleshy pink. In the distance, scarcely visible above the sandstone cliffs, were the far away crests of a somber mountain range.

A small movement near my left foot brought me back to earth. I lowered my eyes and spied the fat, furry body of a ground squirrel who had just popped out of its hole. He was sitting on his haunches, chin lifted, nose twitching, and close enough that I could easily have reached down and stroked his back. But like the squirrel, I, too, lifted my head to the east, and together we watched the sun rise over the mountains and saw the meadows fill with light.

I still hadn't moved when my fat rodent friend suddenly turned about and scrambled down into his hole. Before I had time to wonder what had startled him, I heard the rhythmic thud of hoofbeats pounding the earth. The pulse beat louder and louder until it trampled the morning's stillness, and I whirled about to see a sleek black horse and its rider emerge from the pines just beyond the meadow. The black horse pranced joyously through the purple lupines, tossing its head and side-stepping with the kind of free, proud animal spirit that always makes man feel somewhat a prisoner. As I watched, I saw that same proud spirit in the rider; the same joyous exhilaration in the arch of his body that was present in the animal's beautiful stride. As they drew closer, I noticed he was riding bareback without even a bridle to control the spirited animal. I soon realized he needed no superficial means of control. His entire body spoke to the horse. His black head leaned close to the animal's sensitive ears, his hands gripped the tangled, blowing mane, and his long legs clung to the horse's smooth black sides like a burr.

I drew a sharp breath and rose to my feet as Jay saw me and turned the horse in my direction. My heart began to pound with the rhythm of the hoofbeats and I knew this was what I had been hoping for from the moment I awakened.

Jay brought the horse to a standstill a few feet from where I was standing and brushed a heavy lock of black hair out of his eyes. Sweat glistened on his forehead and throat and his dark eyes were bright and gleaming from the exhileration of the ride.

"You're up early this morning," he said a bit breathlessly.

"I know. Last night I felt as if I could sleep the clock around, but I was awake before the sun. I couldn't sleep and I couldn't just lie in bed, so I came up here. It—it's very beautiful, isn't it?"

"Hmmm?"

"All this. The ranch and—and the morning," I said, sounding rather breathless myself.

Jay's dark eyes didn't move from my face. "Yes. Very beautiful."

My breath stopped halfway in my throat as if it had suddenly forgotten its normal in and out function, and it was a long moment before I was able to look away from those deep-set eyes. I lowered my head and stroked the horse's velvety muzzle. "Your horse is magnificent. What's his name?"

"Her name is Arabesque," Jay smiled, sliding off the animal's back in one fluid motion that seemed to require no effort at all. "And she isn't mine. She belongs to my grandfather. I've just been exercising her in the mornings. She had distemper last winter and hasn't been ridden for a while so she's extra skittish."

"I didn't notice. You handle her beautifully."

"Arabesque isn't hard to handle once you understand her," he said, giving the mare's silky neck a few pats. "We had a good time this morning, didn't we, girl?"

The song of a meadow lark sounded somewhere nearby. Its clear, warbling tones were like a church bell blessing the sweetness of the morning.

Jay stopped fondling the mare and looked at me. "Are you in a hurry to get back?"

"No."

"Then why don't we sit down for a few minutes."

"All right."

Arabesque nudged Jay's shoulder and nickered playfully. "The ride's over, girl. Go home and get your breakfast. Go on!" he said with a grin, giving her black head a shove.

The mare trotted off a few paces, looked over her shoulder at Jay, then with one joyous lunge galloped down the hill toward the ranch. Sunshine burned its golden fire into her glistening black hide and the wind whipped mane and tail into frothing silk.

I sank to my knees in the grass and said softly, "She's like a poem. How does it go? 'Thou dost float and run like an unbodied joy whose race has just begun . . .' "

"Was that Keats or Shelley?" Jay asked, folding his length to sit beside me.

"Shelley. Of course, he wrote the poem about a skylark, not a horse, but somehow the words came to mind just then."

"I think Shelley would approve," Jay said. Neither of us spoke for a while. The sun was warm on our shoulders, the breeze cool in our hair. It was enough just to sit and listen to the day begin.

I felt Jay's hand on my knee and heard him say in a low tone, "You have an admirer. Over there." He didn't point, just gave a slight nod of his head. Out of the corner of one eye I saw that the ground squirrel had ventured forth out of his hole once more and was watching me with curious, button-black eyes.

"Oh, we're old friends," I said smiling. "We watched the sunrise together and enjoyed every minute of it."

"He's a lucky fellow."

I felt myself blushing and said, "What makes you so sure that he really is a he? It could be a lady squirrel, you know."

"Not a chance. I saw the way he was looking at you."

I laughed, feeling a strange mixture of excitement, pleasure and embarrassment at his words.

The squirrel popped down into his burrow once more. He may have come up again, but if so, I didn't notice him. I'm not sure how it began, but suddenly, Jay and I were talking and all the pleasures of the morning faded into insignificance. For some reason, he wanted to know about me. At first, I didn't know where to begin or what to say, but gradually, he seemed to draw me out of myself. His eyes, his voice, his gentle, interested smile peeled away the painful layers of my self-consciousness quite painlessly, letting half-smothered thoughts and feelings come to the surface and breathe freely. All my loneliness spilled out and I was telling him how I wished my mother had married again and how I had always wanted brothers and sisters. But Mother seemed to feel that it was her prime duty in life to provide me with other things—a lovely home, clothes, an expensive education—all the things she thought would bring happiness and security to me. She tried so hard I could never find the courage to tell her how unhappy I often felt. I knew she was acting out of love, so I went along with her ideas for the same reason. When I began college, I was given beaming, loving lectures on how my college education would act as an insurance policy for my future financial needs. Marriage was all well and good, but she didn't want me placed in the same position she had been in when my father died. It was much more sensible to have a solid career underway before I got romantically involved with anyone.

"Your mother sounds like a very modern and practical woman," Jay remarked.

"I suppose she's had to be," I said. "Mother's English, and she doesn't

47

have any family in this country. When my father was killed her whole world crumbled. It's been a terrible struggle for her to build it back again—alone."

"That nice, lucrative career your mother talks about, is that what *you* really want?" Jay asked quietly.

I picked a stalk of lupine and twirled it between my fingers. "Well, I—I really have tried to convince myself that she's right, but—I guess I'm just not as practical and modern as my mother."

"Why do you say that?"

I looked into his face and saw no skepticism, only interest. His dark eyes waited patiently for me to go on and I knew I could never lie to them no matter how foolish the truth sounded.

"I'm not sure I can put words to the feelings I've had for so long, but in a way, I feel I've already had a career—Mother's gift shop. I know it's been necessary for her and I appreciate all she's done, but I keep hoping it won't be necessary for me. I've wondered so many times what it would be like to be a man's wife, to have his children, and make a home for them. My friends think I have no ambition because I want to be a wife and mother—but that is my ambition! Sometimes I'm afraid I want too much, yet others keep telling me that I don't want enough! I don't know." I glanced away from him to study a rock near my left shoe, feeling the hot color in my face and the hard pumping of my heart.

"I have always thought it strange," Jay began thoughtfully, "that white men in our modern world give more praise and credit to the woman who works efficiently for another man, than the wife who understands and works beside her own husband. And likewise, a woman who teaches facts and figures to the children of others is generally thought to be more dedicated and selfless than the mother who spends a lifetime trying to instill intangible things like values and attitudes to the children of her body. Both are important and necessary—but why should one role be given such a glamorous image and the other considered drudgery? I suppose I will never understand."

"Then, you don't think I'm foolish to feel the way I do?"

"No, I don't. But perhaps my thinking isn't very modern or practical either. Indians often disagree with what white men believe is the right way for a person to think and act."

"Do you think like an Indian?" I asked.

"You know, I've never had it put to me that way before," he said with a laugh. "People in the art business are usually curious to know what influence my 'primeval background' has had on my painting, and others have asked me what it's like being an Indian. No one but you has asked me if I think like an Indian."

I smiled into his dark eyes. "Well, do you?"

48

Jay pulled out a long blade of tender grass and chewed on the stem. "In some things—the basic things—I do. But I've had to learn to live by the white man's rules in order to compete with him successfully. I've had a white man's education and lived with a white family, so the adjustment hasn't been too difficult. And yet, there is a part of me—inside—that cannot forget the Indian ways I learned from my mother."

"What are some of those ways? I mean, how does an Indian think differently from a white man?" I asked him, realizing suddenly that this was something I desperately wanted to know and understand.

"Well, take the land, for instance." Jay straightened his broad back and pointed to the wide river valley below us, then to the plains and mountains beyond. "A white man would stand where we are now and say that this land belongs to Judd Bradford; the land to the south is Sam Tyler's, and those mountains far to the east are government owned. Each man has a piece of paper stating that a certain portion of the land belongs to him and no other. Then he works the land, sometimes far beyond its capacity to yield, in order to have more money and material possessions. An Indian would stand upon this hill and look out upon the land as a gift from God to all men. He can't understand how it can be broken into pieces and then claimed by various individuals. To the Indian, land is free—like air and wind and water. He will take from the earth only what he needs, because he understands that the earth is his mother."

"I wish white men believed as the Indian," I said quietly. "Our lives would be so much simpler."

"Not necessarily. Much blood was shed in the old days over the choicest hunting grounds or the finest horses. No one is immune to greed, no matter what his color."

"You said that the land was a gift from God. Do most Indians believe in Him?"

"Many Indians are Christian, if that's what you mean. I happen to be," he said with a wry grin, "but that's partly because the Bradfords were determined not to have a little heathen on their hands. They are like most whites; they don't realize that no matter what name an Indian gives to his god, whether it's the Great Spirit, the Giver of Life, or Christ, that religion is the very essence of his life. Without it he is naked and frustrated."

I met his eyes and saw the richness of the brown earth in their depths and a wisdom that belied his twenty-six years.

"I'm glad you think like an Indian," I said.

Something else came into his eyes then that started my heart pounding like a percussion section. For a moment, I thought I heard bells ringing but that had to be a lot of romantic nonsense. Then I heard it again, a clear ringing sound which came floating up the hillside from the ranch below.

"I did hear bells!" I cried, and scrambled to my feet.

Jay looked at me and laughed. "That's the call to breakfast. Everyone's probably up by now and wondering where you are."

"Good heavens! I completely forgot about the time, and breakfast, too! I'd better run!"

"Hold on!" he called and got to his feet. "Didn't anyone ever tell you you're not supposed to run down hills?"

I looked over my shoulder at him and laughed. "I ran up this one. I might as well go down the same way."

"If you're determined to break your neck I guess I can't stop you, but at least grab my hand."

His lean brown fingers reached out and clasped mine firmly, and together we went bounding down the hillside, leaping over rocks and stumbling through the tall grass. When we reached the bottom and started at a more leisurely pace toward the ranchhouse, his hand still enclosed mine and I made no move to withdraw it.

"I hope Janet's not too upset with me," I told him. "She was sound asleep when I left. Everyone was, in fact. I bet they think I'm a little weird—always taking off by myself."

Jay grinned. "Just tell them you decided to go for a morning walk and happened to run into me again."

I smiled, too, and felt his hand tighten around mine. We walked to the back door and it wasn't until that moment that I realized neither of us had mentioned the previous night the entire time we had been together.

"Well, there you are!" Helen Bradford said as we entered the kitchen. "We were beginning to wonder where you'd gone." She stopped spooning bubbly puddles of pancake batter onto a long griddle, and gave us a warm smile.

Janet, who was scooping out a yellow mountain of scrambled eggs from a large frying pan into a bowl, said without looking up: "I told you Angela was probably out to the barn watching the milking with Thayne." She glanced up, saw Jay beside me, and her ready smile collapsed in the corners of her mouth.

"I woke up early so I decided to take a walk," I explained hurriedly. "I'm sorry if I worried you. It's such a beautiful morning."

"Oh, we weren't all that worried," John Bradford said from the table. "We figured you'd show up as soon as you smelled breakfast cooking."

"And you were right!" I laughed. "It looks wonderful!"

"Well, sit yourself down!" Helen ordered with a chuckle. "There's bowls of mush an' coffee already on the table, an' scrambled eggs an' hotcakes comin' right up."

Jay took my arm and guided me to a place at the table. Across from us, two of Janet's younger brothers and an older man somewhere between the ages of fifty and seventy stopped spooning their hot cereal to watch as Jay helped me into my chair. Janet's two teenage brothers were probably only curious about their sister's roommate, but the older man's squinty hazel eyes were constantly shifting from Jay to me with unusual interest.

Janet placed the bowl of scrambled eggs on the table and asked me a bit pointedly, "Where did you go for your walk?"

I smiled into her dark eyes which were flashing signals right and left. "Oh, I went up on the hillside to see the view. The river valley is so beautiful. Jay was out riding and stopped a moment to say hello."

"Arabesque came trotting back about an hour ago," the older man said in a gravelly voice, but I noticed his small eyes were twinkling as he glanced at Jay. He had the frame of a wiry old billy goat with white stubble on his chin to match. Wisps of salt-and-pepper colored hair curled untidily around his neck and ears, but the crop growing close on his forehead had been tamed by brush and comb. His cheeks and nose were sunburned a shocking pink.

I wondered for a moment if he were Jay's grandfather, then decided definitely against it. For one thing, Janet or her parents certainly would have introduced us by now; for another, there was something too lovable about that weatherbeaten old face for him to be the one Jay had hated.

"Angela, I'd like you to meet two of my younger brothers," Janet was saying. "Stuart is still out helping Thayne with the milking so you'll meet him later. This is Tadd and this is David."

I said hello and the boys mumbled a casual 'hi' in turn, then returned to the more enjoyable process of eating their breakfasts. David appeared to be in his middle teens, and from the length of the lean brown arm that reached for another piece of toast, it was easy to see the rest of his slender body hadn't quite caught up with the growth rate of his appendages. A thatch of brown hair teased his forehead and freckles dusted his nose. Tadd must have been about two years his brother's junior and a full head shorter. He had blondish hair, a wide toothy grin, and brown eyes that were mere slits when he smiled.

"I'm the Bradford's hired man, Bert Tingey," came the gravelly voice once again. The older man shoved a calloused paw across the table and proceeded to shake my hand with gusto. "I sure am happy to meet yuh, Miss Angela."

"I'm happy to meet you, too, Mr. Tingey."

"Aw, hell, call me Bert. I wouldn't know who you wuz talkin' to otherwise," he said with a grin.

"I've called him quite a few names other than Bert, but he always seems to know who I'm talking to," Jay said dryly.

"Don't you pay no mind to that black-haired buck," the old hand told me, giving Jay an affectionate glance.

I watched with what I hoped was concealed amusement as Bert Tingey chomped down on a piece of toast and the white stubble on his chin jerked up and down with the movement of his jaw.

"Angela," he mused, and swallowed the mouthful of toast with a gulp. "That sure is a purty name. You know with a name as nice as that, it'd be a real shame for whoever carried it to have a face as ugly as mine. It's a real pleasure to see that the good Lord blessed you with a face jest as purty as yer handle."

I smiled into Bert's crinkly hazel eyes, but before I could thank him for the compliment, John Bradford broke into the conversation.

"Tell me, Bert, how many ugly old men do you know named Angela?" he asked, then guffawed loudly. Tadd and David joined in the laughter while Bert Tingey's pink cheeks went a shade darker.

"Now John, you knowed exactly what I meant," Bert put in, but chuckled along with the rest.

"What's the big joke?" boomed a voice from the doorway of the dining room. I looked up, startled, as a large hulk of a man entered the kitchen. He was nearly as tall as Jay with the same tough neck and a thick, beefy spread of shoulders and chest, although his face told me he must be three times Jay's age.

"Oh, it's nothing, Grandpa Judd. Daddy was just teasing Bert, that's all," Janet answered quickly. "Come and sit down. Everything's ready."

Judd Bradford gave her shoulder an affectionate pat then seated himself at the head of the table without so much as a glance at Jay or me. Although I tried not to, it was impossible to keep from staring at the man. His eyes were like blue ice, deeply set in a craggy face that looked as if it hadn't tried a smile for years. His bushy black brows were bent in a determined scowl, providing a shocking contrast to the disheveled mass of white hair covering his large head. And there was something about the mouth which disturbed me. I couldn't decide if I read cruelty, grief, or just frustrated old age in those thick lips. Beneath the hoary head and sagging face was a powerful body which could easily have belonged to a much younger man. There was something so authoritative about his very posture that I knew instinctively, here was a man who took orders from no one. He reminded me of a king; a tragic, mad king. King Saul.

Janet poured her grandfather a steaming cup of coffee and said gaily, almost too gaily: "We had a quite a surprise after you went to bed last night. You knew we were expecting my roommate today at noon—well, at eleven o'clock last night, Angela walked in and surprised us."

Judd glanced up sharply and his hooded eyes cut into my face like cold

52

blue metal. "So you're the Miss Stewart Janet's been telling us about."

"Yes sir," I answered stiffly, thinking how automatic the use of 'sir' was in addressing this man.

"How did you manage to get all the way out here from town at that time of night?" he inquired.

"I—I happened to meet your grandson, and he was kind enough to give me a lift out to the ranch."

Judd's lips cracked into what might almost be called a smile. "Kind enough, hell! Thayne knows better than to pass up a pretty face when he sees one."

I smiled a little, vaguely aware that Jay seemed unusually tense beside me. "It wasn't Thayne. Jay drove me out to the ranch."

Judd Bradford set his coffee cup down with a clang that sent the brown liquid splashing over the rim of the cup. "You and Jay—you were with him?"

"I—why, yes," I stammered. "We wouldn't have arrived so late, but the truck had a flat tire and there wasn't a spare so—" I stopped mid-sentence, suddenly aware that Jay's grandfather hadn't heard a word I was saying. He was staring at the sugar bowl, thick lips parted, his eyes a blank, glassy blue. He seemed almost totally oblivious to everything and everyone, and completely immobile except for his hands. They were trembling slightly.

"I've got a stack of hotcakes here, fresh from the griddle," Helen said with forced cheerfulness. "Jay, will you have some?"

"No thanks, I'd better get out and see about the truck," he answered quietly, pushing back his chair.

"But all you've had to eat is a bowl of mush!"

"Quit worryin' about everyone else's stomachs, Helen," John said gruffly. "You haven't had a bite yourself, yet."

Helen set the platter of hotcakes on the table with tight lips and worried eyes.

"And I want you boys out in the fields in ten minutes—hear?" their father ordered. David and Tadd nodded and started gulping their food at an increased pace.

"Let me know about that tire," John said to Jay.

I turned in my chair as Jay nodded to his uncle, uttered a quiet thanks to Helen and strode out of the kitchen, shutting the back door behind him.

I felt something sink inside me after he had gone. What had happened to bring back those lines of strain and tension I had seen in his face last night? And why should the simple fact that I had been with him and not Thayne, trigger such a strange reaction from his grandfather?

Only Bert Tingey seemed completely unruffled. He wiped his mouth on a paper napkin and said calmly, "There's a Hereford cow going to calve

53

any day now. The old girl's pretty big an' I seem to recollect she had one hell of a time droppin' her last calf. Do you think we should bring her into the barn, Judd?"

Judd Bradford turned his head slowly, as if it pained him to do so and mumbled, "Yes. Bring her in. Bring her in." Then, more clearly, "She might need some help. We'd better keep a close watch on her."

"Whatever you say," Bert agreed and helped himself to the untouched stack of pancakes.

Janet cleared away Jay's dishes and sat down beside me with a smile that was almost natural. "How about a horseback ride this afternoon?"

"Sounds wonderful," I replied.

The crisis, whatever it was, seemed to be over, but I couldn't help stealing a side-glance at Judd Bradford, thinking 'King Saul' had proven to be quite an apt name for him, dark moods and all.

Chapter 7

"He had done most bitter wrong
To some who are near my heart . . ."
William Butler Yeats

"There's something I'd like to talk to you about," Janet was saying that afternoon. "I hope you won't be offended at what I have to say," she added.

"Offended?" I queried absently, more interested at the moment in a hawk gliding high above us. The sky was such a piercing blue I had to shade my eyes with my hand in order to see the soaring brown bird. It was a perfect afternoon for horseback riding, the scent of sage was like incense on the breath of the omnipresent Wyoming wind, the air so clear and alive it seemed to shimmer around us.

"Why don't we stop for a few minutes and let the horses graze while we talk," Janet suggested.

I agreed, thinking it must be something serious. She was so subdued. We had been 'exploring the ranch,' as Janet liked to call it, for well over an hour and she hadn't said much more than a handful of sentences. For her, this was more than unusual. It was something of a record.

"Over here," she directed, pointing a finger to a small grove of aspen trees.

I had no idea how far we had come, but as we dismounted and let our horses graze in the tall grass, I could see no evidence of man or civilization; no fences or roads, not so much as a single tin can or scrap of paper blotted the landscape.

"It's so beautiful," I sighed, easing my stiff legs to the ground in degrees. "The whole ranch is just as wonderful as you said. No wonder you love it so."

Janet smiled and flopped on the ground beside me. "I'm glad you're not disappointed. I was a little afraid I'd built it up too much. Of course, things

55

aren't going to be as nice—I mean, when I invited you here for the summer I never expected—" She paused lengthily and rolled over on her stomach.

"Never expected what?"

She yanked up a handful of grass and clenched it tightly in her fist. "I never expected Jay to come back."

"Jay? Why should his coming to visit make such a difference in our summer?" It was a silly question for me to be asking, especially when my brief acquaintance with him had already altered my arrival so drastically. A thought flitted briefly through my mind. Would I still think the ranch was quite so wonderful if Jay weren't here? I refused to give the question an answer, wondering instead why Janet should be so upset over her cousin's visit. She knew nothing of last night so that couldn't account for her agitation.

"It's hard to say," she began. "All I know is, things never seem to go right when Jay's here. He has a way of upsetting people, especially—"

"Your grandfather?" I suggested.

She gave me a quick look of surprise, then shrugged. "I guess you couldn't help noticing the little scene at breakfast."

"I wouldn't call it a scene, exactly, but your grandfather did seem to react rather strangely when I mentioned I had been with Jay last night."

She turned worried eyes to mine. "That's what I want to talk to you about. It may sound like a strange thing to ask, but could you just not mention Jay when Grandpa Judd's around?"

"Not mention him?"

"You know, talk about him, use his name, things like that," she explained.

I was too surprised at her request to give an immediate answer. Her lips tightened and she started plucking blades of grass one by one. The tiny snapping sound was a minute echo of the horses' loud cropping.

"I'm sorry I asked you," she said in a low voice. "You must think I'm pretty ridiculous."

"You're not ridiculous. I just don't know what to say, that's all. I can't understand why your grandfather should be disturbed when people mention his grandson's name or talk about him. Is it because Jay is Indian? Is that it?"

"It has nothing to do with Jay being part Indian—at least, not directly. It— it's because of something that happened a long time ago."

I thought I knew what Janet was referring to, but I remained silent, hoping she would explain without my having to ask her questions about it.

"Oh, Angela, I hate to involve you with family problems. And if Jay hadn't come back—" She sighed again and I felt an uncomfortable knot begin to form in my stomach. "Maybe if I explain a few things you'll understand."

"All right. If you want to."

"If I do, will you promise me you won't mention Jay around Grandpa Judd again?"

I had never seen her quite so desperate. "I'd promise that anyway, Jan. Please don't feel you owe me an explanation."

She looked a little ashamed. "I'm sorry. Now you're angry with me."

"I'm not angry. Only confused. Jay doesn't seem like the kind of person who goes around ruining people's lives."

"It's the reason he's come back that could ruin things!" she blurted out. "It's upsetting everyone, not just Grandpa Judd. Oh, I don't know where to begin. Jay's father is the real cause of all the trouble, I guess. He was my father's older brother. You see, he ran off just before Jay was born and all these years nobody's heard a thing about him. Now, all of a sudden, Jay has this passionate desire to find out what happened to him."

"And that's wrong?" I asked quietly, feeling the knot in my stomach tighten still more.

"It's wrong when it hurts other people! And it's just plain stupid because there's nothing to find out! Everybody around here already knows pretty much what happened to Uncle Jason—even though it's not a very pretty story."

"Perhaps people are mistaken in what they think happened," I said. "It is possible, you know."

"Now you sound just like Jay," Janet said with aggravation. "He thinks the whole town is wrong and it's up to him to find the truth. I don't know why he can't accept the facts concerning his father's disappearance instead of trying to invent some big mystery about it all."

"And just what are the facts?" I asked, trying to keep the edge out of my voice.

"It's really very simple. The trouble all started when Uncle Jason came back to the Triple J and brought an Indian wife with him. About two years before that he ran out on Grandpa Judd and Daddy when the ranch was in serious financial trouble. Then, as soon as things started looking better, he showed up out of the blue with a Shoshoni woman, expecting to be welcomed back with open arms."

She paused for a moment to shift position on the grass and I realized I was literally shaking inside with anger. I didn't even try to analyze why I should accept a stranger's word as truth and consider my best friend's story utter lies. It was evident that Janet believed she was telling the truth, but something inside me refused to accept any part of what she had said. Whoever gave her such information must have been listening to ugly rumor or had carefully twisted the facts to make Jason Bradford appear the type of man who would desert his wife and unborn child.

"Mom and Dad don't talk about it much," Janet went on, "but from what they have said, I gather Grandpa Judd must have given Uncle Jason and his wife a pretty harsh welcome. But hurt and bitterness can make a man do things he wouldn't ordinarily do," she added hastily, "and Grandpa Judd had every right to feel bitter toward Uncle Jason."

But he didn't, I thought fiercely. Why should a father feel bitterness toward a son who sent half his monthly wages home for over a year? Without Jason's help the ranch would never have survived its financial crisis. How could his father and brother sit back after his disappearance and let his name be blackened by vicious rumors and lies?

"Just because Grandpa Judd was upset over Jason's sudden marriage and irresponsible ways doesn't mean that he didn't love him," Janet told me with utter loyalty. "When Jason walked out again—this time without a word to anybody, not even his wife—Grandpa Judd was heartbroken. In fact, he's never gotten over it. He's still suffering, even after all these years."

"Why is everyone so sure that Jason deserted his wife?" I demanded of her. "Is there any proof that he did?"

She looked slightly taken aback. "Well, no—but no one's ever proved that he didn't, either. What other explanation could there be?"

"Something could have happened to him," I suggested. "An accident, perhaps."

Janet shook her head. "The police were called in to investigate his disappearance and half the town was out searching the hills for months afterward, but there was never a trace of him. Not a trace," she said flatly. "That's why it's so useless for Jay to think he can come along twenty-six years later and expect to find out anything."

"But Jay has a right to know the truth," I persisted.

Janet groaned in sheer exasperation. "If there were anything to know other than what I've told you I might agree, but there isn't! All Jay is doing is embarrassing us by stirring up an affair that's dead and buried. And he's hurting Grandpa Judd horribly in the process!"

"How? How could Jay possibly hurt his grandfather by trying to prove that his father didn't desert them?" I demanded.

Janet looked at me incredulously and for a long moment could say nothing. I could see in her eyes that her mind was searching frantically for some defense to what I had just said. Finally, she blurted out, "Because Grandpa Judd has suffered enough misery all these years, and if Jay had any love or respect for him he wouldn't do this! Why, if it hadn't been for Grandpa Judd, Jay would still be living on that filthy Indian reservation. He wouldn't have had a decent upbringing, or an education, or—or anything! And he certainly wouldn't have become the 'brilliant, sensitive young artist' that critics have labeled him. But I guess you can't expect an Indian to appreciate things like that."

Anger pumped through my veins and I found myself clutching the cool grass as fiercely as Janet had.

"You can't imagine what it was like," she went on, caught up in the fervor of her cause, "growing up with a silent, long-legged half-breed who always looked like he'd just as soon scalp you as say hello. I was only about two years old when Jay came to live with us and as far back as I can remember, he's always frightened me. Maybe it's those eyes of his. They look right through you—not at you! And it seemed like he never smiled, let alone laughed. Nothing anybody said could make him mad or lose his temper. He'd just stand there with hatred in his eyes." She shuddered. "I don't know how Mom did it, raising and educating a boy that was more wild Indian than a civilized human being."

"Your mother seems to be very fond of Jay," I said in a dry, tight voice.

Janet smiled skeptically. "She's just soft-hearted, that's all. I suppose she felt sorry for him—his dad running out the way he did, and then his mother dying so young."

I couldn't speak. My mind was suddenly burning with Jay's tormented account of his mother's death. I closed my eyes and felt a deep ache inside for a small boy's suffering as well as a young man's anguish.

"She and Jay were out riding when her horse stumbled and rolled on her," Janet continued. "Jay saw the whole thing happen, but from the way he's acted ever since he came to live with us, you'd think he didn't even care. He's never even mentioned her name. Not once! Indians must not feel things the same way we do!"

My back stiffened and I rose to a sitting position. "And just how do you think Jay should have acted to show you and your family that he was grieving properly over her death?" I demanded, trying to keep the anger out of my voice. I didn't succeed. Janet was staring at me with shocked brown eyes. I took a deep breath and went on as carefully as I could, with a voice that was now strangely calm in spite of the turbulance inside me. "Doesn't the fact that he never smiled or laughed tell you anything? I mean, how can one human being judge another simply by surface appearances? You can't look into another person's soul, so how can you measure his grief? Haven't you thought how terribly alone Jay must have felt—being torn away from his mother's people and tossed into a family who told him that his father was no good and had run out on him and his mother? Can you blame him for being angry? He must have been bleeding inside with loneliness and frustration and yet his pride forced him to remain silent. All these years, the hurt's been getting worse because he couldn't let it out."

Janet slowly drew herself off the grass and a look of reluctant understanding touched her face. "I never thought about Jay that way before." Her brown eyes regarded me closely. "You know, it's strange. I've lived with Jay almost all my life and you've known him only a few hours—not even one day—and yet you make me feel as if I've never really known him at all."

I turned away from her inquisitive stare, feeling hot and fluttery inside.

"You really like him, don't you?" she said wonderingly.

I wanted to smile and make some light answer, but all I could do was nod my head.

Janet pursed her lips and gave me a fatalistic look. "It's like I said before—Jay has a way of upsetting things. Now if you'd only met Thayne first—"

I gave a shaky little laugh. "Oh, Janet! What possible difference could that have made?"

"You mean, it still would have been Jay. Is that it?"

"I didn't say that. What I meant was—"

"You said exactly what you meant!" she said decidedly. "You just didn't intend to, that's all. Oh well, I suppose he is awfully good-looking for an Indian."

"Janet, please!"

"Oh, all right. I'll stop. You're as red as a tomato." She gave me a reluctant smile. "Thayne's going to be awfully disappointed though."

It took a lot of will power to keep from replying to her last remark. Instead, I asked, "Weren't you going to explain why it upsets your grand-father so much for people to talk about Jay? I still don't understand the reason for it."

It was Janet's turn to blush now. "Oh, I guess I did get side-tracked a bit." She gave me a half-hearted smile that was faintly apologetic. "I guess it really isn't Jay's fault that he upsets Grandpa Judd. Most of it is caused by memories—and Jay just happens to be the one who stirs up those memories. I told you how Grandpa Judd has never gotten over Uncle Jason's disappearance—well, having Jay around to remind him of it every waking hour is like putting salt on a raw wound. You see, as Jay grew up he began to resemble his father more and more. Seeing Jay must be kind of like seeing Uncle Jason to Grandpa Judd. It's gotten so that whenever Jay is around, Grandpa is terribly moody. In fact, a few years ago he had spells of depression that nobody could bring him out of."

"Shouldn't those 'spells' have been mentioned to a doctor?"

Janet sighed. "I know what you're thinking, and Mom and Dad tried their best, but Grandpa Judd wouldn't hear of it. He insisted he was just fine. And when Jay wasn't around, Grandpa really was a lot better. Jay left the ranch soon after he finished high school and we hardly saw him after that, except for a few weeks in the summer when he'd come to visit. Then, just seeing him seemed to stir up all Grandpa's old griefs. After a while, Jay stopped coming. We hadn't seen or heard from him for about three years. It was only a couple of weeks before you were due to arrive that my folks got a letter from him. Jay said he'd work and pay for his board and keep, and that he had a very important reason for coming back. Of course, Mother and Daddy had to say yes. What else could they do?"

I nodded vaguely and looked up through trembling, silver-green leaves to an aching blue sky.

"I think if they had known the reason why Jay wanted to come back they might not have agreed to it," Janet told me in a confidential tone. "But Jay didn't announce his so-called quest until dinnertime, the day after he got here. Then he calmly told us all that he knew his father didn't desert his mother and that he was going to stay in Dusk until he found out what really did happen to him. I wish you could have seen Grandpa's face! He looked like death itself that night and he's been extra touchy ever since. So has Daddy, but he doesn't show it as much. You do understand, don't you?" she asked desperately, "and you won't talk about Jay when Grandpa Judd's around?"

"I promise I won't mention him," I told her.

Janet gave a sigh of relief and jumped to her feet, the old spark of gaity back in her eyes and voice. "I knew you'd understand. You always do. I feel so much better for having gotten the whole thing off my chest. It's been driving me crazy ever since you got here. Who knows, maybe Jay will give up his silly notions of solving a mystery and just leave."

There was no point in my commenting on that. I knew that Jay would never leave the ranch—not until he had found out the truth about his father's disappearance. And the source of that truth might prove to be deadly.

I shivered and struggled to my feet, feeling the heavy pull of all my leg muscles.

"Something tells me you're going to be needing a nice, hot bath when we get back," Janet said with a grin.

I gave her a painful smile and hobbled over to my horse. He was muddy brown in color with a darker mane and tail. His legs were short and his belly was round as a barrel. His name was Herman. Silly name for a horse, I thought, but it suited him. Janet's younger brothers had insisted I take Herman because he was so gentle. But it hadn't taken long for me to discover that Herman's gentleness was in his temperament only. His gallop was about as gentle as a pile driver. I swung one leg over Herman's broad back and submitted myself to the hardness of the saddle with a groan. It was going to be a long ride back.

Chapter 8

"Gr-r-r—there go, my heart's abhorrence!"
Robert Browning

Janet was absolutely right about my needing a hot bath. But even after the therapy of a long, steamy soak, I seriously doubted whether I would be able to sit on anything harder than a pillow.

"I think maybe I'd better give you a helpful hint before we go down to dinner," Janet said as she finished combing her dark curls into place.

I sat down on the bed with a groan and began struggling into my clothes. "What sort of helpful hint? Bring a pillow with me?"

"No, just the opposite. No matter how sore you are—don't show it! David and Tadd are just waiting for the chance to tease you to death about today's ride, and if you let out so much as a single moan or walk stiff-legged, they'll never let you see the end of it."

"You mean I have to suffer in silence?"

"More than that. You've got to convince them that you feel wonderful. You see—" She looked at me guiltily. "I have a little confession to make."

I glanced up from buttoning my blouse and gave her a wary look. "All right. Let's have it."

"Well, whenever we have guests on the ranch, my brothers always make sure that somebody gets Herman for their first ride. He's a good horse, really, and as gentle as a lamb, but he's got the hardest, rockiest gallop of any horse on the ranch."

"Janet Bradford! And you went right ahead and let me ride him without saying a word!"

"I know it's a dirty trick, but I honestly thought you were used to riding and hoped that Herman's rocky gait wouldn't get to you. At least, that's what I told my brothers." She gave me an imploring smile. "You're not too mad, are you?"

62

"No. At least you warned me about your brothers. I'm going to make sure they're disappointed tonight. They won't hear one whimper or complaint—even if it kills me!"

Janet winced as she watched me climb into a clean pair of slacks. "Good luck!" she said through her teeth.

Dinner was served in the dining room but it was hardly a formal affair. The men and boys fell upon the food like ravenous wolves, and after a strenuous afternoon of horseback riding, I was fairly ravenous myself.

A large bowl of Swiss steak swimming in rich, brown gravy sat in the center of the table, and there were new potatoes with butter oozing down their thin skins, nearby. I could have written a sonnet about Helen's creamed peas and carrots made with fresh cream and butter, but mere words could never describe the delights of homemade bread and apricot preserves.

My enjoyment of the meal brought a look of satisfaction to Helen Bradford's plain features. "One thing I can't stand," she told me, "is folks who don't appreciate good food!"

"Well, there certainly aren't any people like that in this house," her husband grinned. "Pass me some more spuds, Helen, will you please?"

"You'd better watch out," Janet told me in a warning tone. "If Mother has her way, you'll be waddling back to Ann Arbor come the end of summer."

I smiled at Janet's remark, but Mrs. Bradford looked me up and down critically. "I don't know why you girls like to stay so skinny. Seems to me as if you could stand some more meat on those bones."

"Mother!" Janet said with a tight look.

"Well now, I don't know as Angela needs that much fattening up," Thayne put in with his smooth smile. "I think she's put together just fine."

David and Tadd snickered openly over Thayne's comment, and I turned my head away from his frank blue gaze. As I did, my eyes met those of Janet's seventeen-year-old brother, Stuart. He was a serious looking youth with brown-rimmed glasses in front of equally brown eyes. His manner and expression lacked the mischievousness of his two younger brothers and the forward technique of his older brother, but had the same ready smile and easy-going manner.

"Did you have a nice ride today?" he asked pleasantly.

Tadd and David immediately elbowed one another and exchanged significant glances.

"Yes, I did. I don't know when I've seen such beautiful country."

"Was your horse O.K.? I mean, were you able to handle him and everything?" David asked with round-eyed innocence.

"Herman was just fine and he behaved beautifully. Do you usually have trouble handling him?" I asked in return.

"Well, uh, no—not usually," David stammered and was promptly jabbed in the ribs by Tadd.

Janet gave me a smug grin from across the table and I let out a small, satisfied sigh. Perhaps my aching derriere was worth it, after all.

The only thing lacking from my enjoyment of the dinner hour was Jay's presence. When I first sat down at the table, I found myself counting the place settings almost automatically. I was sure there were enough to include him, but then Bert Tingey had come in and taken the last chair and dinner began without a word having been mentioned about Jay. None of the Bradfords seemed the least bit concerned over Jay's comings and goings, but I couldn't help worrying and wondering where he was. I hadn't seen him since breakfast, and there was always the possibility that something might have happened. The maddening thing was I could have solved the whole dilemma with a simple question—if I hadn't promised Janet that I wouldn't mention Jay when her grandfather was present. Since Judd Bradford was presiding over the meal at the head of the table, and seemed to be in an amiable enough mood, I certainly wasn't going to risk another repeat of this morning's performance by asking about his grandson.

"How's that Hereford cow you brought in today?" Judd asked the hired hand.

"She looks all right to me. I don't think the calf'll be born tonight. Maybe tomorrow. Jay's out checking her now."

I watched Judd's face carefully for some reaction to the mention of Jay's name but none came. If anything, he seemed pleased with what Bert had told him. Then Judd saw me watching him and gave me a questioning look from beneath those bushy black brows. I smiled at him and leaned back in my chair with exquisite relief. Jay was safe.

"If you're not too tired of horseback riding, how about taking a little ride with me after dinner?" Thayne asked me.

"Well—I don't know. I thought I might write a letter to my mother."

"You can write letters any time," Thayne said and stretched his arm casually along the back of my chair.

I looked at Janet for some way out. I could see she was torn between her desire for me to go riding with her brother and the knowledge of how stiff I was.

"I don't know if Herman's up to another long ride—he's not as young as he used to be," she said finally.

"Angela doesn't need to ride Herman," Thayne said and flashed me his disarming smile. "I'll saddle Ginger for you. She's a frisky little mare, but I'm sure you can handle her."

I felt Tadd's and David's eyes on me and knew there was no way out. I couldn't admit how tired and stiff I really was in front of them—not after telling everyone how much I enjoyed my ride and how marvelous I felt.

"That'll be fine," I said, shifting position on the chair.

Before I left with Thayne, Janet took me aside and whispered, "Remember what I said last night. Just give things a chance—you know what I mean."

I nodded and tried not to walk stiff-legged down the stairs. It was horrible to feel obligated to be nice to someone. I might have liked Thayne a lot more if I didn't know that it was expected of me. I wondered then if Thayne were feeling much the same way and purposely trying to please me for his sister's sake. If he were, I would be only too happy to release him from such an obligation.

It was the twilight hour and the soft gray dusk was settling round the hills and valleys like a veil. But as our horses galloped down the gravel road away from the ranch, I was too busy hanging on to enjoy the quiet beauty of the evening. Thayne kept his horse, a saucy gelding called Firebug, at full gallop and Ginger was eager to join in the race. I was forever yanking at the reins to keep her under control. Ginger had a mind of her own though, and obeyed me grudgingly, with frustrated whinnies and a tossing head. Although her gallop was smooth, an entire afternoon astride Herman had taken its toll. Finally, I reined her in, unable to go on.

Thayne glanced over his shoulder at me and quickly turned Firebug's head. He drew in sharply aside Ginger and asked with a teasing smile, "What's the matter? Are you getting tired already?"

"Of course not!" I retorted and tossed my hair back from my face. "It's just—well, the evening's so lovely, I don't see why we need to rush so . . ."

Thayne's blue eyes grew brighter and a pleased smile spread across his face. "Let's stop by the river for a while, then."

The look in his eyes gave me an uncomfortable, crawling feeling in my stomach, but I tried to argue away my suspicions. Most likely, he was being especially attentive to me because of Janet. There was no logical reason why I should be so suspicious of him. In fact, there were probably a dozen girls in Dusk who would gladly trade places with me this very moment. The least I could do was make an attempt at friendship with him.

We guided our horses down into the gulley and, ironically, Thayne stopped near the place where Jay and I had talked only the night before. He helped me dismount and when my feet touched the ground my legs nearly buckled under me.

"Are you all right?" he asked in a concerned voice. "You seem a little stiff."

I made my way to a level portion of the grassy river bank and sat down. "I am more than a little stiff! I am miserably stiff and sore!" I rested my back against the trunk of a cottonwood tree and stretched my legs out in front of me. "But please don't tell your younger brothers. I'd hate to think my performance at dinner was all for nothing."

Thayne laughed and seated himself beside me. "You can count on me! Man, you sure had me fooled! If I'd known you didn't feel like it, I wouldn't have asked you to go riding."

"Oh, that's all right. I should have told you, but I hated to admit what a dude I am in front of the boys."

"You may be stiff and sore, but you're no dude."

"Well, I'm no expert rider either, but thanks for keeping my little secret," I said and smiled at him.

He leaned closer. "It's the least I can do, baby."

The next moment Thayne had me pinned against the tree and his mouth was on mine, forcing my lips apart. Both his hands gripped my arms but I finally managed to wrench my head away and gasp, "Let me go! Please, let me go!"

The bristles of his mustache rubbed against my neck and he murmured, "Why? What's the matter, honey?"

I tried to think what to say and realized with a deep shudder that I was far more frightened than angry. There was something terrifying about his bruising lips and heavy grasp. I knew I couldn't muscle my way out of his arms. My only hope lay in appealing to his ego.

"Look, I know Janet's asked you to be nice to me, but don't you think you're carrying things a bit too far?"

Thayne raised his head to look at me and the surprise on his face was obvious. "How did you know that?" he asked, releasing his hold on my arms. I took the opportunity to struggle to my feet and looked down at him as calmly as I could.

"Janet's my best friend. I think I know her pretty well—and I think her matchmaking ideas for the two of us are ridiculous. So there's no need for you to play the role of ardent suitor all summer."

Thayne grinned and got to his feet. "Who's playing a role? What if Janet did ask me to be nice to you? As far as I'm concerned, the extent of that would be, 'Hello, Miss Stewart. Nice to have you on the ranch.' No, baby. My feelings for you have nothing to do with the promise I made to my little sister."

He took a step toward me and my heart started pounding wildly in my throat. "But, you don't even know me," I said hoarsely, and grasped the tree trunk for support.

"I know you're different from any girl I've ever been with and I want to know you better—a lot better!"

I stepped back and he laughed. "You may keep your distance but you can't fool me. Underneath all that cool you're warm and soft!"

I took another step away from him and tripped over a gnarled root. With the swiftness of an adder, Thayne's hand shot out and grabbed my left wrist, twisting my arm behind my back and crushing me against him. Then his other hand grasped my neck, pulling my head back to meet his lunging mouth. My struggles only brought me pain but I refused to submit to his embrace. When I was finally able to tear my mouth away from his searing kiss, his lips found my neck and he whispered heavily, "Come on, baby. Melt a little."

My voice came out in a breathless whimper. "You're hurting me! Please—let me go!"

Thayne lifted his head to look at me and his blue eyes were hard and brilliant. "Not until you learn to relax, honey. It won't hurt at all if you loosen up a little. In fact, I think you'll like it a lot."

I let myself go limp in his arms, praying he would release my left arm from its torturing position behind my back. He did. One hand now cupped my chin and I saw his completely self-assured smile as he said, "Now, that's better. I always say, if you leave an icicle in the sun long enough, it's bound to melt sooner or later. How about sooner, honey?"

I purposely moved my hands slowly up his chest, letting him think I was yielding to his advances. From the hot gleam in his eyes and the way his hands quickly found the buttons to my blouse, I knew I had succeeded. Then, with a deep breath and a prayer, I pushed him away from me with a strength that surprised us both. Thayne stumbled backward with an angry grunt, and the soft, silky grass of the river bank gave him no footing at all. The next thing I knew, he was making a perfect spread-eagle landing in the stream.

I didn't wait to see what would happen next. Forgetting my stiffness, I ran to the horses and grabbed Ginger's reins. I stuffed one foot in the stirrup and swung my other leg over her back, afraid that any moment Thayne would come lunging after me. I could hear him swearing and sputtering and stomping soggily out of the water even now. In a panic, I reached down and grabbed Firebug's reins, turned Ginger's head and gave her a swift kick in the sides.

"Come on, girl!" I choked. "Let's get out of here!"

The little mare sprang forward into her smooth, easy gallop and Firebug kept up the pace alongside. We took the steep road out of the gulley in a few easy strides. At the top I stopped and let him run free. He and Ginger ran nose and nose all the way back to the ranch and I was barely able to break the mare's stride before we reached the barn. The two horses plodded inside, sides heaving and mouths foaming from their run.

I slumped over in the saddle, suddenly trembling all over and sick with the feeling of Thayne's hands and mouth on my body. Taking the horses at a dead run down the gravel road in near darkness wasn't nearly as terrifying as what I had left behind me.

Bert Tingey came out of a stall and when I saw him my cheeks burned with humiliation. I slid painfully off my horse and clung to the saddle horn for a few moments until I was sure my legs would hold me.

"I'll take care of those horses if you like, Miss," the old hand offered and I gave him a grateful nod, still too breathless to speak.

"You know, as a rule, I get madder'n a hornet when somebody runs these horses along the gravel road," he said, and gave me a scrutinizing glance as he removed Firebug's saddle. "But, mebbe this time I'll let you off easy—if you had a good reason for doin' it."

Was that a twinkle I saw in those hazel eyes? I swallowed hard and gave him another nod, then made my way around the horses to the barn door.

"By the way, just where is Thayne?—if you don't mind my askin'? It's not like him to send his horse on ahead with a purty young lady. No sir, it's not like him a'tall." This time there was no mistaking the twinkle of amusement in his eyes.

"He—uh, decided to cool off in the stream, but he'll be back—in a while."

I hobbled out of the barn and toward the ranchhouse with Bert Tingey's delighted chuckles still ringing in my ears. I remembered the sight of Thayne's startled form toppling over into the water and grinned myself. Then I thought of Janet. What on earth was I going to tell her? I could see her face now, eyes alight and her voice eager. "Well-l-l-l? Did you have a good time?" I could hardly tell her that I detested her brother, and I was too angry and humiliated to go into any details of what had happened. My only way out lay in saying as little as possible.

"Well-l-l?" Janet said expectantly after we were alone in her room.

I had showered and washed my hair and was busy rolling long, wet strands into plastic curlers. I shifted my position on the stool at her dressing table with a groan.

"Well, what?"

Janet was sitting cross-legged at the foot of the bed. Now she bounced impatiently. "Did you give things a chance to develop—you know!"

I couldn't keep back a wry smile. "I didn't need to."

"What do you mean?"

"Your brother doesn't believe in giving things a 'chance to develop.'"

"Angela, make sense. I haven't the slightest idea what you're talking about."

"I guess I'm too tired to make sense."

For a moment she was all sympathy. "You poor thing! As if riding Herman all day wasn't bad enough. I really am sorry about that."

"I know. Don't worry, I'll live."

"He likes you, doesn't he?" Janet prodded.

"Who, Herman? I didn't ask him."

"Angela! I'm talking about Thayne! Does he like you?"

"I suppose so."

"You suppose so! He must have said something!"

I carefully pinned another roller into place, all the while searching frantically for something to tell her. "Well, he did say I was different from other girls he's known."

"You see!" Janet exclaimed triumphantly and clapped her hands. "Didn't I tell you!" Watching her face in the mirror, I saw her brown eyes regarding me closely. "How do you feel about Thayne?"

I took a deep breath and let it out slowly. "At the moment, I don't know if I could find the proper words to describe how I feel."

Janet smiled at me, "Well, like I said last night. You've got all summer!"

Chapter 9

"Hand in hand they went together
Through the woodland and the meadow . . . ."
Henry Wadsworth Longfellow

There was no early rising to greet the sun my second morning on the ranch. I was barely able to crawl out of bed at nine o'clock. Janet had long since dressed and gone so I was free to alternately limp and stomp about her room and bang as many drawers as I pleased. The more I thought about my evening ride with her brother, the more angry I became. It was bad enough that Janet expected me to fall in love with him, but to learn that Thayne himself fully expected me to sooner or later succumb to his charms was infuriating!

I applied makeup, did my hair, then selected a dressy pair of cotton-knit slacks with a coordinated top, both in pale blue. Maybe it wasn't the type of outfit one wore on a ranch, but I wasn't going to get anywhere near a horse today if I could help it. To insure that fact, I put on a pair of thin white sandals. No more Herman and no more Thayne—for twenty-four hours, anyway! I shut the door with a bang and left the room.

The house was stone quiet. I went down the stairs and glanced about the living room. No one was there. Probably, all the men and boys were at work in the fields. It was nearly nine-thirty, so the milking was long since finished and breakfast would be over as well. I certainly wouldn't mind not having to put on a front of cheerful enthusiasm for Janet's younger brothers. This morning it would be asking too much.

I entered the kitchen and Helen Bradford smiled a good morning from her place at the sink. She was scouring the last frying pan and I hated to have her dirty more dishes just to fix me breakfast.

"My, you look pretty this morning," she said. "That shade of blue just matches your eyes. By the way, I saved you some breakfast. Janet said you looked so tuckered out that she didn't have the heart to wake you up." Helen gave me a close look. "How do you feel, dear?"

70

I smiled at her. "Oh, I'll survive. As long as I don't have to ride Herman again, that is."

Helen nodded understandingly. "That horse! If he weren't such a sweet old thing I'd be tempted to tell John to get rid of him. But Herman's kind of gotten to be an institution around here. Whenever folks come back to see us they always ask if Herman's still around." She went to the refrigerator and got out a pitcher of orange juice. "I've got some pancakes keepin' warm in the oven if you'd care to have some."

"Oh, no thank you. I'm really not that hungry. The orange juice will be fine."

"Oh, come now! That's not enough to keep a flea alive! At least have one of my cinnamon rolls."

"You talked me into it," I said. "Where is Janet?"

"She's gone into town with Thayne. I sent them in to pick up the mail and a few things for me."

I managed to hide my relief, but I was infinitely grateful that I wouldn't have to face Thayne as yet. I took a drink of juice then watched rather curiously as Helen opened a cupboard under the sink and started reaching behind the dishwashing detergent and a can of cleanser. She removed a small canister, then, seeing my look, chuckled deeply.

"I don't always keep sweet rolls under the sink," she said. "But when you've got a house full of hungry menfolk, you have to be sneaky sometimes. I knew there wouldn't be one left for you if I didn't hide it. Those boys are always lookin' through my cupboards and drawers for goodies. More'n once they've eaten up a cake or special dessert that I was saving for someone else. So now I hide things," she said with a crafty grin. "Especially the marshmallows. Tadd is always sneaking a handful whenever he can find them."

"Do the boys ever find your hiding places?" I asked.

"Sometimes. Then I have to think of a new one."

"Well, I'm glad they didn't find this cinnamon roll. It's delicious!"

"Thank you, dear. Under the sink is one of my best hiding places. In order to find what I've hidden, the boys would have to move the dish pans and detergent. My boys have never been too eager to wash dishes, so things usually stay hid."

I smiled and said in the tones of a fellow conspirator, "Your secret is safe with me!"

"Well, if anything shows up missing, I'll know who to talk to, won't I?" she said and we both laughed.

There was a light rapping on the back door and then Jay walked in. I hadn't seen him since yesterday morning's walk in the hills and I realized in one swift, piercing moment I had not imagined the impact he had on me. It happened all over again the moment I saw him. This morning he was

71

wearing a pair of corduroy slacks in a deep burgandy hue. His long-sleeved shirt was a complimentary shade of mauve. The outfit was a sultry compliment to his dark good looks.

"Land sakes!" Helen exclaimed. "If you aren't the handsomest thing I ever laid eyes on!"

Jay grinned and gave Helen an affectionate hug. Her eyes were soft as his strong arms went around her.

"You're not all dressed up to impress me, so where're you off to?" she asked with a sniff.

"There's an art dealer up in Jackson who wants one of my latest paintings for his gallery. I thought I'd drive up this morning and deliver it."

"Well, it's a beautiful morning for a drive," Helen pronounced, then looked at me. "We'll have to be sure and take you up to Jackson before the summer's through. It's a fun little town and the Tetons are real close by."

"That would be wonderful. I've always wanted to see those mountains."

"Would you like to see them today—with me?" Jay asked quietly.

My heart started hammering inside my chest. "Well, I wouldn't want you to go out of your way. If you have some business—"

"It won't take me long to deliver the painting," he said.

Helen's brown eyes were sparkling. "I'll pack you a picnic lunch and you can be on your way."

Jay looked at me and smiled. "Well?"

"I'd love to go!"

His dark eyes gleamed. "Good! I'll load my stuff in the Bronco and we can take off."

I sat for just a moment after he had gone, savoring the thought of spending an entire day with him. Had I really been angry and stiff and tired this morning? Ridiculous!

Helen bustled over to the refrigerator and started taking inventory of the contents. "Hmmm, I've got some ham for the sandwiches and there's some apples, cheese, and even some canned soda pop. Does that sound all right to you?"

I got up from the table, walked over to her and put my arms about her. "Thank you," I said.

She gave me a tender smile and a ferocious hug. "You can pack some of the food while I make the sandwiches," she said. "There's a picnic hamper down in that end cupboard."

Ten minutes later Jay was helping me into the front seat of his Ford Bronco and Helen Bradford was waving goodbye to us. "Have a good day!" she ordered.

Jay smiled at me and gave Helen a wave of his hand. "We will!"

It seemed strange at first, driving back along the road where Jay and I had walked the night of my arrival. Everything looked so different in the daytime. The gulley wasn't quite so steep and forbidding, there was no aura of danger lurking behind the trees and bushes. The countryside was peaceful and content to bask in the mild rays of the morning sun. It was easy to forget what had happened two nights before until we approached a large clump of trees.

"Is this where—" I began hesitantly.

"Yes."

I glanced at Jay who didn't seem the least bit disturbed by memories of two shots fired at the truck. "Have you found out anything?"

"No. Nothing. And I don't want you worrying about it. Today you're going to fall in love with Wyoming and forget everything else."

I smiled at him. "Is that an order?"

He grinned back. "That's an order. And to help you enjoy our trip I've got a little present for you in the back seat."

"A present?"

He nodded over his shoulder. "Take a look and see."

I turned around and glanced behind me. "How did you know I needed this?" I asked with an embarrassed smile, and reached over the seat to grasp a large bed pillow.

"I knew you were out riding yesterday afternoon on Herman, then Bert told me you went riding again last night. I'm surprised you can walk at all."

I looked at Jay suspiciously, wondering what else Bert had told him, but he kept his eyes on the curving brown road and his face told me nothing.

"Thanks for the present," I murmured and slipped the pillow under me with a sigh.

Jay's Bronco ate up the miles and it seemed no time at all until we were approaching the sharp curve in the road.

"Isn't this where I went swimming the other night?" I asked lightly.

"It sure is," he said, then added casually, "and I hear you've been giving Thayne swimming lessons in the creek."

My cheeks went scarlet and there was a long, confused moment before I could think of anything to say. Finally, I mumbled, "Where did you hear that?"

"Well, Bert told me you came high-tailing it back to the barn last night with the horses all lathered up, and Firebug minus a rider. A while later, he saw this wet rooster come dripping along the road and sneak up the outside stairs to the house. Seeing as how Thayne's idea of a good time usually isn't a dip in an ice cold creek and a long walk home, it wasn't too difficult to figure out what happened." Jay slowed the Bronco to round the sharp curve and when he spoke again, all traces of amusement were gone from his voice.

73

"Did he hurt you, Angela?"

I lowered my head and almost involuntarly, my right hand moved to cover the ugly bruise on my left wrist. I heard Jay mutter, "Damn him!" under his breath and the Bronco jerked forward as his foot hit the gas pedal.

I clenched my hands together and stared as the Bradford's red-panelled truck came lumbering around a curve just ahead of us. Thayne gave several blasts on the horn and I saw Janet waving frantically out the window. The truck came to a quick stop on the dusty road, and with tense jaw and flashing eyes, Jay pulled the Bronco alongside it.

"Hey, where are you two headed?" Thayne called out.

"I have a painting to deliver to an art dealer and thought I could show Angela some of the country on the way," Jay said.

"Sounds like fun," Thayne commented with a tight smile. "If you're not in too much of a hurry, maybe you could wait until we drop off the mail and Mom's packages back at the house. Then we could go with you."

"Some other time," Jay said and shifted the Bronco into first gear.

Thayne's mouth hardened and Janet's head suddenly popped out of the window beside her brother's. "Where are you going?" she asked. "Maybe we could meet you somewhere later on and have lunch."

Jay's hand tightened on the gear shift and I quickly slid over beside him. "Your mother's already packed us a lunch," I told her with a smile. "We'll see you tonight!"

Jay grinned at me and the Bronco surged forward with an eager roar. Jay didn't mention Janet or Thayne again, but I noticed he pushed the Bronco quite hard until we were well out of Dusk and on the highway leading north to Jackson. Then he drove at a more leisurely speed, content to pull over to the right and let other cars pass us at will. I was surprised though, when he steered the vehicle off the highway and brought it to a stop near a grassy field. Jay jumped out of the car, came around to my side and opened the door.

"Will this do?" he asked.

"Do? What do you mean? Why are we stopping here?"

"So you can stand in the middle of a field of wild flowers, of course."

I smiled and gave him my hand.

We strolled out into the open meadow and Jay pointed out flowers with strange, wonderful names I had never heard before: Oldman-Whiskers, Goatsbeard, Scarlet Gilia, and Mule Ears. We lingered until we felt "the personality of the place," as Jay put it, and then drove on.

We stopped another time for my first view of the Wind River mountain range.

"They make me feel almost uneasy," I told Jay. "Most mountains are rugged and majestic, but these are so—so awesome! It's hard to explain how they make me feel inside."

Jay nodded and said, "Whenever I see them, I think of those ghostly peaks as the home of the manitou."

"The manitou? Who is that?"

"It is one of the names the Indians give to the Great Spirit, the Power, the One who Rules Nature."

I looked at the towering peaks where winter snow still lingered and clouds drifted through jagged crevices. "The home of the manitou. Yes, I see what you mean."

Jay brushed a heavy lock of black hair out of his eyes. "Far across those mountains, past the wilderness country, lies the Wind River Indian Reservation and the grave of my mother."

"Where is she buried?"

"In a little cemetary in Fort Washakie. It's a barren place," he began, then stopped himself. "She's in good company though," he continued in a lighter tone. "Sacajewea and Chief Washakie himself are buried nearby."

"I would like to see her grave."

"One day I will take you there," he said quietly.

He stood for a while, thinking his own thoughts, lifting his face to the wind. The sadness in his eyes made me ache inside so I said to him, "Is the manitou smiling today or are his thoughts full of sadness?"

"I will ask him," Jay replied seriously and raised both arms out in front of him in a solemn gesture. "Manitou!" he called, and his voice was carried on the wind in a long, melodious cry. "Manitou!"

I stood motionless and for a moment the mountains seemed to look down upon us with their solemn granite faces. Even the wind lowered its voice to a hushed whisper.

Jay let his arms drop slowly to his sides and said, "The manitou is just and wise. But he is also a jealous god. I think he would like to leave his lonely home in the clouds and take my place today."

I was too moved by his words to speak, but when he stretched out his hand, I took it and clutched his lean brown fingers tightly as we walked back to the car.

We passed a lot of what Jay termed great cattle country. The most popular breed was the white-faced Hereford, but we saw many Black Angus cattle as well, their dusky coats shining like smooth black satin in the sun. Once or twice we saw the creamy Charolais breed, but when we passed by a small tan animal standing in sagebrush and high grass, I took an excited second look over my shoulder.

"Jay! Was that a deer?"

"Where?"

"In the sagebrush over on your side of the road. It's still there! Jay, it's an antelope! I'm sure it's an antelope. I've never seen one before!"

75

"Let's go back and get a closer look, then," he said and began slowing down. One lone car passed us, then Jay made a quick U-turn and started back.

"Can you still see him?"

"Yes, there he is!" I said, pointing.

"I'll have to find a place to turn off the highway. The drop-off is too steep here."

"There's a little side road up ahead," I suggested.

"That'll do fine."

Jay turned the Bronco onto the dirt road and parked it while I kept glancing anxiously at our antelope to make sure he hadn't run away. I could barely see his trim, pointed horns and pert black nose above the tall grass, but he was there, about one hundred yards away.

A wire fence separated the open rangeland from the highway area and Jay said to me, "If we keep down low and follow along this fence we might get pretty close to him before he gets scared off. I've got a pair of binoculars so you can get a better look."

I followed Jay off the dirt road and down into a low, weedy section of land between the highway and fenced-off fields. As we stalked around sagebrush and dry twigs, keeping our backs hunched, I thought how curious we must appear to motorists passing by. "Do you suppose people will think we've lost a contact lens?" I asked, trying to stifle my laughter.

I heard Jay's low chuckle, then he whispered, "We should be pretty near him now."

Slowly, we straightened up and peered out over the grass and gray-green sage. He was there. A beautiful little buck with black almond eyes staring right at us. For a few seconds we watched one another, Jay and I with silent admiration, the antelope with unblinking wariness. Then I took two steps toward the fence for a closer look. The buck decided that was two steps too close and bounded off through the field, his white rump a sharp contrast to the dusky green sage.

"He's gone."

"No, he isn't. Look! He's just gone back to join his family. There are more antelopes out there."

I followed Jay's directing finger and saw four, tiny brown dots near some sage-covered hills. Jay handed me the binoculars and the four brown dots became a handsome antelope family. "There's a little one out there," I told Jay, then, in surprise: "They're looking right at us!"

"Sure they are. Antelopes have excellent eyesight. I'm surprised we got as close as we did to that buck."

I handed Jay the binoculars and he watched them intently for a few moments, then put the glasses back into their case and took my hand.

"Shall we go? Our next stop is lunch."

"Good! Let's be on our way!"

We ate Helen's picnic lunch somewhere in the Gros Ventre Mountains along the Hoback River, then took to the road once more. I was delighted that it followed the rushing course of the Hoback through the mountains until it joined the Snake. Jay explained that the Snake River eventually met the mighty Columbia whose waters flowed into the endless sea. But our course was not down river. Instead, we followed the Snake up through the mountains to the little town of Jackson. I fell in love with it at first sight. It was largely a tourist haven but even that did not lessen its charm and Old West atmosphere. The multitudinous pairs of sunglasses and dozens of cameras slung across the shoulders of visiting tourists were all a part of Jackson's unique personality.

We drove along the main street, past elkhorn arches and boardwalks until we came to the art gallery. This was located in a building that was typically Old West in design and structure. Jay led me up a flight of wooden stairs and through swinging doors into a fairly large room with white plaster walls. All manner of Western art was displayed, including some sculpture, and I busied myself with looking at the various paintings while Jay went to find the art dealer. There were several paintings of the Tetons, none of which did the mountains justice, and some good Charles Russell prints, but most intriguing to me were the pieces of wildlife cast in bronze. I looked up from two stallions locked in vicious combat to see Jay walking toward me with a middle-aged, heavy-set man at his side. The man had thin, sandy hair and large, freckled hands. He was wearing a Western shirt with a string bow tie and around his ample waistline was a leather belt with a monstrous silver buckle. I pried my eyes off the buckle to smile a greeting.

"Angela, I'd like you to meet Frank Reynolds. He owns the gallery here and deals in Western art. Frank, this is Angela Stewart, a friend of the Bradfords. She's staying at the ranch this summer."

Mr. Reynolds gave my hand a quick shake and said before I could acknowledge Jay's introduction, "Won't you come into my office with us, Miss Stewart? I'm sure you're as anxious as I am to see Jay's latest painting." He looked longingly at the oblong package wrapped in heavy brown paper which was tucked under Jay's arm, then turned and walked rapidly toward the back of the gallery.

"Is he always this abrupt?" I whispered to Jay as we followed the art dealer to his office.

"Always," Jay said with a smile. "I usually manage to get on his nerves because I refuse to be hurried and Frank loves to hurry."

Frank Reynolds unlocked his office door, ushered us inside, and motioned to two black leather chairs. He moved to his desk with quick steps and sat down in a swivel-type chair.

"Now then, let's unwrap that thing and have a look," he said eagerly.

Jay gave me an amused glance and proceeded to undo the brown paper wrappings quite leisurely.

The art dealer swung about in his chair and tapped the desk with the tip of a pencil. "Come on, Bradford! I've been waiting all morning!"

"I don't remember telling you I would be here at any particular time," Jay said.

"I know, I know, but a couple from New York were in here a little while ago and they were asking lots of questions about the local artists. When I mentioned I'd have one of your paintings here today they got pretty excited. They're coming back sometime this afternoon to see it. I wouldn't be surprised if they bought it on the spot."

"Then again, they may not like it at all," Jay said and held up his painting for Mr. Reynolds to see.

"The woodpecker-like tapping of the pencil ceased immediately and the art dealer stared at the painting for a long moment. Then he said, "Stand back a little, will you? I want to see it from a distance."

Jay stood up and moved back with the painting. I turned in my chair so I could see it, too, and felt the same tugging inside that I had experienced when I saw his other paintings for the first time.

"Good Lord," Reynolds muttered. "How do you do it?—take a hunk of canvas and some greasy pigments and turn them into living things!"

Before us was the portrait of an old Indian man. He wore a shirt of tired purple and a ragged band of red cloth was tied about his gray hair. One gnarled hand was reaching upward, the fingers outstretched. The details of the painting were so fine I could see the prominence of blue veins traveling a weary course under his leathery brown skin. A wreath of wispy gray smoke circled the old man's head and crept across the bottom of his chest. Jay's technique was incredible and his use of subdued color was perfect in setting a mood of wisdom and old age. Like the portrait of his mother, the most outstanding feature of this painting was the old man's eyes.

I leaned forward to examine the portrait more closely and said, "He's blind, isn't he?"

"What makes you say that?" Frank Reynolds demanded. "His eyes seem a little sad perhaps, but look how bright and penetrating they are! Look at the wisdom in that face!"

"I know there's wisdom in the face," I said to him. "But there's something more. The old man looks as if he is seeing things the rest of us could never comprehend. Visions of his own—" I turned to Jay. "Am I right? Is he blind?"

Jay smiled at me said, "The Shoshoni call this old man, 'One-who-sees-light-through-the-darkness.' He is the wisest man on the reservation and he has been blind from birth."

"Good Lord," Reynolds muttered again. Then, to me: "You're a very perceptive young woman, Miss Stewart. Are you an artist, too?"

"No, I'm not."

The art dealer shook his head and took another look at the painting. "It's good," he pronounced. "If I could afford it, I'd buy it myself. You ought to get at least $800 for this one."

"Thanks, Frank. You can reach me at the ranch if you need to."

"Aren't you going to be in Jackson for a while? You could show Miss Stewart the sights, wander through some of the stores, then drop back here around five or so." He gave me the first genuine smile I had seen since our introduction.

"I'm sorry, but Angela and I are headed for the Tetons right now. I have to be back to the ranch tonight, so I hate to waste any more time waiting around here."

Frank Reynolds cocked a fuzzy eyebrow. "I've never known you to be in such a hurry, Bradford, but—I can't say I blame you. Goodby, Miss Stewart. Come back again."

When we were outside once more and walking down the boardwalk toward the car, Jay took my arm and said with a pleased smile, "You know, you really surprised old Frank."

"Because I thought the Indian was blind? Why should that surprise him so much?"

"Well, Frank's never been overly fond of the weaker sex, and I don't think he believed brains could be associated with beauty."

I smiled at him then looked out toward the street. "Jay, we just passed your car."

"I know."

"But I thought you were in a hurry to get to the Tetons. Where are we going?"

"You can't go hiking in those shoes. How would you like a pair of moccasins?"

He stopped suddenly as we came to a clothing store and ushered me inside. "They have some beautiful moccasins here."

"Jay, I don't know what to say."

His white teeth flashed a broad smile. "You're supposed to say, 'Yes, Jay, I'd love a pair of moccasins.' "

I couldn't help laughing. "But you don't need to buy them for me. If you're thinking you owe me something because of my suit—"

"That's only part of it," he said. "I know I don't need to buy you some moccasins, but I'd like to. Will you let me?"

For a long moment I was conscious only of the light burning deep in his earth-brown eyes. Then I realized we were standing directly in the center of a narrow aisle, and people were having to edge their way around us on either side. One hefty-looking woman who was poured into a pair of Levis and a ridiculous Western shirt with bright orange braid bouncing across her bosom, tried unsuccessfully to pass by on either side and finally stood her ground and glared at the two of us.

"Excuse me, please!" she said and it was a command, not a request.

"I'm sorry," I mumbled, and Jay stepped quickly to one side of me with an amused grin.

"They're either going to have to start making these aisles bigger or the tourists smaller," he whispered and I giggled helplessly. Then he said, "Well? What about those moccasins?"

"May I have a pair with beads on top?"

Jay slipped an arm about my shoulders. "One pair of moccasins with beads on top, coming up!"

I will never forget the surprise and thrill of seeing the Tetons for the first time. After driving a few miles out of Jackson, suddenly, there they were, rising thousands of feet from the flat, sage-covered area known as Jackson Hole. I must have sounded like an awe-struck child to Jay, but I couldn't stop exclaiming over them.

"I know a place where we can get a fantastic view of the Tetons and all of Jackson Hole," he told me.

"Where is that?"

"On top of Signal Mountain. That's our next stop."

I expected a rough climb in order to have the fantastic view Jay talked about. Instead, there was a paved road leading almost to the top of the pine-covered knoll. There were several people ahead of us, already enjoying the view, but as Jay and I stood hand in hand on the windy summit, I felt completely alone with him. Not only did we have a panoramic view of the entire Teton range and all of Jackson Hole; the rugged beauty of the Gros Ventre and Absaroka mountain ranges were on display as well. Through it all, we could follow with our eyes the winding path of the Snake River.

"I wish I could memorize all this forever," I said and felt Jay's hand tighten around mine.

"Excuse me, Mister. Excuse me, but my wife was wondering if—well, if you're an Indian."

Jay and I turned from the magnificence of mountains, meadows and forests to see an elderly couple standing behind us. The man came barely to Jay's shoulders and a straw hat covered his gray hair. Clutching his arm was a plump little woman with round blue eyes and a quivering mouth.

"Yes, I'm Indian," Jay replied, smiling into their inquisitive faces.

"Oh!" The word came out in a tremulous little sigh. "I told you, Henry!" the elderly woman said, then looked up at Jay. "I told Henry the minute we saw you, that you had to be an Indian. Of course, you aren't dressed like one, but with that black hair and those high cheekbones, I knew—"

"Martha!" her husband said in an admonishing tone.

"Are you folks from around here?" Jay asked.

"No, we're from Detroit, Michigan. I'm Henry Carlson and this is my wife Martha."

"I'm glad to know you. I'm Jay Bradford and this is Angela Stewart." Jay shook both their hands and when his long, bronze fingers clasped Martha Carlson's plump little hand, her blue eyes were as big as china saucers.

"We're practically neighbors," I said. "My home is in Ann Arbor."

"Is that a fact?" Henry Carlson said with pleasure.

"You know, you don't talk like an Indian either," Mrs. Carlson said to Jay and there was genuine disappointment in her face.

I glanced up at Jay and saw his mouth twitch with amusement. He folded his arms across his chest and said with deep solemnity, "Me go to white man's schools. Learn—many things."

"Oh! Oh, I see," the little woman breathed, staring at Jay as if she were in a trance.

"Martha!" Mr. Carlson said again. "I think we'd better be going."

"Would you mind very much if we took your picture?" she went on, ignoring the hand on her elbow. "Our grandchildren would be so thrilled to think we saw a real Indian!"

"Come on, Martha," her husband urged.

"But, Henry—!"

"The camera's out of film, anyway," he whispered and pulled her down the trail after him.

"Oh, all right," she agreed petulantly, and turned back to wave her hand. "Goodby! Goodby!"

I gave her a little wave and tried to choke down my laughter as Jay raised one arm in a stately gesture of farewell. He grinned at me. "Shall I let out a war whoop and really give them something to remember?"

"Don't you dare!"

As the afternoon wore on, we sat on the pebbled shore of Jackson Lake and Jay made stones skip happily over the water. I listened to the wind in the pines and the comfortable lapping sound of the water against the rocks, knowing what he would say soon and hating to hear it. I wished this day could go on and on.

"It's four o'clock. I'm afraid we'd better be getting back," he said, and the regret in his voice was some consolation.

The drive back to Dusk would have been just as enjoyable as the rest of our day, except I was fighting a strange sadness. It was late afternoon and the sun cast long shadows on the valleys and hills. I looked out the window, telling myself that the day was still beautiful and there was no reason to be so despondent. I tried to make some conversation but Jay didn't seem to be in a mood for talking either. When we reached Dusk and turned onto the gravel road by the railroad tracks, my despondency increased and I gave up trying to fight it. We drove for perhaps ten miles without saying a word to each other, then Jay turned the Bronco off the road and parked it near a grove of cottonwoods. He shifted about on the seat to face me, resting one arm on the steering wheel and the other along the back of the seat.

"What's the matter?"

"Nothing, really." I tried to smile but his dark eyes saw through my pretense.

"Yes, there is. What is it?"

I looked down at my hands. "It's silly. We've had a perfect day. I know I should be feeling happy and grateful. Instead, I'm miserable because it's over."

"It hasn't been quite perfect," Jay said and took me into his arms.

I found myself leaning forward slightly to meet his bent head. My eyes closed with his, then I felt the warm pressure of his mouth on mine. His kiss was gentle; asking, not demanding. Never before had I experienced such a beautiful sense of belonging.

When his lips left mine, he drew back slightly to look at me. "Now it's perfect," he said with a husky sigh, and kissed me again.

Some time later, the Bronco floated back to the ranch. I'm quite sure we must have been at least a foot above the ground as I don't recall a single bump or chuckhole in that lovely road. When we pulled up in front of the bunkhouse, Bert Tingey came running out to meet us.

"I sure am glad yer back!" he panted, his rosy cheeks even redder than usual.

"Why? Is something wrong?" Jay asked quickly.

"Old Jane has finally gone into labor and she's havin' one hell of a time. Pardon my French, Miss," he said, nodding to me.

"Have they called the vet?"

"Yeah, they called him, but he ain't comin'. He's out to Peterson's tendin' to a sick horse and can't leave. Judd's fit to be tied, but I told him you could handle the old girl as soon as you got back."

"I'll try," Jay said, getting out of the car and coming around to open the door for me. "Angela, will you tell Helen I'll have to miss dinner? I'd better change clothes and go straight to the barn."

I nodded and climbed out of the Bronco, feeling a little stiff and tired, but not the least bit despondent. Jay reached for the wicker hamper and I said, "I'll take that back to Helen if you like."

"Thanks."

"Thank you," I murmured softly so Bert wouldn't hear me, "for today."

Jay put both hands on my shoulders and kissed me hard on the lips. "I'll see you later," he said.

Chapter 10

"Now is the time of tension between dying and birth . . ."
T. S. Elliott

It was almost getting to be a ritual—my having to face the Bradfords after being with Jay, but this time I didn't care what they said. John could look at his watch and frown his frowns, Thayne could make his snide remarks, and Janet could toss me her disapproving looks. What did it matter when I could still feel the strength and tenderness of Jay's arms around me, and my lips were still warm and smooth from his kisses.

I reached the back porch and paused for a few seconds, trying to compose my face. If I walked in now, my smile alone would reveal everything that had happened as plainly as a newspaper headline. It took a great deal of effort to replace my exalted expression with one more placid.

As I entered the kitchen, conversation ceased and eight pairs of eyes glanced my way. I placed the wicker hamper on the counter and murmured a greeting, fully aware of the frosty disapproval in Janet's glance and the hot anger in Thayne's eyes.

"Did you have a nice day, dear?" Helen asked.

"Oh, yes. We had a perfect day," I told her, unable to keep back a soft smile. "The Tetons were so wonderful—everything was," I finished, feeling the color rise in my cheeks. "Oh, Jay asked me to tell you he's sorry, but he'll have to miss dinner. He went straight to the barn with Bert."

"Well, I'm not sorry!" Thayne muttered, shoved his chair away from the table and left the room.

"Sit down, dear," Helen said hurriedly. "There's a place set for you over by Stuart."

I moved to the indicated place and noticed Judd Bradford staring at me with a strange expression on his face. His chilly blue eyes made me shiver, but I managed a tremulous smile in his direction. Across the table, Janet's father was looking at his watch with a frown. I was sure he was going to make some comment about how late Jay and I were in returning, but instead, his words were addressed to Janet and Helen.

"If you two girls are goin' to that shindig in town, you better get a move on. It's past seven now."

"My goodness, so it is!" his wife exclaimed. "I didn't realize it was so late!"

Janet looked at me and said, "I forgot to tell you. There's a bridal shower tonight for one of the girls in town. You're welcome to come along if you'd like to."

The forced cordiality in her voice hurt me far more than Thayne's ridiculous dramatics. "Thanks, Janet, but I am tired. I thought maybe I'd write a letter to Mother and go to bed early, if you don't mind."

"Why should I mind?" she retorted flippantly, and her mother put in quickly, "You have had a busy day. There'll be plenty of other times for you to meet the folks in town. Janet, we'd better get these dishes cleared up if we're going to get to that shower on time."

"Please don't worry about doing the dishes," I told her. "I'll be happy to do them. You and Janet go ahead and get ready for the party."

"Why thank you, dear. That's real sweet of you."

"Oh, I don't mind," I murmured as Janet left the room without another word. I glanced down at my dinner plate with a sigh.

Twenty minutes later, Janet and Helen were on their way into Dusk, the boys were sprawled in front of the television set, John and Judd were closeted together working out ranch business and I was alone in the kitchen. I scraped the plates furiously and stacked the dishes, glad to have something to keep my hands busy.

Outside the bay window, clouds the color of thin, liquid gold were hovering in a blue-green sky. The gold diffusion of light intensified the green of nearby trees and fields so that each leaf and blade of grass seemed luminous in itself. Yet, even as I watched, the colors subtly changed and darkened.

I picked up a stack of plates and carried it over to the sink with a sigh. I had thought it wouldn't matter what the Bradfords said, but I was wrong. It hurt to have Janet so upset with me, and all because I had spent today with her cousin. Why did it have to be this way? Why was there this tense undercurrent of animosity toward Jay? And now, because I liked him, I could feel a strong portion of that current directed toward me. There was so much I didn't understand.

I got out the dishpans and filled them with hot water.

A voice behind me said, "Need some help? I'll dry if you like."

I swung about in surprise and saw Stuart Bradford with a dishtowel in his hands and a smile on his lips.

"Why thanks, Stuart. Are you sure you don't mind?"

He shrugged. "It's O.K. Just this once."

I smiled back, feeling a sudden bond of friendship between us. He was only three years my junior and his quiet manner put me at ease. He was so quiet, in fact, that for a while neither of us spoke. Several times he seemed to be on the verge of saying something. Finally, I gave him an encouraging smile and said, "Is there something you want to tell me?"

His serious brown eyes met mine hesitantly. "Well, yeah. I'm just not sure how to say it."

"By some chance, would it have something to do with Jay?"

Stuart gave me a slow grin. "Yeah, I guess it does. I'm not tryin' to be nosy, but I think there's something you should know, and Jay, too."

"All right. What is it?"

"Well, Thayne's awful mad and some of the things he was sayin' to us boys have got me worried just a little."

I stopped washing a plate and looked at Stuart. "What was he saying?"

"Well, usually the morning after a big date, Thayne's struttin' and crowin' his head off to us boys—sayin' how he did this and that and how his girl did such and such—if you know what I mean."

I nodded. "Yes, I think I know what you mean."

"Well, this morning he wasn't talkin' at all and I sort of got the impression that he didn't score too many points with you last night. And then when you left this morning with Jay—" Stuart raised his eyebrows and whistled. "Man, I've never seen him so steamed up!"

"But why should he be so angry? I've done nothing to encourage him."

"I know. That's just it. You see, Thayne's pretty used to gettin' his own way with girls." Stuart's tanned cheeks reddened. "Then you come along and well—anybody can see he's throwin' out the line but you're just not bitin.' 'Course, just between you and me, I'm kinda glad you're not hooked on him."

I turned grateful eyes to his. "Thanks, Stuart. I wish Janet felt as you do."

"Maybe this'll teach her a lesson," he said. "She's always tryin' to play matchmaker. 'Course in a way, you might say her matchmaking did pay off. If she hadn't invited you out here, you never would have met Jay."

A bowl slipped from my grasp and landed in the rinse water with a splash. "Somehow, I've gotten the impression that no one is very happy I've met Jay—especially Janet."

Stuart laughed. "Maybe she isn't, but I think it's great you and Jay got together. Yesterday morning when I was bringin' in the cows I saw you with him up on the hill."

"You did?"

"Yeah, and tonight, when you came in—well, the way you looked—I guess I'd be jealous, too, if I was Thayne. The trouble with Thayne is, he's a rotten loser. He's played some dirty tricks on guys who tried to make time with girls he was dating."

"What do you mean? What kind of dirty tricks?"

"Well, don't tell nobody I told you this, but he's let the air out of a few guys' tires, and one time he put sugar in a guy's gas tank and ruined the whole engine. He's beat up a couple of dude's before, too. I got to thinkin' about it after I heard him say something this afternoon."

My heart started to beat uncomfortably. "What did he say?"

"Oh, Tadd and Dave were giving him a bad time, sayin' how it looked like the Indians were really beatin' the cowboys and gettin' the girl—stuff like that. Man, Thayne really blew up! He said, well, these aren't his exact words, but he said Jay would sure as hell be sorry he'd ever messed around with you."

My hands lay idle in the soapy water and I asked in a low voice. "What do you think he'll do?"

Stuart shrugged. "I don't know. I just felt like I ought to tell you. I know Thayne's my brother, but—I like Jay, too. He's all right. You know what I mean?"

"Yes, I know," I said softly. "Why does Thayne dislike Jay so much?"

Stuart twirled the dish towel around his arm. "There's lots of reasons. Ever since we was kids Thayne's always had to be the best there was in everything, and then Jay would come along and top him without really trying. Jay didn't do it on purpose—he was just naturally better than Thayne in some things. One of the things that really bugs Thayne the most is that he can never get Jay mad enough to lose his temper. No matter what he'd say or do, Jay would never lose his cool, and if there's anything Thayne can't stand, it's bein' ignored." Stuart looked at me and grinned. "Maybe if Jay would let go and really belt him one it might clear the air a little. And if he ever does, man, I'd like to be there!"

"Well, I don't want to be there!" I told him and emptied the dish pans. "And I certainly hope nothing happens because of me. I'm not trying to make Thayne jealous or angry, but I can't pretend to feel something for him that isn't there."

"Don't worry, Angela. Maybe he'll cool off. I didn't mean to scare you—I just thought you should know."

"I'm glad you told me, Stuart. Thanks for your help with the dishes. It looks like we're all done."

Stuart threw his towel over the dish drainer. "Well, I'll see you. I think I'll go challenge Thayne to a game of chess. He'll beat the heck out of me and maybe that'll make him happy for a while."

I gave him a grateful smile as he left the kitchen and thought, Bless you, Stuart.

I wiped the draining board then got out the cleanser and scoured the sink, feeling more tense than ever. The sudden squeak of the screen door made me jump and scald my hand under the hot water. I relaxed when I saw the grizzled face of the hired man.

"Evenin', Miss. I see they've got you doin' a few chores."

I smiled at him. "Janet and Helen have gone to a bridal shower in town so I offered to do the dishes, that's all."

"Is there anything left worth nibblin' on?" he asked. "Jay hasn't had no supper and I thought mebbe I could bring somethin' out to him."

"Let's see. I think there's a little roast beef. I could put some slices in a couple of rolls. Oh, and there's Helen's chocolate cake. I'll fix something for Jay right now."

"Thanks, Miss. That's real good of you."

I fixed the sandwiches then cut a generous piece of cake. "Has the calf been born yet?" I asked Bert, hunting through the kitchen drawers for something to wrap the food in.

"Nope, the old girl's really been havin' a time of it."

I found a carton of small plastic bags and placed the rolls and roast beef inside one and the piece of cake inside another.

"Ah, that's jest fine," Bert said as I handed him the food.

He turned to go and on impulse I asked, "Do you think Jay would mind if I came along, too?"

"Hell, no!" the old cowhand said and beckoned to me with a twist of his head and a sly wink. "Jay won't mind and it's a sure thing the cow won't object. In fact, Old Jane'll probably be glad to have a woman around," he added with a chuckle.

I smiled and followed him out of the house, completely forgetting about Thayne and Stuart's warning.

Marshall and Dillon bounded about our heels as we walked across the back lawn and through the pines. When we drew near the bunkhouse, Bert paused and said, "Seein' as how you wanted to come along, I wonder if you'd mind too much takin' this stuff to Jay. I'm feelin' a bit tuckered and it sure is temptin' to go inside and put my feet up fer a spell. 'Course, if Jay needs me, you tell him all he has to do is holler."

I smiled into his crinkly hazel eyes and took the plastic bags from him. "I'll tell him."

"Thanks, Miss. Somehow, I don't think Jay'll mind my not bein' there, too much."

He ambled off to the bunkhouse with a pleased grin on his face and I hurried on toward the black, angular shape of the barn. The two dogs trotted along beside me until the cry of some night bird sent them racing away to the open fields. I watched them go, amazed how quickly their lithe shapes melted into the furry gray dusk.

Six more steps brought me to the barn. With parted lips and a pounding heart I walked inside. The surrounding darkness was thick with the pungent smell of hay. The air was warm and alive, almost breathing. As I walked past saddles, bridles and harnesses hanging from nails and over wooden rails, I could have sworn I heard the comfortable creaking of the leather. A strong white light led me to the far left-hand corner of the barn and I stopped suddenly, listening to the labored breathing and moans of an animal in pain. I approached the last stall rather timidly, feeling like an intruder in something very personal. A gas lantern hung from a nail on a wooden beam in the far corner of the stall, illuminating the entire area with its harsh white brilliance. I saw that fresh, clean straw had been spread on the earthen floor and a pile of old flannel blankets were folded neatly in one corner. In the center of the pen, Jay was kneeling beside a white-faced cow with bulging red sides. I watched his hands move gently and expertly over the cow's body, first giving an encouraging pat to her head, then a probing feel of her sides. His back was to me so he wasn't aware of my presence until I moved closer. Then he heard the crunch of my footsteps in the hay and glanced quickly over his shoulder. His dark brows lifted in surprise and the sudden smile that parted his lips sent a pang of pure joy shooting through me.

I climbed onto the bottom slat of the stall and dangled my plastic-wrapped excuse for coming to see him over the side. "I brought you some food. Bert said he'd be in the bunkhouse if you wanted his help."

He nodded his thanks and continued to stroke the Hereford's red neck.

"Is she all right? Bert said she was having a bad time."

"Her calf is taking too long in getting here. As far as I can tell, it's in a good position, but the old girl is just too worn out to push. Her contractions are weakening instead of getting stronger." Jay got to his feet and opened the gate of the stall. It grated along the floor with a protesting squeak. "Why don't you come inside if you want to watch," he said, motioning to a corner where a few bales of hay were stacked.

I crossed to the corner of the pen he had indicated and was about to ask what he was going to do when the cow suddenly stumbled to her feet and began ambling nervously about the stall. When she turned away from me I saw that two tiny hooves and forelegs were already protruding from her. I stared at those pointed little hooves, my mouth gaping open. It seemed incredulous to me that the cow could move about while giving birth to her calf.

Jay was trying to calm her but she shied away from him into a corner, snorting and breathing heavily. I backed further into my own corner.

"Steady girl, steady there. I'll help you. Yes, yes, I'll help you."

Jay's low voice quieted her a little, but she eyed him dubiously, her long tongue lolling out of her mouth. Jay continued to speak in the same soothing tone and glanced at me. "I'm going to pull the calf. Will you get me the rope that's hanging on that post behind you? Move slow and easy now. Yes. That's it."

"Pull the calf?" I said nervously, wondering if I really wanted to watch this, yet too fascinated to look away.

Jay took the rope from me, made a loop, and moved slowly around the cow's backside. Her liquid brown eyes watched him warily and I knew she was ready to bolt any second. Jay was too fast for her. In one rapid motion he had the loop around the calf's forelegs and tightened it. She did bolt then! I held my breath and braced myself for whatever might happen. Jay dug the heels of his boots into the ground and kept a tight hold on the rope. The cow uttered a pitiful bellow of pain and I clutched my own stomach with a shudder and shut my eyes.

When I opened them, only moments later, a wet, shiny creature was lying on the hay blinking dazed brown eyes. I watched with an aching sort of rapture as the mother stood close beside her newborn, dutifully licking it with her tongue. She was so placid and content, one could almost believe that the pain and tension of a few moments ago had never existed.

Jay finished pitching the dirty hay out of the stall, washed his hands in a bucket of soapy water, then dried them with a clean flannel rag. I raised my eyes to his face, hoping that he wouldn't say anything because I knew I wouldn't be able to answer him. A lump was rising in my throat. I had never before witnessed the moment of birth, and sharing it with him had moved me more than I thought possible, even if the new life entering the world were only a white-faced calf.

Jay walked over to me, smiled a crooked smile that had a hint of gentleness in it, then sat down beside me without a word. There was a moment of contented silence between us, then he glanced at my lap and said dryly, "Was *that* supposed to be for me?"

I looked at the mangled rolls and cake I had been clutching unconsciously during the tense moments of the calf's birth and couldn't help laughing. "Well, yes, it was," I said, lifting the plastic-wrapped disaster with two fingers to inspect the damage.

Jay's dark eyes surveyed the food with amusement. "It looks delicious," he said, taking it from me. "And I'm starving!"

I watched him devour the rolls and cake with manly enthusiasm. When he had finished, he rumpled the plastic bags, stuffed them into a pocket of his jeans and stretched out his long legs with a satisfied sigh.

"Thanks for the food," he said. "And the company," he added as an arm went around my waist.

We were both startled by a sudden bellow from the cow. I jerked my head around and saw she had stiffened with pain and was standing with all four legs spread apart. Jay leaped to his feet and was at her side in the same instant—just as she "dropped" her second calf.

"Twin white-faced calves," he breathed in amazement. "No wonder the old girl was having such a hard time!"

I got up to look at the tiny animal lying so still on the bloody hay. "Jay, is it all right?"

"It's a lot smaller than the first calf and doesn't seem to be as strong. The cow's long labor may have weakened it." He stood over the second calf and glanced anxiously at the Hereford who, after a disinterested glance at her newest arrival, began licking the firstborn as placidly as before. Jay shook his head and gave me a worried look. "I don't think she's going to accept it. This sometimes happens when a calf is born sickly."

"It won't die, will it? If the mother won't accept it, surely there must be something we can do!"

He smiled gently. "Don't worry. It's not going to die. There are some flannel blankets in the corner by the lantern. Would you mind getting them for me? First thing we've got to do is clean this little one off and get him warm."

I went quickly for the blankets and brought them back while Jay took care of the afterbirth. I watched him for a few moments as he wiped the calf clean with the soft flannel, then dropped to my knees beside him. I spread one of the blankets across my lap to support the calf's head and began wiping the small white face around its eyes and nostrils.

Jay stopped drying the calf's haunches and looked at me. "You don't have to do that."

"I want to help."

His glance started a warm glow inside me. "Are you sure the mother won't accept it?" I asked.

"We'll know soon enough."

When the calf was completely dry, Jay lifted it in his arms and placed it next to the firstborn. The cow greeted this gesture with nervous snorts and backed away. Jay tried again, this time holding the wobbly little creature up to its mother's side. With an angry bellow the cow lowered her head and kicked at the calf with her hind legs. Jay ducked quickly out of the way of her hooves and turned to me. "It's no use. She's made up her mind."

I looked at the first calf which was making a clumsy effort to straighten its spindly legs, then at the rejected little animal in Jay's arms. "What will happen to it now?" I asked, stroking the soft, russet coat.

"We'll have to put him in another pen. We might be able to get another cow to play nursemaid to him, if not, he'll have to be bottle fed. If he's strong enough, he'll make it."

"May I help feed him?"

He smiled. "Yes, if you like. Will you get the lantern for me? I think it's time we got this little one into his new bed."

I went for the lantern and lifted it off the nail, then followed Jay to the gate of the stall which he opened with the toe of his boot.

"We can put him in the next stall down on the other side," he said.

I held the lantern at shoulder height and as we walked, grotesque shadows danced and bobbed about us. Beyond the friendly radius of light, thick darkness loomed. I have never been overly afraid of the dark so I couldn't account for the sudden feeling of fear which struck me. I glanced nervously at Jay. The calf was licking his hand. He laughed and buried his dark head in the animal's soft red neck. Still, the feeling persisted. I'm not sure, but perhaps it was that ominous presentiment which made me look up just then. I felt—rather than saw the thing swinging silently toward us. I screamed a warning and the calf started violently in Jay's arms. Then it hit. The heavy, thudding impact of metal on bone made me cold all over and I thought I was going to be sick. Jay was hurtled backwards by the blow and fell to the ground. He lay motionless on the dirt floor of the barn with the calf beside him, a thin stream of blood spreading to form a grisly halo around its head.

There was one agonizing moment when it seemed as if time had stopped and with it all motion and life. I could only stand there, staring at the calf, the blood, and Jay's silent face. The lantern slipped from my fingers and I fell to my knees. I bent low over his body and something warm and wet oozed between my fingers that clutched his shoulder. I put my head on his chest and with relief that was almost pain, felt it heaving against me in hard, ragged attempts to regain breath.

"Jay! Are you all right? What happened?"

He wasn't able to answer but his eyes were open and staring up toward the loft. I felt his body tense beneath me, then his right arm came around my back pulling me close against him. He uttered a strangled sort of "Shhh," and I lay still in his arms, feeling the pulse beating wildly in his throat.

Somewhere above us in the darkness, there came a frenzied scuffling, then the scrape of hard shoes against wood. I lifted my head slightly and looked toward the doorway of the barn but the darkness was too thick to see anything at all. My ears caught the sound of running footsteps escaping into the night, then all was silent except for the lantern's hiss. I shut my eyes to its harsh white glare and turned my face into Jay's shoulder. After a long moment, he released me. I sat up and he managed to raise himself on one elbow. He stared at the calf and a look of pain came into his eyes.

"It's dead," he whispered.

I turned away from the bloody animal and put my head between my knees, waiting for the waves of nausea to pass.

Jay put a hand on my shoulder. "Please, don't cry."

"I'm not crying."

"My shirt's all wet where I was holding you."

I put a hand to my face and felt the tears for the first time. "I thought you were dead," I told him. "After it happened, I thought you were dead."

"The calf took the brunt of the blow. Thanks to your warning I just had the wind knocked out of me for a minute. Angela, how did you know? Did you see it?"

The feelings of nausea and light-headedness began to pass and I tried lifting my head to look at him. "No, not really. What was it that hit you? I'm not sure yet what happened."

"This," he said and got stiffly to his feet. He pointed to a heavy iron hook, longer than his forearm and nearly as thick, which hung from a long cable that stretched up toward the rafters of the barn. "When a steer or sheep is slaughtered, it's strung up on the hook here to be cleaned and skinned. The cable's attached to a pulley in the rafters so the hook can be raised or lowered and move quite freely."

I stared at the metal hook as it swung, harmlessly now, like a slow-moving pendulum. When I spoke, my voice was curiously flat and dry. "That thing may be able to move quite freely, as you say, but not on its own."

Jay straightened his shoulders with a grimace of pain then reached down and offered me his hand. "I know. Someone was up in the loft and let it go."

I struggled to my feet on legs that didn't want to support me. "Then the noise we heard—?"

"Was someone running away."

"Someone," I breathed and looked up into his face. "Jay, do you think it was the same person who fired those shots at the truck?"

"I don't know. I don't see how—and yet, who else could it be?"

The impact of Stuart's warning hit me so hard I couldn't speak. I tried taking a deep breath to quell the trembling inside me but it sounded more like a series of short gasps.

Jay was looking toward the open barn door, his eyes searching the darkness.

"What is it?" My voice was barely a whisper and my legs felt hideously weak.

"Someone's coming," he hissed and hurriedly unlatched the gate to a nearby stall. "In here! Quick!" Jay clutched my arm and shoved me inside the pen, entered himself, then shut the gate behind us. We had just crouched low against the wooden sides when I heard shuffling footsteps enter the barn. My heart was pounding so loudly in my throat, my ears and my head that I thought Jay must surely hear it. His body was tensed close beside mine, as if he were ready to spring, cat-like, at the person moving steadily toward us.

The footsteps halted directly outside the stall where we were hiding. Through the slits in the fence I could make out the bent figure of a man examining the dead calf.

"Jay? Miss Angela? Where are yuh?" came a gravelly voice.

My pent-up breath came out in a gush and I slumped against the side of the stall. Jay stood up quickly and said, "We're in here, Bert."

"What the Sam Hill?" the old man gasped. I got to my feet and saw Bert's astonishment turn rapidly to anger. "Are you tryin' to give me a heart attack or somethin'? What the hell are you doin' in there and what happened to this poor little critter out here?"

"Bert, did you see anyone around on your way over here?" Jay asked in quiet urgency.

"No, and who in the blue-blazes was I supposed to see?"

"Did you hear anything? A horse or the dogs barking?"

"No, I didn't! And I'd sure as hell like to know what's goin' on here!" He glanced at me and his angry red face softened a little. "Are you all right, Miss? You look as white as a sheet."

"Someone tried to kill Jay with that hook over there, but it hit the calf instead," I said hoarsely. "When we heard you, we thought whoever did it was coming back."

All the anger drained out of Bert's face and he turned disbelieving eyes to Jay. Jay brushed a lock of black hair out of his eyes and nodded a brief affirmation to my statement. Twice, the old man opened his mouth to speak and twice he clamped his lips shut in utter shock.

Jay ushered me out of the stall and said in that grim, quiet voice, "Bert, will you help me bury the calf? I know there's a lot of explaining to do but it'll have to wait a few minutes."

"Bury the calf!" I burst out, not giving Bert a chance to answer. "Why on earth do you want to bury the calf?"

"Because the Bradfords musn't find out about this. You know that."

"Now hold on here!" Bert demanded. "Before I do any buryin' or anythin' else, I want to know one thing. Why would someone be wantin' to kill you, boy?"

Jay's tall form slumped against the wooden slats of the stall. "In order to stop me from finding out what happened to my father. The night before last, somebody took a couple of pot shots at the truck, and a few days before that, a note was left on the seat of my car warning me to 'stop meddling' with the past. Well, I'm not about to stop meddling until I find out who's behind all this!"

Comprehension filtered into the old man's eyes and the gravelly voice softened considerably. "Why didn't yuh tell me before, son? Didn't yuh think I'd care or understand?"

"It wasn't that, Bert. I just didn't see how you could help, and I didn't want to get you involved in something that might turn out to be dangerous."

"Didn't want me involved in somethin'—didn't want me involved!" Bert sputtered. "And what about Miss Angela, here? What makes you think she can handle somethin' dangerous better'n me?"

"My involvement in all this was purely by accident," I explained quickly. "Jay was driving me out to the ranch when the shots were fired. Whoever it was expected Jay to be alone and Jay thought if neither of us mentioned the incident, this person may not find out I had been with him."

"Well, now, that's fine and dandy, but what about tonight?" Bert countered. "Do you think whoever swung that there hook expected Jay to be alone this time?"

I stared at Bert, my mouth too dry for speech.

"Where were you when it happened?" the hand demanded.

"Right beside Jay—holding the lantern," I whispered.

Jay moved away from the stall and put an arm about my shoulders. "Stop it, Bert! You're frightening her."

"I'm not tryin' to frighten her! Lord knows, it's you I'm tryin' to get through to. Don't you see the danger you've put this girl in? Who's to say that the person after you was such a good aim that he could be sure of hittin' only you with that thing?"

I shuddered involuntarily and Jay's arm tightened around me in a fierce grip.

"Damn it, Bert, I know that! Ever since it happened I've been asking myself why whoever did it would take such a chance! And I haven't come up with any answers unless the guy is some maniac who doesn't care who he hurts." Jay paused and drew me closer to him. "If you think I want anything like this to happen again—"

Bert met Jay's dark eyes for a moment then nodded and cleared his throat. "It's gettin' too cold to stand here an' argue. We can talk all this out a lot better in the bunkhouse over coffee. Right now, well, I guess I better be huntin' up a couple of shovels."

I felt some of the tenseness leave Jay's body and he managed a tight smile. "Thanks, Bert."

"All right, son. Where'll I meet you?"

"How about in the field behind the sheds? It's out of sight and the ground's fairly soft. We've got to bury the calf deep enough so the dogs won't get at it."

The old man nodded and shuffled off, leaving us alone.

I stared down at the dead calf, wondering what would happen now. I couldn't rid my mind of Jay's words to Bert. Was the man after him really a maniac who didn't care who he hurt, or was tonight's accident Thayne's way of getting back at both of us?

I felt Jay's eyes watching me and looked up into his anxious face. "What do you want me to do now?" I asked him.

"I guess you have two choices. You can stay with Bert and me—at least until we get a few things talked out—or, I'll take you back to the house and you can tell the Bradfords everything. I won't ask you to remain silent for my sake—not now."

Jay bent down for the gas lantern which still lay on the floor where I had dropped it. I watched him rather dazedly, suddenly realizing that it was all up to me. I could go back to the ranchhouse and tell Janet's father and grandfather everything that had happened—but would it really do any good? Especially, if Thayne were the one responsible for tonight's accident.

I turned away from Jay to lean heavily on the top rung of the wooden stall. Nearby, the Hereford cow and her calf were blissfully unaware of anything save each other.

Finally, I said, "The only reason I wanted to tell the Bradfords about this was I thought they might be able to help you. Maybe it's a terrible thing to say, but suddenly I'm not at all sure they would believe one word of what happened tonight." I turned my head to look at Jay and said quietly, "I know I'm a burden to you and I'm sorry for that. I wish there were something I could do to help, but right now I'm too frightened and confused to know what's best, so—if you don't mind too much—I'd like to stay with you."

Jay hung the lantern over a post and moved close beside me until his face was only inches away from mine. With both hands he smoothed back my hair, then lifted my face until my eyes met his. In that moment I forgot about the Bradfords, my fears, and everything that had happened. It was as if only my senses existed and all thought had ceased. I saw black fire burning deep in his eyes, felt the gentleness of his strong brown hands on my face, breathed in the warm, musty barn smells and heard the contented suckling noises of the little calf.

Suddenly, Bert's voice barked out from the doorway, "I've got the shovels. Are we goin' to bury that critter or not?"

Jay swung about sharply and his voice was slightly breathless as he answered the old man. "We'll be right there, Bert." Then he turned to me. "After I pick up the calf, will you turn out the lantern? I think it would be better if no one saw us leave the barn."

I nodded, wondering if the moment which had passed between us had actually taken place or if it existed only in my imagination. It had happened so quickly—a brief interim of tenderness in the bloody business of reality—and yet, I was still trembling inside from his touch.

Jay hoisted the dead calf in his arms, strewed hay and dirt over the blood-stained earth, then motioned for me to turn out the lantern. Thick blackness closed about us and I had to fight the sudden spurts of fear which rushed up inside me.

"Jay?"

"I'm right here."

His voice came out of the darkness nearby. I reached for him and touched the bloody calf instead. I gasped and my hand sprang back from the animal.

"Are you all right?" he asked quickly.

"Yes, but I can't see a thing."

"Take my arm. Your eyes will adjust to the darkness once we get outside."

Gingerly, I reached out once more and this time linked my hand through his arm. Together, we walked out of the barn to take the little calf to his new bed. Only now it was not a warm bed of straw which awaited him, but the cold dark earth.

Chapter 11

"The blossoms shall fall in the night wind,
And I will leave you so, to be kind. . . ."

Anna Wickham

I stood silently with my arms folded across my chest while Jay and Bert buried the calf. Above me was a night sky thick with stars that glittered in frosty colors of blue, white, red and gold. Below me came the rhythmic chunk of the shovels with an occasional ear-jarring scrape as the head of a shovel glanced off a rock. Then the shovels ceased their work and the night kept its silence while Jay placed the calf into the black hole.

I swallowed hard and thought what a pitifully short life this little creature had had. To go through the trauma of birth only to be rejected by its mother, and now this.

Jay and Bert filled up the hole and packed the earth down with the heads of their shovels. After strewing some brush around the spot, Jay handed his shovel to Bert and walked over to me.

"You're cold," he said.

I just stood there, looking down at the crude grave.

Jay put an arm about my shoulders. "Come on. Let's go over to the bunkhouse. Bert'll make some hot coffee and you'll feel lots better."

"I keep thinking about the calf—"

"I know," he said gently. "I know."

When we entered the bunkhouse the first thing I noticed was its comforting warmth. A chubby black stove stood in the far right-hand corner of the room with a hearty orange blaze burning in its belly.

Bert went immediately to a small nook in the opposite corner and took a can of coffee from the middle of three wooden shelves which ran along the wall. "While you two clean up, I'll get the coffee on," he said over his shoulder.

I glanced at my blood-stained hands with a little shudder and noticed the front of my blue-knit top was streaked a sticky red.

Jay fingered the collar of my top and said, "I'm sorry, Angel. If you'd like to wear something of mine, I'll put your blouse in some cold water."

His use of my father's pet name for me sent a wave of bittersweet pleasure over me. I thanked him faintly and mumbled, "Blood stains would be rather difficult to explain to Janet."

"Oh no! I forgot all about Janet! I'm surprised she isn't out here looking for you!"

"She and Helen have gone to a bridal shower in town. I doubt if they'll be back much before ten-thirty or eleven."

"Good! That ought to give us enough time to talk," he said, taking hold of my arm, and steering me toward the bedroom. He groped about in the chilly darkness just above our heads, till his hand met a slim cord. He gave it a yank and the light went on with a click. I blinked several times as the harsh glare of one bare bulb illuminated an equally bare room. The walls were painted a flat, brownish color and cold, cracked linoleum covered the floor. The only furnishings were two sets of bunkbeds and a small chest of drawers which crowded its way between them. Both top bunks were made with military neatness while the blankets on the lower beds had only been pulled up haphazardly to cover the pillows. Jay's clothes hung on wire hangers from the metal frame of the top bunk to my left.

"There's not much to choose from, but help yourself to whatever you like," he said.

It was too cold in the room to spend much time deliberating what to wear. A turtleneck sweater of navy blue caught my eye and I slipped it off its hanger, saying to Jay, "This will be fine, thank you."

Jay stripped off his bloodied shirt and I noticed his slacks were also badly stained. "I'll let you wash and change in the bathroom," he said. "I can clean up at the sink and change in here."

I nodded and left the room, trying desperately not to stare at him.

The bunkhouse's tiny bathroom was little more than a closet with its ancient metal shower, a basin and toilet. I took off my blouse, then gave my hands a vigorous scrubbing with a strong-smelling green soap. I splashed cold water on my face, hoping it would cool the fire burning inside me. What on earth was the matter with me that my emotions should be touched off so violently by the mere sight of him? I pulled Jay's woolly sweater over my head and pushed back my hair. The face in the cracked mirror over the basin was not the Angela Stewart I used to know. I thought of what Thayne had said to me last night and smiled. The icicle was indeed melting.

I picked up my soiled blouse and went out into the main room where the pungent smell of freshly brewed coffee was strong in the air. "May I help with anything?" I asked Bert, who was reaching for cups and saucers on one of the wooden shelves.

"Things is just about ready, Miss," he replied. "I've got a bucket of cold water here by the sink. Why don't you stuff that blouse in and let it soak awhile."

I doused my knit top in the bucket which already held Jay's shirt, then walked over to a wine-colored wicker rocking chair near the pot-bellied stove and sat down. A multi-colored rag rug warmed the center of the floor and to my right was a lumpy sofa with an ugly green throw covering its worn spots. A small desk of pine stood next to the sofa. By far the most interesting piece of furniture in the room was a high-backed chair hewn of rough pine. The back and seat were made of animal hides and strapped to the frame with leather thongs. It was a little wild-looking as well as rustic and I had the distinct feeling that sitting in it would be a unique experience. Hanging on the wall just above the high-backed chair was one of Jay's paintings. There was no need for me to check the small signature in the right-hand corner to know it was his.

Bert saw me looking at the landscape and said, "Jay gave me that picture a long time ago. It was one of his first paintings. That boy sure knows how to burn up a canvas with color, don't he?"

I looked at the ominous canyon with lion-colored rocks and black pines silhouetted against a blood-red sunset. "That describes it exactly. Is this place somewhere around here?"

"Yep, that canyon's a few miles up the cattle trail, southwest of here."

I rocked back and forth and said reflectively, "You know, I don't think I've seen one of Jay's paintings over at the ranchhouse."

Bert poured the coffee and a slight frown creased his brow. "I imagine there's reasons for things, but sometimes it's best not to go into 'em."

I didn't pursue the conversation further, realizing that Jay's paintings were undoubtedly as sore a subject with Judd Bradford as Jay himself.

Bert shuffled over to me and held out a steaming cup of black coffee. I took it from him and noticed the embarrassed grin lurking around the corners of his mouth. "If you'll pardon me for sayin' so, Miss, that there sweater sure looks a heap better on you than it ever did on Jay."

"I'll go along with that!"

I glanced up as Jay entered the room wearing a clean shirt which hung unbuttoned against his brown chest. He took a cup of coffee from Bert and sat down in the high-backed chair. I knew I was staring again, but I couldn't help it. The effect he had on me was maddening—and one over which I had very little control.

"That's such an unusual chair," I said to him. "Is it very old?"

"Yes. My father made it. He and my mother lived out here after they came back to the Triple J."

"Out here?"

His jaw tightened and he gave a brief nod to my question. I said no more.

Bert eased himself down on the sofa and took a noisy slurp of coffee. "All right, son, let's have it. But before we talk about what happens next, I need to know a few things that have gone before. How about fillin' me in?"

Jay gave Bert a brief account of Parley Evans' information, then explained his own theory concerning his father's disappearance. "Well, what do you think?" he asked the old ranch hand. "Does it make any sense at all to you?"

Bert heaved a sigh. "It makes sense, boy. 'Course, I wasn't workin' for Judd back then, so I don't know much about what went on. But I sure am glad about your pa. Somehow, I never did hold to the idea that he walked out on your ma. Just seein' 'em together the few times I did was enough for me to know that Jason would never walk out on a woman like that. Yessir, I sure am glad about your pa." He took another slow slurp of coffee then said, "One thing bothers me, though."

"What's that?" Jay asked.

"I jest can't figure how this feller knew you was goin' to be out to the barn tonight. I didn't see nobody hangin' around and like you mentioned before, I didn't hear no horse. An' the dogs didn't set up a ruckus the way they usually do when somebody comes around."

"I know," Jay said with a puzzled shake of his dark head. "That bothers me, too."

I set my cup and saucer in my lap and said to Jay, "I should have told you before—the person who swung that hook at you might not be the same one who fired those shots at the truck."

Jay's lengthy form straightened up in the chair. "What do you mean? Who else could it be?"

"Thayne! Stuart as much as warned me that Thayne might do something to you because—well, because he's upset about our spending the day together. It worried me at the time, but I didn't think he would resort to anything this dangerous."

"Thayne's always been a jealous fool when it comes to women," Jay said. "Everybody knows that. But what happened tonight was pretty drastic—even for him. You might have been hurt, too, and I know he wouldn't want that. What do you think, Bert?"

Bert shifted position on the lumpy couch and smacked his lips. "I think there's a damn good chance it was Thayne! Just before I left to go check on things out at the barn, he came by lookin' for Miss Angela. He thought she might be in here and came chargin' through the place like a bull after a heifer. When I told him Miss Angela was out to the barn with you he left. And he wasn't just a mite perturbed neither. He was mad as hell!"

Jay's cheeks darkened and his eyes flashed black fire, but his voice was even and cool as he answered Bert. "Then, I guess we'd better accept the possibility that it may have been Thayne. But it's still just a possibility. I can't accuse him of anything. What if he didn't do it? Then he'd find out about this other business and I can't let that happen."

Bert got up to pour himself more coffee and Jay said, "Bring that pot over here while you're at it, will you Bert?"

The old man poured more coffee for Jay and glanced at me. "Care for another cup, Miss Angela?"

"No thank you. This is fine."

Bert took the coffee pot back to the hot plate and returned to his place on the couch with another heavy sigh. "So what are you goin' to do, son? We can't just ignore the whole thing. Another time, you and Miss Angela, here, might not get off as easy as you did tonight."

Jay slouched low in the chair and stretched his long legs out in front of him. "I know, I know," he said impatiently. "Just let me think a minute, will you?"

"O.K. Don't get riled at me," Bert grumbled and gulped down his coffee.

After several moments of silence I got up and said to Bert, "I'll take your cup to the sink if you're through."

"Thanks, Miss."

I took his dishes and mine over to the sink and rinsed them off under hot water, then looked at Jay with a little sigh. He was staring at the floor with fierce concentration, and the lines of worry were deep in his face. Finally, he raised his head. "I think," he said slowly, "that I'd better leave."

"Leave?" I echoed in a voice that sounded totally unlike my own.

"For a while, anyway. I don't want any more accidents and the way I see it, the only way to prevent them is for me to go. If the man responsible for my father's death is the same person who swung that hook, then he'll probably think he's scared me off and forget about you. If it was Thayne—well, I'm sure he won't shed any tears over my going."

"Where will you go?" I asked in that same unknown voice, my hands gripping the counter top.

Jay's dark eyes met mine briefly. "I was thinking of a place not too far from here. Bert, do you remember that old cabin in the hills overlooking the summer range?"

"Yeah, sure I do."

"I was thinking of getting some food and my gear together and staying up there for a while. You and Angela could tell the Bradfords that I've gone

102

off to paint in the hills. You don't know where and you don't know for how long. Understand?"

Bert nodded. "I understand and I like it. That'll get Thayne off your back and make things a lot easier for Miss Angela, too."

"How far away is this cabin?" I asked.

"If you take the cattle trail along the ridge, it's little more than an hour's ride on horseback. Then there's a dirt road that leads right to it from Tyler's place," Bert told me. "Nobody uses the cabin anymore, so it's the perfect place for Jay to lay low."

I wanted to smile at Bert's use of Western movie terminology, but somehow, I just couldn't.

Jay got to his feet, looking even taller in the small, low-ceilinged room, and crossed the floor to stand beside me. I lowered my head, examining the minute cracks in a plastic cup.

"I—uh,—think I'll get a few of yer things together," Bert said gruffly and cleared his throat.

"Take your time," Jay said to the older man as he moved toward the bedroom.

"What about your sweater?" I asked Jay, still looking down at the cup.

"You'd better keep it for now. Bert can get your blouse to you sometime tomorrow." He moved behind me and put both hands on my shoulders. "Tell me something. Are you holding that counter down or is it holding you up?"

I couldn't help laughing a little and he said softly, "That's my girl."

I turned around and went into his arms. "When will you leave?"

His lips moved against my hair. "Tonight."

There was so much I wanted to say to him and that made saying anything at all nearly impossible.

"I don't want to go," he said, "but I can't take the chance of something happening to you because of me. I won't be gone long. Maybe a week."

My arms tightened around his back and I whispered against his chest, "Please, be careful!"

He released me and stepped back to look into my face. "You're the one who's got to be careful! Promise me something, Angel." I nodded and he went on in an urgent tone. "Don't let yourself get caught alone with Thayne. It may be hard—both he and Janet will be thinking of ways to throw you two together—but do what you can to avoid him!"

"I will. Believe me, I don't want to be alone with him. He frightens me a little—especially after last night."

"Just what did happen last night?"

I felt hot color seep into my face. "Maybe he only wanted a few kisses, but I just couldn't—"

"He wanted more than a few kisses!" Jay said roughly. "He wanted you! Hell, I wish there were some other way. Maybe I shouldn't go."

"No! No, you mustn't stay! The only thing worse than your going would be something happening to you!" The words came out in a rush before I could think what I was saying. The next moment I was being kissed with the kind of violence that made Thayne's embrace seem like the peck of a schoolboy. And yet, I was not frightened. Nor did I struggle in Jay's arms as I had in Thayne's.

"I've got most of your stuff ready." Bert's voice came from the doorway of the bedroom and Jay's arms dropped away from me.

"I thought I told you to take your time," he said in a voice that was breathless and unsteady.

Bert blushed and wiped a hand over his grizzled chin. "I know, son, but it's nearly ten-thirty. I think maybe you'd better git Miss Angela back to the house before Janet and Helen come home."

"Yeah, I guess you're right." He started buttoning his shirt and said to me, "Just let me grab my jacket and I'll walk you over to the house."

He went to the bedroom and I asked Bert, "What's this cabin like where Jay's going? Is there any heat?"

"There's a fireplace. He won't freeze as long as he can light a fire."

"You will see that he takes some warm blankets along, won't you?"

Bert's small hazel eyes crinkled in a smile and he patted me on the shoulder. "Now, don't you go worryin' yer pretty head about Jay. He ain't half Injun fer nothin' you know."

I looked at him imploringly.

"Oh, all right. I'll tuck in an extra blanket or two if it'll keep you from frettin'. Laws, those big eyes of yers could make a man do anything!"

Jay came out of the bedroom and I went quickly to his side. He opened the door and the night air huffed a chilly greeting in our faces. I turned back to give Bert a little smile, then the comforting warmth of the bunkhouse was shut firmly behind us.

We walked in silence through the pines and across the back lawn. Blossoms blew in the wind and the darkness was colored with the rich purple scent of lilacs.

When we reached the back porch Jay said, "I think I'd better see you up to your room. Thayne might be waiting up for you and I want him to know you're not alone."

We entered the kitchen and Jay shut the door soundlessly behind us. The only light burning was a small globe over the stove and the only sounds I could hear were the workings of the electric clock, the faint whirring vibrations of the refrigerator, and the pounding of my heart. We went silently through the dark house, up the stairway and along the somber hall.

Jay pointed to Thayne's door which was slightly ajar, allowing a path of soft amber light to creep into the hallway.

"I thought so," he whispered.

We made a somewhat noisy approach to Janet's room and Jay said for the benefit of Thayne's open door, "Well, I hope you had a good time today."

"I had a wonderful time. Thank you for taking me along."

"We'll have to do it again, sometime, but I won't be seeing you for a while."

I turned the doorknob with hands that were cold and shaking. "Oh? Are you going somewhere?"

"I thought I'd pack some of my gear and go paint for a while."

"Where will you go?" I asked hollowly. Why was it so difficult to act natural when one had to make a point of doing so?

"I don't know yet. Wherever the spirit moves me, I guess."

I held out my hand to him and whispered, "Goodbye," feeling my throat tighten as I said the word.

Jay took my hand and pressed my palm to his lips, then he turned and walked away, leaving me there with my arm outstretched and my hand still cupping the memory of his kiss.

Chapter 12

*"A lamentable tale of things
Done long ago, and ill done."*

John Ford

The next morning was Sunday and Thayne drove Janet and me into Dusk to attend church services. The rest of the family followed behind as there were too many to ride comfortably in one automobile. It was a bright, cloudless day and the air was warmed even more by a strong, southerly wind.

On the way into town, Janet was her old self, gay and talkative. Thayne was polite and friendly, but not at all aggressive. He never mentioned Jay and I could hardly pounce on the subject of last night without cause or reason.

The Bradfords paused on the stone steps of the little church to greet people and introduced me to many of the townspeople and ranchers. There wasn't a shifty-eyed person in the bunch.

The sermon was delivered by a balding man with a deeply tanned face and a broad white forehead. The line where the brim of his cowboy hat had shaded his face couldn't have been more marked if he had painted it on. He had a low, pleasant voice but after a few minutes I could no longer concentrate on the sermon. My mind was too busy trying to visualize a small cabin in the hills. Vaguely, I heard the minister quote a passage of scripture, saying: " 'Ye are the salt of the earth, but if the salt hath lost his savour, wherewith shall it be salted?' " I straightened my back against the hard wooden bench and gave a small sigh. Life without Jay was like food without salt—flat and tasteless.

A Sunday dinner on the Triple J was not flat and tasteless, however. When we returned from church the lusty smell of pot roast and onions met us at the front door. Helen immediately set Janet and me to work peeling potatoes and by the time we had finished our task, the sink was full of peelings and a large, heavy pan was equally full of clean white potatoes.

106

Helen Bradford took a knife and began cutting the peeled potatoes into smaller pieces for cooking. She gave me an anxious glance and asked quietly, "Did Jay say where he was going or for how long?"

"No. He wasn't very specific about time or place."

"What does it matter where Jay goes or what he does?" Janet put in. "He's a grown man and shouldn't have to report to us."

Helen looked at her daughter with a little frown. "I know that Janet, but it was rather sudden. I can't understand why he would take off in the middle of the night that way. It worries me."

"Things that Jay does don't always make sense," Janet said philosophically. "What's there to worry about if he decides to go paint somewhere for a while?"

"I suppose nothing," came her mother's doubtful reply.

Janet rinsed her hands under the tap and asked, "What tablecloth do you want me to get?"

"I think it would be nice if we used the best linen cloth today. Angela, would you reach that stack of china plates for me—then I won't have to get a chair. Thank you, dear. Janet, the best cloth is still out in the utility room with some of the other ironing I did yesterday."

"I'll go get it."

The moment Janet had gone, Helen turned to me and I knew the worried look in her eyes meant more questions about Jay. "Did you really have a good time yesterday?" she asked, carrying the pan of potatoes over to the stove.

I put the stack of china plates carefully on the counter. "We had a wonderful time. I'll have to show you the moccasins Jay bought me. They're so beautiful!"

A look of delight instantly replaced her troubled expression. "Jay bought you some moccasins?"

"Yes. We got them in Jackson after he delivered the painting."

"Land sakes! I nearly forgot!" Helen cried out. "Last night after I got home from town, John told me that some art dealer in Jackson telephoned us."

"That would be Frank Reynolds," I said and Helen gave a nod.

"Yes, I'm sure that's who John said it was. He called to say he had sold one of Jay's paintings to a couple from back East somewhere. New York, I think." Helen's voice lowered to a confidential whisper. "Do you know how much they paid for it? Eight hundred and fifty dollars!" She accented each syllable with increasing amazement.

"They got their money's worth," I said.

"Oh, I'm sure they did," she agreed. "But can you imagine anybody having eight hundred and fifty dollars to plunk down for a painting? Laws, I feel guilty paying twenty dollars for a pair of shoes!" I smiled at her and she went on, "Of course, that's no concern of mine. What bothers me is John didn't tell Jay about the call last night. When it came, he was out to the barn tendin' to the Hereford, so John just took down the information. I can't understand why he didn't go out afterwards and tell Jay."

"I suppose he thought it could wait until morning," I said, thinking how disastrous it might have been if John had gone to the barn and discovered the dead calf.

"Maybe so," Helen conceded, "but now Jay's gone and all that money's coming here. I feel just terrible!"

"I'm sure there's nothing to worry about. Mr. Reynolds will probably send a check through the mail and that will be perfectly safe."

"Do you really think so?"

I smiled at the way she took reassurance from my words and asked for more at the same time. "Of course. And Jay won't be gone too long."

Helen snatched eagerly at this last statement. "Then you're sure he'll be back?"

"Yes," I said. "I'm sure."

Helen Bradford served simple, basic foods and prepared them in a simple, basic way, but to me, the end result rivaled that of the most lavish restaurants I had visited. It took only one mouthful to know why a Sunday dinner on the Triple J would always be a memorable occasion. There was a bowl heaped with mashed potatoes, with a fat dab of golden butter melting lazily right in the middle. In another bowl were tender carrots cooked in a sweet butter sauce. Making frequent trips around the table was a silver bread tray laden with a pyramid of soft rolls, still steaming from the oven. The pot roast itself was as tender as the finest cut of sirloin. Especially tasty was a tangy, homemade relish consisting of grated cucumbers, onions, and vinegar. I couldn't resist taking a second helping when it came my way.

Thayne observed this with an amused smile and said, "A little of that stuff goes a long way. It's dynamite on your breath."

"I promise I won't breathe on you," I told him, smiling, and took another spoonful.

"That's real nice of you, Angela," David put in, "'cause I'd sure hate to see ol' Thayne explode like he did yesterday."

Stuart choked back his laughter by stuffing a hot roll in his mouth, but Tadd let out a loud hoot before Thayne elbowed him, none too gently in the ribs.

"Bert told me this morning that you watched the calf being born last night," Judd Bradford said in his low, rumbling voice.

I looked toward the head of the table in surprise. Janet's grandfather had spoken very few words to me since I had arrived at the ranch, and every time he did I felt strangely unnerved.

"Yes, I did. It was the first birth I've ever seen."

And the first time I had seen death come, as well.

"That must have been quite an experience for you," John said between mouthfuls.

I nodded and said simply, "It was wonderful."

Judd's bushy black brows lifted slightly. "It didn't bother you then—what you saw?"

I suddenly found it difficult to swallow the forkful of potatoes I had just put into my mouth. They went down like a rock and I said hoarsely, "No, it didn't bother me too much. The cow had a bad time and that made things rather tense for a while. Finally, Jay had to pull the calf and everything was fine after that." The irony of my statement rang hard in my ears and Judd Bradford continued to stare at me with a puzzled, measuring expression in his cold blue eyes.

"It's hard to believe you actually enjoyed all that blood and gore," Thayne said.

"I've always associated blood and gore with death—not birth," I answered, keeping my gaze level with his.

"You may have a point there," he said easily and flashed me his ever ready smile.

All that afternoon I was hoping for an opportunity to go out to the bunkhouse and talk to Bert, but I was never alone for more than a few minutes. After dinner was over, the three younger boys went outside to throw darts. They set up their target on a big poplar tree adjacent to the bunkhouse which made it impossible for me to get past them unnoticed. And try as I might, I simply could not come up with a casual way of explaining why I had left my blouse in the bunkhouse the night before.

I dumped the panful of wet garbage and scraps I was carrying into a ditch and started back toward the house. It had taken me ten minutes to accomplish this simple task because I had spent most of my time looking for a trash can. When Helen asked me to take the wet garbage out by the fence I was ignorant of the fact that the Bradfords threw their food scraps into the ditch for the magpies to eat. I'm sure Janet's brothers must have thought I was slightly crocked as I wandered back and forth along the wire fence with a pan of garbage in my hand. Finally, Stuart had come over and asked me what I was looking for. When I told him, I could see it took great control on his part to explain the matter without collapsing on the ground in a fit of laughter.

I was discovering by experience that it took nearly as long to clean up after a meal on the ranch as it did to prepare one. It was sublimely satisfying to see the last dish put away and the last pan scoured, and be able to go upstairs to Janet's room and write a letter to Mother.

I wrote her a lengthy paragraph describing the beauties of the ranch and the interesting character of the ranchhouse itself. I gave her a mouth-watering summary of the meals and finally assured her that the Bradfords were a wonderful family and had done their best to make me comfortable and happy. I wanted to tell Mother about Jay and my day with him, but suddenly, I was at a loss to know where to begin. I made several attempts and crumpled them all. Probably, no matter what I told her, Mother would read through, around, and in-between the lines and think that I was in love with him.

I snatched another sheet of stationery and wrote a few inane sentences before the pen locked itself between my fingers and refused to write another word. Was I in love with him? The question demanded an answer. I sat staring at nothing for a timeless moment. I didn't feel like I was falling in love. My appetite was just fine. In fact, if I didn't watch myself, I would be "waddling" back to Ann Arbor as Janet had laughingly predicted. I didn't feel confused or silly or any of the other emotions people usually ascribe to those who are in love. No, I wasn't "falling" in love. "Rising" was more the word. Every part of me felt more alive, more complete. It was as if I had suddenly become fine-tuned to a deeper awareness of life itself. Was that love? I knew one thing for certain. Jay's happiness meant far more to me than my own.

After the sun went down, the wind increased. Its mournful voice whined around the windows of the big gray house and John Bradford built a roaring fire in the fireplace. The family gathered around its cheery warmth and everyone seemed to be in the mood for story telling. The air was full of 'remember when's' . . . "Do you remember when the old barn burned down and our best stallion had to be shot?" "Do you remember the time we had a house full of guests and little Tadd jumped into bed—right on top of Great Aunt Minerva?"

I watched their faces as they relived incidents from the past, some comic, some harrowing, and a few tragic. The two younger boys were sprawled before the fireplace on a braided rug. They reminded me of young pups—their brown eyes were alight and their mouths were open. I could almost see their tails wagging. Stuart was posed in a straight-backed chair on the perimeter of the braided rug, listening in his own serious attitude. Judd was seated in the big brown recliner with Janet curled up, kitten-like, on the floor at his knee. I was sitting on the sofa with John and Helen to my left and Thayne on my right.

I didn't know whether to smile or shudder as John related an incident where he had locked Janet in the outdoor food cellar for misbehaving.

"I wanted to teach that little tomboy of mine a lesson," he said, "but after twenty minutes had gone by I started feelin' like I'd acted a bit hasty and went out to check on her. I opened the door but no Janet. Helen would have liked to tan my hide she was so worried, but after a minute's searching we found the little rascal curled up behind a sack of spuds sound asleep."

Janet gave me an impish smile. "Daddy never did shut anybody in the cellar after that."

"I don't know how you stood it," I said to her. "If there's anything I hate, it's feeling all closed in."

"It doesn't sound so bad to me," David said with manly bravado.

"Yeah, you'd eat our whole food supply and die happy," Thayne quipped and everyone laughed.

The wind sent a little shower of sparks swirling up the chimney in a golden shaft and I suddenly wondered if Jay were sitting alone before a fire somewhere high in the hills. Might he be thinking of me, or were his thoughts centered around the puzzling and dangerous events of the past few days? I remembered his voice saying, "I don't want to go," and contented myself with that.

"Grandpa Judd, you haven't told us a story yet," Janet was saying.

I turned my gaze from the fire to Judd Bradford's craggy features. The hoary patriarch was surveying his offspring with eyes that were mellow and soft.

"Tell us about the range wars!" Tadd begged.

"I want to hear about the winter when you were stranded in the blizzard!" David cried.

Judd chuckled deeply at his two grandsons, then fastened his blue gaze on me. "I was thinking of going back even further than those days," he said. "Since Miss Stewart, here, will be spending the summer with us, maybe she'd like to know how the Triple J got started."

I smiled into his forbidding face. "Why yes, I would. I'd love to know more about the ranch!"

"Before you start, let me add another log to the fire," John said and his father gave an assenting nod. Once John had returned to his place on the sofa, Judd sent a sharp-eyed glance about the room to make sure he had everyone's attention. Then, after a satisfied grunt, he began to speak.

"My father, Joseph Bradford, was a wealthy man with a large estate and some of the finest Hereford cattle in all of England when he first heard about a place called Wyoming. He and my mother, Sara, had three daughters who were pretty near half-grown and well on their way toward becoming fine English ladies. In most men's eyes, my father had all that a man could ask for in this life. Then, one evening, a friend dropped by and that one visit changed the course of my father's whole life. This friend had recently returned from a trip to the United States and he was full of tales about a new territory out West. This territory had mile upon mile of open rangeland just perfect for raising the Hereford breed.

"There was new earth and sweet water for raising crops. There were hundreds of acres of timber land, too, and great mountain ranges with strange names like Absaroka, Gros Ventre, and Teton. The name given to this new territory was Wyoming." Judd's deep voice rolled over the word like the sonorous music of ocean waves. "Wyoming," he said again. "That one word started a vision in my father's mind—a vision of what he wanted most in life: a cattle ranch in Wyoming with strong sons to work by his side.

"Within a year's time my father had sold his home and land and made all the necessary preparations to leave England and come to America. I'm sure it must have been hard for my mother to leave her beautiful home. She had all the luxuries any woman could wish for—servants, clothes, fine furniture. But she loved my father more than all those things so she went with him. After they came to Wyoming and found this river valley, I'm sure she felt like my father did—that they were home." Judd's voice rose in strength and his eyes shone with pride. "My father started right in to build this house and get a crop of alfalfa in for the cattle and horses he'd brought with him. It was hard work, but he thrived on it. He knew he was building a home for generations of Bradfords to come.

"About a year and a half after they settled here, I was born. My father was more than proud. The vision he'd had back in England was coming true right before his eyes. My birth weakened my mother some because she didn't have the kind of help she was used to back in England. Then, too, she wasn't a young woman any more. She still hadn't got all her strength back when she found out she was going to have another baby. She died a few months after my brother John was born. But at last the vision was complete. My father had a cattle ranch in Wyoming and two strong sons to stand by his side. He named the ranch in honor of the three of us—Joseph, Judd, and John—the Triple J!"

Judd's pride in the ranch and its history was like a living thing glowing inside him, and I could see from the faces about me that they shared in his pride. I didn't want to say anything that would tarnish the glow of their rich heritage, but I couldn't stop the tender ache of sympathy inside me for Sara Bradford. Sara, the gentle Englishwoman, who was unused to the rough life of a wild, new country. Uncomplaining Sara, who had given her life to fulfill a dream of her husband's. The fact that his mother had died for them didn't seem to bother Judd at all. Probably, in his mind, any sacrifice would not be too great in order to bring about the conception of the Triple J. I wondered than about Judd's younger brother, after whom I'm sure he must have named his own son.

"Does your brother have a ranch around here, too?" I asked him.

I was completely unprepared for his thunderous answer.

"The only thing my brother has around here is a grave!"

I sat rigidly on the sofa while John's mild voice came to my ears so faintly, it was almost as if he were in another room. "Don't upset yourself, Dad. Angela didn't know."

"I'm not upset!" Judd bellowed. "And since Miss Stewart is so interested in the ranch, I'm sure she'll want to know what part Indians have played in its colorful history!"

His large hands gripped the arms of the chair and he glanced feverishly around the room to see if he would have to put down any more interference, but the entire family was as still and motionless as the chairs they were sitting on. I saw Janet's hand leave her grandfather's knee and she moved quietly away from him to lean against the couch.

I wasn't sure whether Judd Bradford was obeyed through fear or respect, but one thing was certain; no one dared raise his voice in opposition to his wishes, not even his son.

"Now then," Judd began again, and his chilly blue eyes were focused directly on mine. "After my mother died, my three older sisters mothered me and Johnny-boy, but one by one, they all married and moved away. Then, it was just the three of us. Lord, we had fine times," he said softly. "Just me and Dad and Johnny.

"In those years the ranch grew and prospered. We had the sleekest, fattest cattle in these parts. When roundup season came we always hired on more cowhands to help with the work, and one year my father signed up a couple of redskins." Judd's black brows narrowed and he peered at me with an uncompromising stare. "I warned my father at the beginning that those Indians would make nothing but trouble, but he insisted we were short-handed and needed them to get the work done. Well, things went pretty smooth until after the cattle were all shipped out—then the hands really let loose. They all came back from town one night pretty high on booze, and those two Injuns were ten times worse than all the rest. A fight got started and Johnny went out to the bunkhouse to see if he could calm them down some. He opened the door and got three bullets right in the chest. When I heard the shots I came running to see what had happened and found my brother lying dead on the floor with one of those filthy varmits bending over him, trying to take his scalp, but so dead drunk he didn't know what he was cutting. The other one was dancing and whooping it up around him, while all the rest of the hands just stood there like their boots were nailed into the floor. I grabbed the mangy cuss who was trying to scalp my Johnny and stuck his own knife through his gizzard. Then I took the other red devil and slammed him into the wall so hard he died of a broken neck before I could do anything else to him." Some of the red flush died in Judd's cheeks but his hands were still trembling as he said in a low whisper, "My father never stopped grieving for Johnny. I think that's what killed him in the end, and it taught me a hard lesson." Once more his eyes cut into my face. "There isn't an Indian alive that's worth spittin' on!"

I looked down at my hands which were clenched so tightly the knuckles showed hard and white. No one said a word. The younger boys slipped silently away and Helen got up from the couch looking drawn and pale. John took her arm and they left the room together.

I felt Thayne's hand touch my shoulder briefly, and he said in a tight voice, "I don't know about you, but I've had enough history for one night. See you in the mornin.' "

Janet got to her feet, giving me a look of mute apology and I stood up from the sofa like one in a daze. Judd Bradford had slumped back into the deep cushions of the recliner and was staring into the fire. He looked more than ever like King Saul must have when a dark mood was upon him. I wanted nothing more than to get away from his gloomy presence, but even stronger was the feeling that I must speak to him before I left. I knew he had told the story of his brother's violent death for my benefit, but I didn't understand why.

"I'm sorry about your brother," I said slowly. "I'm especially sorry you felt you had to tell me about it. I don't want to cause you any grief. Honestly, I don't!"

Judd stared into the glowing coals like one in a trance.

"You're tired, Grandpa Judd, and it's getting late," Janet said softly, giving one of Judd's thick shoulders a little squeeze.

"It's not the Triple J, any more," he mumbled sadly. "Not like it was then."

"Yes, it is," I said, thinking only to comfort him. "There's you and John and Jay—"

His large head jerked away from the cushions. "He's not part of the Triple J and he never will be! And you can tell him I said so," he added with a peculiar look in his eyes.

Fear shot through me in that moment. I turned quickly and walked away from him, feeling cold all over. Janet hurried after me, for once not knowing what to say. When we reached the stairs I said to her, "I didn't purposely try to upset your grandfather tonight. Please, believe me!"

"Of course I believe you! I can't imagine what got into Grandpa tonight—that terrible story about his younger brother, and the way he talked right to you. It was all so strange. Angela, I never knew how his brother died. None of us did. Mom and Dad told us once that he died a long time ago, but not how. I'm not sure they even knew. I wonder what made him want to talk about it tonight?"

"I don't know," I whispered as we walked down the hall toward her room. "But I had the feeling he thought it should mean something to me."

"Don't let it bother you," she said. "We're used to Grandpa's moods and usually they go away as fast as they come. Tomorrow, everything will be fine. You wait and see."

Chapter 13

"And turning round, much terrified,
Her darkest fears were verified . . ."

Guy Wetmore Carryl

Monday morning Helen Bradford woke up with a severe migraine headache. She made a valiant attempt to cook breakfast as usual, but her face was gray and her eyes dull with pain. John came into the kitchen and promptly ordered her back to bed.

I asked Janet if her mother often had headaches like this and she replied with a concerned shake of her head, "She hasn't had one this bad in months. If it gets any worse we'll have to call the doctor."

After breakfast and dishes were over, Janet and I had the weekly washing to contend with. I soon discovered that this involved a great deal more than sorting clothes, tossing them into a machine and turning a dial. Janet tried to show me how to operate a dangerous-looking contraption with a wringer and two metal tubs for rinsing, but after one or two tries at getting clothes caught in the wringer and scaring myself silly, she wisely assigned me the task of hanging out each load while she washed and rinsed the others.

I picked up a basket of wet laundry and carried it out to the clotheslines, hoping that a little fresh air and sunshine would lift my spirits more than the dreary, cement-floored washroom with its brown, plywood walls. Outside, the sky was a clear, cornflower blue with mere puffs of white clouds skimming about. And, as always, there was a wind. This morning's merry breeze must have been the mischievous younger brother to last night's mournful gale. It seemed to take special delight in snatching the sheets and towels out of my hands as I tried to pin them on the lines, and soon it was dancing a lively jig with the shirts and dresses.

I listened to the chorus of birds over in the pines and smiled. There was something deeply satisfying, almost comforting, about hanging out clean, sweet-smelling clothes and feeling the morning sun upon one's back. Soon I

116

was humming a little melody and revelling in the luxury of reliving my day with Jay. The lines were laden with sun-bright laundry long before my mind had finished the journey from Dusk to Jackson Hole and back again.

Janet and I carried the last load out between us. I took one look at the heavy-hanging clotheslines and asked, "Where are we going to hang the stockings? I don't think there's an inch of clothesline left anywhere."

"Just lay them down on the grass to dry here in the sun," she said, giving me a grateful smile. "I really do appreciate your help this morning. I knew Mother wasn't up to doing it, and it takes forever when just one person does the wash."

"I believe you! I don't know how your mother keeps up with everything the way she does!"

"Mother thrives on hard work!" Janet said, "and ranch life means a lot of it."

"Do you want to live on a ranch after you're married?" I asked her.

"Well, I guess that all depends on who I marry, doesn't it?" she laughed.

"Do you have anyone in particular in mind?"

A sudden, painful gleam of remembrance burned in her eyes, but she answered lightly, "Oh, I did, but that's all over now."

I laid the last stocking on the warm grass. "What happened?"

"Oh, it was all so stupid!" she blurted out and picked up the empty laundry basket with a vengeance. We started walking back to the house and she said wistfully, "Last summer at this time, Reed Tyler and I were practically engaged. I guess I've only been in love with him all my life. He and Thayne have been best friends ever since they were old enough to sit a horse and hold a fishing pole. And I was always tagging along behind. I was such a tomboy! It's no wonder Reed thought of me as nothing more than Thayne Bradford's scrawny little sister—up until last summer," she added with a soft little smile.

We entered the washroom and Janet pulled out the rubber stopper on a hose connected to the washer. A gray torrent of water crested with soapy foam gushed out into a nearby sink.

"Well, aren't you going to tell me what happened?" I prompted.

She smiled self-consciously. "There isn't all that much to tell, really. Thayne and Reed planned a fishing trip in the mountains east of here and like always, I went along to help with the cooking and stuff. Nothing really earth-shattering happened, but that first night out I knew that Reed was aware—really aware of me for the first time. I guess our feelings for each other must have been pretty transparent though, because when we got back, Mom put her foot down. I was not allowed to go camping with the boys anymore!" She laughed. "Mom never could figure out why I obeyed her new edict without a fuss. I didn't tell her that Reed had promised me we'd go camping on our honeymoon." Then she sighed.

"Reed and I started making some plans and he didn't know whether to stay here in Dusk and work on his dad's ranch or go away to school. I wanted him to stay here so we wouldn't have to wait so long, and I guess I put too much pressure on him. We had a fight and he went away to some university on the West coast. After Reed left, I couldn't stand being around here anymore, so I decided to go to a university back East and get as far away from him as I could."

I looked at Janet with new understanding. I had often wondered why she had chosen to attend Michigan State when there were excellent universities much closer to her home.

"I haven't seen or heard from Reed since he left, but one of the girls in town told me that she heard he'd gotten engaged this past winter."

"You know how rumors are," I said gently. "Maybe he'll come back."

She shook her dark head. "No. He'll never come back." Then she glanced at the watch on her wrist. "Oh, rats, it's almost time to start lunch. We'd better go check on Mom first, though. I hope she's feeling better."

But this was not the case. Mrs. Bradford's headache had worsened to the point that Janet, thoroughly alarmed, called their doctor. He prescribed some powerful pain pills and a sedative, and since no one else was available at the time, Janet decided to drive into town herself to get the prescriptions. I would gladly have gone in her place but she dashed out the back door before I could utter a word, calling over her shoulder that the meat was already in the oven and would I get some potatoes out of the cellar and put them on to boil. I looked up at the kitchen clock and nearly panicked. The men would be in from their morning's work and expecting a hot meal at half past twelve. Already, it was nearing high noon and the potatoes would take a full half hour to cook.

I went to one of the cupboards, grabbed a large pan and hurried outside to the Bradford's underground food cellar. The grass growing over its humped ceiling of earth was long and thick. The sloping green mound reminded me faintly of a grave. I tossed away my grisly comparison and unlatched the wooden bar from the heavy door. I pulled the door all the way open and flung it back on its hinges against the grassy side of the cellar, then walked down the earthen ramp. The air inside the cellar was cool with the taste of earth on its breath. Coming from the brilliant sunlight of noonday made it even harder for my eyes to adjust to such intense darkness. At first, all I could see were assorted black shapes, then my eyes made out some wooden shelves along the walls which contained canned goods, bottled fruit and preserves. On the floor were several metal bins and lumpy burlap bags. The bags were in the furthest corner of the cellar and I examined them first.

Luckily for me, the second one I opened held the potatoes. I began filling the pan, wondering if there were some other vegetable I could serve or whether I should prepare a salad.

Suddenly there was a sharp squeaking of hinges. I looked up, only to have darkness slammed in my face and hear the heavy thump of the wooden bar falling into place. I jumped to my feet, knocking over the pan of potatoes. They rolled lumpily in all directions as I plunged through the darkness and up the short incline of the ramp.

I don't know what stopped me from pounding on the door and shouting for help. My fists were raised and my mouth open to cry out, when for no reason, my body froze in that position. Slowly, my arms dropped to my sides. I held my breath and listened. Inches away, through the bulky wooden door, another form was standing quite still and listening also. I couldn't hear him, but stronger than all the other senses combined, I could feel his presence. What if he should open the door now? What would he do? Dear heaven, why did I drop the pan? At least I could have had some sort of weapon.

I let out my breath and tried to think what to do. The answer came from some unknown source within me and I didn't pause to analyze it or even think twice. I knew that I must not cry out for help. Whoever was outside the cellar door must not know how terrified I felt.

I swallowed hard and said clearly, "Tadd? David? Is that you? Please let me out. I've got to fix lunch." Nothing. "All right, you've had your joke. Now let me out or you won't get a hot meal." I pressed my ear against the smooth dry wood and waited. After a long moment I heard the snap of a twig and what might have been footsteps, then nothing. The sick, paralyzing fear left me and I knew he had gone. I sank down upon the earthen floor of the cellar, as the tenseness left me in a series of violent shudders.

I knew I must fight the closed-in, smothering feeling of earth and darkness all around me. I must! If I heard the boys walking by I could call out to them, but other than that there was nothing I could do until someone found me. Who would think to look for me in here? No one. Perhaps, not even Janet. Nonsense! When she returned from town and found a house full of hungry, grumbling menfolk, she would immediately ask where I was. No one would know, but she would remember how she had asked me to get some potatoes from the cellar, and when she saw that there were no potatoes boiling on the stove she would come straight out here. Yes, of course she would! But Janet wouldn't return from town for an hour, maybe longer. How could I endure this cold, black prison for an hour? I fought another wave of panic by burying my face in my hands and shutting my eyes. Somehow, that kind of blindness wasn't nearly as frightening as staring into black nothingness with my eyes wide open. I raised my knees and rested my head against them. It was a comforting illusion which allowed my thoughts to proceed more rationally.

I didn't believe that Janet's younger brothers had locked me in here as some sort of cruel joke; especially after I had mentioned my claustrophobia in front of the entire family only last night. If it had been the boys, they certainly would have answered me when I called out to them. Tadd and David might be a pair of mischievous rascals but they were not malicious. Who could have done it and why? It seemed incredulous to me that I could have become such a threat to the man after Jay that he would risk a stunt like this in broad daylight! It was more than incredulous—it was impossible! That person would have to possess omniscient faculties in order to know Jay's and my whereabouts at all times. How else could he be waiting in that dark grove of trees, hiding in the hay loft, and now, wandering openly about the ranch to see me go into the cellar. Yes, it was impossible. Unless . . . Unless . . .

My hands fell away from my face and I stared blindly into the darkness, seeing the truth clearly for the first time.

Minutes dragged by, but their slow passage gave me time to think. Piece by piece, tiny facts fell into place. The puzzle was far from completed, but the picture was becoming more and more clear.

Someone from the Triple J would have known the approximate time of Jay's return from town the night the shots were fired. In fact, it had been Janet's father who insisted that Jay take the spare tire in to be repaired that evening. All of the Bradfords knew that Jay was in the barn tending the Hereford cow. The only unexpected factor in both incidents was my presence. It must have been quite a shock for someone when I arrived with Jay that first night. He must have been wondering why I made no mention of two shots fired at the truck. And again, after the accident with the calf, I had said nothing. Was it any wonder he felt threatened and worried?

Why must life contain these sudden, vicious stabs of irony? Jay had gone away to protect me. I had tried so hard to keep from revealing anything about him and what had happened—and yet it was silence itself which had condemned me.

What did this new knowledge do to Jay's carefully thought out theory about his father's disappearance and the Triple J's missing horses?

I got up and tried to move about, but the darkness and my rushing thoughts made me dizzy.

Jay's theory might be logical, but so often in life, the way things really happen don't make sense at all. Jay would never suspect a member of his family. How could he? My own heart twisted inside me when I considered the very real possibility that one of the Bradfords was responsible for Jason's death and now, the attempts on Jay's life.

I thought of John Bradford's friendly blue eyes and teasing manner. The idea that he might have killed his own brother was ludicrous. And then

120

there was Judd. He was an old man with a tragic, violent past. I had no way of knowing what strange griefs or hatreds might form a strong enough motive for murder in his twisted mind. But could there honestly be a motive strong enough to perpetrate the murder of his own son? Surely not a handful of missing horses, as Jay had theorized. And what of Thayne? Was it simple jealousy that triggered his actions toward Jay or did he know something of Jason's disappearance? He might be trying to protect his father or grandfather by getting rid of Jay.

I edged my way up to the door and sat down again. It was all getting too complicated. And it was horrible to be compiling a list of murder suspects from my best friend's family. As yet, I hadn't included Bert Tingey, but I had to trust someone. Jay trusted him. Surely, that meant something! Besides, I hadn't seen Bert since Sunday morning at breakfast. If only I could talk to him—or Jay! I could almost see the stark look of anguish in Jay's dark eyes when he learned that it was a member of his own family he was looking for. I put my face in my hands again and tried to stop thinking.

I had no idea how much time had gone by. It felt like hours. I pressed my body close to the door and tried to keep my mind occupied with simple, mundane things. But after a while, nothing helped. My ears invented furtive rustlings and small scratching noises. My eyes created dark, furry shapes that lurked in the corners and thin, wavering shadows that pulsed and dilated in the air around me. And I was cold. Every time I took a breath it was like swallowing, thick, cold molasses. I almost panicked with the thought that I might suffocate before someone found me. Perhaps more than just a scare had been intended for me after all. I stumbled to my feet and for the first time began pounding on the door and calling for help.

Suddenly, it opened and there was Janet staring at me open-mouthed. I staggered past her out into the sunlight and stood squinting in its blessed warmth, hugging myself.

"Are you all right?" she asked quickly.

I gave her a jerky nod.

"How on earth did you get locked in the cellar?"

I stared at her for a moment then said, "I—I don't know. I was getting some potatoes when suddenly, the door banged shut. I thought you'd never get back."

She bit her lip and looked at me with worried eyes. "Are you sure you're all right? You look so white."

"Yes—really, I'm—fine." I tried to give her a smile but I couldn't stop shuddering. "It's just—that I hate feeling closed in—and it was so dark—and cold."

"Angela, I'm so sorry," she said helplessly. "When I got back from town Dad was in the kitchen getting a make-shift lunch on the table and

121

everyone said they thought you had gone with me. I couldn't imagine what had happened until I remembered that I'd asked you to get some potatoes out of the cellar, and saw there weren't any cooking on the stove. Then I came straight out here. I—I'm so sorry."

I looked up at the gray stone house as we turned our steps toward it. "It's all right," I told her. "It wasn't your fault. The wind must have blown the door shut."

Chapter 14

"Death at a Distance we but slightly fear,
He brings his Terrors as he draws more near."

Susanna Gellett

The Bradford family reacted with proper amounts of shock and sympathy when Janet told them I had been locked in the cellar. John sternly suggested that Tadd and David might know who was responsible and the two boys erupted with righteous anger at his implied accusation. I found myself observing every reaction with new eyes—eyes made wary and cautious, even cynical by my knowledge of the situation. Was John really concerned about the possibility of his boys having locked me in the cellar, or was he merely putting on an act for my benefit? Was Thayne as sympathetic as he seemed, or was he laughing at me behind those brilliant blue eyes? True to form, Judd said nothing at all. He was still moody and morose from last night's story telling and I made a special effort to keep out of his way.

It was another problem altogether trying to keep out of Thayne's way. That evening he asked if I wouldn't like to drive into town with him, have a few drinks, and meet some of his friends. Somehow, I managed a smiling, "Not tonight, but thanks anyway," and headed for the living room.

But Janet's brother was not easily discouraged. His next suggestion was a rabbit hunt which he proposed for the following morning, complete with his own brand of special instructions on how to shoot.

Janet, overhearing her brother's invitation, pounced on me with bright-eyed enthusiasm. I had been trying to wangle my way out of the situation, using Helen's illness as an excuse. I really hated to leave, I told Thayne, when Janet and Helen might need my help around the house.

"Oh, don't worry about that!" Janet put in quickly. "You're here for a vacation, remember? I can handle things just fine. You and Thayne go ahead."

I sat down on the sofa with a little sigh. Now what could I do? Thayne leaned over me and twirled a strand of my hair around his finger.

"I know just the place," he drawled, giving me a pleased grin. "Miles away from everything—and everybody."

I felt like screaming. Instead I had to sit there and suffer his fingers to fondle my hair while Janet beamed benevolently at the two of us.

Stuart glanced up from the book he was reading and looked directly at me. "A rabbit hunt sure sounds like fun. It's been ages since us boys have gone on one."

I grabbed at his words the way a drowning man reaches for a life preserver. "Why don't you come with us, Stuart? And Tadd and David, too. I'm sure I'll need a lot of help learning how to shoot. I've never fired a rifle before in my life. You don't mind, do you, Thayne?" I asked sweetly.

There were ten seconds of silence while Thayne Bradford stared at me with his mouth hanging open, then he cleared his throat and said, "No, no, I don't mind—if Dad doesn't need the boys' help tomorrow morning," he added, turning to his father for help.

But Tadd and David were already barraging the man for permission to go, and John, listening to their pleadings and promises of work that would faithfully be made up, gave me an amused smile.

"I guess it'd be O.K. for you boys to go along—but I expect you to leave plenty early and be back before noon. I don't want the whole day wasted."

Tadd and David were jubilant. Stuart gave me a knowing grin and went back to his book. I ignored Thayne's and Janet's dour expressions and said cheerfully, "Well, since we're going to be getting an early start, I think I'll go up to bed. See you in the morning!"

We left the ranch well before dawn while the stars still showed pale in a blue-violet sky. Tadd and David were in the back of the truck, happily shouting insults at one another, and Stuart joined Thayne and me in the front. For someone who was usually quite noncommunicative, Stuart did a beautiful job of maintaining nonstop conversation all the way into town. I remembered very well Stuart's telling me that the one thing Thayne couldn't stand was being ignored, and yet the devil in me just wouldn't stop. All my smiles and laughter were directed to the younger boy, while Thayne's silence grew more and more ominous.

When we reached Dusk, Thayne turned right, away from the main street and onto a gravel road. This eventually led us away from town altogether. Soon, even the outlying ranches were left behind and the truck was jostling along a dirt track through the wildest country I had ever seen. Barren, desolate hills blended into an ash gray sky, while the face of the land was scarred and pitted with rocky knolls and deep ravines.

Totally without warning, Thayne shoved his foot on the brake pedal and switched off the ignition. "This place looks as good as any," he growled.

At first, it seemed like a game to me. I never really stopped to think that we were out here to find and kill rabbits. I was too caught up in the singular pleasure of walking through totally new country. Wild and desolate it certainly was, but in the soft light of early morning the land became beautiful to me. Once we saw the great wings and shirred, feathery head of an owl returning to its nest after a night of hunting, but other than that, we saw no other living creature.

The sun was just coming up and the sky was slightly overcast as we made our way down the nearest ravine. The soil was dry and rocky, and down in the gulley we found numerous pockets of tumbleweeds meshed with other dry bush. Then, always unexpected, the first rabbit leaped out from a fat clump of brush. Tadd nearly stepped on it and in his excitement could only utter a string of unintelligible syllables and point with his finger. David and Stuart raised their rifles and two shots ripped the air. Almost the same instant, two patches of earth exploded into dust behind the rabbit's hind legs. The terrified animal darted away with frenzied, zig-zag leaps. Two more shots followed him, but in a matter of seconds he was too far away for the boys to get another shot.

In our wanderings, Tadd and David found several beer cans and an old bottle, and Stuart set them up on the remains of an ancient rail fence for target practice. Thayne did not get the opportunity to demonstrate his skill as a teacher because all three of the younger boys were eager to instruct me in the finer points of aiming and firing a rifle.

"Now just keep your eye on the sight and you'll do fine," David was saying with the lofty air of supreme knowledge possessed by all fifteen-year olds. "Try hitting that can on the end of the post."

I squeezed the trigger and was surprised by the sudden release of power exploding from the rifle. My bullet only pinged the bottom of the can, but it was enough to earn a nod of approval from the boys.

Thayne seemed content to stand aside and watch while his brothers shattered the bottle and knocked cans off the rail fence. After my first blinding success as a marksman, I managed to kill a rock or two and wound several clumps of sagebrush. Then, after the cans had been blown off the fence for the third time, Thayne called out: "Tadd! David! Set those cans up again. It's time for the 'old master' to show you guys how it's done."

I stepped aside with Stuart as Thayne sauntered back several yards further than where his brothers and I had been standing.

After Tadd and David had arranged an elaborate, if somewhat battered pyramid, Thayne yelled, "All right! Move out of the way! The fireworks are about to begin!"

I stood very still, gripping my rifle with white hands while Thayne blasted each can off the pyramid with incredible speed and accuracy. When the last can went flying, Tadd and David let out a whooping cheer, obviously impressed. And so was I. It wouldn't have been difficult in the least for someone with Thayne's skill to fire two shots at a moving truck. He would probably enjoy it.

"He's awfully good, isn't he?" I commented to Stuart in a dry voice.

"He oughta be with the teachers he's had," Stuart said with a grunt.

"Oh. Who were they?"

"Dad and Grandpa Judd. They're both crack shots."

John and Judd. Somehow, it always came back to them.

After another hour of tramping through dry, washed-out gulleys, I was good and ready to go back to the ranch, but, remembering the boys' teasing, I didn't want to be the first one to suggest it. After that first rabbit, we hadn't seen so much as a lizard, and the clouds had long since blown away. I stopped for a moment to tie my shoe lace and realized Tadd was waiting beside me. I looked up into his youthful face with a tired smile.

"Me and Dave didn't lock you in the cellar," he blurted out suddenly. "We've played tricks on guys before, but—we wouldn't ever do that to you! Honest, Angela!"

I looked into his earnest brown eyes. "I know you didn't, Tadd. I never for a minute thought that you did. Honest!" I added with another smile.

He glanced away with a pleased but embarrassed grin and hurried off to catch up with David.

"It's getting too hot to hunt anymore," Thayne said as I picked up my rifle and headed after the boys. "We'd better be getting back to the ranch."

"Whatever you say," I answered.

I watched him wipe the sweat off his forehead and fought to keep back a smile. I'm sure our little excursion had turned out quite differently than he had originally planned. We might be miles away from "everything" but certainly not "everybody" as he had expressed it.

Suddenly, only a few yards away, a long-legged jackrabbit leaped out of some brush. Thayne called out, "This baby's mine!" and fired before his brothers even had a chance to raise their rifles.

I had thought that rabbits made no sound, but as the bullet tore into its soft brown body, I heard a pitiful, high-pitched scream. The animal seemed to stop for a moment in mid-air, then fell flinching and kicking in the dust.

Stuart cried, "It's not dead yet! Shoot it again!" and Thayne was quick to oblige him.

The flinching stopped. My stomach heaved within me as I stared at the mutilated carcass. I put a hand to my throat and swallowed hard. So this was

126

how the game ended. My eyes lifted from the bloody remains to Thayne's exultant gaze. I stared into that hard blue brilliance, but all I could see were dark eyes—dark eyes filled with pain as they looked at a dead calf. I turned without a word and walked away.

After the noon meal, Helen insisted that I take a rest. "You look all frayed around the edges," she said with a frown.

Accordingly, I went up to Janet's room and stretched out on the bed. I pulled a quilt over me and closed my eyes. I seriously doubted whether I would be able to sleep, but I was glad of any excuse to put distance between me and the Bradford men. How could I possibly endure an entire summer of tension and fear? If only I could be with Jay, I wouldn't feel so frightened. I clutched my pillow and thought desperately, I'd give anything in the world to be up in that mountain cabin in his arms right now!

When I awoke, long shadows hovered on the walls and I was sure several hours had passed. The room was pleasantly warm and I could hear the squawking of the magpies just outside the window. I felt completely rested and lay for just a moment, savoring the calm. Then I turned over on my back and stretched. As my arms moved across the pillow I felt something small and smooth brush against my skin. I sat up and saw a neatly folded piece of paper lying innocently on the pillow. I stared at the white paper for several seconds, feeling my chest grow tighter with every breath. Finally, I reached out a hand, but gingerly, as if the note were something which might strike out when touched. I opened the neatly creased folds and saw one word printed in black ink across the paper: LEAVE.

Chapter 15

"Fate snatch'd her early to the pitying sky . . ."
Alexander Pope

The small scrap of hope I had that Jason's killer might not be a member of his own family, crumpled like the note paper in my shaking fist.

I got off the bed and paced about the room. The moss green carpet was soft under my feet, the daisies on the wall were smiling in the late afternoon sunshine that poured through an open window and I was cold, a clammy, shuddering cold. Someone had come into this room while I was sleeping to deposit a single word of warning and I could neither say nor do anything about it—at least not to the Bradfords. Perhaps Bert Tingey could help me— and Jay must know the truth! I couldn't afford to wait any longer.

I ripped the note into small pieces and tossed it into a waste can. Behind me, the door opened with a soft click. I whirled about with a sharp intake of breath but it was only Helen Bradford's gentle voice and smile that greeted me.

"Did you have a nice rest, dear?"

"I—yes, I did."

"I always say this Wyoming air can do wonders to settle a body down."

"Yes, I feel much better."

"You know, I never did get the chance to see those moccasins Jay bought you," she said.

"That's right, you didn't. Let me show them to you now." I went to the closet while Helen sat down on the bed with a weary sigh. I bent down for the brown shoe box then turned about to face her. "Is your headache still bothering you?"

"No, not too much. But they always leave me feeling real washed out. I'm not even worth my salt today."

128

I put the shoe box in her lap and watched her face with enjoyment as she removed the lid and lifted out the moccasins. Her worn hands caressed the soft, fragrant leather, then she raised her head to look at me.

"You must mean a great deal to him," she said soberly. "Jay doesn't give presents lightly—or his love, either. Most of his life, I think he's been near starved for love. I tried to make a good home for him here after his mother died, but I know how alone he's felt most of the time." Her usually mild voice was suddenly tight and constricted with emotion. "There's just too much bitterness and old hatreds in this house to let the love grow. I don't know as I've ever told him so right to his face—but I love Jay every bit as much as I do my own boys!"

I put a hand over one of her work-roughened ones. "I know you do, and so does Jay. He told me how good you've always been to him. He loves you very much."

"Jay told you that?"

I smiled and nodded.

Helen bent her head and dabbed at her eyes with the hem of her apron. "Land sakes, I never meant to get so blubbery. What I came up here for in the first place was to see how the idea of a big Western party appeals to you."

"A party?"

"That's what I said. I couldn't help noticing how that chin of yours has been draggin' on the floor lately, and menfolk are a bunch of ninnies if they think horseback rides and rabbit hunts will cheer a girl up. What you need is a party with lots of good food and dancing and other young folks."

"It—it sounds wonderful," I said, returning the moccasins to their box, then going to the closet.

"Of course it does!" she declared with a broad smile. "Laws, the fellows in town will go crazy when they see those big eyes and that sudden, sweet smile of yours. Thayne will be hard put to get a dance now and then, I tell you! Not that it will do him any good, of course," she sniffed, then added with twinkling eyes. "Maybe that runaway nephew of mine will leave off from painting long enough to come down out of the hills and put Thayne in his place. Not that you haven't been doin' a real fine job of it so far. That boy of mine has needed puttin' down a peg where girls are concerned for a long time," she chuckled.

Try as I would, I couldn't keep the laughter from bubbling up inside me and some of it escaped to the surface.

"That's better," Helen said crisply. "We haven't been hearing that laugh of yours near often enough. I knew this party would be just the thing."

"Hi!" Janet poked her head in the doorway. "I take it Mom has been telling you all about our party plans."

"I was just getting started," her mother said. "You can fill Angela in on all the details."

129

"Mom and I thought it would be fun to have everyone come in real Western dress, and we could have a big barbeque dinner outside," she said, joining us on the bed. "Then, after dinner we could come in the house for some square dancing."

"And a few waltzes!" Helen ordered.

"And a few waltzes!" Janet conceded with a grin.

"There'll be plenty of room for dancing in the living room if we take out some of the furniture. The rest can be moved against the walls," she went on. "Elmer Potter will be glad to call the square dances and old Floyd Thacker is always looking for an excuse to get his dance band together."

"You really have thought of everything," I said, secretly wondering what 'old Floyd Thacker's' dance band sounded like.

"Well, we thought it might be a nice way for you to meet some of the folks in Dusk and have a bit of fun at the same time," Helen said.

"Are you sure you feel up to having such a big party?" I asked her. "I know it will mean a lot of extra work."

"Pshaw, I can't think of a better excuse to get my cleaning done. Besides, John and the boys will take charge of most of the barbeque fixin's. John's famous for his barbeque sauce for miles around!"

"It's the wildest stuff you've ever tasted" Janet promised.

"And I'm sure there will be a few things you girls can do to help out," Helen added.

"You can count on that," Janet groaned. "Mom's a real slave driver!"

"Organizer is a much nicer word, Janet," her mother corrected with laughing eyes.

"Did you say everyone would be wearing Western style clothes?" I asked them. "I don't think I have anything to wear—except jeans, of course, and they aren't very partyish."

"That's no problem! There are tons of trunks up in the attic just full of old clothes!" Janet told me.

"There ought to be two or three, anyway," Helen amended with a dry smile.

"Why don't we go up to the attic and look through the trunks right now?" Janet suggested.

Helen glanced at her wrist watch. "I suppose we have time. I was only going to fix a light supper tonight."

I followed them out into the hall, thinking how ironic it was that while Janet and her mother were happily planning a party to brighten my stay at the ranch, another member of their family was hoping I would leave.

Helen opened one of the doors along the hall which I had supposed might be a linen closet. Instead, I saw a flight of steep, wooden stairs leading upward. She flipped a switch on the wall to her right then proceeded up the stairs. Janet went eagerly on her mother's heels and I followed behind. Where the stairs ended, a huge, shadowy garret began and stretched the entire length of the house. Two bare bulbs dangled on cords from wooden beams in the ceiling, but their harsh light did little to alleviate the musty darkness.

"I'm afraid everything's terrible dusty up here," Helen apologized, wrinkling up her nose.

I gazed with interest at the assortment of forgotten, discarded items which had once belonged to the Bradford family's past. A three-legged table, a cracked oval mirror with a heavy gold frame, antique wardrobes and cupboards, were just a few of the items I saw at first glance. There were many cardboard boxes filled with newer items, but somehow they did not quite belong in this dusty realm of the past.

"What is it about an attic that always makes me want to whisper?" I said. "Sometimes I think that if I were to look quickly over my shoulder I would see someone's great-great grandmother standing behind me dressed in cobwebby lace."

"Don't say things like that!" Janet pleaded. "You give me the shivers!"

I smiled at her. "I didn't mean a skeleton or ghostly hag. I was just thinking how interesting it would be to talk to those who have gone before us. Think of all we could learn."

Helen dusted off an ancient rocker with her apron and sat down in it. "I know just what you mean, dear. There are times when I'd love to talk to my mother again—tell her about the chidren, things they've done." She sighed and rocked for a moment in tryst with memories of her own.

"The trunks are over there by that big wardrobe," she said finally. "I don't believe they're locked, so you two girls can rummage through them to your hearts' content."

One of the trunks contained keepsakes and books but no clothing. Janet and I each took one of the two remaining trunks and dragged them across the floor closer to Helen where the light was better. Janet's trunk opened almost immediately but I had to struggle for a few moments with the big, old-fashioned clasps and hinges on mine.

"These must be Grandma Bradford's," Janet exclaimed and lifted out some dainty shirtwaist dresses with big, puffed sleeves and yellowed lace around the cuffs and collars.

"Let me see. Hold them up, dear. Yes, those are your grandmother's clothes," Helen pronounced. "She was a tiny little woman—no taller than you, Janet—and she had the snappiest brown eyes you ever saw. You're a lot like her, you know."

My own trunk finally yielded and I lifted the lid back to peer at its contents. The frills and tucks and bits of lace on Janet's grandmother's dresses were not to be found on the clothes I examined. And the skirts were of a noticeably longer length. Halfway down I found a long riding skirt made of heavy brown cotton with shiny brown buttons going down both sides of the divided skirt.

"Oh! I love this!" I stood up and pressed the skirt close to me to check the length.

"Why, it's perfect for you, Angela. Look, Mother!"

Helen stopped rocking and stared at the riding skirt a little strangely. "I wonder if those clothes belonged to Nora," she said.

"Who was Nora?" I asked.

"Judd's first wife," she said slowly, still staring at the skirt. "I never knew her. She died when Jason was still a baby."

"Then Jay's father and your husband are really half brothers."

"That's right. Judd married Grandma Bradford a few months after Nora's death. My mother told me all about it years ago. Funny, how just seeing that skirt has brought it all back. When Nora died, there was an awful lot of talk going around Dusk, but Mother always had a way of sorting the truth out of the rumors. Besides, she and Lizzy Woodruff were best friends."

"Lizzy Woodruff?" I said blankly.

"My grandmother, Grandpa Judd's second wife," Janet supplied and stopped sorting through the clothes to listen to her mother.

I sat down on the dusty floor and folded the riding skirt in my lap. "How did Nora die?"

"Pneumonia. It was a real tragedy. Judd fairly worshipped the ground she walked on. Folks said it wasn't natural—to love a woman the way Judd loved Nora. When Jason was born, everybody said you never saw a happier man on the face of the earth than Judd Bradford. Little Jason was only six months old when Nora took sick and died. Nobody knew what went wrong or how she got so sick. She didn't have any trouble at all when Jason was born and she was a tall, strong girl. But when the doctor was sent for she was pretty much gone. Nora's death nearly killed Judd. And Jason, too. I don't know what those two would have done if Lizzy Woodruff hadn't stepped in the way she did. Mother told me that Lizzy had been in love with Judd for a long time—long before he married Nora. After Nora's death, Lizzy used to go out to the ranch and cook meals for Judd and clean up a bit. And like I said, she took care of the baby, too, or the poor little mite probably would have died like his mother. When spring came and the worst was over, Lizzy put it to Judd real plain. That woman always had plenty of spunk, I tell you! Just imagine, if you can, a tiny, brown-eyed lady, barely five feet tall, standing up to Judd Bradford and saying: 'I know how much you loved your

132

wife and I don't aim to take her place. But you need someone to care for you and your son, and if it's all right with you, I'd like to be the one to do it.'

"Well, Judd was fond of Lizzy so he agreed and they got married. Land, how folks talked! A couple of years later John was born and folks stopped waggin' their tongues when they saw Judd Bradford smiling again. I know Lizzy would have liked to give Judd more children, but it wasn't possible. None of us ever knew about it, but she had a bad heart. Laws, the way she worked herself you woulda thought she had the strongest heart in the world! But then, Lizzy was never one to complain. She died real sudden, not too long after Jason disappeared."

I sat pondering all this history and the personal tragedy that seemed to follow Judd Bradford throughout his life. Then I looked down at the brown riding skirt.

"Do you think Judd would mind if I wore Nora's clothes to the party? I wouldn't want to upset him."

Helen waved this worry aside. "Men don't remember things like dresses and such. If you want to wear that skirt, you go right ahead."

"You're sure he won't mind?"

"Why should he mind if you wear Nora's riding skirt?" Janet said. "I'll be wearing one of Grandma Bradford's dresses, so what's the difference?"

"I guess you're right," I agreed, but it bothered me just the same.

Chapter 16

"We never know how much we learn
From those who never will return
Until a flash of unforeseen remembrance
Falls on what has been."

Edward Arlington Robinson

I slept badly that night and my dreams were haunted by a marching procession of the dead. I awoke in the early dawn, cold and trembling, with visions of Nora, Johnny, Lizzy, and Jason Bradford still vivid in my mind. In my dream they were all locked in a room that had neither doors nor windows, and yet, strangely, I could see their faces plainly as they called to me.

Judd's younger brother wore the face of Janet's father, and Lizzy Woodruff resembled Janet. Nora Bradford had somehow become Jay's mother and Jason was embodied with the tall figure of his son. They were all pleading with me to help them and I was searching frantically for a key to the room. Then, something came. I didn't see or hear it, but its presence was malignant and overpowering. The faces in the room stopped crying out and faded away. I felt myself being smothered by an unseen hand and cried out for Jay to help me.

It was then I awakened, beads of perspiration forming on my body and the unseen fear still pressing upon me. I sat up in bed, hoping that would force me out of my terrifying dream and into reality again. But was reality any less terrifying? I had to get out of this house! I looked at Janet, sleeping so peacefully. Didn't she feel it? Dear heaven, it was all around us!

I got out of bed, stripped off my nightclothes with fumbling hands and dressed hurriedy. On impulse, I reached into my drawer and pulled Jay's woolly sweater over my head for warmth, and left the room.

I escaped from the silent house and ran like a wild thing across the back lawn, through the pines, and nearly collided with Bert Tingey.

"Whoa, there!" he cried out in surprise, then chuckled at me. "Now where are you off to in such a hurry?"

I shook my head and tried to catch my breath. "No where—anywhere. Just—away!"

The crinkly smile left his face. "What's the matter, Miss?"

"Is there somewhere we can talk? I've been hoping for the chance to see you for days now. There's something—something important you and Jay should know."

Bert took this in without comment or question, but I saw lines of worry replace the friendly smile around his eyes and mouth. "I was jest on my way to mend a fence out yonder," he said, pointing to the north pastures. "The cattle have been gettin' through and trompin' down the crops. Why don't I saddle you a horse and you kin come along."

I gave him a grateful nod and followed him to the barn.

"Old Duke is in the corral here, but we'll have to go on down to the fields an' catch you one," he said.

Accordingly, Bert took a length of rope, made a lasso, and we walked past the barn toward grassy fields and a stream bright with new sunshine, where many of the Bradford's horses were grazing.

"There's Arabesque!" he cried. "I'll see if I kin get her for you!"

The silky black mare was standing apart from the rest of the herd and when Bert ambled toward her with lasso in hand she immediately raised her head and watched him with big, intelligent eyes. Bert kept her attention with a low, warbling whistle then raised the rope. Arabesque frisked up her heels and cantered away with a playful nicker. I smiled as Bert ran after her with his bow-legged shuffle.

"Come back here, you finicky female! This ain't the time to play hard to get!"

The mare allowed Bert to get just close enough to throw his lasso, then galloped away with a haughty shake of her black head.

"You git back here!" Bert yelled. "You heard me, you black devil! Come on back!"

Arabesque turned her head and gave the old hand a look that held pure disdain.

Bert came puffing back to me with crimson cheeks. "It looks like I'll have to go on back to the barn and saddle Duke, Miss Angela. That smart-alecky female won't get away from me on horseback. You jest wait here!"

When he had gone, I stood for a moment, feeling the sun on my back, watching its golden rays dance on the white creek water, then walked out into the field toward the horses. Arabesque saw me coming and stood with feet apart and ears cocked forward, watching my approach. I got within five yards of her and stopped, seeing her nervous movements.

"Hello, girl. Want to go for a ride?"

135

Arabesque plowed the moist earth with one hoof and blew through her nostrils.

"Oh, I know you'd much rather have *him* on your back, but he can't come to you now. Won't you come here, girl? Please!" I stretched out my hand to her and waited.

The mare shook her silky head as if she couldn't quite decide what to do, then took a few cautious steps toward me. She paused about a yard away and I smiled at her.

"You really do need the exercise, you know. A girl has to think of her figure. Come on, Arabesque."

She came. I smiled in delight and wonder as the horse sniffed my outstretched hand, my hair and my clothes, especially the sweater.

"Why you know it's his, don't you!" I laughed, and buried my head in her thick mane.

"Well, I'll be!"

I turned my head to see Bert Tingey mounted on a big brown stallion just behind me.

"Now how in hell's name did you get that finicky piece of horseflesh to be so cooperative?"

"Oh, I just talked to her."

Bert sniffed. "You womenfolk sure stick together!" He tossed a bridle at my feet and said, "Here. Since you caught her you might jest as well bridle her."

"How do I do it?"

"Jest slip it over her head—now behind her ears—that's the way. Can you handle her bareback or do you want me to go back for a saddle?"

"Oh, good heavens! I'd never be able to stay on her without a saddle!"

"Sure you can. Arabesque has a gallop as smooth as honey and she's not so round that you might slip off her."

"Well, if you really think I can," I said doubtfully.

"Jay always rides her bareback and she's kinda gotten used to it."

That settled it. "How do I get up?"

Bert chuckled and urged his horse close to Arabesque's side. "Jest stuff yer foot in my stirrup and swing yer other leg over Arabesque. That's the way. U-up you go!"

I settled myself astride the black horse and looked at Bert with a foolish grin. "It—it feels all right."

"Sure it does! Now jest hang on with yer legs and keep yer knees close in."

Bert gave his horse a swat on the rump with the reins and headed him toward the north pastures. I leaned close to Arabesque's sensitive black head and whispered, "I'll try if you will. Let's go!"

I had visions of myself plummeting over her head or tumbling off on either side, but after a few precarious moments of slipping and sliding around, I began to get the feel of it. Arabesque had a clean, beautiful stride and it wasn't long before I gave myself up completely to the excitement of the ride. Ahead of us, I saw that Bert had brought his horse to a halt before a barrier of wire fencing. I pulled on the reins and shared Arabesque's reluctance to bring our ride to an end. When she came to a full stop I patted her head, slid off her back and staggered toward Bert Tingey.

"Well now, you done jest fine!" he pronounced with a toothy grin.

"Thanks, but I wish I didn't have such a hard time walking afterwards. Everytime I get off a horse my legs give up!"

Bert chuckled and took a pair of wire cutters from one of his pockets. "That's O.K. At least you stayed on her. Jay would've been right proud to see you flyin' across the fields thataway. Yes sir, you sure wuz a purty sight."

At the mention of Jay's name, I remembered with a sickening twinge my reasons for coming out to talk with Bert and the pleasure of the ride faded.

Bert went to work on a trampled section of wire fencing and I sat down on a sawed off stump. Arabesque stood close beside me, content to graze in the long grass.

"Jest what is it you've got to tell me, Miss?"

I watched the old man's tough, stubby fingers deftly string new wire into place and said slowly, "The person after Jay isn't someone from another ranch as we thought—he's right here on the Triple J."

Bert shot me an unbelieving, almost accusing glance. "I hope you have a damn good reason for sayin' that, Miss."

I rubbed my palms nervously against my Levis. "Do you think I'd dare say anything like that if I didn't? Bert, I didn't want to believe it either—but I have to! I know what this will do to Jay, but it will be even worse if he doesn't know. Surely, you can see that!"

Bert cut a piece of fencing with a vicious snap of his wire cutters. "Let's hear yer reasons, then I'll let you know how I feel about it."

I twisted my hands together and stared at the tender blue morning sky. I had hoped Bert would understand, but I had forgotten that years of loyalty to the Bradfords would make him resentful of anything I might say against them, and rightly so. Looking at his gruff, disgruntled expression, I began to wonder if telling Bert were a wise thing to do. But what other choice did I have?

"I suppose you heard that I was locked in the cellar Monday afternoon," I began.

"Yeah, Judd mentioned something about the wind blowin' the door shut and nobody knowin' where you were until Janet got back from town."

"That's what I told Janet and her family, but the wind didn't blow the door shut! Someone locked me in! Bert, I laid that door flat on its hinges against the side of the cellar before going inside. While I was getting the potatoes, it suddenly slammed shut and I heard the bar falling into place."

"Well now, I don't blame you for feelin' frightened, Miss, but it was probably jest Tadd or Davy playin' a trick on you."

"I thought of that, too, but Tadd told me they didn't do it and I believe him. Bert, if it had been the boys, I know they would have let me out. They may like to tease, but they're not malicious. The more I thought about it, the more I knew it had to be the person after Jay. Only I couldn't understand how he could be roaming around the ranch like that in broad daylight. I don't want to believe that one of the Bradfords is responsible for everything, but it explains so much. Take the accident with the hook. Jay wondered why the dogs didn't bark and how this person knew we were in the barn. And those two shots fired at the truck—someone here at the ranch knew Jay had gone into town, and he also knew the approximate time of his return."

"What yer tryin' to tell me is, you think John or Judd is the one after Jay—is that it?" Bert said, giving me a scowling glance from beneath his bushy brows.

"Yes. Yes, that's what I think."

"Well, I sure as hell don't!" he exploded. "Yer gettin' locked in the cellar don't prove a blamed thing! Probably, Thayne's the one behind all this. He's so jealous of Jay, he'd do anything to get rid of him."

"Maybe. But Thayne didn't know I would be with Jay the night those shots were fired. He had no reason to be jealous then. And there's something else. Whoever it is that wanted Jay to leave the ranch is now very anxious for me to do the same thing."

Bert's scowl lifted and he looked at me with interest. "Now what makes you say that?"

"Yesterday afternoon I was resting in Janet's room. When I woke up there was a note on my pillow."

"A note? What did it say?"

"Just one word—leave!" Bert stopped mending the fence and stared at me. "How could someone outside the ranch know that I'm involved?" I asked him. "And how could this person walk into the ranchhouse, upstairs, and into Janet's room—and then just disappear without anyone seeing him!"

Bert rubbed his chin with a grimy paw and cleared his throat. "I'm still not sayin' I believe all this, but—I kin see you're right about one thing. We'd better tell Jay. After that, it's up to him."

I breathed a sigh of relief. "How soon can you get to the cabin and talk to him?"

Bert thought for a moment, then a smile flickered across his gruff features. "I think there's a way we kin both git up to see him. Tomorrow mornin's the cattle drive when we take the first group of Hereford's up to the summer range. It's only a small bunch—30 to 35 head is all. I'll try and work it out so's you kin come along, then afterwards we'll go on up to the cabin and talk to Jay."

"Tomorrow morning?" I said breathlessly. "Tomorrow morning! Oh, Bert, that's wonderful! I mean—do you really think it would be all right for me to come along?"

"Oh sure, sure. Won't be no trouble," he said, sounding amiable once more.

I gave his sunburned cheek a little kiss, then stood on the stump and climbed onto Arabesque's back. "Even if you don't believe me, thanks for listening," I said and rode away.

"You'll just love Aunt Kate and Uncle Al," Janet was saying that afternoon as we headed for the bunkhouse armed with mops, soap, rags and buckets. "They live down in Rock Springs so we don't get to see them very often—not nearly as often as we'd like. I'm so glad they chose this weekend to come up for a visit! Now they can come to the party and Aunt Kate will be here to help Mom. It's just perfect!"

Just before noon, Kate Thompson, a younger sister of Helen's, had telephoned to ask if it would be all right if she and her husband and their five children drove up to spend the weekend with the Bradfords. Helen immediately agreed and I assumed this was good news because Janet and her brothers were positively jubilant over the prospect of seeing their cousins. Seeing their excitement, I felt a brief pang of envy at the Bradford's having such a large family and sharing such closeness with aunts and uncles and cousins. The only relative I had met more than once was Mother's older sister Mildred, and her marriage had been a childless one.

The arrival of the Thompsons meant drastic changes in sleeping arrangements for everyone. Within minutes of the phone call, Janet and Helen were planning who would be sleeping in which bed. Aunt Kate and Uncle Al would take over Tadd's and David's room; eighteen-year-old Randy would move in with Stuart; twenty-year old Larry would share Thayne's room, and the two youngest Thompson boys would sleep in the bunkhouse with David and Tadd. There was a bit of a problem deciding where to put sixteen-year-old Marsha until I offered to sleep on a couch downstairs. My offer was accepted with gratitude and relief. All the bodies were accounted for.

I set my bucket on the linoleum floor of the bunkhouse with a clank. Helen had insisted the entire place be scrubbed from top to bottom before the Thompson's arrival, and looking about the room, the job ahead of us made it seem larger than I remembered. I glanced into the bedroom where

Jay's clothes had hung from the top bunk. Only empty metal hangers remained. I let my eyes wander about the main room, passing over the ugly green couch, the makeshift wooden cupboards, the wicker rocking chair, the pot-bellied stove and finally, the high-backed chair with its rustic leather thongs and smooth animal hides. Was it only a few days ago I had seen the breadth of his shoulders relaxed against the frame, bronze fingers holding a chipped coffee cup, the sooty warmth of his eyes . . .

"Angela, what on earth are you staring at? Oh, that horrid chair! Have you ever seen anything like it? Mother's begged Bert to get rid of it a thousand times, but do you think he will? Not on your life! Oh, well. What do you say we start in the bedroom? It takes two to turn the mattresses and change all that bedding."

Some two hours later the bedding was freshened and changed, dishes were washed and cupboards put in order, the floors were scrubbed and shining with a fresh coat of wax. Intent on her job, Janet had waxed herself into a corner near the pot-bellied stove and the bathroom.

"Good grief, you'd think I'd know better," she said in exasperation, then giggled.

"Maybe it's a good thing," I said from the opposite corner of the room. "We haven't cleaned the bathroom."

"Ugh! And that's the worst job of all!"

I laughed and tossed a can of cleanser across the room to her. "It's all yours! If you like, I can dust and clean this desk a bit while the floor dries."

"Don't strain yourself," she teased and retreated into the tiny bathroom.

It took very little time to dust and tidy the scattered group of magazines and papers that crowded the top of the old pine desk. I was about to pronounce the task finished when I noticed the bottom drawer on the right side of the desk wasn't shut all the way. I gave it a hard shove with my knee, but it wouldn't budge. When I knelt down to open the drawer, I discovered my shove had only jammed it more tightly in its crooked position. It was really a minor thing, but irritating, so I grasped the round wooden knob on the drawer, took a deep breath, and gave it a vicious yank. The entire drawer came out that time and its sudden release nearly sent me toppling over backwards onto the newly waxed floor. I sat down on a small oval rug near the desk and was about to put the drawer back in place when a faint, metallic gleam from within the dark rectangular hole of the desk caught my eye. I bent down and peered inside but I couldn't distinguish what the object was. I reached inside and felt about. Lodged between the bottom of the desk and the framework where the drawer had lain was a book. I took it out and carefully wiped many years accumulation of dust from its cover. It wasn't very large, just about the size of a pocket book, with a semi-hard cover and a

140

metal clasp. As I held the book in my hands I felt an excited crawling in my stomach and a queer tightness of breath. I opened the cover to the first page and saw with some disappointment it was merely a ledger of accounts. I thumbed through the yellowed pages, glancing casually at meaningless facts and figures concerning cattle and crops and machinery repairs. Halfway through I came upon some lined pages and stopped to read the masculine scrawl that filled them.

"I know I can make things work. With time and patience
the old man's heart will have to soften. No one could look at her
without loving her. Not even him."

My breath caught in my throat and I clasped the book more tightly. This book was more than just a ledger—it was also a kind of diary! I turned the page and read:

"We're sure now. The baby will be born in the spring, the
end of May. When I try to convince her that I'd love a girl just as
much as a boy, she smiles at me and says quietly, 'We will have a
son. I know this. And he will be called Jason, after his father.' "

I closed the book with trembling hands and for a full minute knelt there on that old rag rug with my head bowed, letting the wonder of my discovery break over me in waves. Those were Jason's words! The mystery of his disappearance might very well be solved within those yellowed pages.

The flush of a toilet and Janet's cheerful whistling brought me out of my reverie with a frightening jolt. I knew I must get the book out of the bunkhouse and keep it safe until I placed it in Jay's hands tomorrow. But how?

"Well, I'm done!" Janet called from the doorway of the bathroom. She reached out one foot and tested the floor gingerly. "Hooray, the floor's dry! What do you say we go back to the house and get a couple of tall glasses of lemonade?"

"That sounds wonderful."

Janet gathered her bucket, mop, and rags together and tiptoed across the floor.

"Do you think Bert would mind if I borrowed a few of these magazines?" I asked her.

"I don't see why. Most of them are ours, anyway. We bring them out here when we're through with them."

I picked up my bucket and followed Janet out of the bunkhouse, with the magazines under my arm and their precious contents tucked safely inside.

Chapter 17

"Had she come all the way for this,
To part at last without a kiss?"

William Morris

The Bradfords offered no objections to my going on the cattle drive; in fact, John and Helen gave open approval to the idea. Janet was a trifle confused by my excitement over the venture and more than once I caught her watching me closely, as if she weren't entirely convinced that a cattle drive could be so appealing to me. She said as much at dinner and Thayne looked at me with teasing blue eyes. "Maybe Angela knows some exciting steer up at the summer range." I smiled at him and said smoothly, "I didn't think steers were capable of much excitement." The boys hooted and even Judd's thick lips cracked a smile. "You better watch what you say in front of this young lady," he told Thayne. "She's a clever one."

I was very careful of what I said that evening, but still, it was all I could do to keep from bursting apart with excitement. Jason's words—pieces of his life—were contained in a small brown book locked safely in one of my suitcases. How could I possibly act calm and sedate?

Morning finally came. I bathed and dressed carefully and somehow managed not to take the stairs two at a time going down to breakfast. When I walked into the kitchen and saw only Janet and Helen at the big oval table, my first reaction was sheer panic.

"Where is everybody?"

"Grandpa Judd's gone into town, Bert and Stuart are out finishing up the milking, and the rest were up hours ago rounding up the cattle," Janet informed me.

"Janet! You shouldn't have let me sleep so late! I didn't know they would be starting this early!"

Helen smiled and motioned for me to sit down with them. "Don't worry, dear. You haven't missed anything. The herd is still quite a ways from the ranch. The men have to round them up from the lower pastures first, then drive them up to the cattle trail. You and Bert and Stuart will take them the last leg of the trip. Once they get the cattle up on the ridge trail, the summer range is only a few hours away."

I poured myself some orange juice and said, "Then, there'll only be the three of us?" wondering how on earth Bert had been able to manage such a feat.

"Thayne wanted to go along but Dad said he needed him around here this morning," Janet apologized.

"It's not too big a herd," her mother added. "I think the three of you will be able to handle them just fine."

I smiled and reached for a piece of cinnamon toast. I didn't know whether to thank luck, providence, or Bert Tingey, but I was infinitely grateful that I wouldn't have to worry about any of the Bradford men this morning.

"With your fair complexion you'd better wear a hat on the drive," Helen advised, "and gloves, too, to protect your hands."

"I have some black leather riding gloves you can wear," Janet offered.

"What about a hat?" Helen persisted. "Janet, didn't I see a black hat on your closet shelf a while back?"

"Do you really think I'll need a hat?" I asked her. I hated hats.

"It gets mighty hot and dusty in the hills. And the sun is so direct. You don't want to get a bad sunburn with the party coming up tomorrow night. It's too bad you and Janet don't wear the same shoe size, then you could wear her boots."

"I'm sure my loafers will do just fine."

But Helen shook her head. "The 'Mohawks' are mighty thick this time of year—go right through your stockings, that thin blouse, too."

"Mohawks! What on earth are they?"

Janet giggled, "Mosquitoes, Angela. Mother, stop! The next thing we know, you'll have her in a suit of armor!"

I escaped the armor, but Helen Bradford was adamant about the black hat and gloves. I rode away from the ranch feeling like Black Bart. All that was missing was my trusty six-shooter. Stuart managed to suppress his grin when he saw me so that his mouth only twisted in a lopsided smirk, but I knew David and Tadd wouldn't be so kind. As soon as we rode over the first hill away from the ranchhouse, I persuaded Bert to stuff Janet's hat into one of his saddlebags, along with my sack lunch containing the diary.

"Are you sure you don't want to wear it, Miss?" Bert asked. "You're liable to get a good burn before the mornin's through."

"A little sun will do me good," I told him. "Besides, I feel so much better without the hat—like myself again."

"Whatever you say, Miss," he said and we urged our horses into a gallop.

The cattle trail lay about a mile and a half southwest of the ranch-house. The broad, dusty track was beaten into a sage-covered shelf which curved along the perimeter of the hills. I shaded my eyes with my hand and saw how clearly the naked brown line of the shelf was etched into the contours of the land, dividing the gentle pastures below from the rough terrain above.

"Herd's straight ahead!" Stuart yelled, motioning to a cloud of dust which mushroomed above the rounded edge of the next hill.

We galloped along the dust-choked trail until the cloud engulfed us and we were in the midst of some thirty head of bawling, red-backed Herefords. Urging them along with shrill whistles and yee-haws were John Bradford and his three sons.

I stared at the timeless scene of Western Americana before me with a nostalgic thrill and a little shiver of dread. These men and boys were experienced cowhands; a lifetime of hard work and know-how was behind the effortless riding and expert handling I was watching. Whatever possessed Bert to arrange for my part in the drive? And why hadn't I tried to think of some other way to arrange a meeting with Jay?

Looking at the wide grins on Tadd's and David's brown faces, I knew my coming on the cattle drive must be the most hilarious event of the summer.

Janet's father left his place at the front of the herd and rode back to meet us. "They're movin' along real good," he said to Bert, then added with a sideways glance at me, "you shouldn't have any trouble."

That small addition added a fifty-pound weight to my already sinking confidence.

"Hope you enjoy the ride," he said to me, politely touching his hat. "Helen should have given you a hat to wear though."

"Oh, I'll be just fine," I assured him, feeling a guilty twinge about the hat stuffed into Bert's saddlebag.

Thayne lingered behind to give me lengthy, detailed instructions for the drive, not one of which I remembered a moment after he had gone.

Bert barked out orders for Stuart to ride up front on the outer edge of the herd, I was to flank the middle and he would take up the rear. Maybe it was expecting too much on my part, but I had hoped Bert would give me a little friendly advice or conversation along the way. The only time he said anything was to cuss at a poky steer or swear at the mosquitoes and flies. One thing was certain—now was not a good time to discuss John and Judd, or to tell Bert about the diary.

Actually, it was a relief to have something else occupy my mind for a change. Time passed and I was aware solely of the physical, earthy things around me—dust and cow dung, the nostril-twitching pungency of sage and warm animal flesh. The air was alive with the sounds of earth and her creatures—bawling cattle, sharp hooves thudding along the trail, and the constant buzz and hum of insects.

As the drive progressed, we climbed higher and higher into the hills. The sun was bright in a cloudless sky and the air was so bitingly clear I was half afraid of becoming intoxicated by breathing too much of it. Then, up ahead, I saw that the cattle trail suddenly split in half. A broad, left fork ambled in a general southwest direction toward rounded hills and lush, green valleys, while the right fork pursued a narrower, steeper course towards rocky cliffs and canyons.

Bert yelled and whistled for Stuart and me to keep the cattle moving on the left trail. Some were balky and confused, but most of the Herefords seemed to sense which direction to take and agreeably turned left along the assigned course. Naturally, there had to be a rebel.

In front of me, a low-bellied cow broke away from the rest of the herd and charged straight toward the rocky canyons of the Right Fork.

I glanced back at Bert for help, but he waved his arm and shouted, "That one's yers!"

I had no time to think. With a quick jerk of the reins I turned my horse's head and gave her a sharp kick in the sides. We were off through the brush in an instant, the sage crackling under her hooves and whipping against my legs.

Instinctively, I found myself leaning with the horse as she made a sharp turn and deftly cut around the stubborn cow. With bawls of protest all the way, the animal was finally persuaded to rejoin the herd.

Stuart looked over his shoulder and grinned at me. "Nice going, Angie! You can ride with me, anytime!"

"The horse did all the work!" I said with a laugh, but his praise made me glow inside.

"Princess is a great cow pony," he agreed, "but you still handled her real good."

I permitted myself a small sigh of satisfaction and glanced back to the Right Fork. It was rough, overgrown and fascinating in a wild sort of way. Even in the cloudless sunshine of a hot June day, the cliffs and craggy summits held a sinister look.

"You'd do better to keep yer eyes straight ahead and not back there," Bert said gruffly, riding up beside me.

"I was just wondering what was up there."

"Nothing that would interest a young lady like you. That trail branches off into canyons that even a mountain lion could get lost in. It's not the kind of place you'd go for a Sunday picnic."

"Is it Bradford land?"

"Most of it. But nobody goes up there anymore."

"Why not?"

"Cause it's wild country, that's why!" he snorted. "A few years back, Thayne and some of his buddies got a huntin' expedition together. They hadn't been gone twenty-four hours before they were good and lost. Them fellers was mighty cold and hungry by the time we found 'em. After that, Judd laid down the law that nobody was to go up the Right Fork."

Something in Bert's voice made me shiver in spite of the heat. "I wasn't interested in going up there," I assured him hastily. "I just wondered what it was like, that's all."

"Well, now you know," Bert said curtly and rode back to his place at the rear of the herd.

It was nearly one o'clock when we reached the summer range; a long, broad valley with furry, sage-covered hills on one side, a natural barrier of steep, pine-covered slopes on the other, and a man-made barrier of barbed wire stretching across its broad north end. Leading directly to the fenced end of the range was a gravel road. I remembered Bert's and Jay's conversation that night in the bunkhouse and realized the road must have its source on the Tyler ranch some miles away. My eyes followed the gravel road past the summer range until it disappeared among the aspens and pines. The cabin had to be up there somewhere. Perhaps even now, Jay was watching our approach.

We drove the cattle up to the main gate and I was only half aware of what we were doing. In a few minutes' time I would be seeing Jay again and suddenly, I was scared silly! I licked my dry lips and wiped the sweat off my forehead with my hand. I knew I must look wretched—windblown hair, sunburned face, dusty clothes. Ugh! And there wasn't a thing I could do about it.

"How about you eatin' yer lunch and watchin' things here for a while?" Bert said to Stuart once all the cattle were inside the fence. "I thought mebbe Miss Angela might like to see the view from the ridge before we start back."

"That's fine with me. I could stand a rest," Stuart said and headed his horse for the nearest shade.

"Ready, Miss?" Bert asked me.

I gave him the fatal nod and we turned our horses toward the ridge where dark fingers of pine and spruce clasped the hillside.

It was only a matter of minutes now. I looked up at the piercing blue sky and drew a shaky breath. What would I say to Jay when I gave him his father's diary? For that matter, what would he say? And after reading it, what would he do? If it answered the question of his father's disappearance and the affair was settled, would he leave the ranch? Of course he would. That was all he came back for in the first place. But if the diary were inconclusive, what then? Jay would return to the ranch and there might be another accident. If anything happened to him . . .!

"You feelin' all right, Miss?" Bert inquired, giving me a sideways glance.

"I'm all right."

"You sure there's nothin' on yer mind?"

"Well, there is something I should tell you."

Far below us, I heard what sounded like a horn. Impossible. Who would be coming up here? Then I heard it again, a long, loud blast. Bert and I turned in the saddle and looked behind us. On the dirt road below, the Bradford's red-panelled truck was racing toward the summer range, a cloud of dust boiling up behind it.

Bert swore viciously then spat on the ground. "It's Thayne! I mighta knowed!"

I glanced at him in a panic. "Bert, what are we going to do now? I've got to see Jay! I've got his father's diary!"

The old cowhand's sunburned cheeks blanched considerably and he stared at me with wide, unblinking eyes. "You've got what?" he croaked.

"Jason's diary! Yesterday afternoon, while Janet and I were cleaning the bunkhouse, I found it wedged between the bottom drawer and the framework of the pine desk."

"Does Janet know about this, too?" he asked quickly.

"No! No, of course she doesn't. She was cleaning the bathroom when I found it. I managed to hide the diary inside some magazines and get it back to the house without her knowing. Then I locked it in one of my suitcases until this morning."

"Have you read it?" he demanded.

I stared at him for a moment, surprised at the question and his demanding tone. "Well, not really. That is, I only read enough to realize what it was."

A dazed expression came into the old man's eyes, and his mouth split into a grin. "Lordy, Miss, I knowed you was a smart one, but I never expected this."

I glanced away from him, the expression in his eyes making me feel strangely uncomfortable, and saw that the truck had nearly reached the fenced end of the range. "Bert, Thayne's almost there! What are we going to do?"

"There's nothin' fer you to do but ride back to the ranch with him. I

147

hadn't planned on things workin' out this way, but it's too late fer anythin' else now. You'd better give me the diary and I'll take it up to Jay."

"Bert, I don't know—isn't there anything—?"

"Don't argue with me, girl! Thayne's come up here for you and he's too stubborn to leave without takin' what he came for. Now give me the diary!"

I glanced hastily at the truck, then at Bert's gruff features. Confusion, disappointment, and something else I couldn't quite put a name to, swept over me.

"Come on!" he urged. "You don't want Thayne to find out about this, do you?"

"You—you have it already," I said. "It's in my sack lunch in your saddlebag."

The old hand gaped at me then reached over and unbuckled his saddlebag. The first thing he found was Janet's hat which he tossed carelessly at me, not even bothering to look where he threw it. The black hat was caught in a little rush of wind and swept over my head. I watched it go by, then turned my head to see a look of relief and satisfaction spread over Bert's face as his fingers felt the book.

"It's here," he breathed.

"Bert—"

"You'd better git on back, Miss."

"What shall I tell Thayne? He'll want to know why you're not coming back with us."

"Doesn't matter. You'll think of somethin'. It doesn't matter." He gave his horse a sharp swat on the rump and galloped up the ridge trail without a backward glance.

I watched his retreating figure on horseback until it disappeared into the pines. Suddenly, the hillside was a green blur. I wiped my eyes angrily on the side of my sleeve and yanked on Princess' reins. There was no reason for stupid tears! No reason! Bert had the diary and he would give it to Jay. Mission accomplished. Why did I feel so frightened? That's what the other feeling was; something more than fatigue and disappointment.

I found Janet's hat caught in some brush and leaned over the side of my horse to snatch it up, then urged Princess on down the trail. By the time I got back to the summer range, Stuart was leading his horse up the ramp into the truck.

Thayne gave me a friendly wave as I approached. "After bein' in the saddle all mornin', I thought you might appreciate ridin' back in the truck," he said and came forward to help me dismount.

"Thanks. I am a little tired." When my feet hit the ground, the feeling in my legs was so dead and wooden, I could have sworn they belonged to someone else. For once, I was glad of Thayne's supporting arm.

He helped me to the truck and said with genuine concern, "You better take it easy the rest of the day. I'd sure hate to see you feelin' punk for the party tomorrow night."

"I'll be all right."

Thayne tilted my chin up with a gloved hand and looked into my face. "You don't look all right, honey. You got a lot of sun today. Are you sure you feel O.K.?"

I nodded and looked away from his probing blue eyes. "I'm all right. I'm just tired, that's all."

Thayne helped me into the truck and slammed the door. "By the way, where did Bert take off to?"

"I—I'm not sure. He said he'd be back to the ranch later."

Thayne's brown forehead creased into a frown. "He sure is a funny old coot sometimes. I wonder what he's up to?"

A chill suddenly knifed up my back, but I gave Thayne a noncommital shrug and managed a smile.

"You just sit tight, honey," he instructed. "I'll get your horse loaded in the back, then we'll head for home."

I swallowed hard and focused my eyes on the pine-covered ridge where Bert would be making his way toward Jay. Fear tightened my chest and twisted my stomach, but my mind kept repeating the words: Everything will be all right. Bert is taking the diary to Jay. Everything will be all right. Jay trusts Bert. I trusted him, too. After all, I had given him the diary.

Suddenly, the air inside the truck was stifling, too stifling to breathe. I felt as if I were being strangled by doubts and fears I could do absolutely nothing about. What if I had trusted the wrong person? If I had, then I was sending Jason's murderer to kill his son, and given him the only evidence in the world that might prove his guilt.

The ride back to the ranch was endless. Both Stuart and Thayne kept voicing their concern for me and somehow the outer shell kept insisting I was fine when inside I felt as if I were being torn apart.

Bert could have fired those warning shots at Jay just as easily as Judd or John. The night the calf was born, Bert had suggested I take the food out to Jay with the excuse that he was too tired. He could have followed a short while later, let go the hook and run away, only to return acting innocent and concerned. Thayne might never have come out to the bunkhouse that evening. Bert could have lied about that, making Thayne the scapegoat for his own actions.

Fragments of sentences from Bert's lips kept coming back to me, seen now in a different light. " . . . I hadn't planned on things workin' out this way, but it's too late for anythin' else now . . ." ". . Have you read it?" "Don't argue! Give me the diary!" "Give me the diary!"

And I had given it to him. But what if Thayne hadn't come for me? What if I had taken the diary to Jay as planned? Did Bert have a convenient accident planned for me as well as Jay? If he had, no one would be left to cast any blame on him. No one would suspect Bert . . .

As Thayne turned the truck onto the shady, tree-lined drive leading to the ranchhouse, Stuart called out, "Hey, that's Uncle Al's car!"

"It sure is!" Thayne said and smiled at me. "I know they'll all be real anxious to meet you—especially Larry. I'm going to have to keep an eye on him the whole time they're here."

His words floated over my head and I allowed him to take my arm and lead me to the house. We walked inside the back door and I was vaguely aware of a crowd of people sitting around the table, eating, laughing, clanking dishes. The room was warm with laughter, and the tangy smell of fresh apricots. Thayne steered me toward the table and Janet wriggled out of her place to start the introductions. Somehow, the outer shell that made automatic replies to Thayne and Stuart on the ride back, managed to smile and nod in turn as Janet attached names to the various personalities seated around the table.

Aunt Kate was a younger, plumper version of Helen Bradford with honey-brown hair and a healthy chuckle. Al Thompson was long and thin with stringy dark hair and friendly eyes. The Thompson's sons were all straight and slim like their father, but their only daughter, Marsha, already showed a tendency toward resembling her mother in shape and size. "Square" is the only word that could accurately describe her proportions.

Helen came to the table, plates of hot apricot cobbler in each hand, and when she looked at me her eyes widened.

"My goodness, dear! You're sunburned! Didn't you wear Janet's hat?"

Thayne saved me from answering by saying in a low voice, "I think Angela should take it easy for the rest of the day. She's had too much sun."

I asked Helen for a glass of water and mechanically followed her to the sink. Why was Janet staring at me that way? John was staring, too. And Judd. I shuddered and drank the water in hurried gulps.

"Aunt Helen?" Marsha piped from the table. "I thought you told Mother last week that your nephew was visiting at the ranch, too."

"Oh, you mean Jay? He was here, but he's off painting somewhere in the hills right now."

I set the glass down on the counter, seeing Bert's figure on horseback riding up the ridge. I shut my eyes.

"Oh, well. We just wondered why we hadn't seen him around," Marsha said nonchalantly.

"You mean, *you* were wonderin' why you hadn't seen Jay around!" one of her brothers corrected with a sneer. "Old Marsha has a nose like a bloodhound for sniffin' out men!"

"Jay must have heard you were comin' and headed for the hills to hide!" another boy quipped and they all laughed.

"Will Jay be back soon?" Marsha asked, happily ignoring her brothers.

"I don't know, dear," Helen said kindly.

The outer shell quietly and completely dissolved.

"Angela, what's wrong?"

"She looks ill."

"I told you—too much sun."

"Come along upstairs, dear. You'll feel much better after you've had a rest."

I looked about helplessly but all the faces were a blur. "I'm sorry. Please forgive me. I'm sorry."

"You'll be all right, dear. Everything will be all right once you've had a rest."

"Do you think we should call the doctor?"

"Give her to me. I'll carry her upstairs."

I shook my head and said. "No. No, please. I can walk." I felt Helen's arm about my waist, steering me out of the warm room, toward the stairs. I turned my head, slowly, painfully, to look into her kindly brown eyes. "He can't come back," I told her with tears streaming down my face. "He can't come back now, and it's all my fault!"

When I awoke my eyes were dry and burning, and my skin felt hot and tight. But my mind was cool, clear and deliberate. The shadows on the walls told me I must have slept for several hours and the clock on Janet's dresser confirmed this. Five-thirty. The time couldn't be better. The boys would be off somewhere with their cousins and most likely John or Judd, perhaps both, were in the barn doing the milking. Janet and her mother would be down in the kitchen making preparations for dinner and having a good visit with Kate Thompson and Marsha. Yes, the time was right.

I sat up in bed and took off my robe, tossing it carelessly across the end of the bed. Then I went to the closet and got a sleeveless summer dress and my sandals. Strange, I didn't feel the least bit afraid now. I applied fresh lipstick, brushed my mussed hair and left the room.

I couldn't risk going down the stairs and meeting one of the family so I walked to the end of the hall where large windows opened to the roof and a flight of white-washed stairs. I hurried down the stairs and across the back lawn without seeing anyone. I went straight to the bunkhouse, knowing Bert would be there. Opening the door, I saw him sprawled on the lumpy green sofa. A large black fly was buzzing about his head, but the insect's drone was completely obliterated by the old man's snores.

I shut the door behind me with a purposeful bang and Bert awoke with a surprised snort. His squinty eyes blinked open and when he saw me standing over him in the small room, he immediately struggled to a sitting position and fumbled with the buttons of his shirt.

"I'd like to talk to you, Bert."

"Why, uh, sure, Miss. Sit down."

"No thank you. I want to know why Jay didn't come back with you." The steady coolness of my voice surprised me as much as it did Bert.

"Well, now, he'll be back, Miss. But he couldn't come right away. There were things—well, he just couldn't, that's all. But, he'll be back. Don't you worry."

I looked calmly into his flustered pink face and said, "I don't believe you. I don't believe he's ever coming back—now!"

Bert's squinty hazel eyes opened wider. "Now, Miss! Don't get all upset! 'Course he's comin' back!"

"He's not!" I cried. "How can he, when you—when he's—!" I swallowed a sob and fought for control. "You planned everything, didn't you? And if Thayne hadn't come for me, I wouldn't have come back to the ranch today, either. I even gave you the diary, so now you've got all the evidence. There's not a thing I can do. But please, won't you tell me why—why in the name of heaven did you do it?" My voice broke and I collapsed on the geeen sofa, no longer able to keep back the tears.

I heard Bert say, "Lord, Miss . . ." in a tone I had never heard him use before, and I looked up to see him wipe an unbelieving hand over his face. "I kin see now what you're thinkin', but it just ain't so. I didn't kill him! I never done anything. You've got to believe that!"

"I don't know who or what to believe, anymore. How can I know if you're telling the truth? How can I know?"

The old man rubbed his grizzled chin and shook his head. "There's not a thing I kin say to prove it to you, Miss. I could tell you that I love Jay more'n I do my own cussed hide, but it'd still be up to yer woman's heart to decide if I was speakin' truth or a lie. It's jest up to you, Miss."

We faced one another and through my tears I looked into the old man's eyes for a long moment. I saw hurt, bewilderment and honesty in their depths, but no malice. No malice at all.

"Forgive me, Bert," I whispered and reached out to clutch one of his tough, calloused hands. "Please, forgive me."

A smile turned the corners of his mouth and he gave my hand a squeeze.

The horrible dread that had been crushing my heart ever since the cattle drive suddenly released its hold and melted away.

"You really do love him," I said softly, and tears filled my eyes.

Bert took his handkerchief from his pocket and put it into my hand. "Not near as much as you do, Miss," he said with a tender smile. "Not near as much as you do."

I wiped my eyes, blew my nose and breathed a long, shuddering sigh. "I didn't want to believe it was you, but you seemed so distant and angry today on the cattle drive—especially when I told you about the diary. I was so hot and tired and disappointed, I guess my imagination ran away with me."

Bert grinned. "I guess I was a mite cantankerous at that. But you see, I had a few things on my mind, too. All the way up I was arguin' with myself as to whether lettin' you come along on the drive was the right thing to do or not. I jest couldn't believe what you told me yesterday—about someone here—well, you know what I mean. I've known Judd and John and this family for a good many years and it really stuck in my craw to have you come along and say that one of them might be responsible for Jason's death. Then, when you told me about findin' Jason's diary, I was so kerflummoxed I didn't know what to do!"

"How did Jay take it—when you told him about the diary and everything?" I asked.

Bert looked me straight in the face. "That was the strangest thing of all, Miss. Here I was dreadin' havin' to tell him and sure as hell that you were wrong, and Jay—well, he jest looked at me with that sad quiet look of his and said: 'I was right then. I've had the feeling all week that something was wrong at the ranch; that she was in danger.'

"Can you beat that, Miss? Here I was shakin' in my boots over what I had to tell him an' he knew all the time!" Bert smiled at me and his hazel eyes were suspiciously bright. "Oh, Miss! I wish you coulda been there when I handed him that diary. I felt like I'd brought his dad back to him. I truly did."

I blew my nose furiously, determined not to get misty-eyed again. "Do you have any idea when he'll be back?"

"Not exactly, but it shouldn't be too much longer. When I walked in the cabin he had his gear packed and was all set to come back to the ranch right then. I've never seen such a caged lion as that boy! But now that he's got his father's diary, well, he wanted to take time to read it real careful, and then be alone while he was decidin' what to do. It's the Indian in him, Miss. If I know Jay, he's probably roamin' those forests up there right now, gettin' all the facts straight in his mind and preparin' himself for what's to come."

I sat quietly for a moment, wondering just what was to come, then gave Bert his handkerchief. "I'd better get back to the house. Janet might be looking for me."

I got to my feet and Bert heaved his tired body off the couch. "Oh,

153

Miss, before you go, there's something I was supposed to give you." He walked stiff-legged across the room and reached into a saddlebag that was slung across the high-backed chair. He hobbled back to me with a pleased grin on his face and put something into my hands. "Jay asked me to give this to you along with his thanks."

Resting in my palm was a jade pendant on a silver chain. I turned the green stone over to see a man and a woman's profiles carved in intricate detail. "This belonged to Wenona," I said softly.

"That's right, Miss. Jason gave it to her before they were married, so Jay told me."

I stared down at the pendant, caressing the cool jade with my fingertips. "Jay can't have many things that belonged to his mother. Are you sure he wants me to have it?"

"Sure I'm sure!" Bert said with twinkling eyes. "He never woulda give it to me if he didn't. You better scoot now."

"Oh, yes. I suppose I'd better." I moved to the door in a daze, gently closing my fist around the necklace and wondering if Bert could hear the hard, happy thumps of my heart.

He opened the door for me, then said with a wry grin, "By the way, Miss, I wonder if you could settle jest one little thing for me?"

"What's that?"

"If I had been the one after Jay, jest what was you plannin' to do about it?"

I gave him a blank look and shook my head. "You know, I never thought about that."

Chapter 18

"And lightly dance
A triple-timed romance
In coupled figures and forget mischance."
Thomas Hardy

After I had assured Janet for the tenth time that I really didn't mind sleeping on a sofa in the living room, she bade me goodnight and ran up the stairs two at a time to her own room. I turned out the lamp, making a mental note that I would have to rise early if I didn't want the Bradford boys and their cousins traipsing through my boudoir, as it were. Then I snuggled down into the blankets with Helen Bradford's special (very smelly) concoction of a wonder cure for burns smeared over my face and neck, and a deep, satisfying peace in my heart. The situation at the ranchhouse was still the same; one of the Bradfords knew what had happened to Jay's father and was not afraid to take drastic steps to prevent anyone else from knowing. But now, Jay had this knowledge plus the diary. My own safety was practically guaranteed by the arrival of the Thompsons. With so many people in the house and a party planned for the following night, I felt sure there would be no further attempts made to frighten me into leaving the ranch. My sleep was calm, dreamless, and undisturbed.

As soon as breakfast was over the next morning, preparations for the barbeque dinner and dance began. Judd and Bert offered to do the always necessary chore of milking so the boys would be available for other tasks. Stuart and Randy were assigned the jobs of mowing and raking the back lawn and the younger boys had the dubious honor of stringing lanterns from the pine trees. Janet, Marsha and I tackled the huge living room with Thayne and Larry on hand to roll up the rugs and move some of the heavier pieces of furniture.

The nose-twitching aromas of boiled eggs, potatoes, and warm yeast were heavy on the morning air. Kate Thompson was busy tripling her recipe for potato salad and Helen was thumping out the dough for soft rolls.

155

After a light lunch, everyone dived into work once again. Now the kitchen was filled with the spicy smell of baked beans and barbeque sauce. Janet's father and Al Thompson had borrowed several dozen folding chairs and some long banquet tables from the town hall, and the boys were busy unloading them from the truck and setting them up on the back lawn. Janet and I were putting finishing touches on the living room and dining room— wild roses along the mantle, lilacs and roses as a centerpiece on the dining room table, and candles to light both rooms after dusk.

Marsha Thompson's contributions to the afternoon's work were amusing if not productive. One minute she was taking what she called "little snitches" of the food being prepared in the kitchen, the next she was commenting on our flower arrangements in the living room. Another time, I looked out one of the windows to see her sashaying between Stuart and Randy as they set up chairs. As the afternoon wore on, I couldn't help noticing that Stuart was the prime recipient for most of her beaming smiles and incessant chatter, albeit reluctantly. I wasn't surprised when he came slinking into the dining room, casting several anxious glances behind him.

"Here's a letter for you, Angela. Dad brought it back from town with the rest of the mail. I just haven't had a chance to get it to you yet," he added with a scowl and backwards glance.

I saw Mother's familiar handwriting on the envelope and eagerly tore open the gummed seal.

"Do you need any help with this stuff?" Stuart asked Janet, the 'stuff' being a lovely silver candelabra and a box of crystal punch cups.

Janet grinned at her brother. "What makes you think you can escape Marsha in here?"

"Anything's worth a try!" he said desperately. "Come on, Sis!"

"Oh, all right. You can wipe some of these cups."

I smiled at the two of them and sat down on a dining room chair to read my letter. Everything back home was just the same; business at Mother's gift shop was brisk and the summer was unbearably hot. Aunt Mildred was going to Europe in July, and if I had not been so hasty and reckless in my decision to come out West, I could have gone with her.

"Think of it, Angela dear! Mildred will be touring all over England and you know how much I've always wanted you to visit my home. Perhaps it's not too late. If you flew home now, there might still be time to make the necessary arrangements. Surely, your little ranch couldn't hold as much fascination as a trip to Europe. At least, give it some thought, dear. You'll probably never get a chance like this again. If you decide you want to go, please phone me and I'll make arrangements for you to fly home as soon as possible."

156

I sat for a long moment, pondering this new development. If I wanted one, here was a perfect excuse to leave the ranch. No one would connect my going as having anything to do with Jay. Perhaps, if I were to put six or seven thousand miles between us, I might even be able to forget. . . .

"Oh, Stuart!" a shrill voice called out.

The next second, Marsha came bouncing into the room, pink cheeks aglow and her round face wreathed in its perpetual smile.

The youth groaned and muttered, "Oh, no! 'Jane Oink' has found me again!"

"Don't be crude!" Janet admonished in a whisper as the younger girl joined us.

"Everything looks so beautiful!" Marsha exclaimed. "I just know this is going to be a super party. Don't you think so, Stuart?"

"Yeah, sure," came the grumbled reply.

The rest of the afternoon breezed by and suddenly it was time to wash and dress for the party. With fifteen people and only two bathrooms, every precious minute was rationed out. I came back to Janet's room after my brief allotment and found Marsha already dressed and Janet with towel in hand, ready for a quick shower.

"I hope you left some hot water for me."

"There ought to be a drop or two if you hurry," I said as she dashed down the hall.

"Do you think I look all right?" Marsha asked me, looking at her plump reflection in the mirror with a worried frown. "Aunt Helen told us to bring something Western for the party, and this was all I could think of."

'This' was a bright orange and white gingham dress with puffed sleeves and yards of material in the gathered skirt. The color and style of the dress did little to disguise the girl's plumpness. Actually, it added a few extra pounds to Marsha's more than ample figure. With her round arms and neck protruding out of the bright orange material, she reminded me of Peter Pumpkin Eater's wife newly-stuffed in the pumpkin shell. There are times, however, when tact must excuse a "little white lie." Looking into the soft, eager shine of her eyes, all I could say was, "You'll look as Western as anyone. I have an orange ribbon for your hair if you'd care to borrow it."

"Oh, I'd love to!" she responded eagerly. "Thanks a lot, Angela!"

While Marsha primped and fussed with the ribbon, I put on the clothes I had chosen for the party. Nora's brown riding skirt had been cleaned and pressed and I had found a blouse of pale green muslin to go with it. I buttoned the long, full sleeves in snugly at the wrist, then stepped into the riding skirt. Marsha was quick to help me fasten the hooks and shiny brown buttons.

"What I wouldn't give for a tiny waist like yours!" she sighed. "The skirt fits just perfect—like it was made for you!"

I smiled at her, feeling a strange, excited racing of my heart. I put on the soft, brown moccasins Jay had given me, then on impulse, tossed away the brightly-colored scarf I had planned to wear and reached into my jewelry box for Wenona's necklace. I fastened the slim, silver chain about my neck, took a comb and began braiding my hair.

Marsha sat down on the bed and for the first time today, her chattering ceased as she watched me. When I had finished, two thick plaits hung down past my shoulders. I put down the comb and stepped back to view the entire effect of my costume. Yesterday's sunburn had darkened my usually pale skin to a healthy bronze, and a touch of mascara and eye shadow made my eyes appear even larger.

Janet came into the room and did a beautiful double-take when she saw me. "Angela?" she said doubtfully.

I smiled at her. "I think so."

"What made you do your hair that way?"

"Don't you like it?"

"Oh, it's not that. You just look so—so different."

"I feel different. Not quite like myself, and yet I like it. I suppose it's the clothes."

"I think you look wonderful!" Marsha said with a wistful glance.

I thanked her then turned to Janet. "Come on! Now it's your turn!"

It had taken a lot of coaxing to persuade Janet to wear one of her grandmother's frillier dresses and she grumbled the entire time she slipped on layers of stiff crinolines. I lifted the dress over her head and Marsha helped fasten the long line of cloth-covered buttons down the back. The dress was of pale yellow voile with a tightly fitted bodice and short, capped sleeves. Janet took one look at the low bodice and groaned, "Good grief! I won't be able to bend over all night long!"

"Turn around and stand still!" I ordered.

Finally, after she had brushed her hair into a soft mass of dark curls, I handed her an old-fashioned cameo brooch fastened to a black velvet ribbon. "Your mother brought this up for you a little while ago," I said.

Janet tied the ribbon about her slender throat and stood quite still, looking at her reflection in the mirror. Then she whirled about with a soft swish of her ruffled skirts and her pert red mouth turned up in a delighted smile. "I do like it," she admitted. I stood beside her and she gave me an impish grin. "Anyone who didn't know us would swear I was the Eastern guest and say you were the born Westerner!"

The sun was beginning to relinquish its high, fiery post in the sky and the barest hint of an evening breeze was blowing down from the hills when

Janet and I went outside, leaving Marsha in the kitchen happily indulging in a few more of her "snitches." The afternoon had lost its sultriness and was mellowing into the sunset hour of brilliant sky and quiet land. Far away sounds seemed strangely near—the long, mournful whistle of a train passing by, the cry of a hawk, the contented lowing of cattle. The air was a tantalizing mixture of growing things, warm earth, and lusty, barbequed beef.

Helen and her sister were arranging the food on a long table as we walked across the back lawn. They were quick to voice their delight in our costumes for the evening.

"John! Judd! Leave that beef for thirty seconds and come look at something a lot prettier!" Helen ordered.

The two men left the smoky barbeque pit and walked toward us with obliging grins. I stood quietly aside while father and grandfather commented on Janet's appearance.

"You're the image of your grandmother," Judd said with tenderness in his eyes. "You've got a lovely young woman for a daughter," he told his son gruffly, as if John had never been aware of the fact.

"I know it," John answered proudly. "Every young feller in Dusk is going to be begging you for a dance," he told Janet. "Do you think you could save one for your old Dad?"

Janet gave her father a quick little hug and Helen put in with well-intentioned forcefulness, "And doesn't Angela look wonderful?"

Judd's eyes shifted in my direction and a sudden look of pain and anger flashed in their frosty blue depths. His entire body went rigid. The anguish in his face made me tremble and I knew of a surety that he was seeing someone else, not me.

John tried to make up for his father's silence by saying rather awkwardly, "I hardly recognized you in that outfit. I don't know why, but you remind me of someone—"

David and Tadd came running up to us. "Hey, the Willards are here!" David announced. "And old man Cooper's truck is comin' up the road!" Tadd finished breathlessly.

"Thanks, boys," John said. "You tell them where to park and we'll do the rest."

"Hey, Angela! You look just like an Indian!" Tadd cried out before running off with his brother.

Judd turned and walked heavily away.

Ranchers and townspeople from Dusk arrived in a steady stream after that and I had little time to worry about Judd's reaction to my clothes. In the midst of arrivals and introductions, Thayne and his cousin Larry sauntered over to say hello. Thayne gave Janet an appreciative whistle and said, "It's a good thing curtsies are out of style or you'd really be givin' all of us a show."

Janet gave her brother an appropriate jab in the ribs and said, "Be sure to save us a place by you at one of the tables."

Thayne gave me a swift, appraising glance that ended in a frown. He was looking especially handsome this evening in a bright blue Western shirt that must have been color-coordinated to match his eyes, a brown leather vest and tight Levis belted around his narrow hips.

Larry Thompson touched his brown Stetson and gave me a shy smile. "You sure look pretty tonight, Angela."

Thayne added with a sneer, "Yeah, if you don't mind lookin' like a squaw," and walked away.

Janet stared after her brother and I said hastily, "I think I'll go see if your mother needs any help serving the food."

By seven-thirty, most of the guests had arrived and were happily making their way along the food laden table. I watched plate after plate go by heaped with potato salad, hot baked beans, soft rolls, and a fat slice of roast beef with sizzling barbeque sauce slopping over its edges, and felt my own stomach gnaw with hunger.

"I think we've met everyone," Janet said finally. "Shall we go get something to eat before it's all gone?"

"I thought you'd never ask!"

As we turned away, I saw a young man hurrying across the lawn behind us. He was tall, with dark hair and eyes, and for a moment my heart took a painful leap. I snatched a quick second look over my shoulder and realized it wasn't Jay after all. Disappointment slowed my heartbeat to a dull thud. The young man was making straight for Janet, who as yet, had not noticed his approach. The next moment he had both hands on her waist and was saying, "Hello, little squirrel! Mind if I crash your party?"

Janet swung around and when she saw who was holding her, her face went white to the lips with a hot spot of color burning in each cheek.

"Reed! When did you—how did you—everyone told me—that is, I thought—"

The young man's skin darkened under his ruddy tan. "We can go into all the whens, hows, and whys later. Do you think you could find something to eat for a no-good, hungry cowpoke who's missed you a hell of a lot?"

"Oh, Reed!"

I suddenly became conscious of my awkward position in their little tableau and made a move to step away unnoticed.

But Janet roused herself with a happy sigh. "Angela, you haven't met Reed." She lifted glowing brown eyes to his face and said, "This is Reed Tyler, one of Thayne's very best friends. Reed, I'd like you to meet Angela Stewart."

I smiled at her introduction and shook hands with him. "Janet and I were just going to get something to eat. Won't you join us?"

"You'd have a mighty hard time gettin' rid of me," Reed said with an attractive grin and eyes that were only for Janet.

The rest of the evening was uncomfortably long. I smiled, laughed, and talked with the rest of the happy crowd, and yet, inside me was a hollow ache of loneliness. Janet and Reed were in a world of their own that quite naturally could not include me, and Thayne was doing a marvelous job of keeping four or five girls purring and contented. Even Marsha had found someone other than her unwilling cousins on whom to foist her attentions. I saw her sitting next to a thin, gangly fellow with a wide, crooked grin and a brown thatch of hair sticking out from beneath his battered straw hat. The uncommon length of his arms and legs had earned him the nickname, "Stretch," but I heard Marsha calling him Delbert in honey-sweet tones.

Evening stars were making their pale appearance in a blue velvet sky when John and Helen began herding their guests back to the house for the dancing. I assisted Kate Thompson in clearing away the dishes and any leftover food. I dumped a stack of paper plates into a trash can and saw Thayne along with three of his friends, making their way toward the barn, bottles in hand. Behind me, I heard low laughter and caught a glimpse of Janet and Reed disappearing into the darkness of the pines. With a sigh, I picked up a bowl that still held a few spoonfuls of potato salad and walked back to the house alone.

Janet's plans for square dancing had been cancelled at the last minute as the caller had come down with a sore throat, but no one seemed to mind. In fact, I'm sure the change in plans was a relief to all those whose stomachs were overloaded with barbequed beef and baked beans.

The dance band was actually a five-piece ensemble consisting of drums, bass fiddle, guitar, piano and accordian. Floyd Thacker played most of the lead melodies on his accordian and his pencil-thin frame looked barely sturdy enough to wield the instrument. Floyd's wife accompanied the group on the piano, pounding out each tune with sturdy fingers and keeping strict time with one foot. Mabel Thacker was a robust example of a rancher's wife with her no-nonsense coronet of brown braids wound about her head, her ample bosom stuffed into a bright calico dress, and her strong freckled arms moving in vigorous rhythm to the music. The men playing the drums and guitar were easily identified as ranchers by their sunburned faces and white foreheads. Marsha's conquest of the evening, whose full name I learned was Delbert Eborn, played the bass fiddle. Marsha had arranged herself on a chair nearby and every time the youth glanced away from his fiddle into her beaming pink face, his ears turned a violent crimson.

What the little ensemble lacked in musicianship they made up for twice over in enthusiasm. Their repertoire was limited to old-fashioned waltzes and fox trots, but anything more modern would have been completely out of place. The familiar, sentimental tunes were in complete harmony with the rustic charm of the old ranchhouse. The glow of candlelight and the warm smiles of simple, honest people made an indelible impression upon my mind.

Helen saw to it that most of the ranchers or their sons asked me to dance, but after the initial questions, "Are you having a nice summer?" and, "How do you like Wyoming?" there was nothing much to say. The evening wore on, and I finally managed to slip away from Helen's kindly but watchful eyes. I made my way around the edge of the crowd and found a vacant chair hidden away in a shadowy corner near the fireplace. To my right, three matronly ladies from Dusk were resting their substantial figures on a sofa, taking note of the various couples in the room and commenting on the state of the world as they saw it.

"Isn't that Barbara Jennings dancing with Bill Rupert?" asked a lady dressed in calico.

"None other!" came the emphatic reply delivered from the woman on her right, dressed in gingham.

"He's ten years her senior if he's a day!" was the crisp comment from the lady to the left, dressed in startling polka-dots.

"I think they're a sweet couple," sighed the calico lady.

"That may be true, but what about twenty years from now? He'll have one foot in the grave and she'll still be in the prime of life," the gingham lady said gloomily. "and the Rupert men were always short-lived anyhow."

"Didn't I see Reed Tyler here tonight?"

"As ever was. But all he could see was little Janet Bradford," the calico lady responded with a smile.

The polka-dot lady sniffed and stuck out her chin with a superior air. "Well, all I can say is, it's about time he came home. A fine lot of good it did him to go gallivantin' to the coast!"

"It'll be wedding bells for them two, I say," predicted the gingham.

"Most likely, but they'll probably have to wait until the hayin' season's over."

"I'll bet Helen wishes that rascal Thayne could find a match and get himself settled down," the calico lady said, to which the gingham lady replied in a confidential tone, "Rumor has it that Thayne may have met his match at last."

Both her companions leaned forward to catch every word and so did I.

"According to Emma Scott who overheard Jack Miller and Dave Peterson talking last Sunday after church, Thayne is 'clean gone' over Janet's friend, that Stewart girl."

"That may be true, but I'm not so sure she's 'clean gone' on him," the polka-dot lady said archly.

"Why not?"

"How do you know?"

"Well, for one thing, if that Stewart girl had taken a shine to Thayne, you can be sure he'd be in here dancing with her now instead of out behind the barn nursing his wounded pride in a bottle of beer."

Her companions agreed with clucks of the tongue and heart-felt sighs, and I found myself grinning broadly, thinking there was probably very little that escaped the eyes of the polka-dot, gingham and calico ladies—except perhaps the fact that I was sitting nearby listening to their every word with a sense of guilty enjoyment.

"I haven't seen Jay here, tonight," commented the gingham, and my heart skipped a beat.

"Helen told me he was away painting or something."

"He's such a handsome boy," said the calico lady with another sigh. "It's a shame things are—well,—the way they are." Polka-dot and gingham both nodded in complete understanding.

"He's been asking a lot of questions about his father. Did you know?"

"I saw him coming out of the sheriff's office last week—no, I guess it was about ten days ago," the polka-dot lady said. "But what can the poor lad expect to find after twenty-six years?"

"Shhh! Here comes Judd!" warned the gingham and all three women devoted instant and complete attention to the dancing once more.

I shrank back in my chair, wishing I could melt into the shadowy corner as Judd sauntered through the crowd to stand in front of the fireplace, only a few feet away. He gave a courteous nod to the three women seated on the couch, but if he saw me he gave no sign.

The music ended followed by a fairly large migration of guests moving into the dining room to visit the punch bowl. During the lull, the front door opened and Thayne came swaggering in, a trio of his faithful companions close behind.

"Where ish she? Have any of you guys seen a big-eyed squaw around here? Where is she?"

I winced and heard disapproving clucks from gingham, calico, and polka-dot alike, but no one else seemed to be paying him much attention. I began to think that seeing Thayne in an intoxicated state wasn't an uncommon occurance to those who knew him.

Thankfully, the music began again and Floyd Thacker's whining voice called out, "This is the last waltz, folks, so find yer favorite gal and enjoy it!"

The melody was old, familiar and bittersweet. I watched couples glide gracefully past and felt the ache of loneliness begin again. Then, to one side,

I heard a gasp and the words: "Jason—my God!" uttered in a hoarse whisper. I swung around on my chair and realized it was Judd who had spoken them. He was leaning heavily against the mantlepiece for support, his face a chalky white—and his eyes! I shuddered and followed their catastrophic gaze past the crowd of dancers to the dining room. At first, I could see nothing there that would cause the look of dazed horror on Judd's face, only the laughing confusion of guests around the punch bowl. Then, near the drapes, touched by the softness of candlelight, I saw a tall figure dressed in buckskin. A sharp gasp tightened my own throat. I think I spoke his name. I know one hand clutched Wenona' jade necklace. After that I didn't think at all. I got to my feet and moved forward with thick, heavy steps, as if I were wading through water. The next moment I was seized roughly by the arm.

"I been lookin' all over for yuh, honey," Thayne said with a slow, liquored smile. "What were ya doin' hidin' way over there in a corner?"

"I wasn't hiding," I told him and glanced quickly toward the dining room. The tall figure had gone.

"I been tellin' my fren's here all about you," Thayne said, nuzzling my cheek with his mustache. "Yessir, I tol' them I never thought I'd see the day when I'd wanna lay my hands on no squaw, but then, I never met one as sweet smellin' and soft as you."

I flinched at his touch and turned to go, but Thayne laughed and tightened his hold on my arm. "Come on now, honey, I know you been mopin' aroun' all night 'cause I ain't been payin' you no mind." His free hand played with one of my braids then rested on my shoulder. "But I jes' thought I'd give you a taste of your own med—your own medicine and see how you liked it."

"I like it fine so let me go!"

"Whee, she's a fiery little devil when she get's riled up," one of his friends said and broke into a silly drunken giggle.

"Come on, Thayne! Let's see you tame yer squaw—if you can!" taunted another.

"I'll tame her," Thayne boasted in a tone which terrified me. "You jest watch an' maybe you'll learn somethin.' "

One of his hands was on my neck, pulling my head toward his, and the other bit into my arm more savagely than ever. I twisted my head away from his and saw the wide eyes and open-mouthed shock of gingham, calico and polka-dot ladies alike. This would certainly make for a juicy tidbit of gossip to spread around town the next day! My cheeks flamed with humiliation at the thought.

A large hand suddenly grabbed Thayne's shoulder and yanked him away from me. Unbelievably, it was Judd!

"Leave her be!" he growled and Thayne's drunken grin turned into an ugly scowl.

"Why should I?" he demanded.

"Because I'll smash your face in if you don't!" came the answer, but it wasn't issued from Judd.

I swung around to see Jay standing squarely behind me, his mouth set in a thin, hard line and anger blazing in his eyes. Thayne gawked and Judd glared, but Jay didn't give either one of them a chance to speak. Turning to me, he said: "It's the last waltz," and took me into his arms. We moved into the crowd, leaving both men staring after us with looks not lawful to be uttered.

Somehow, it didn't seem the least bit incongruous that I should be waltzing with an Indian dressed in buckskin. I was only half aware of the music and the movement of other couples around us. It was as if they existed in a different dimension, separate and apart from Jay and myself. Somewhere outside the black flame burning in his eyes, I saw Janet's parents glide past and felt the curious glances of others following our movements.

"Everyone is staring at us," I said.

Jay's eyes left mine briefly to glance about the room. "So they are. Do you mind?"

Entirely of its own accord, my left hand suddenly found its way around his neck and my fingers knew the softness of his thick black hair. "Mind? I'm too happy to mind."

Jay's arm tightened about my waist, pulling me closer to him. The heady aroma of buckskin stirred my senses. I felt his lips touch my forehead, then move against my hair. It took a moment for me to realize we were no longer dancing. Then I heard Jay's voice in my ear, "I need to talk to you, Angel. Let's get out of here."

He took my arm and we left the crowded living room just as the dance was ending. His lengthy stride brought us quickly through the dining room and kitchen, then outside, where the night air met us with a glad rush of fragrance. I drew a welcome breath of its coolness as Jay led me around the back of the house. Across the lawn, the lanterns danced to the rhythm of the wind's music, their amber light making graceful shadow patterns on the lawn.

Jay's footsteps halted in a dark patch of shadow and his arms reached out for me, erasing all traces of darkness between us.

"You said . . . you wanted . . . to talk to me?"

"There's so much I want to tell you, so many things to explain—but now . . ."

"You couldn't wait to get your filthy hands on her again, could you, halfbreed?"

Jay's hands fell away from me and I whirled around with a start, my heart racing and my limbs as weak as water. Thayne and his companions had come around the side of the house and were watching us with contempt.

Jay moved out of the darkness into the lantern light. "What do you want, Thayne?"

"I wanna know what kinda trick you use to turn her on, thas what I wanna know! I never thought I'd see a woman who liked the stink of Injuns bettern'n the smell of a white man, but every time you come aroun' she sure gets hot. Maybe if I lived with dogs for a while like you did, she'd be hot for me."

Jay's face went rigid and there was a threatening rumble to his voice. "Get out of here, Thayne! Go sober up!"

"Who do you think you are, tellin' me where to go an' what to do?" Thayne demanded and took a swaying step towards Jay. "You can't tell me nothin'! You with yer no good father and yer dirty red-hide mother!"

Jay's hands clenched into fists and a muscle twitched in the tight line of his jaw.

One of Thayne's friends glanced at Jay and grabbed Thayne by the arm. "Come on, buddy. Let's go cool off!"

"You go cool off!" Thayne blustered. "I ain't finished with this Injun yet." He stepped forward and took a wild swing at Jay which was easily avoided.

"Sorry, fellah," Jay said, shoving him away. "I don't fight drunks."

"Who's drunk?" Thayne bellowed. "I can hold my liquor better'n any damn Injun!"

I glanced around and saw that several people were leaving the house and casting curious glances in our direction. "Thayne, please don't make a scene!" I pleaded. "Not after your parents have worked so hard to make it a lovely evening!"

"Lovely evening!" he snorted. "I've had one hell of a time watchin' you turn yer nose up at me! Then the minute this stinkin' halfbreed walks in yer all over him! You're no better'n he is, you dirty little—"

Jay's fist suddenly plowed into Thayne's face, cutting off any further descriptive comments right at the source. The blow sent him staggering backwards with a startled grunt of pain. He crumpled on the ground like a rag doll.

Jay rubbed his knuckles and gave a curt nod to Thayne's friends. "Why don't you guys thank the Bradfords for a nice evening and then disappear." His suggestion was heeded immediately and without comment. The three turned and stalked back to the house.

166

"Looks to me like he's going to be out for the night," came an amused voice behind us. "Between the two of us, I think we could lug 'sleeping beauty' up the back stairs without causing too much of a fuss."

Reed Tyler had appeared out of the shadows near the pines with Janet close beside him. I looked at the pair rather incredulously, knowing that Reed was one of Thayne's closest friends. Yet, neither he nor Janet seemed the least bit disturbed over the fact that Thayne was lying on the grass with blood trickling from his nose to his mustache and down his chin. Already, his mouth was swelling to an ugly size.

Jay must have been having thoughts similar to mine because he glanced from Reed to Janet with a puzzled frown. On Janet, his gaze lingered.

She flushed under his glance and said contritely, "Reed and I saw what happened just now and we couldn't help hearing the awful things he said. I know Thayne drinks too much once in a while, but I've never seen him act so—so—" She looked down at her brother in disgust, then back at Jay and me. "I'm sorry for what he said. I feel just terrible."

Reed chuckled. "Thayne's going to feel terrible, too—especially when he wakes up in the morning. You girls had better get back now and say your adieus to the guests. Jay and I can handle things here."

Janet agreed and raised adoring eyes to his face. "And after that—?" she asked demurely.

Reed grinned and planted a kiss full on her lips. "And after that, little squirrel, we'll go talk to your father. And not about your brother's bad manners, either."

Jay and I exchanged glances and I felt his fingers close around mine.

From around the side of the house we heard the sound of running feet and suddenly Stuart burst into our little circle.

"Hey, what's this about a fight?" he asked eagerly. Then, looking down at his older brother's bloodied face, the youth gave a disgusted sigh. "Oh hell! I missed it!"

Chapter 19

"Then will I lay my cheek
To his, and tell about our love,
Not once abashed or weak . . ."

Dante Gabriel Rossetti

The last of the furtive laughter and whispers went out into the night. The screen door slammed. I heard a chorus of frantic "shhhs!", then nothing.

I lifted my head off the pillow and looked toward the dining room, content that feigning sleep was no longer necessary. I had been wide awake when Tadd and David and their cousins had come creeping into the house to make a raid on the refrigerator. The boys knew, of course, that I would be sleeping on a couch in the living room and had taken every precaution during their nocturnal visit not to awaken me. I had to smother my smiles and laughter in the pillow not to disappoint them. Once Tadd bumped into a chair and was soundly chastised by the others. Then one of the boys had clanked a dish and a whole round of "shhhs!" followed, completely obliterating the innocent noise.

But now they were gone and I was alone with my thoughts once more. After Janet and I had bid goodnight to departing guests there had been much to do in the kitchen. I hadn't had the opportunity to see or talk to Jay again, except for a quick glimpse of him as he helped the Bradfords fold up chairs and stack them against the side of the house.

My mind recalled the low urgency of his voice saying there were things he needed to tell me. Did I dare let myself hope that what he had to say concerned the two of us?

I tossed my blankets aside and sat up on the couch with my legs tucked under me and my arms resting across the back of the sofa.

Outside the window, a white wave of moonlight spilled across the lawn and the leaves of the cottonwoods were rippling silver.

I sat there for some time, breathing in the calm beauty of the night, hoping some of its tranquility would ease my restlessness. Then, although there hadn't been so much as a sound, I knew I was no longer alone in the room. A prickle of fear crept along my skin and my relaxed pose turned rigid.

This time there had been no tell-tale squeak of the kitchen door, no muffled laughter and jumbled footsteps of mischievous boys. This time, every taut nerve in my body told me that one, solitary presence was nearby.

I turned, slowly, until my eyes were staring straight toward the curved archway of the dining room. There, etched in blackness, was the tall form of a man. My heart began to pound with heavy, suffocating beats as he came out of the shadows into the moonlight. He moved directly to the couch and I said breathlessly, "Do you Indians always have to be so stealthy? You nearly scared me to death!"

A smile eased the tenseness of his face. "I'm sorry. I wasn't sure if you'd be sleeping."

Jay stood before me, swathed in moonlight. He was wearing the buckskin shirt and trousers I had seen him in earlier, but now the shirt hung unbuttoned outside the pants.

"How did you know I was here?" I asked in my best reserved manner. My serene composure lasted about two seconds. The sleeve of my nightgown suddenly slipped off my shoulder and I heard Jay catch his breath. I jerked the sleeve back up with clumsy fingers, wishing to heaven I'd worn a different nightgown. Although the gown was long and the sleeves reached down to my wrists, the neckline was low and the elasticised bodice had long since grown limp from years of wear and many washings. I was trying to find the courage to ask Jay for my robe which lay at the other end of the couch when he sat down—right on it.

"I was in the bunkhouse when the boys came back with the spoils of their midnight raid," Jay explained. "They were pretty cocky about pulling the whole thing off without disturbing you. But knowing my cousins, I figured that was just about impossible. Anyway, I hoped you were awake because I needed a chance to talk to you before tomorrow." Jay paused and rubbed his palms against the sides of his leather breeches. "I thought you'd want to know what I found out from the diary."

I slumped back against the sofa and spread my flannel gown over my bare feet. The diary. So that was all he wanted to tell me.

"I hope you don't mind," Jay was saying. "I know it's late."

"No. No, of course I don't mind. I couldn't sleep anyway, and I've been so worried all week—that is, I've been wondering if the diary was of some help. Do you know—does it give any clues—?"

"Yes. I know now. Not all the details, but those will come tomorrow."

Tomorrow. I looked at Jay's somber features molded by moonlight—his deep-set eyes, his high cheekbones with finely cut hollows beneath them, and the mouth, tightly set.

"Is—is everything going to be all right?"

"I think so. I hope so!" he added fervently, regarding me with an expression that I couldn't read in the darkness.

I looked away from his probing glance and fidgeted with the soft folds of my gown, during which time the other sleeve fell down. I yanked it back on to my shoulder.

Jay cleared his throat and asked, "Do you think we could risk turning on a light? I've brought the diary with me and some parts are better read than explained."

"I don't know. If someone came in—wait! There are some candles and matches on the mantle. That would be better."

I got up quickly and moved across the vast, empty space of the living room, praying I wouldn't trip on the hem of my gown. Although the fireplace was in darkness the candles were easy to find, for Helen's treasured candelabra shone dully against the darker background of wood and stone. A box of matches was right beside it. I snatched them up and returned to the couch.

Jay sat in silence while I placed the candelabra on a small coffee table in front of the sofa. I leaned over the table and struck a match to one of the wicks. A small burst of flame smothered the moonlight around us. I lit two more candles, then glanced up to find Jay's eyes upon me. I straightened up to a more modest position and blew out the match—and one of the candles as well. I groaned inwardly and reached for another match, but Jay said, "Never mind lighting another. This'll do fine." He reached inside his buckskin shirt and brought out the small book I had discovered just two days before. His long fingers turned the yellowed pages gently, almost reverently.

"Yesterday, I got to know my father," he said. "I understand now why my mother never stopped believing in him."

Jay was silent for a long moment, then continued in a more matter-of-fact tone. "The diary begins shortly after my parents were married and returned to the Triple J. I'm afraid they didn't have much of a homecoming. My father had written Judd that he was coming back but he hadn't told him about his marriage. That alone was quite a shock. And when Judd saw my mother was an Indian he was furious. He not only refused to speak to her, he wouldn't even let her set foot inside this house. Lizzy, my grandfather's second wife, tried to reason with him, but it didn't do any good. She did get him to agree to let my folks stay in the bunkhouse, and without Judd knowing she brought over some new curtains, a rug or two, and even one of her precious geraniums, to make things homier for my parents.

"The situation was pretty tense between my father and grandfather, but

Dad was determined to make amends. He kept hoping that Judd would calm down and listen to reason as far as my mother was concerned. But my grandfather wasn't a reasonable man. Months went by and things never got any better. I'm sure that's why they wanted to keep the news of my mother's pregnancy to themselves. Lizzy was the first to find out and she thought it would be better if she were the one to break the news to Judd. They all hoped that a baby on the way would mellow him."

I looked at Jay hopefully, but his voice was hard and bitter. He put the book into my lap and I took it without comment.

"Thursday—February 7"

"Walked in on Dad and Mother today right in the middle of a fight. Actually, Dad was doing all the yelling and Mother was just coming back in that calm way of hers that drives him crazy. I came into the kitchen just in time to hear him say: 'I'm not going to let that squaw whelp a redskin brat on this ranch!' I've never laid a hand on my father, but right then I wanted to flatten him good. I probably would have if Mother hadn't stepped between us. What she said flattened us both. She called Dad a hypocrite and said he had no cause to object to me marrying an Indian because he'd done the same thing himself. She told Dad that she'd known for years that my real mother was half Indian, even though Dad had done his best to keep it a secret from the whole town. Dad got an awful look in his eyes then, but she went right on. She said it was time I knew the truth; that it was my privilege to carry Indian blood in my veins; that it was something I should be proud of, not ashamed.

"For once, the old man was speechless. He looked at me, then Mother, and walked away. After he had gone, Mother started to cry. I've never seen her cry that way before. Nothing I could say was any comfort to her. It isn't easy for a woman to know she's second best. I know if anything ever happened to Wenona, I could never love another woman the way I do her."

My hands began to tremble and I couldn't read further. "Jay! I wore her clothes to the party tonight! Nora's clothes! And the way I did my hair. No wonder Judd looked at me the way he did! I'm sure he thought I wore those clothes just to torment him, but I didn't know! Janet and Helen said it would be all right to wear them, but I had a feeling—a feeling about Nora and Judd. If only I'd known!"

"You couldn't have known," Jay said. "Like Lizzy said in the diary, no one in Dusk knew about my grandmother being an Indian. I'm not sure if Judd even knew when he married her. That part's still a mystery to me. But

171

I'm glad Lizzy had the courage to tell my father the truth. Read the next page."

I turned a yellowed leaf carefully and looked down at Jason's heavy black scrawl once more.

"February 25"

"My anger towards the old man never seems as strong when I realize Wenona and I are of one blood now as well as one heart. And our son will carry the blood of a proud people in his veins! I wish I had known my mother. I think about her often now. Somewhere up north, our child has relatives who should know about his birth when that time comes. Maybe I could find them. It's only three months now until the baby's due. At night, when our bodies find love and warmth together, I can feel the life stirring inside her and I wonder how one man could be so lucky . . ."

As I read Jason Bradford's intimate thoughts, I felt his son's eyes upon me. Warmth flooded my cheeks and I gave the diary back to Jay without looking into his face. I didn't trust myself to make comment on the latter part of Jason's words so I asked instead, "Did your father learn anything more about Nora's family?"

"No, he never had much chance. Work on the ranch kept him pretty occupied, and after the last upset with Judd, my father began to feel an urgency to get away, to make a new life somewhere else. The main things stopping him were money and a job. All he knew was ranching and he didn't have enough cash to buy a spread for himself. John and Lizzy both wanted my parents to stay at the Triple J. I guess they kept hoping that after the baby came, Judd would soften up. Then, too, my father had expressed a desire for his child to be born on the ranch. I guess all those things held him back for a while, but when spring came, Dad made his decision. He wrote to Parley Evans and asked for his old job back. The rest we already know, except what happened the day before he disappeared, which was also the day he wrote to Parley for the last time."

"Does the diary tell what happened that last day?" I asked quietly, hoping that it did and yet afraid to know.

Jay nodded and I saw sadness in the lines of his face. "This is the last entry," he said, and together we read Jason's final words.

"May 15"

"Rode up into the hills this morning looking for strays and checking the fences. I was half-way up the cattle trail when I saw an Appaloosa grazing up the Right Fork. I didn't need to get closer to know it was Shiloh. I'd know those markings anywhere even if I hadn't raised him from a colt. I took off after him and the spunky devil led me quite a chase. Even if my horse hadn't

172

been tired I don't think I'd have caught him. Shiloh always could outrun any horse on the ranch. He was heading for some box canyons when I last saw him and that set me to thinking. How the hell could Shiloh be running wild on our own land when my father insisted that he and nine other horses were stolen two years ago? By the time I got back to the ranch I had it pretty well figured out. The old man was lying to me all the time. Those horses were never stolen. He just didn't want to sell them so he cooked up that rustling story. Last fall, when Wenona and I came back to the ranch, he must have hidden them somewhere up the Right Fork. Sometimes I wonder if he's really right in his mind!

"I confronted Dad with the whole thing this afternoon and all he could do was sputter and rave. He never admitted a thing, and he wouldn't tell me which canyon they were in. Finally, I lost my temper and told him I'd had enough of him and the whole damn ranch. I told him that four of those horses were mine and I was going to go back up in those hills the next day and take what belonged to me. After that, I told him I was leaving for good. Dad got a scared, desperate look in his eyes then and told me if I ever left the ranch it would be with nothing but the clothes on my back. I just walked away. What can you say to a man who's sick in the mind with greed and hatred?

"Wrote to Parley and told him that Wenona and I would get to his place sometime this week. If it weren't for those horses I'd leave tonight, but selling them will pay all the doctor bills for the baby and maybe give us enough to start saving for our own ranch. I'd sure like to keep old Shiloh, though. Wenona would love riding him."

The remaining lines on the page were blank and so were the pages following. Jay closed the diary and I felt a sudden impulse to stop him. It was as if as long as the book were open, Jason was still alive. Now I knew he was dead.

I lifted my head to look at Jason's son. Even the blend of candlelight and shadow could not soften the tenseness of jaw and mouth. Nor could it hide the agony in his eyes.

"Then it's Judd," I said at last, my voice sounding flat and dry.

"Yes, it's Judd," Jay stated in quiet affirmation. "My father must have gone to look for his horses the next morning and Judd stopped him." Jay was silent for a long moment, drew in a deep breath and said with frightening grimness, "I hope it was an accident!"

With a little shiver I forced myself out of the tragic past and back to the present. There was a question more important to me now than the grisly details of how Judd Bradford had killed his own son.

"What will you do after you find out—after you know what happened to your father?"

Jay leaned against the sofa with a weary sigh. "The only thing I can do—leave the ranch. I feel the same way my father did about it now. I want nothing more to do with the Triple J or anybody on it. As far as the law is concerned, I can't see going to the sheriff and having Judd arrested—even if what he did was intentional. He's been living with his guilt all these years and he'll go on living with it. That's punishment enough. My father's name will be cleared when we—when we find the body," he said and cleared his throat. "The family can say he was killed accidentally and that will be the end of it."

I was thankful Jay couldn't see my face. I looked down at my clenched hands and tried to fight the sick, numb feeling that was spreading through my body. Of course Jay would leave. I had known that from the beginning.

"Angela—"

My throat was constricted in a hard tight knot and there was no way I could answer him. I tried to swallow and nearly choked on the tears that were coming.

One of Jay's hands moved over mine. "Angela—when I go, will you come with me—as my wife?"

I raised my head to look at him, unbelieving, unsure, and horribly afraid that I was only imagining what I wanted to hear.

"I know we haven't known each other very long—only a few days—but I can't risk losing you because of that. I'm sure time will make my feelings grow stronger—but I don't need more of it to tell me *how* I feel. I love you, Angel," he said softly, the words sounding new and unused on his tongue.

Happiness was rising inside me like a sunrise. Jay took me into his arms and the tears of frustration and disappointment which I had been struggling to keep back, spilled freely down my cheeks as tears of joy.

"I've been so afraid this would never happen," I said against his shoulder. "Afraid I had no part in your future."

Jay gave a shaky laugh and held me closer. "And just what kind of future would I have without you, love? Why do you think it took me nearly two days of wandering around in the hills to decide what I should do? After I finished reading the diary I was so angry—so torn apart!—all I wanted was to come down here and tear Judd apart. Maybe that makes me sound like a bloodthirsty savage, but I couldn't help it. Last night I lay awake for a long while. I tried not to think of you because every time I did, I felt less angry—and I wanted to be angry. Finally, I made a fire and read through the diary again. I thought of the love my father had for my mother, and the joy they knew in giving me life. I thought of the future they dreamed about but never had, and I knew I wanted that kind of future with you."

Jay held me slightly apart from him and looked into my face. "I don't want to end up like my father. I want to see my children! I want to watch them grow! And I want you to be their mother. Will you come with me, Angel?"

My answer was neither timid nor weak. What I told him then, I never thought I would have the courage to say to any man. And perhaps even more amazing was the sweet sense of pleasure I felt in giving such free utterance to my love for him.

Jay's response was immediate and so thorough that words weren't possible or necessary for a long while. When, at length, I leaned back against the couch pillows to gaze up at him, I saw the corners of his mouth turning up into a wry grin.

"You know, I owe your nightgown an apology," he said. "I was cursing it pretty heavily for a while tonight, but right now, I have nothing but good things to say about it."

My laughter joined his. "You weren't the only one cursing it. If that sleeve had fallen down one more time I don't know what I would have done!"

"I know exactly what I'd have done," Jay said huskily, as his fingers took a firm hold of the front of my gown. "Or what I'd have liked to do, at any rate. Every time it slipped off your shoulder my brain went blank. I don't think I could have recited the abc's, let alone tell you about the diary."

The warmth of his fingers on my skin made me feel lightheaded and I knew he must feel my heart's wild pounding. The flickering light from the candles was dim and hazy compared to the black flame burning in his eyes. Jay's fingers loosed their hold on my gown and a sleeve promptly fell off my shoulder. This time I made no move to replace it. One of Jay's hands closed firmly about my shoulder, the other slid around my waist, pulling me down on the couch.

Then from above, scuffling footsteps sounded in the hall, followed by the sound of running water in the bathroom. Jay quickly leaned over me and blew out the candles. We lay still in each other's arms. A moment later the footsteps retreated and all was quiet.

Jay's voice was breathless and unsteady in my ear. "I forgot this isn't the most private place in the world. I think maybe I'd better go before somebody decides to come downstairs for something." His lips took mine for a long moment then he straightened up. "I'll see you in the morning, love."

I sat up quickly and reached for his hand. "Jay, you will be careful, won't you? Your grandfather might try something dangerous when he realizes how much you know. Look what he's done already!"

175

"I know, sweetheart, but tomorrow will be different. This time I'll be the one taking him by surprise. And don't forget, my uncle will be there, too. I want John as a witness to everything that's said and done. I've already talked with him and he's agreed to meet with me and Judd tomorrow after chores. So there's nothing for you to worry about. Everything's going to be all right!"

"Oh, I hope so! But after all that's happened, I can't help worrying!"

"Well, maybe there is one thing you should worry about," he said with a smile in his voice.

"What's that?"

"A certain very important phone call will have to be made to your mother. I hope she doesn't have a heart attack when you tell her about us."

"Good heavens! I forgot all about Mother!"

Jay laughed. "I don't care what you tell her. Just make sure she understands that I don't believe in long engagements."

"What would you consider a long engagement?" I asked, smiling at him through the moonlight.

"Right now, twenty-four hours seems too long!" he said and kissed me with a fierceness that was altogether wonderful.

The next moment he released me and disappeared into the night.

Chapter 20

"It seemed that out of the battle I escaped . . ."
Wilfred Owen

I was awakened early the next morning by voices and footsteps coming down the stairs. I heard Jay's name mentioned and instantly I was wide awake and listening.

"If you don't feel up to doing the milking this morning I suppose I could ask Jay and Bert to help out. Ordinarily, the boys would do it, but I promised them they could go horseback riding with their cousins."

"That sounds good to me. Wouldn't hurt you to take it easy this morning, yourself. Jay can drive the truck into town."

"I suppose he wouldn't mind. He wants to talk to us about something. Said it was pretty important."

"That can wait! I suppose you know he got into a fight with your son last night."

"Yes, I know. I also know Thayne deserved what he got! He's had it coming to him for a long time."

I lifted my head off the pillow slightly and saw Judd and John standing at the foot of the stairs.

"Any time I'd let a dirty redskin make a fool out of my son and not do anything about it!" Judd retorted in an angry growl.

"Dirty redskin? You're talking about my nephew and your grandson! Or have you forgotten whose son he is?"

John didn't wait for an answer to his question but strode angrily through the dining room toward the kitchen. Judd stood watching him for a moment, then turned in my direction. I quickly shut my eyes and held my breath as his footsteps came nearer. He paused beside the couch and I could hear his heavy breathing as he stood over me. Then, when I felt a scream tearing at my throat, he moved away. The front door opened and closed behind him.

I wanted to jump off the sofa and run, but it took several seconds for the sick, clammy feeling to release me so I could move at all. Then I snatched my robe and scrambled up the stairs to the safety of Janet's room. I entered quietly, but found both girls awake and eager to divulge confidences from the night before.

Marsha pounced on me first and if I hadn't seen Delbert Eborn with my own two eyes, I would have believed him to be a tall, dark, inscrutable hero that would melt any maiden's heart after listening to her rose-colored description.

"Delbert's three years older than I am—eighteen!" Marsha declared in a tone that made me feel at least forty. "And he has his own car and works part time at the service station in town. And do you know what else? We were talking and found out that the same doctor delivered both of us! And his favorite sandwich is peanut butter and banana, the same as mine!"

"I assume you're referring to Delbert and not the doctor who delivered you," Janet said, struggling to keep back a smile.

"Well, of course, silly!"

"You certainly have a lot in common," I told the younger girl.

"We really do," she sighed. "Why, it's almost as if—as if—"

"As if the fates decreed that you should meet," I finished for her in dramatic overtones.

Janet suddenly coughed into her pillow but Marsha agreed with another rapturous sigh.

"That's it exactly," she said, picking up her toothbrush from the dresser. "As if the fates decreed that we should meet." She moved to the door with a dreamy expression on her face. "You know, we even use the same brand of toothpaste!"

Somehow Janet and I managed to control the wild desire to laugh until after she had gone, then we collapsed on the bed and howled shamelessly.

"I shouldn't laugh at her, but I can't help it," Janet gasped.

I hugged my sides and asked weakly, "Tell me something. Do you and Reed Tyler use the same brand of toothpaste?"

Janet giggled, but her eyes grew soft. As I had suspected, she and Reed had settled a good deal more than a lover's quarrel. Their wedding date was set for the first of September.

"We're going to be married in the church in town," she told me with a rosy flush on her cheeks and shining eyes. "Thayne doesn't know it yet, but he's going to be best man!" She laughed then looked at me with a touch of hesitancy. "It would mean a lot to me if you would be my maid of honor. Even if you don't marry Thayne, you'll always be as close to me as a sister."

I gave Janet a hug and assured her that I would love to be her maid of honor, wondering to myself if perhaps the title would have to be altered to matron of honor by September.

Something must have come into my face because Janet gave me a swift second glance and demanded, "Angela, what's happened! Something's happened! You look too calm."

I got off the bed and hunted through the closet for something to wear. I wanted to share my own happiness with Janet but I felt unsure about this being the right time. If I did tell her, she would naturally ask a lot of questions—especially about why Jay had come to see me in the middle of the night. And I couldn't tell her about the diary.

"Does it have something to do with Jay?" she asked shrewdly. "Has he asked you out again?"

I slipped a light summer blouse off a hanger and smiled. "Well, yes. He has."

This morning, the rules in the kitchen were everyone fend for himself. When Janet and Marsha and I came downstairs, Helen and her sister were already at the table enjoying a leisurely cup of coffee and some sweet rolls that Helen must have brought out from her special hiding place under the sink. I thought the younger boys might be a bit bleary-eyed after their midnight escapade but they came bounding through the back door, laughing and eager for their horseback ride. Already, Stuart and Randy were out rounding up the horses. Tadd and David and the two Thompson boys made a frantic dash for the cupboards and proceeded to argue over who wanted which cold cereal as I sat down at the table beside Helen.

"Did you have a good time last night, dear?" she asked. "Seems like I never did have a chance to talk to you."

"It was a wonderful party."

"It sure was!" Marsha agreed ecstatically.

"I sure wish I could have been there to see ol' Thayne get flattened out," Tadd said with relish, as Al Thompson and his son Larry entered the room. Behind them was a tousle-haired, red-eyed, swollen-jawed personage who vaguely resembled Thayne Bradford.

Tadd gulped and choked on his orange juice. There was absolute silence as Thayne made his way to the table with careful steps and sat down.

"Looks like I better fill the coffee pot again," Helen said cheerfully and went to the stove.

Thayne looked around at the various assortment of smiles and growled, "The first one who makes a wise-crack is gonna look a hell of a lot worse than I do, understand?"

Helen returned to the table and gave Thayne a scrutinizing glance. "I don't know if that's possible, son. Laws, but you do look awful!"

The boys' strangled laughter broke free and even Thayne couldn't keep back a crooked, but rather painful grin. "Aw right! Aw right! You've had your joke!"

Helen shushed her sons' riotous laughter with, "You boys finish your breakfast now and get on outside, or you won't have time for that horseback ride."

"They might not get to go riding anyway," Judd Bradford pronounced from the kitchen doorway. "It looks to me like we're in for a bad storm today."

I avoided the old man's eyes as he sat down at the breakfast table and turned around in my chair to look out the bay window. The sky was hazy and gray. Not a leaf trembled on the big cottonwoods along the drive and the sun was only able to cast a sallow light through the low clouds.

Then I noticed a horse and rider racing up the gravel road. In a few seconds they were close enough for me to see it was Stuart on Arabesque. I remembered the mild scolding Bert had given me for running Ginger along the road and wondered what reason Stuart had for keeping the black mare at such a frantic pace. Moments later, the boy came bursting into the kitchen, eyes wild with panic and his face white to the lips.

"There—there's been an accident!" he gasped, and it was several seconds before he could get enough breath to speak again.

In the interim Al Thompson demanded, "What sort of accident? What happened?"

"The truck—the truck's crashed down in the gulley!"

My heart jerked convulsively and I stared at Judd's craggy features where there wasn't the barest trace of surprise at Stuart's news. You've done it! I thought, wanting to scream the words out loud. You've done it! You've killed Jay!

"Is anyone hurt?" Helen asked, her brown eyes wide in her pale face.

"It's Dad!" Stuart choked. "He's hurt real bad! I—I couldn't get to him 'cause the truck's in the creek."

Helen gave a low moan and clutched the back of a chair for support. I stared at the faces in the room. Everyone was seized by shock and disbelief—stunned seconds when the brain registers what has happened and at the same time tries to deny the horror of reality.

Judd suddenly wrested all the attention upon himself by knocking a platter of toast off the table with one swipe of his hand.

"You're wrong!" he bellowed. "It can't be John! Jay was supposed to drive the truck into town this morning. Don't you see? There's been a mistake! A mistake!" he cried desperately. "It can't be John!"

"Grandpa Judd, I'm sorry," Stuart said hoarsely. "But it is Dad. I saw him."

I turned away from the old man's angry confusion. Relief, harsh and

180

wonderful was sweeping over me. I shut my eyes for a moment, thinking, thank God he's safe!

Thayne stood up and shook himself like one coming out of a daze. "The shock's been too much for him. Mom, I think Grandpa Judd had better have one of those strong sedatives the doctor prescribed. He won't be any help to us or Dad right now. You boys! Stop sitting in your chairs like a bunch of idiots and go get some tools—rope, a crowbar, an ax—anything you can find! Put them in my car and I'll be with you in a few minutes!"

It didn't matter that Thayne's orders came out in a slightly garbled fashion from his swollen jaw and thick lips. The boys shoved back their chairs and hurried outside without saying another word.

After his outburst, Judd was a shaking, shrunken old man. He allowed himself to be led upstairs to his room without protest.

Al Thompson got up from the table and said to those of us remaining, "If John's hurt as bad as Stuart said, we're going to need some medical supplies. And I think we'd better plan on driving him directly to a hospital. Larry, you and Randy clear out the stuff in the back of our stationwagon. Janet, I think we could make your father a stretcher of sorts if we could borrow a mattress off one of the beds. Angela, you and Kate round up some bandages, a clean sheet, anything you think we'll need. All right, let's get going!"

There was no time to think, to wonder what had happened or how it had happened. Every minute and every particle of energy had to be used toward one objective: to get John out of the truck and on his way to a hospital as quickly as possible. Al Thompson, Thayne and Larry were the first to leave the ranchhouse. Stuart followed close behind, driving the younger boys in the Bradford's family car. Marsha Thompson and I put the last of the medical supplies in the back of the stationwagon then climbed in quickly. Helen came out of the house, her face ashen and her lips trembling, but otherwise calm and composed. Kate Thompson got behind the wheel of the big stationwagon, Janet climbed in beside her mother and the car roared out of the driveway.

"I can't imagine how it happened," Helen said. "John is always so careful. I've never known him to drive recklessly."

"Maybe the steering failed—or the brakes," her sister suggested. "He might have lost control of the truck."

"That's impossible!" Janet argued. "Dad and Thayne drove the truck into town just yesterday to get the tables and chairs for the party, and neither one of them noticed anything the matter with the truck. Dad always keeps it in top shape. Doesn't he, Mother?"

"I just hope he's all right," Helen said fervently.

I bit down on my lower lip and remained silent. I knew full well that

181

Judd must have tampered with the truck early this morning, but that knowledge wouldn't help John now.

As the stationwagon moved down into the steep gulley, I could see the path the truck had taken. The tire tracks missed the sharp left turn entirely and went screaming off into heavy brush, over a steep embankment of rocks and down into the stream. Helen drew in a tense, tight breath as the truck came into view, and Janet clutched her mother's arm.

The entire left side of the vehicle was plunged into the rushing water. The right front wheel was thrust up on some rocks and the right rear wheel barely skimmed the surface of the water. Thayne was hip-deep in water, working to pry open the door on the driver's side, while Al and Larry Thompson were making an effort to brace the truck's precarious position by trying it with ropes and securing them to trees on the bank. The impact of the crash had crushed John against the steering wheel and from what I could hear of Thayne's and Al Thompson's remarks as we approached, one of John's legs was broken and tangled in the brake and clutch pedals.

I stood a few feet behind the rest of the family who were gathered on the very edge of the creek, knowing that if Judd's intents and purposes had come to pass, it would be Jay's dark head slumped over the steering wheel, not John's.

Stuart walked over to stand beside me, his face grim.

"Are they getting your father out all right?" I asked.

The youth frowned and shoved his glasses back up on his nose. "They're getting him out. But it's going to be a while yet."

"Where's Jay and Bert? Shouldn't they be here, helping?"

"They rode up to the summer range first thing this morning."

"The summer range? What are they doing up there?"

Stuart ran a hand through his straight brown hair. "Old man Tyler called and told Dad that a bunch of our Herefords had wandered over the hills and down onto their land. They were tramping down the alfalfa and Sam was pretty peeved, so Dad asked Jay and Bert to go round up the steers and get 'em back inside the summer range. We sure could use their help now!"

A long, anxiety-filled half hour passed before John was freed from the wreckage and his unconscious body placed on the mattress-stretcher inside the stationwagon. Helen climbed in beside her husband, still calm and silent, but with tears slipping down her sallow cheeks.

The closest hospital in miles was located in Jackson but Al Thompson said it would be faster to drive down to Rock Springs. Kate insisted that the Bradford family stay at their home as long as was necessary, and Helen gratefully accepted the arrangements. I was the logical choice for someone to stay behind and tell Jay and Bert what had happened.

182

Thayne offered to drive me back to the ranchhouse, but I declined, saying, "It's not far to walk. You go ahead with the others."

"I don't know when we'll be back," he said. "It all depends on how bad Dad's hurt. Jay and Bert will be able to handle the chores."

"Call when you know."

He nodded. "Take care now."

I watched his car take the steep road out of the gulley and disappear over the lip of the hill, then turned my steps away from the stream and the crippled truck and walked swiftly up the avenue of maples.

The air was still and heavy, almost oppressive. Trees and fields were green and still, basking in a false peace that would end when the warring black clouds above gave their thunderous battle shouts.

I kept a rapid pace along the gravel road, fear of what lay ahead in that gray stone house quickening my heartbeat. I forced my mind to repeat sensible, reassuring thoughts. Jay and Bert would be back soon, only a couple of hours from now. Thayne had said Judd was deep in a sedated sleep and would probably remain so for a long while yet. There was nothing to worry about.

Once inside, I found myself tiptoeing through the silent house, hardly daring to make a sound. Nothing could make me go upstairs to Janet's room when I knew I would have to walk past her grandfather's bedroom first. I spent the remainder of the morning in the kitchen, clearing away the food left from breakfast and washing the dishes.

At eleven-thirty, I telephoned the Tyler ranch to find out if Jay could be reached. Mrs. Tyler was sorry but all the men were out working and she wouldn't be able to get a message to Jay until lunchtime. I thanked her and hung up the receiver. I took a breath and tried to loosen the tight threads of fear and worry that were winding themselves about me. At least Judd was still asleep, and for all I knew, Jay and Bert might be riding back to the Triple J this very moment.

At twelve-fifteen I telephoned the Tyler's again and asked if the men had returned from their morning's work.

"No, I'm sorry," came the polite voice on the other end of the line. "My husband and sons should be back any time, though. Is this Angela? Yes, dear, I'll be happy to give them a message."

I told Mrs. Tyler about the accident and explained that Jay and Bert were needed back at the Triple J to take care of the chores until the Bradfords returned.

"Is John hurt bad?" she asked. "Is he going to be all right?"

"I—I don't know. I hope so."

"How's Helen taking it?"

"Pretty well. She and the rest of the family have gone down to Rock Springs."

"Are you alone, dear?" Mrs. Tyler asked.

It was a simple question. No reason for me to freeze up this way. "Yes. No—Judd's here, too. But just now he's asleep. He became very upset when he heard about the accident and Helen gave him a sedative."

"Is there anything I can do?" the woman inquired kindly. "Would you like me to come over there?"

"No, I don't think so. But thank you, anyway. As soon as Jay gets back everything will be all right."

Mrs. Tyler couldn't have known what I meant by that, but she agreed comfortably, and assured me once more that she would telephone the minute her husband returned from the summer range.

I replaced the receiver and stood before the bay window, looking out on a landscape that was dark and fitful. It hadn't begun raining, but the rolling masses of black clouds that weighed heavily upon a thin border of filmy gray sky, seemed to be waiting only for the proper signal to begin. The ancient cottonwoods along the drive were shuddering in the wind and I could hear their restless moaning even inside the house.

Waiting. Would it end with Judd's waking or Jay's return? My eyes lowered to a black fringe of dead flies along the window sill and I pressed a hand to my stomach, hating the sick feeling of dread inside me. This would never do! The best thing for me was to keep busy. When Jay and Bert returned they would be hungry and expecting a hot lunch. I left the window and went to the refrigerator. My eyes stared at the loaded shelves, but my brain was suddenly incapable of making even simple decisions. But even in my present state, soup and sandwiches shouldn't be too difficult to manage. I grabbed a platter heaped with leftover roast beef, set it on the counter, then hunted through the various cupboards until I found a can of condensed soup. It was two minutes more before I located a can opener. I dumped the soup into a sauce pan, added water, and placed the pan on a burner to heat. Now where did Helen keep the bread? And butter. Hadn't I just seen it a moment ago in one of the cupboards? Or was it in the refrigerator?

My eyes wandered to the kitchen clock on a wall beside the doorway. Twelve-thirty. Dear heaven, what could be keeping them! Judd wouldn't sleep forever! Even now, he might be awake! I left the sandwiches and went to the window once again. Only an empty road met my anxious gaze.

A loud, bubbling hiss startled the heavy silence of the room. I whirled around with a gasp to see soup boiling over the sides of the saucepan. I grabbed a dish towel that lay on the counter near the sink and quickly lifted the pan off the burner. Nerves, anyway! If I didn't calm down, I would be setting the house on fire with my foolishness!

184

"Has everyone gone?"

I slammed the saucepan down on the counter with a suddenness that sent some of the seething liquid splashing over my hand.

Judd Bradford repeated the question as he entered the room, and it seemed minutes instead of seconds before I was able to answer.

"Yes—I—that is, the family have all gone to the hospital, but Jay and Bert should be back from Tyler's any minute now." I struggled to keep fear out of my voice and added, "I was just fixing a little lunch. Are you hungry? I've made some sandwiches . . ."

Judd ignored my question. "You sound very anxious to have them return."

I dried my hand with the dish towel. "I—well, Jay doesn't know about the accident yet."

A spasm of pain passed over the old man's face and he said in a low tone, "Jay should have been driving that truck."

The dish towel dropped from my hands and for a moment I felt physically ill. "What did you do to the truck?"

Judd didn't make any attempt to deny my question or its accompanying accusation. "I loosened the connectors on the brakeline so the fluid would leak out. It's a simple thing to do. I knew by the time Jay started down the gulley the brakes would be pretty well shot. He always drives too damn fast, anyway! No one would blame me if he broke his fool neck!"

I stared at Judd, knowing what I was hearing and wondering at the same time if this were really happening. I heard my own voice saying quite calmly, "Just the way no one could blame you for two shots fired at the truck—or a heavy iron hook swinging loose and killing a little calf."

Judd nodded and kept his eyes riveted to my face. "That's right. Only I didn't kill that calf. I went out the next morning to check on him and there he was, looking fit as can be. They're strong little buggers. The way that hook hit, it should've been killed instantly."

"It was," I whispered. "There were twin calves born that night. Jay buried the one you killed."

Judd's hooded eyes widened in surprise. "Pretty clever, weren't you? Keeping quiet about the whole thing. You and that red-skinned devil! You thought you'd fool an old man, but I know what you're after. I know what you're trying to do! You want to destroy me—and everything I've worked so hard to keep! But I won't let you! I won't let you, do you hear!"

I gripped the side of the counter and faced the old man's anger with words that struggled out of my throat no louder than a whisper. "Jay and I don't want to hurt you. Please believe me! All Jay wants is to learn the truth about his father."

Judd's mouth twisted and he took two menacing steps in my direction. "He'll never find that out from me!"

I backed away. "You can't be sure of that. Jay has his father's diary and he already knows most of what happened. The rest won't remain a secret much longer."

"Ja—son's diary?" he faltered and the sagging flesh on his cheekbones paled. "Jason never kept a diary! You're lying!"

"I'm not lying! I found the book myself a few days ago. It was wedged between the framework and bottom drawer of the pine desk in the bunkhouse."

Judd's tongue passed over his thick lips and there was uncertainty in his eyes. "I still say you're lying," he insisted, but no so strongly as before. "Jason never kept a diary! I'm his father. I ought to know."

My terror of the old man gave way momentarily to pity. "There's so much you never knew or understood about your son. You were blind to all his efforts to please you. It was his money that kept the ranch going, and his hard work! And you let everyone in Dusk think that Jason had deserted—run out on you!"

"That's enough!" Judd bellowed.

"But there's more! And it's all in the diary. Do you believe me now?"

"I believe you know too much, Miss Stewart."

Suddenly, there was nothing more to say. My eyes went involuntarily to the bay window, but there was no sign of Jay. Along the hills and through the windy sky, thunder grumbled toward Dusk. When I glanced back at Judd, he was watching me with eyes that shone like cold, hard metal.

"Why—are you looking at me that way?"

He smiled a sick, sneering smile and said, "I'm trying to decide what I should do about you—what sort of little accident I should arrange."

Madness was in his eyes, paralyzing my thoughts as well as my body. He moved closer.

"No—please—" Inane, senseless words came from my mouth. I was trapped and he knew it. Positioned in the long, dead-end section of the kitchen, Judd Bradford's menacing hulk stood between me and the door. I took one step back and my left hand went up in a helpless gesture of defense. Judd's right arm lashed out and his thick fingers seized my wrist in a crushing grip. That initial moment of contact freed me from fear's paralysis and loosed all my fighting instincts. I struggled and fought to escape his grasp and in doing so my free hand bumped against the hot pan of soup sitting on the edge of the counter. My fingers found the handle and the next second I had flung the scalding liquid at Judd. He gave a surprised bellow of pain and let go of my wrist.

I knew I would have no second chance. While Judd groaned in pain and rushed to the sink, I bolted for the back door and wrenched it open. In an instant, I was outside and running, with the screen door banging shut behind me.

The wind fought and blew against me as I raced across the back lawn. The wild air tore at my lungs. I tried to force my legs to go faster, but I felt as if I were living a nightmare where one runs and runs but never covers any distance. I reached the open courtyard and paused for a few precious seconds to catch my breath. Where could I hide? Certainly not in the barn or sheds. I could think of nothing worse than being trapped like a hunted animal while Judd closed in for the kill. I glanced around wildly, but all the cars were gone and the corrals were empty.

Then, above the wind, I heard a nervous whinny. I put a hand to my pounding heart and stood perfectly still, straining to hear the sound again. It seemed to be coming from the direction of the barn. I ran toward the wooden structure and flung a hurried glance inside. Nothing but empty stalls and musty darkness. Perhaps in my desperation, I had only imagined what I wanted to hear. But no, there it was again—the unmistakable whinny of a frightened animal.

As I turned away from the barn, thunder roared like a cannon, exploding the air all around me. I covered my ears and turned my head to see that the wood on the side of the barn was splintered open. I fingered the torn, smoking wood, for a moment confused and uncomprehending. Then I looked across the courtyard to see Judd Bradford striding towards me, rifle in hand. Terror spurted through my veins and sent me racing around the side of the barn where I would be out of sight for a few moments.

Suddenly I saw her, grazing in tall grass along a wire fence and still saddled from earlier in the day when Stuart had ridden her. My knees nearly buckled under me and I felt like dropping to the ground and weeping with relief, but I forced myself to approach the mare at a calm walk.

Arabesque's black head lifted instantly and her big eyes blinked in recognition, but the wind and approaching storm had made her jumpy. As I moved closer, she jerked her head and shied away.

"Arabesque! Stay girl! Stay!"

Any moment now, Judd's stalking figure would appear around the side of the barn.

I tried to call the mare once again but my voice tightened into a sob. All I could do was hold out my hand to her and pray she would come.

Arabesque whinnied low, and, nodding her silky black head, advanced a few steps in my direction.

I swallowed hard. "That's a girl! Come on! Come to me, girl!"

The mare gave me one more appraising glance and trotted obediently to my side.

"That's a good girl," I murmured, grasping her reins with hands that were moist and shaking. I moved around to her left side and had one foot in the stirrup as Judd Bradford came into view. When he saw me he stopped dead and raised the rifle to his shoulder.

"All right! Just hold it right where you are!"

My hands gripped the saddle horn but I didn't dare lift myself up into the saddle. Judd's thick lips were set in a threatening line. He lowered the rifle a few inches.

Thunder grumbled through the clouds above us and Arabesque gave a nervous snort, side-stepping and tossing her head. I kept a tight hold on the reins and hopped after her, one foot still in the stirrup. Now, Arabesque was between me and Judd's rifle. I knew, instinctively, that he would never shoot the horse and leaped into the saddle.

"Let's go, girl!" I shouted, giving Arabesque a hard kick in the sides. No further urging was necessary. The mare burst forward with the energy and suddenness of an electric shock. Judd Bradford took one look at the black fury charging straight for him and made a frantic sideways dive. I dug my knees into the mare's smooth black sides and leaned forward with her into the wind as we streaked across the fields toward the cattle trail and Jay.

Chapter 21

"I wake and feel the fell of dark, not day.
What hours! O what black hours we have spent
This night!"
Gerard Manley Hopkins

Time and distance went unmeasured as Arabesque plunged up the cattle trail with me clinging to her back. I gave her full rein, thinking only that the faster we went, the sooner we would reach Jay. The mare seemed to share my need and surged along the dusty ridges with black fury that could only be matched by the storm threatening to break around us. It wasn't until the sky overhead was ripped in half by lightning, with thunder coming soon after like a convulsive roar of pain, that my terror of Judd Bradford began to recede and another fear, perhaps even more deadly, had its beginning. That first roll of thunder brought about a sudden increase in the mare's speed and every boom and rumble thereafter spooked the sensitive horse even more. I tried reining her in, but Arabesque's strength sparked by fear was too great for me to control. I leaned down closer to the sleek black head and spoke a few reassuring words, but my voice was swallowed up by a sudden gust of wind that spewed dust and dry bits of sage out of its mouth. My cheeks stung from the needle-like particles and my eyes burned from the dust. Another flash of yellow-white seared the sky and a scant second later the hills trembled from a deafening explosion of thunder. The terrified horse broke into a dead run. I clutched the saddle horn with one hand as she shot forward, and prayed I would be able to hold on.

The rain came down; first in large, hard drops that pelted the dusty trail, then in great gray sweeps that soaked Arabesque and me in a single gush. On and on we went, headlong into the storm. The rain was so heavy I could no longer distinguish the trail ahead. I gave up trying to see where we were going and cowered in the horse's mane, thinking if Arabesque's speed were any measure of distance covered, we should be very near the summer

189

range. In fact, we should have met Jay and Bert by now. Where were they? Or perhaps, a better question to ask might be, where was I?

I lifted my head slightly to peer through gray torrents of rain. I could just make out the heavy growth of pine and fir growing close on either side of the trail. Beyond that, I could see nothing. Arabesque's frantic pace had slowed somewhat and I knew by her heavy, ragged breathing and labored efforts that we were climbing steadily over rough terrain. I could recall nothing like this on the cattle trail. The mare's hooves went plunging into rushing water, clattering precariously over smooth stones in the stream bed. I gripped the saddle horn more tightly and felt my heart lurch inside me as the horse slipped, then regained her footing. Arabesque clambered up the bank, her breath coming in snorts and gasps. I pulled in hard on the reins and her gait slowed to a heaving walk, allowing me a brief glimpse of our surroundings. Through the soaking rain and mist, cliffs rose to great, lonely heights with dense pine forests huddling at their base. Suddenly, lightning sliced through the branches of a pine tree a mere ten yards away. The sharp crack and ear-splitting boom which followed shook the ground and sizzled the air.

My horse could take no more. Arabesque reared with a terrified scream and for a few seconds I felt the sudden freedom of nothing but wind and rain swooping around me. Then, came the comforting release of blackness. . . .

I had no way of knowing how long I was unconscious. It may have been a few seconds, or even minutes, but probably no more than that. When I came to, I was lying on my back with cold rain pounding my face and running down my body in rivulets. My clothes were soaked through and splattered with mud, feeling even colder than the rain itself. At first, I was afraid to move, but other than a throbbing head and general soreness, I didn't think I was badly injured by the fall. Slowly, I sat up. Cliffs, pines, rocks and rain were all I could see. Arabesque was gone. Even more slowly, I got to my feet.

The sky flashed white and I clapped my hands to my ears as thunder burst forth again. I had no earthly hope of finding Arabesque or the cattle trail as long as the storm lasted. I wiped rain and hair out of my eyes and peered about for a place of shelter. Only a few yards away, a massive pine flouted the storm's violence and I staggered toward it.

I knew perfectly well that getting under a tree during a thunderstorm was against all the rules, but I didn't have many alternatives. It was either risk the possibility of getting struck by lightning, or die of pneumonia by standing out in the rain. I ducked under the low, spreading branches of the tree and huddled down against the trunk. I was still drenched and shivering, but at least the wind and rain could no longer reach me. I settled down to wait out the storm, sharing the cozy inner world of the ancient pine with several birds and a few squirrels. I could hear the flutter of wings and rustling on the boughs overhead, and the squirrels did a first-rate job of scolding me for invading their privacy. I looked up through the denseness of needled boughs but could see neither bird nor squirrel. After a while, the chattering ceased and I assumed I had been accepted as a temporary resident of their home.

As the storm raged on, I became more and more grateful for my resin-scented shelter and the dry, needle-covered earth I sat upon. Peering out through the branches, the sky was very dark and I wondered what time it was. Jay must have returned to the ranch by now. I remembered Judd's tormented face, his big hands gripping a rifle, and said a fervent prayer for Jay's safety.

Thunder rolled across the cliffs and my head began to throb more insistently. I was so tired, so cold . . . I straightened my back against the scratchy trunk and tried to fight sleep, but it came creeping over me just the same.

When I awoke, my little shelter under the pine was very nearly dark and the troubled skies were still weeping. I realized the storm might last into the night and I couldn't control the sudden stabs of fear which set me trembling any more than I could control the elements which had trapped me. I buried my head in my lap to shut out the sounds of the storm and almost missed hearing another sound, moving in hollow rhythm with the rain. I sat up, straining forward to hear it again. The rhythmic clopping was louder now. My first thought was that Arabesque had found her way back to me and I scrambled out from underneath the pine tree, calling her name. But it wasn't the mare after all. Making its way up the canyon was a sturdy buckskin with a tall rider on its back. I shielded my eyes with my hand, but I couldn't be sure who it was. For one horrible moment I thought it was Judd coming after me, then the rider lifted his face into the storm and called out my name.

I started to run forward to meet him and fainted dead away to the ground.

Consciousness returned slowly, painfully. The first sensation to greet me out of the blackness was a queasy stomach and then hot dizziness. I was vaguely aware that my muddy blouse and Levis were being peeled away; then came the rough, masculine warmth of blankets and strong hands rubbing my chilled skin back to life. I wanted to open my eyes but the lids were too heavy. It was odd, concentrating so hard on such a simple thing. I heard a low voice repeating my name and finally my eyelids raised.

Jay was bending over me, his black hair dripping water down a face that was taut with anxiety. I looked into his eyes and smiled. The tight line of his jaw relaxed a little and he continued to massage my legs and feet. His touch

191

started a warm glow inside me that had nothing to do with the blankets or an increase in circulation.

I took a quick little breath and whispered, "I can't believe you're really here—that you've found me!"

"I've been half out of my mind for the past four hours!" His voice was harsh with relief. "I was beginning to think I'd never find you in this storm!"

I sighed and mumbled, " 'To an Indian, even the hummingbird leaves a trail through the air.' "

Jay's lips parted in a smile. "Come again? Where did you get that tidbit of knowledge?"

I tried to shake away the warm buzzing inside my head. "I—don't know. I think I read it somewhere. I don't know why I said that. I guess I'm the one who's half crazy."

"Shhh, just rest, love. You'll be all right now," he said gently, smoothing back my tangled hair with his long fingers.

I looked into his dark eyes and asked, "How did you find me?"

A worried look tightened the muscles of his face, but all he said was, "The important thing is, I did find you. We can talk later, after I've built a fire. Will you be all right for a few minutes while I go look for some wood?"

The thought of being alone again sent panic shooting through me but I gave him a quick nod and looked away from his concerned glance.

"Where are we?"

"In a cave, not too far from where I found you. I didn't dare risk taking you back to the ranch in this storm. Just stay put now and I'll be right back with some wood."

"I'm not exactly dressed to go exploring," I said, pulling the blankets around me more closely.

Jay grinned and got to his feet. The cave was fairly high-ceilinged, but not enough to allow straight passage for his six feet plus. He put on his hat and walked stoop-shouldered to the entrance, then out through the heavy gray curtain of rain.

I shivered in my blankets and glanced about our stony shelter. In the semi-darkness it was difficult to see much of anything, but the cave appeared to be five or six feet wide. I wasn't sure how far back it went, and staring into such gaping blackness made me feel even more nervous. More than once I was positive I heard something moving further back in the cave. It was a relief to hear the friendly clomp of Jay's boots outside.

He ducked his head as he came in and a stream of water poured off the brim of his hat. He looked at me through the gloom and asked, "You all right, love?"

"I am now."

Jay dropped the assortment of kindling he had been carrying and knelt down, rubbing his palms together. "I'll have a fire going in just a minute."

"How will it burn? The wood's all wet."

"Not all of it. I found some dry sage and twigs under the rocks and trees. Have a little faith in my ability to perform like my noble ancestors!"

I smiled and watched as he set about building a fire near the cave's mouth. From the way he quickly and expertly arranged the wood, I knew that making a campfire was about as difficult as breathing for him. Soon there was a merry little blaze shutting out the wind and damp and lighting the cave's dark walls with its warm glow.

I tried to sit up and my head issued forth a pounding protest. Jay noticed my movements and said, "Don't try to move, Angel. I'll go get something that should make you more comfortable."

He dived out into the storm again without putting on his hat, to return minutes later, dragging a saddle behind him. He took off his jacket and rubbed the saddle dry, then placed it on the rocky floor beside me. "Here you go. Lean back on this."

I rested my head on the saddle and gave him a grateful smile.

"How do you feel?" he asked.

"Well, I ache all over, but it's heaven to be warm and dry." A low growl came from beneath the blankets and I looked at Jay with an embarrassed grin. "My main complaint is I'm starving to death. I didn't eat any lunch and now that I think about it, I didn't have much chance for breakfast either."

"You're on your way to becoming a good Indian," Jay said, putting a brown hand to my cheek. "Many tribes made it a practice to fast quite regularly. It's good for the soul."

"Right now, I think I'd settle for a soul that wasn't quite so good and a stomach that wasn't quite so empty."

"I think I can oblige you," he said, smiling. "Helen packed lunches for Bert and me before we left this morning, and mine's right here in my saddle-bag. I didn't have time to eat it once we finished rounding up the cattle." Jay placed the leather pouch in my lap and added, "Knowing Helen, she probably made enough for an army."

I grabbed the bag and eagerly inspected its contents. There were three sandwiches stuffed with fat slices of roast beef, two carrots, a hunk of cheese, a monstrous piece of apple pie and a thermos filled with lemonade.

"Oh, this is marvelous! I never expected a banquet!"

"You go right ahead and eat. I've got to get some more wood."

"More wood? Don't we have enough?"

"Not nearly enough to last all night. And by the looks of this storm, that's how long we're going to be here."

"But you're soaking wet, and your jacket—"

"I'm fine. I've got to get as much wood as I can before dark."

193

"It's already dark."

"All right. Before it gets any darker."

I relented with a sigh and he bent down to kiss my lips and my throat. I traced the hollow under one of his cheekbones and whispered, "If you take too long, I can't promise there'll be any food left."

Jay gave me what Janet would have described as a 'deep, dark look' and said, "I'll be sure to hurry then."

After he had gone I watched the firelight make dancing shadows on the cave's dark walls and ate my little meal, leaving half for Jay. The roast beef sandwiches were wonderful, and I didn't mind that the cheese was a little dry, the carrots rubbery. The pie was pretty well squashed and the lemonade lukewarm at best, but I enjoyed every morsel.

I had just finished eating when Jay's hunched over figure entered the cave. Raindrops dripped off his nose and glistened on his black hair. He dumped the load of branches and twigs onto the first pile of wood, flashed me a smile, and went out into the rain once again. Jay made several trips before the woodpile was of a size to satisfy him, but his last load was not kindling. Instead, he entered the cave with his arms full of wet pine boughs. Their fresh, living smell intertwined with the pungent aroma of woodsmoke and the blend was intoxicating.

"Well, that does it," he pronounced, setting the pine boughs carefully aside from the firewood.

I stared at him with open curiosity. "What are the boughs for?"

"Our bed," he answered, tossing away his soaked hat.

"Our—? Oh!"

Jay's mouth bent in a crooked grin and amusement was bright in his eyes. I knew he saw me exactly as I was: a completely inexperienced and rather nervous girl of twenty.

"You won't believe how comfortable a pine bed can be until you've tried it," Jay said, sitting down cross-legged opposite me.

"Won't it be rather—er, wet?"

"Not a bit. Once I've finished making it, I'll cover the whole thing with the waterproof ground cloth Bert used to wrap the blankets in." He unfastened the buttons on his shirt, then stripped it off and flung it aside. "I promise you, this will be a night to remember."

My eyes must have popped wide as an owl's, but I managed to keep my mouth from falling open. Jay's mouth was definitely twitching as he got up to add more wood to the fire. I watched as he broke a few branches over his knee to make smaller pieces for burning. His black hair hung wet and shining around his face and firelight danced across the muscles of his bronze chest.

"You know, you're the first girl I've ever built a pine bed for," he said without looking up.

I swallowed and cleared my throat. "Maybe you'd better explain that last statement. Does that mean you've built other kinds of beds for other girls?"

Jay looked at me and said quietly, "It means you're the only girl I've ever wanted to share any kind of bed with."

I felt the effect of his words deep inside me. A breathless moment passed before I could speak. "Then, you've never—"

He smiled and shook his head.

"Then why did you let me think?—Oh! You and your night to remember!" He burst out laughing and I picked up one of my sneakers and flung it at him. It was a futile gesture because Jay caught the shoe neatly in one hand.

"Why don't you toss the other one over here and I'll put them by the fire along with your clothes," he suggested with another laugh.

"You're terrible," I told him, throwing the other shoe, and laughing myself.

"I know. Is there anything else you'd care to contribute to the cause?"

Jay had draped my blouse and Levis over a long pole held up at either end by two forked sticks. Now he added his shirt and jacket to the pole and placed my shoes underneath.

"My underthings have dried very nicely where they are," I said.

Jay left the fire and moved close beside me. In his dark eyes, all traces of amusement had vanished. I pushed the saddlebag between us and said, "I left half the food for you."

"Oh, thanks. At least one of my appetites will be satisfied."

I smiled and kissed him on the ear.

"You keep that up and I'll forget about the food," he warned.

I laughed and pushed the damp masses of hair back from my face. "I don't know how you can stand to look at me! What I wouldn't give for a comb!"

Jay swallowed a mouthful of roast beef and said, "Why don't you do it the way it was last night. I liked that."

"You mean braids? I suppose I could, but it takes both hands and right now I need one hand to hold up this silly blanket."

Jay's dark brows lifted. "I'll be glad to help."

A high whinny sounded above the rain and wind and I said abruptly, "What was that?"

"My horse. Don't worry, he's out of the storm. I found a sheltered place under the cliffs. He'll be fine 'til morning."

I sighed and looked past the fire to the pouring rain. "I hope Arabesque is all right. I hate to think of her running scared out there somewhere."

"She's not. She came back to the ranch about a half hour after Bert and I got back from Tyler's."

"She did? Is she all right?"

"She was pretty frightened and dead beat, but Bert'll give her a good rubdown and keep a close watch on her."

I was silent while Jay finished eating. He took a gulp of lemonade and pulled a face. "This stuff is awful! How did you stand it?"

"It's a little warm, but I thought it tasted quite good."

He screwed the cap back on the thermos and put it aside. "What happened, Angel? Did Arabesque throw you?"

I nodded. "But it wasn't her fault. She was terrified of the storm. I just wasn't able to control her. It was all I could do to hang on! After a while, she tired and I was able to rein her in. But by that time we were good and lost. Lightning struck a tree a few yards away from us and Arabesque reared and threw me. I was unconscious for a short while and when I came to she was gone. I crawled underneath a big pine tree to get out of the storm. If you hadn't come, I suppose that's where I'd be spending the night."

Jay's arm came around me and he pressed my head against his chest. His skin was warm and smooth and smelled faintly of woodsmoke. I snuggled closer within his arms.

"You still haven't said how you found me," I said after a while. "Arabesque couldn't have left much trail to follow with the rain as heavy as it was."

"No, she didn't leave a trail. Not one that I could find, anyway. Looking back, I don't know how I knew where to look for you. Maybe it was that 'trail through the air' you talked about . . ." I lay still in his arms, feeling a sudden tenseness in his body. "If Arabesque hadn't come back when she did, I never would have known you were up here."

"What happened after you and Bert got back from Tyler's?" I asked with a tenseness akin to his.

"Well, the first thing we noticed was that all the cars were gone and nobody was around. That had me pretty worried. I found my grandfather up in his room, just sitting and staring out the window. I asked him where the family was and he said everyone had gone to the hospital—that there'd been an accident, something about John being hurt. When I asked if you'd gone with the others he wouldn't answer. All he would tell me over and over was that 'everyone's gone.' I was leaving the house when the phone rang. It was Mrs. Tyler calling to let you know that Bert and I were on our way back. I found out from her that you had been trying to reach me all morning and that Uncle John had been hurt in an accident with the truck. She told me you had stayed behind to take care of my grandfather.

"When I hung up the phone I was ready to go back upstairs and beat the truth out of the old man if I had to, but then, Bert came tearing into the kitchen to tell me that Arabesque had just come back, riderless and reins dragging. I didn't know, but I figured you must have gone looking for me up the cattle trail and become lost in the storm. Bert grabbed some heavy blankets and wrapped them in the ground cover while I saddled a fresh horse. It was just a wild guess that made me think you might have gone up the Right Fork instead of the Left."

"Is that where we are?" I moved out of Jay's arms to face him in astonishment. "Bert told me once how easy it is to get lost up here, what wild country it is. You might never have found me."

Our eyes met in wonder and silent consideration of what had happened. Then Jay said, "I'd better get started on the bed. While I work you can tell me what happened this morning—and why you rode off on Arabesque to find me," he added with a tightly set mouth.

I leaned back against the saddle and explained to Jay that I had overheard his grandfather and uncle discussing plans for the day, and that Judd had insisted Jay be the one to drive the truckload of milk into town. When I described the accident, Jays' hands ceased their work with the boughs.

"Is John all right?"

"I don't know. He was hurt quite seriously, I think. It took so long for Thayne and the others to get him out. He was unconscious when they put him in the back of Thompson's stationwagon."

"What about my grandfather? Where was he while all this was happening?"

I looked away from his probing glance, wondering just how much I should tell him. "Well, after Stuart told us that John had been hurt, Judd began acting strangely and saying things—"

"What did he say?" Jay asked quietly. I looked at him and he said, "It's all right. I want you to tell me."

"Well, Judd kept insisting that it couldn't be John who was hurt—"

"Because he had intended it to be me," Jay finished, and the expression in his eyes made my heart ache.

"Jay, your grandfather is ill! The thoughts of anyone finding out what he did to your father have made him desperate! I—I can't make myself believe that he hates you or really wants to hurt you. It's just that he's so afraid."

Jay was concentrating fiercely on breaking and arranging the pine boughs. "Go on. What did the others think when Judd started acting up?"

"Oh, they all thought the shock of what had happened was too much for him. No one really paid much attention to what he said. Thayne and

Helen got Judd upstairs to his room and gave him a strong sedative. He was asleep when everyone left for the hospital."

"And you were left alone in the house—with him," Jay said slowly.

I wrapped the blanket about my shoulders and stared into the greedy orange flames of the fire. "I called Tyler's several times trying to reach you, as Mrs. Tyler said. I kept hoping you'd get back before your grandfather woke up, but—but he—" I bit down on my lower lip to stop its trembling.

"What happened? What did he do to you?"

I swallowed hard and tried to smile away the look in Jay's eyes. "Nothing happened. I was frightened, but I got away before he—nothing happened."

"Angela, if you won't tell me, I'll get it out of Judd one way or another. I don't care if he is my grandfather! I want to know what happened!"

I looked away from his angry face and leaned my head back on the saddle. On the cave's black ceiling, leaping shadows of flame made grotesque patterns.

"I was waiting in the kitchen—to be near the phone—when Judd came downstairs. The minute he began talking I knew he was still very upset. He seemed to think I was a threat to him, that you and I were trying to destroy him! I thought if I could talk to him and keep him calm until you got back, everything would be all right, but—I only upset him more. I told Judd that you had your father's diary, and soon everyone would know the truth of what had happened. I guess that panicked him. He—he grabbed hold of me, but I got away from him and ran outside. I didn't know what to do. There weren't any horses in the barn or corrals. Then, I heard thunder—only it wasn't thunder. The bullet hit the barn just above my head. Judd was coming. I saw the rifle in his hands. I ran—I ran behind the barn and saw Arabesque. Judd told me to stop but I didn't. We made straight for him. He jumped aside just in time. I think he dropped the rifle, I'm not sure. I never looked back . . ."

Jay was sitting motionless with a wet pine bough across his lap.

"That's all," I said. "You know the rest."

"That's all—that's all!" he repeated hoarsely, his hands clenching the branch so tightly the knuckles showed white.

I clutched my blanket with one hand and made my way over to his side. He flinched when I touched his shoulder.

"Jay, I'm so sorry," I murmured, knowing there were no words I could speak which would take away his anger or ease his anguish. My hand dropped from his shoulder.

"Maybe it doesn't matter, but even after what happened this afternoon, I can't hate your grandfather. I'm afraid of him—and I feel sorry for him, but—I don't hate him. And I don't think you do either," I added softly.

Jay broke the branch over his knee with a vicious snap. "I wish I could hate him! If that bullet had hit you! If I'd come back today and found you—"

I leaned my head against his shoulder and laid a hand across his chest. "Don't think about something that didn't happen. I'm safe, and you're safe—and we're together!"

The muscles of his chest eased their tightness and I could feel the surge in tempo of his heartbeat against my palm.

"Thank God for that!" he whispered fiercely and crushed me to him. His mouth found mine then wandered to the curve of my neck and my shoulders. Somehow, my blanket had slipped down to my waist and Jay's hands encouraged it.

"Jay, darling—maybe we shouldn't—"

He released me and I drew the blanket up around my shoulders once more. We looked into one another's eyes.

"Every time I hold you I forget this cave isn't at all like the place I had in mind for our honeymoon," he said in a husky tone. "I'm sorry, Angel. I'd better finish that bed."

Jay started to work on the boughs once more and it moved me to see that his fingers were trembling.

"What's it like?" I asked softly.

"Hmmm?"

"The place you had in mind for our honeymoon."

"Oh. A friend of mine has some land and a cabin outside of Jackson Hole. I go there often to paint. The cabin's completely secluded and pretty rustic. There's no telephone or electricity, but it has a big natural rock fireplace and an old cast iron stove nicknamed 'Belch-fire' that can bake the best biscuits you ever tasted. Behind the cabin is a big stand of pines and aspens with wildflowers that are almost unbelievable. Below it there's a stream and a clearing. It's the kind of place where deer come in the morning, and at night the sky is so thick with stars you can hardly see the blue."

"It sounds like heaven!"

"With you there, it will be," he said quietly. "Well, your bed's just about ready. I'll just spread the ground cover over the boughs. It's not very fancy but it'll be a lot softer than bare rock. Care to try it out?"

I moved over to the bed and lay down rather gingerly, as if it were a bed of spikes instead of boughs. I was surprised to find the framework of boughs made a soft, resilient mattress. I relaxed full length upon the bed with a sigh. "It is comfortable! And it smells wonderful! Is there a pine bed in our honeymoon cabin?" I asked him, smiling.

Jay bent down and kissed the tip of my nose. "No. Just a big old iron

199

bed with springs that squeak every time you roll over."

I thought about this for a moment. "I guess it's not possible to oil bed springs, is it?"

Jay looked at my face and laughed. "I'm afraid not, Angel-love, but that's all right. There'll be no one but the squirrels to hear us."

I reached up suddenly and pulled his dark head down to meet mine, pressing my lips against his with a fervor that took him completely by surprise.

"Oh, Angel," he moaned against my mouth. "Do you have any idea how much I want you?"

I let go my arms from around his neck and Jay raised himself on one elbow. We looked at one another, each feeling the strain of emotions crying out for release, and aching with a need that as yet, was unfulfilled. I pressed my palms against his bare chest and whispered, "I love you, Jayhawk!"

His eyes darkened into black flames and his words were both a promise and a vow. "One day very soon, you will know how much I love you. But for now, try to get some sleep, Angel."

"What about you?"

"I don't feel like sleeping. Besides, I've got to keep the fire going." He moved to the woodpile and added a few branches to the fire, then sat down cross-legged before it, one hand lying idle across each knee. His straight black hair hung down on either side of his face, with firelight accentuating the high cheekbones and deep-set eyes.

I lay on my side, watching his strong, erect figure and thought I had never seen him look so completely Indian as now. I felt a deep sense of wonder that I was loved by a man such as this.

The fire snapped and hissed, sending up tiny, orange-blue waves of flame that lapped at the air. Outside the cave, the rain added its wet rhythm to the night's music. I closed my eyes, but found after minutes had passed that sleep was slow in coming. Jay's dark eyes were still brooding before the fire.

"What are you thinking about?" I asked softly.

For a moment I thought he hadn't heard me, but then he turned his gaze away from the flames and said, "I was remembering another time, years ago, when I came up the Right Fork trail. Strange, how looking into a fire can stir up the embers of memories you think have grown cold." He poked at a blackened branch with the tip of his boot and smiled to himself. "I was only thirteen—no, fourteen years old."

"Why did you come?"

Jay glanced at me. "Do you know anything about initiation ceremonies that Indian boys used to take to become men?"

"Weren't they strength or endurance tests of some kind?"

"Yes. The test varied a little depending upon the particular tribe, but they all had the same basic purpose. A boy was to go away from his family and tribe, usually into rough wilderness, and remain there for a period of time, living off the land, enduring hardship, to prove he was a man."

"Wasn't there some religious significance as well? Something about a vision—or an animal?"

Jay nodded. "You're thinking of the guardian spirit who would guide the boy throughout his manhood. The Indians believed this spirit would manifest itself in the form of an animal which the boy would see in a vision sometime during his ordeal. After the test was over, the boy returned to his family and told them of his experiences. Then one of the old men of the tribe selected a new name for him.

"When I was a child, I loved to listen to the stories of the old men on the reservation. I can still remember my mother telling me the story of her grandfather's initiation ceremony. She told me many times that she wanted me to have an Indian name when I reached manhood, as well as my given one. After she died, I made a vow that I would somehow take a test to prove my manhood—even if I had no one to prepare me for it or listen to my experiences afterwards. And, if necessary, I would choose my own name."

My heart tugged within me at his determination, and the struggle it must have been to keep his identity as an Indian.

"I had been living at the ranch about six years when I decided the time had come. It was my fourteenth summer. I didn't really know what I was going to do or how I should go about it, but early one morning before it was light, I ran away from the ranch and headed for the hills."

"Didn't you tell John or Helen where you were going?"

Jay shook his head and grinned at me. "No. I was afraid they might try to stop me if they knew. I suppose I could have told Bert, but I didn't want him to get into trouble if the family asked him where I was. All I took with me was an old knife which had belonged to my mother's father. I'd heard a lot about how wild and rugged the canyons were up the Right Fork, so that's where I headed. It took most of the day, just walking, before I was satisfied that no one would find me. By nightfall, my belly was beginning to feel like a big, empty hole and my throat burned like it was full of sand."

"Oh, Jay! You should have taken the time to pack some food! Wasn't there any water you could drink?"

He gave me an indulgent smile. "Yes, there was plenty of water. And food, too, if I had wanted it. Most initiation ceremonies only require the boy to live off the land, but I chose a more difficult test for myself. I guess, partly, because I wanted to prove to myself and the world, that I could do anything a full-blooded Indian could."

He looked deep into the fire and when he spoke again, his voice had taken on a new timbre, low and vibrant. "I'll never forget that first night in the mountains—the stars, the sounds, and the stillness. I didn't think I'd ever be able to sleep, but when I did, I dreamed my father's spirit was calling to me. I don't remember anything in particular that he said, but he felt—nearby. I awoke in the middle of the night calling his name and my face was wet with tears."

Jay poked at the fire with a blackened branch a minute longer than was really necessary, and I kept silent, realizing that this memory must be a sensitive one to recall, let alone share with someone.

"The next morning I explored the canyon I was in and tried to look for some sign or animal that might give me my Indian name. Nothing happened of any importance. Once, I caught a glimpse of a mountain lion sunning himself on a rock, but he didn't look much like a guardian spirit to me, so I took off in another direction. By mid-afternoon, I was feeling pretty weak and dejected. The sun was hot and there wasn't so much as a breeze to move the air. I could hear a stream just below me and that cold, rushing water was getting more tempting every minute. I sat down to rest and noticed a young hawk in some brush a few yards away. Its talons were caught in the undergrowth and he couldn't free himself. I don't know how long he'd been there, but he looked even more hungry and thirsty than I was. When I approached him we looked at each other and I felt inside that this hawk was to be my guardian spirit. I told the hawk that he must trust me and I would help him. I went down to the stream, took off my shoes and filled them with water then came back to the hawk. I could see how much he wanted the water but he still had enough fight left in him to beat his wings and hiss at me.

"I talked to him for a minute, then poured the water in a slow trickle, just above his head and let him drink. When he had his fill I went down to the stream and drank also. I've never tasted anything sweeter in my life than that cold mountain water! The hawk was quiet and still the whole time I cut him loose and when he was free, he perched on my hand. His talons cut up my wrist a bit, but I was proud because now we were brothers. I told him he was free and the hawk looked at me as if he weren't sure what he should do. Then he took flight and I watched him soar up to the cliffs.

"I started back for the ranch late that afternoon, walking pretty shaky but feeling every inch a man. I'd gotten as far as where the Right Fork joins the cattle trail when I met Uncle John. He'd been riding the hills and hunting for me for two days and he was plenty mad. I remember staggering up to his horse and him asking me where the hell I'd been, and if I enjoyed worrying people to death."

"What did you tell him?" I asked with a sleepy smile.

"Just that I'd gone to prove my manhood the Indian way. John told me

202

if I ever tried anything like that again he'd prove his manhood to me behind the woodshed with a willow switch. Helen was pretty upset about the whole thing, too, but she tended to my hand where the hawk had clawed me and never said a word." Jay chuckled, then sighed. "I really put those poor folks though a lot."

"What about Bert? Did you tell him anything about your experiences?"

"I told him all of it—except the dream about my father. You're the only one who knows about that. Bert was the one who suggested my Indian name. He thought 'Jayhawk' sounded good."

"Jayhawk," I repeated softly, looking at the black-haired figure seated before the fire. "It is a good name."

Jay laughed softly to himself. "I remember Bert telling me afterwards that 'you gall darn Indians sure go to a hell of a lot of trouble jest to change yer name!' "

I smiled, then yawned, feeling relaxed and drowsy.

"Jayhawk talk too much," he grunted in mock Indian fashion. "You sleep now."

Whether my mind was merely acting upon the experience Jay had related to me earlier that evening I didn't know, but during the night I dreamed of Jason, his father. Jason's face was never clear to me, but his presence was so overwhelmingly real I awoke with a start, my heart thudding and my eyes wide. I saw at a glance that the fire was nearly out. Only a few orange coals remained, glowing brightly amid the charred wood and ashes. Beyond the fire, the cave was very dark. But I could make out Jay's figure, his head slumped over his chest in sleep. Outside the cave, the fury of the storm was spent and the wind was still. My ears could barely hear the light, drizzling rain that fell.

I knew of a surety that I was wide awake, that the dream was gone, and yet the sense of Jason's presence remained. The feeling became too much to bear. I sat straight up and called his name aloud.

My voice and sudden movement roused Jay from sleep and he sprang to his feet, knocking his head on the low ceiling.

"Angela! What is it? What's the matter?"

"Your father," I whispered, starting to tremble all over.

Jay dropped to his knees beside me and gathered me in his arms. "It's all right, sweetheart. You must have been dreaming, that's all."

I couldn't explain to him what I had felt. It was still too real for me to speak. I could only cling to him, letting the warmth of his body flow into mine. Jay held me until my trembling had ceased, then said softly, "I'd better get the fire going again. It's a good thing you woke me when you did or it would have gone out."

He crawled away from me to kneel before the dying embers. He fed them small bits of sage and twigs, gently blowing life back into the coals. As these were consumed, he added larger pieces of wood to the flames until the fire was once more blazing high and filling the cave with its crackling warmth.

My fears gone, I could be practical again. "Are my clothes dry yet?" I asked him. "I think maybe I'd better get dressed."

Jay felt my Levis and blouse, then pulled them off the pole. He brought them to me with a smiling offer of assistance. "Need any help?"

I clutched my clothes in one hand and my blanket with the other. "Look, I know this is going to sound silly because—well, because you undressed me in the first place—but do you think you could—"

"Go take a walk in the rain, maybe? That sounds like a good idea, but it's practically stopped raining."

"You don't need to go outside," I said, smiling at him. "Couldn't you just fiddle with the fire, or explore the cave or something for a few minutes?"

"Well, since you've given me a choice, I think I'll go exploring. I'm curious to see how far back the cave goes."

Jay picked up a pine branch bare of needles with a cluster of sticky pine cones on one end, and thrust the cones into the flames. They ignited immediately, providing him with a brightly burning torch.

I watched him move stoop-shouldered toward the back of the cave and said, "I suppose if there were any mountain lions back there we'd have heard them by now."

"More likely, we'd have smelled them," he said with a grin. "I'll give you three minutes to get dressed, love."

My clothes were warm and dry and smelled wonderfully of woodsmoke. I got into them eagerly, then put on my stockings and shoes. When Jay didn't return in the prescribed three minutes I assumed he must have found something of interest farther back in the cave. I sat contentedly before the fire, braiding my hair.

More minutes passed and I could hear nothing of Jay's return. I could hear nothing at all. I got to my feet and spoke his name but my only answer was cold, empty silence. I stood for several seconds, staring at the blackness of the cave where Jay had gone, feeling fear drive itself deep into my heart. Then I took slow, careful steps forward, my arms outstretched and my hands feeling the black air for any obstacles. After a few blind steps, I found the walls narrowed on either side so I could reach out and touch bare rock with both hands. I felt my way along a narrow passageway and discovered that it made a sudden curve to the right. Up ahead, I saw the wavering flame of Jay's torch. The meager light revealed another room, smaller than the first, with a lower ceiling. It was here I found him, kneeling at the head of a humped mound of rocks.

"Jay—what is it?"

He kept his face averted from mine but reached out his hand. I stooped low and entered the dark chamber, walking around the odd mound to where Jay was kneeling. I gave him my hand and his fingers grasped mine so tightly I winced.

He raised the burning branch to the head of the rock mound where a wooden marker had been fixed. I bent forward to read the roughly carved words.

"Here lies my son Jason
May God forgive me"

"Oh, dear heaven!" I whispered and sank to my knees beside him.

I knelt with Jay on the rough stone floor while the torch slowly burned itself out and thick darkness closed around us. When his fierce grip on my hand lessened, I sensed that he wanted to be alone. I pressed my cheek to his hand, then gently withdrew my fingers and left.

I found my way back to the campfire, feeling dazed and numb. I sat down on the pine bed and stared dully into the flames. Twenty-six years. For twenty-six years this forlorn place had been Jason Bradford's tomb. Unknown. Undiscovered. Until tonight. Now, Jason had a son to mourn his death.

I was exhausted but I couldn't sleep. Not as long as Jay kept his lonely vigil beside his father's grave. Minutes lengthened into hours and I began to wonder if Jay were going to spend the rest of the night in that small dark chamber.

The night was still and silent. The only sound in all the world was the crackle and hiss of the fire.

I buried my face in my hands and prayed he would come back. Some time later, I heard slow, dragging footsteps and Jay appeared out of the cave's inner blackness.

"Angela—I thought you'd be asleep."

"No. I wanted to wait for you."

He avoided my eyes and sat down beside me on the bed of boughs.

I wasn't sure what to say, or even if anything should be said. We sat wordless before the fire for a long while. Finally, I placed a hand across his thigh and asked, "Aren't you tired?"

"I don't know. I guess so."

The dull, tortured look in his eyes brought a familiar ache to my throat, making it difficult to speak.

"Would it help if you talked about it? I'm not asking you to, but—"

Jay's lips parted in a thin smile and he covered my hand with his. "Don't look so sad, Angel. I'm all right. I've known for a long time that he was dead, only—" His voice suddenly tightened up and he wasn't able to go on. After a moment he drew a ragged breath and cleared his throat. "Even though he's been dead for twenty-six years, I feel like it happened tonight. You think you're prepared for something—and then it happens and you find out you weren't ready for it at all. He's dead. I know it, but I don't want to believe it! I wish!—I wish I could have known him!"

Jay turned his head away, but not before I saw moisture brimming in his dark eyes. This moved me more than all his self-control and strength. My own lashes were wet as I reached out for him. I laid my cheek against the dark hair that hid his face from me. With head bent low, he turned and put his arms about me, then slowly drew me down onto the bed of boughs. We clung to one another out of desperation as well as love, discovering a depth of peace and consolation in each other's arms that mere words could never bring.

Chapter 22

"Let age speak the truth and give us
peace at last."

Robert Browning

Pale daylight filtered into the cave, diluting the darkness to a ghostly gray and making it a much more fearsome, forlorn place than it had been the night before. With a storm raging in the night, the cave had been our shelter, a haven of warmth and protection. Now, it felt as cold and lifeless as the blackened wood and gray ash of the campfire.

I rolled over and discovered that Jay no longer lay beside me. I was alone. This realization and the chill of early dawn forced me to my feet. I snatched up the blanket that had covered me and made for the entrance.

Outside, a tender sky of pale blue belied the raw chill in the air. My breath went out in frosty puffs before my face and I wrapped the blanket about my shoulders.

The cave was only a small hollow cut into the face of a steep, wooded hillside, but its location gave me a wide vantage point of the surrounding country. Below the cave, dense, tangled undergrowth eventually gave way to a clearing and the stream Arabesque had plunged through the day before. A trail, narrow and rocky, led my eyes away from the clearing and down canyon where trees and foliage were soaking in a cold mist. My gaze lifted from the winding canyon to a rugged horizon where bony ridges of rock were thrust against the pale sky like gigantic vertebrae. The profile of the eastern mountains was etched with a fine line of silver. As I watched, the contrast between jagged peaks and pale sky sharpened to an intense point of clarity. I blinked, and the next moment the line had softened, the silver warming to a hazy gold. I bowed my head as the sun reached blinding fingers of yellow-white over the mountains, feeling a little guilty that the beauties of a sunrise should still move me after last night's sobering discovery.

The whinny of a horse, sounding like husky shivers of air, came from somewhere nearby. I turned my head to see Jay leading the black-maned buckskin out of a sheltered cove of rocks slightly downhill from the cave. I walked down to meet him, noting that his face was haggard and drawn. Even so, he gave me a smile and tugged at one of my braids.

"You're walking a bit shaky on your pins this morning," he said.

"Oh, I'm all right."

Jay bent his head to give me a kiss. "We can leave just as soon as I pack the gear."

"Can I help?"

"No. Just pull up a rock and sit yourself down."

I smiled at him and said, "I love you," then glanced away, still unaccustomed to giving such free expression to my feelings.

Jay tied the horse's reins to a sturdy bush and turned back to me. "You can say that as often as you like. I don't mind."

He placed both hands on my shoulders and looked into my eyes so deeply and for so long that I finally hid my face against his shoulder, a blush warming my skin. His arms moved around my back and mine went around him. We stood close together with the hush of morning around us and the gentle sun touching our shoulders.

A sudden scurrying in some brush nearby brought us out of our embrace, and we looked to see a gray squirrel dart across the path. He gave Jay and me a sharp, black-eyed glance then scampered past the cave, heading for a narrow trail which scraped its way through rocks and brush along the very edge of the mountain. Both squirrel and trail disappeared in a steep tumble of rocks some fifteen to twenty feet high.

I noticed Jay's dark eyes taking in every detail of the rockslide with unusual interest and asked, "What is it? What do you see?"

He shrugged. "Nothing. Just the slide. But it suddenly hit me that somewhere around here my father was killed." His gaze wandered from the mountainside to the canyon below, then back to the steep rockslide. "I'd like to climb that trail to the slide and have a look around," he said. "That is, if you think you'll be all right for a few minutes."

"I'd like to go with you."

"Do you think you're up to it?"

"I can make it."

Jay took my hand. "Let's go then."

Hunger and weakness made the climb seem much longer and steeper than it actually was. When we reached the rockslide my heart was pounding in my ears and my legs were shaking. I leaned against the rocky face of the cliff to catch my breath while Jay looked over the edge of the precipice.

"Come look at this," he said. "Down below is the trail you took last night."

I went, rather reluctantly, and peered down some fifty feet or so into a thickly wooded ravine. There were wildflowers, a swiftly moving stream of white water, and as Jay had said, a trail. It first appeared out of a tall stand of aspens some thirty yards away, then wandered at will through the underbrush until it passed directly beneath the rockslide. I backed away from the edge and sat down on a large rock at the base of the slide.

"What do you expect to see—or find?" I asked.

"I don't know. All morning I've been trying to figure out what might have happened—trying to piece all the facts together and see what sort of picture they make." He looked out over the canyon and sighed. "I know from the diary that my dad found one of his horses somewhere up the Right Fork, and that the rest were probably hidden in a canyon up here somewhere. Since Judd wouldn't tell him where, Dad must have left the ranch early the next morning to look for the horses himself. My grandfather followed him and—" Jay cut himself off sharply.

"We know Judd was here, but I don't believe he killed your father in cold blood. Even after all that's happened, Judd doesn't seem like the kind of man who would value ten horses more than the life of his own son."

"Maybe not. I'm not saying what happened couldn't have been an accident, but—whatever it was—my father died somewhere near here." Jay was silent for a moment then turned away from the deep ravine and looked up at the slide. "I'll bet this trail continues on the other side of those rocks," he said suddenly.

"What if it does?"

"Well, my dad came up here looking for horses. If Judd hid them somewhere near here, it would be in a place where they couldn't roam too far or get back to the ranch—maybe in a side canyon with an open meadow that would be good for grazing."

"You think Judd hid the horses somewhere up this trail?"

"It's possible."

"But how could he get ten horses over the rockslide? It blocks the trail completely and the dropoff is too steep to try and go around it."

"Maybe the slide wasn't here when he hid the horses. That was twenty-six years ago." Jay nudged one of the boulders with the toe of his boot. "These rocks look too sharp and loose to have been here for too long a period of time."

"It does look as if part of the hillside sort of fell away. Maybe an avalanche of snow during the winter."

"Could be. I'd like to have a look at what's on the other side."

"You're not going to climb the slide?"

Jay smiled at my concern. "That's the best way I know to get to the other side." He reached down and took both my hands in his. "I won't be gone long—just fifteen minutes or so. Then I'll get you right back to the ranch. My idea may be all wrong, but I've got to find out. I've got to know!"

I nodded my understanding. "I'll wait here."

His lips brushed mine, then he released my hands. I tilted my head back to watch him climb nimbly up the slide, his practiced eye choosing fairly stable footholds on the loose rock. At the top, he paused and shouted down in jubilant tones: "I was right! The trail picks up again and goes way back into the canyon!" The next moment he was over the top and out of sight, with only the dubious assurance of clattering rock to signify his presence. I let out a tense breath as I heard him land neatly on stable earth and take off down the trail at a fast sprint. Then I leaned back against the rocky face of the cliff to wait.

Across the canyon, the sun was warming the great cliffs and pine forests, but as yet, the rockslide was still in the shadow of the hills. I sat in contemplative silence, wondering where, in all this peace and loveliness, a man had been killed. Soon, sunlight was spilling over the far edge of the rockslide and I moved over to feel its warmth. I stared down into the ravine where wildflowers were tasting the mildness of mountain sunshine. Indian paintbrush, blue lupines, and milky white columbines with golden throats swayed in the clear, cool air. A brown shadow splashed across the green glade and I tilted my head back to see a hawk sailing along rain-fresh currents of air. I followed his smooth flight, envying his winged freedom to explore the jagged canyons and mountaintops along aerial pathways. Suddenly, he plunged downward toward the forest, disappearing in a dense cover of pines and aspens. At that precise moment, a horse and rider moved out of the trees and into the sunlight.

I stared at the thick, powerful figure astride a big brown stallion, my heart choking me and my brain numb with disbelief. In all the maze of trails and canyons up the Right Fork, how could Judd have known we were here? It wasn't possible, and yet, here he was, guiding his horse along the canyon trail below me.

Instinct insisted that I crouch down, for there was always the chance that Judd might glance up as he passed by, but fear held me in its grasp. I could only sit in rigid silence and watch as Judd rode directly beneath the rockslide, his blue-eyed scowl searching the heavy growth of trees and brush growing along both sides of the trail. I realized then that Judd didn't know we were here, but in all the world, this was the one place he didn't want us to be. Fear had driven him up the Right Fork.

The soft forest earth yielded no sound as the big stallion carried his master toward the hillside cave. The only sounds were the cheerful twittering of a forest bird and the splashing stream below. I couldn't see Judd, but I heard the nickering of his horse and the answering whinny of another. Moments later, his stalking figure appeared out of the brush, moving in slow, deliberate silence toward the cave. A rifle was clenched tightly in his hands. Judd paused at the cave's entrance, cocked the rifle, and crept inside.

The instant he had gone I whirled about and started clambering up the rockslide. At best, I would have only a few seconds before Judd realized we weren't inside the cave. I knew, instinctively, where he would look next. The rocks were sharp and treacherous under my feet, but desperation made it impossible to tread quietly. Each falling stone sounded like an avalanche. I was slightly more than halfway to the top when an insistent, dry rattle halted my frantic climb.

The snake must have come out of the rocks to warm itself and was probably as startled by my sudden appearance as I was his. I took one look at the fat, leathery coils on a rock just above me and leaped backwards with a terrified scream. Rocks rolled and shifted under my feet. The sky was pushing me down toward the ravine. Another cry tore out of my throat as I fought for balance, my arms waving wildly at my sides. With a painful lunge, I pushed the sky away and threw my body face downward on the slide. My fingers clawed among the sharp rocks for a handhold while my body slithered down toward the edge of the cliff. I saw one large boulder jutting out from the rest and threw my left arm around its solid girth. Thankfully, it held fast, although the slide was restless and grumbling. Small stones and gravel skipped over the edge and down into the ravine, but my own fall had come to a precarious standstill.

I was lying face down on the slide with my left arm locked around the boulder and my left leg stretched out across jagged rock; my right hand clutched a tough, spiny plant that grew among the loose rocks and my right leg dangled helplessly over the edge.

Then from above and below, I was aware of the sound of running feet.

"Angela! What happened? Angela! Are you all right?"

Jay's shouts carried clearly from the other side of the rockslide, but I couldn't answer him. I was afraid the sound of my own voice would be enough to send me over the edge of the slide. I heard him climbing up the rocks, and on the trail behind me the running came to a sudden halt. Judd! It was Judd! I lifted my head, hoping to warn Jay and the rocks beneath me grumbled a warning at this slight movement. Then I saw his tall form silhouetted against the sky and heard his voice calling down to me.

"Don't try to move! I'll be right there! Just hang on!"

He had begun a careful descent when a voice suddenly boomed out from the trail below. "Hold it right there! Don't take another step!"

There were a few seconds of startled silence, then I heard Jay's voice, sounding strained and tense. "Judd, for God's sake, put down that rifle! She can't hang on like that much longer!"

"I said not another step, boy!"

"I'm going down! If you want my blood on your hands as well as my father's, then go ahead and shoot! But I'm going down!"

I heard Jay's boots scrape against a rock, then a thunderous report shattered the air. The shot echoed across the canyon walls, flooding the mountains with sound. I buried my face in the rock, feeling like my own life had come to an end. Perhaps it would. I waited for another shot.

The echoes stopped and I heard a calm voice saying, "Hang on, sweetheart! I'm almost there!"

I didn't believe the voice, but moments later I felt a hand grasp my elbow and another grip my belt. Slowly, I was dragged back, away from the edge of the slide. When I realized I was safe, the strength of will that had kept me clinging to the boulder suddenly gave way and I was too weak to stand.

"Try to walk, love. We've got to get off this slide. The rocks might give way again. Come on, you can do it!"

Jay's arm came around me, solid and hard, pulling me to my feet. The thoughts of another landslide provided enough impetus to keep my feet moving, but my legs were trembling so I would have fallen if he hadn't held me. When we set foot on firm ground, I collapsed with a groan. Jay dropped beside me and pinioned me in his arms. His breathing was as ragged as mine.

"You're all right," he whispered and kissed me. Then, with a thread of doubt in his voice he asked, "You are all right, aren't you?" I nodded and he kissed me again.

"The girl looks pretty cut up to me."

I flinched at the voice and looked up to see Judd Bradford standing nearby, surveying us with what appeared to be honest concern in his eyes.

"You're mighty lucky to get away with just a few cuts ane scratches," he said to me, "but they need to be tended to just the same."

I put a hand to my chin, then my left cheek, suddenly aware that my face was hot and stinging.

"I've got some water in my canteen down below. I'll go get it," Judd said and started down the trail.

"I don't understand," I murmured slowly, looking up to Jay for an explanation of his grandfather's behavior. Violence and moodiness I had come to expect from Judd Bradford, but gentleness and concern seemed foreign to the old man's nature.

Jay stared after his grandfather and shook his head.

"But the shot—" I said. "When I heard the shot I thought he—"

"He killed a rattler. If he hadn't, I would've stepped right on it."

My breath came out in a shudder. "The snake—I almost forgot. I was climbing up the slide to warn you Judd was here and nearly stepped on it myself. That's when I slipped on the rocks. I was afraid—so afraid Judd had come up here to kill you!"

Jay looked down the steep trail where his grandfather was laboring his way back up to us with a canteen in one hand. "He had his chance. I wonder why he didn't?"

Sunlight added gold to the silver of the old man's hair and gleamed in the perspiration on his brow. His big chest was heaving when he reached us and he shoved the canteen at Jay. Then, finding a low, flat rock to sit upon, he drew a handkerchief out of his shirt pocket and fervently mopped his face.

Jay ripped off a portion of his shirt, poured some water from the canteen onto the cloth and, with a wary look at his grandfather, knelt beside me.

"I can do that," I told him. "There's no need for you—"

"Yes, there is," he insisted gruffly. "I'll try to be careful," he added in a softer tone.

The water was icy cold and numbed the stinging cuts almost immediately.

"Your hands are bleeding," Jay said and poured some water into my cupped palms.

"I saw your campfire over in the cave," Judd began in a quiet voice. "I suppose you know—I guess you must have seen—"

"My father's grave? Yes, I saw it," Jay supplied in a voice that was calm and detached.

Judd looked at his grandson and drew a deep breath. "I'd like to tell you what happened—how it was with your father."

Jay put the wet cloth into my hands and set the canteen on the ground with movements that were slow and carefully controlled. Then he looked at his grandfather.

Judd's blue eyes rested on the bronze face of his grandson for several seconds, then he bowed his head. "I'm not sure how much you know already. The girl—Angela—told me that you have your father's diary."

"Yes, I have it."

"Did he—did Jason mention anything about some horses that were stolen from the ranch years ago?"

"Yes, only the horses weren't stolen. You hid them."

The old man's face blanched, but he gave Jay an affirmative nod. "Yes, I hid them. But before you say anything, I want to explain why. There was so much that happened before. So much . . ." Judd wiped a hand across his face.

"I guess Jason was about your age, maybe a little younger, when Dusk had one of the worst winters on record. All the ranchers were hard hit, especially the Triple J. We lost nearly all our beef cattle. The ranch was in a bad way. Jason wanted to take ten head of our best horses and sell them to help make up for some of the loss, but I was against it. We argued back and forth and then, without telling me a thing about it, Jason left the ranch and headed for Rock Springs to find a buyer for the horses. That boy was always so damn stubborn! Like his father, I guess," Judd said with a sigh. "A few days later, Jason called to tell me he'd found an interested buyer who would pay us a good price for the horses. That's when I knew I could never sell them. Those horses were part of this ranch—part of me! I told Jason the first thing that came into my head—that the horses had been stolen. He got real angry and we both said things we shouldn't have. That was the last I heard from him for nearly a year and a half. His being gone did something to me. I found out too late how much I needed your father—how much I depended upon him. I felt ashamed and angry because I'd never praised him or told him how much he meant to me.

"Every month I got a check, but Jason never told me how he was or what he was doing. The envelopes were all postmarked in Lander, so I satisfied myself that at least he was still in Wyoming. Then, one day in September, I got a letter from him saying he'd like to come home. Lizzy and I were heart glad of it, though I never did let on how glad I really was. About a week later, Jason drove up to the ranchhouse. Lizzy and John ran out to meet him, but I sort of stayed behind. I saw him get out of the car and hug Lizzy, then go around to the other side and help someone out. When I saw her, I felt like someone had just run a branding iron clear through my insides. I heard him introduce his wife to John and Lizzy, but all I could see—all I could see—" Judd broke off, his rugged jaw trembling visibly.

"All you could see was an Indian!" Jay spat out bitterly. "I know how you treated her—how much you hated her!"

"No, son! No!" Judd turned tortured blue eyes on his grandson's face. "I know that's what your mother must have thought, your dad, too, but that's only because—because I couldn't tell them the truth!" He bit down hard on his lower lip, then blurted out, "I was afraid! Afraid if Jason ever found out what I did to his mother he'd never forgive me. I've never forgiven myself!"

Jay leaned forward and stared at his grandfather, bewilderment wiping away the bitterness and anger on his face.

"I never wanted to hurt Nora," Judd went on brokenly. "I loved her—loved her more than I've ever loved anyone—but what happened to her was my fault."

"Helen told me that Nora died of pneumonia," I said quietly. "How could that have been your fault?"

I don't think he heard me. His face turned skyward and his eyes were burning with a light I had never seen before. "Nora," he breathed. "I haven't let myself speak her name outloud in years, but she's never been out of my thoughts. Lizzy was a good woman and a fine wife; I loved her as best I was able, but I only had half a heart left to give her after Nora died." Judd's gaze lowered from the brightening sky to the dark eyes of his grandson. "I've never told you about your grandmother—I didn't think I could—but, I'm telling you now so someone will remember her after I'm gone. She was the kind of woman that shouldn't be forgotten," Judd rubbed his big hands on his pantlegs and cleared his throat before going on.

"I met Nora at a time when my love for life was all but gone. Two years after my brother John was murdered by Indians, I buried my father in the ground he'd come to love more than his own native land. I was only twenty-four, and all alone on a ranch of more than 20,000 acres. I remember feeling like the Triple J was nothing more than a graveyard for all those I loved. I decided to go away for a while that summer, see some new country, and think things out. I hired a man to handle the ranch while I was gone, then traveled up north to Montana. While I was passing through Bozeman I thought I'd look up an old friend of my father's. He introduced me to his daughter. I knew the first time I saw those dark eyes and that slow, sweet smile that I had to have her. When autumn came I brought Nora back to the ranch as my wife, and before the first snows fell we knew she was carrying our child. Those were happy times and when your father was born our joy was full. He resembled Nora more than me—he had her dark eyes and dark hair—but we both knew right away that he had the Bradford temperament—strong-willed and stubborn!

"Your dad was almost six months old when we got word that Nora's father was ill and wanted to see his little grandson before he passed on. I took Nora and the baby and we went back to Bozeman. We were sitting around the fireplace one night, Nora and her father and me, and he started talking about his wife. He told me he couldn't get over how little Jason reminded him of her—Singing-in-the-Clouds, he called her. I said, that sounded like an Indian name and he said, 'That's right. My wife was a Dakota-Sioux.'

"Nora must have thought that I was crazy, the way I carried on after that. She hadn't told me about her mother being Indian 'cause she didn't think it mattered. And she couldn't understand why I was so upset because she didn't know how my brother had died. And I could never tell her about it. Instead, I just let it fester inside me. I felt deceived and tricked into marrying someone I had vowed to hate. And I had a son with tainted blood!

"We never argued and I never laid a hand on her. It was silence that came between us. As the months went by, things got worse and worse. I couldn't stop loving her and at the same time, I couldn't stop hating what she was. And when I looked at Jason—" Judd's shoulders sagged and he ran a hand through his white hair. "Nora thought I didn't love her anymore and that I hated our son. When I'd come in from doing chores I'd find her crying. Even the baby knew something was wrong. He started fussing all the time and he'd never been that way before.

"Then one day in the middle of January, I came back to the house and found Nora and the baby gone. At first, I couldn't believe it, then I got blazing mad! I told myself it was all for the best—that I was a fool to marry her—but I started searching just the same. None of the ranchhands had seen Nora since early that morning and I couldn't believe she'd be so crazy as to try and walk all the way into town in the dead of winter, especially with a baby! A storm started blowing in from the north and when it started to snow I was too scared to be mad. I grabbed a horse and took off down the road. The snow was blowing real hard and I'd covered half the distance between the ranchhouse and town before I found her. She was lying by the road. I almost passed right by. She looked just like a small white heap near some trees. But I heard the baby crying. She'd wrapped him inside her coat to keep him warm. When I lifted her onto my horse, her face was so white—I'd never seen her face white like that!" Judd covered his face with his hands and it was a long moment before his voice possessed enough control to speak clearly.

"I asked God to let her live and take me instead. I was the one who should have died. I told Nora that I loved her—begged her to forgive me—but she died."

Judd wiped a hand across his eyes then looked at Jay. "I'm telling you this because when your folks came back to the ranch that fall, it was like seeing Nora and me. Your mother had the same soft smile Nora had, the same dark shine to her eyes. I couldn't stand it! I knew your folks thought I acted the way I did out of hate, and I let them go ahead and think it. But it was myself I hated, not your mother! Try and understand if you can!"

I glanced from Judd's pleading eyes to Jay, whose dark head was bent low over his chest. He considered his grandfather's words in silence and refrained from commenting on them. Instead, he asked, "What about the horses? You haven't explained yet how they fit into all this. When did you hide them?"

Judd shifted position on the rock with a grimace. "I took the horses into the hills just before Jason came back to the ranch with your mother."

"Not until then?" Jay asked in surprise. "You mean those horses were sitting right here on the ranch the whole time my father was away working for Parley Evans and sending you money?"

Judd couldn't meet Jay's cold, accusing glance, but he nodded briefly.

"What about John? Was he in on the whole thing, too?"

"No! No, John never knew that Jason had found a buyer for the horses. He thought Jason had run out on us when the going was rough and I—I didn't tell him any different. When I got Jason's letter—when I knew he was coming back—I started getting worried. I knew how mad he'd be when he saw those horses. I was afraid Jason would take the horses that belonged to him and never come back! And I couldn't let that happen! I couldn't lose him again!"

"Did John know you were going to hide the horses? You must have told him something," Jay said.

Judd swallowed hard. "I told John your father was coming back and that he still wanted to sell our horses. I said there was no need for that now and Jason didn't have any right to them. John agreed with me. John always agreed with me. I told him I was going to take the horses and pasture them somewhere off the ranch for a while so Jason wouldn't find them. I told John to tell his brother that the horses had been stolen over a year ago, if he happened to ask about them, and let me handle the rest. John didn't know I was going to hide them up the Right Fork. And I knew Jason would never think to look up here."

Jay shook his head and uttered a sigh of disbelief. "So after you hid the horses, then what? Were you planning to leave them here all winter long? You must have known they'd never make it through."

"I was going to bring them back down," Judd said quickly. "I had it in my mind all along to bring them back down once I'd settled things with Jason. Then, when he came back with an Indian wife I was so upset I forgot about the horses. Fall wore on and I remembered, but I kept putting off coming up here. I guess I knew deep inside that what I'd done was crazy and I was afraid what Jason's reaction would be. The first snows came early that year and it was heavy. I knew there was no way to get to the horses. I felt bad about it, but I was relieved, too, because I figured Jason would never know what I'd done. But it didn't work out that way. When spring came, one of the horses broke through the barricade I'd put across this trail and Jason found him running loose. He came back to the ranch madder than hell and demanded to know where the rest of the horses were. I wouldn't tell him. I denied everything. Jason told me he was going to come up here and search until he found them and after that he was leaving for good. Something happened inside me when he said that! I knew I couldn't let Jason leave, and I knew once he found those horses that nothing could stop him. I had to do something fast, and somehow, I thought if I could only keep him from finding the horses he'd have to stay. That same afternoon, after I'd talked to Jason, I went into town and bought a few sticks of dynamite."

Jay's back stiffened and his face went rigid at the old man's words. "Dynamite?" he repeated slowly.

Judd nodded. "I knew it wouldn't take too much to block this trail. That way the horses wouldn't be able to get out and Jason would never find them. It was such a simple thing. I didn't see how anything could go wrong. I left the ranch before dawn the next day and came straight up here. There wasn't much to do. Just stick the dynamite in the rocks above the trail and light the fuses." Judd's tone was matter-of-fact, but there was horror in his eyes and his hands were trembling. He clenched them together and said, "I was in the cave when the charge went off. Afterwards, I came out to see if the trail was blocked and—found my son. I didn't know he had followed me up the canyon! I swear to you, I didn't know!"

Jay swallowed and his voice was unsteady. "Where? Where did you find him? Was he—buried by the slide?"

"No. No, he was lying right down there, near the stream." The old man pointed a wavering finger to the ravine below us where a clump of blood-red Indian paintbrush grew.

"Jason must have been riding up that trail down there when the charge went off. It looked to me like he was hit in the head by falling rocks and knocked off his horse. He was dead when I got to him," Judd said painfully and could say no more. He glanced at Jay briefly, grimaced, and wiped his forehead with the damp handkerchief.

Jay remained completely motionless for several seconds, his dark eyes staring down into the ravine.

"I guess we'd better be getting back," Judd mumbled, starting to rise.

"Not yet," Jay said quietly but with a firmness that put Judd back down on the rock.

"I've told you everything," he said wearily. "There's nothing else."

"Why didn't you tell my mother what you've just told me? Why did you let her suffer for eight years, never knowing what happened to my father? Why!"

The old man's jaw started to tremble and he clamped his thick lips together. When he spoke, the deep, rumbling voice was only a pitiful whine. "I wanted to, and I knew I should—but I just didn't have the courage to look into those sad, dark eyes of hers and say that I'd killed her husband. I convinced myself that it was better if she didn't know. She went away not long after you were born—back to her own people. I know she suffered, and it cuts deep to know that I was the cause of it! But I suffered, too! God knows how many times I've wished it was me buried in that cave over there and not Jason!" he cried with all the anguish of his soul.

Jay got to his feet and moved slowly over to his grandfather. He placed a hand on the old man's shoulder and Judd's white head lifted. "I don't blame you for hating me," Judd said. "After what I've done, you've the right to hate me!"

"No one has the right to hate," Jay said.

Something broke and shattered in the old man's face. A hardness that had been there for too many years. He struggled to rise and Jay grasped his arm, helping him to his feet.

I looked away from the two of them, blinking back sudden, unbidden tears, and dabbed the wet cloth against my cheek. When I glanced up again, Judd's blue eyes were regarding me with painful awareness.

"About yesterday—" he began, then stopped. He cleared his throat and tried again. "I guess you thought I was crazy. Maybe I was. Those damn pills always put me in another world. And I was scared. You knew too much! Anyway, I'm glad now that I was so upset, because—I haven't been known to miss a shot very often."

Jay released his grandfather's arm and stepped away in a movement of revulsion. "Is that all you can say? That you were scared? Since when does being scared give someone the license to kill? You talk about begging God to take you instead of my grandmother—then you tell me you wish it were you instead of my father in that cave down there—but it's all a lie! It's just a cowardly lie to ease your conscience! You've never had the courage to say 'I'm sorry,' to forgive someone, or to face the truth about yourself. What makes you think you'd have the courage to die?" Jay's voice lowered to an intense pitch. "I'll tell you one thing. If I'd come back yesterday and found Angela hurt—or dead—" He stopped himself and struggled for control.

Judd's nervous glance flickered in my direction and his tongue passed over his lips. "I—I didn't know she meant so much to you."

"She means everything to me!"

"Well, I—you don't need to worry about anything else happening. I mean, I'd never hurt either one of you. I swear it! Things'll be different now. You'll see."

Jay appraised his grandfather with a hard, measuring stare. "Maybe they will, but I won't be around to see it. I only came back to the ranch to find out what happened to my father. Now that I know, you won't be seeing me again."

A desperate look came into Judd's eyes. "When Jason told me he was leaving, I thought I'd die!" he whispered. "And now—you say—"

"You won't die," Jay said. "You've been living with fear and guilt since the day my father died and you'll have to go on living with it. Maybe, if I'm not around to remind you of him—your burden won't be quite so heavy," he added softly.

Judd shut his eyes and lowered his head. "What are you going to do now? I mean, about the rest of the family. Will you tell them?"

"I don't know. We can talk about that later." Jay turned to me. "Let's go." He bent down and picked up the canteen, then helped me to my feet. He kept his eyes averted from mine and his face had the closed, Indian-look that told me he was deeply troubled.

I wanted to cry out, to beg Jay not to go, to plead with both of them to forget the past and start now, but my throat was so tight I couldn't speak.

"Are you coming?" Jay asked his grandfather.

Judd shook his head. "No. No, you two go on down and load your gear on my horse. I'd kind of like to be alone for a little while."

Jay nodded his understanding and took my arm.

The old man turned away from us with a sigh and I saw his glance travel up the rockslide. "You don't suppose—" he began wistfully.

Jay looked at him inquiringly and Judd said, "You don't think there's a chance that—that any of the horses could've survived, do you?"

"Not after all these years. If the winters didn't kill them off, the big cats would."

Judd sat down on a boulder at the base of the slide. "I guess you're right, only—"

"I got up as far as the meadow," Jay told him, "and I didn't see any sign of horses."

Judd gave a brief nod and turned away to stare out over the canyon.

Jay and I walked down the trail, slowly and silently. About halfway, I stopped short and said, "Jay, he doesn't want you to go! He needs you!"

Jay's dark eyes met mine, for a moment unguarded and open in their misery. "I don't know what to do."

"Go back! Tell him you'll stay—just for a little while!"

Jay considered my words, then his fingers tightened around mine. "Wait for me at the cave," he said in a rush.

Suddenly the canyon was flooded with shouts from below. We looked to see three riders taking the trail out of the forest.

Jay said, "It's Bert and the Tylers!"

The next moment we heard a startled cry and the clatter of falling rocks. Jay glanced behind us and a look of horror spread across his face. The next second he was lunging back up the trail toward the rockslide where his grandfather was slipping down a cascade of loose rock.

I stood frozen in the center of the trail with tightly clenched hands, my breath locked in my throat, watching Judd's big hands claw at the rocks, only to have each one, in turn, give way under his fingers. I heard his cry for help and Jay's breathless shout, "I'm coming! Just hang on!"

The old man struck out in a desperate attempt to gain a firm hold on the rocks and lost what little balance he had. Jay reached the slide just in time to hear his name tear out of Judd's throat and see his grandfather's body drop over the edge.

I couldn't move until I heard the snap of breaking branches and a hard thud, then I ran the rest of the way up the trail to where Jay stood, staring down into the ravine.

I let my eyes flicker downward, afraid of what they would see, yet demanding to know. No grisly scene of death met my gaze, no mangled, bloody corpse. Instead, I saw an old man with a heavy shock of white hair lying on his back near a stream of swiftly moving water. His attitude was relaxed, one hand lying idle at his side, the other across his breast. If I had not known, I might have supposed that, being weary, he had only lain down to rest and fallen asleep, except his blue eyes were open and staring fixedly into the blue sky. And the peace of the mountains was on his brow.

Chapter 23

"Oh, yet we trust that somehow good
Will be the final goal of ill;
To pangs of nature, sins of will;
Defects of doubt, and taints of blood."

Alfred Lord Tennyson

Mountain birds were singing riotous praises to the new day, their songs rippling through sun-bright, rainwashed air, as a grim procession traveled down the canyon. I was seated behind Jay on his sturdy buckskin; behind us, Bert Tingey led Judd Bradford's horse with its lifeless burden draped in blankets across the saddle. Sam and Reed Tyler brought up the rear.

It wasn't a very grand manner for such a proud man to come home, I thought, but at least he would never have to face his family and friends with the truth of what had happened to Jason. Perhaps that would have been even more cruel than the death he suffered.

I tightened my hold around Jay's waist and rested my head against his broad back, shutting my eyes to the glaring sun. In my mind, I could still see Judd Bradford lying at the base of the cliff, red and yellow wildflowers nodding gently beside his head. Death had given him a look of peace that I had never seen while he was alive.

When we reached the ranchhouse, Mrs. Tyler came running out the back door, worry fresh on her face. She was a small, slender woman with fair hair rapidly turning to gray. Just now, a frown troubled her forehead and fear stared sharply out of her eyes. When she saw Jay and me, relief spread quickly across her features.

Jay dismounted and helped me off the horse. I leaned heavily on his arm. Standing required all my effort and concentration.

"Take care of Angela for me, will you Ruth?" he asked.

"Of course I will! Thank heavens, you're both all right! Oh, my Lord! What's happened? Who's that?" She cried, clutching a hand to her breast as Bert Tingey rode forward, leading Judd's horse.

222

Jay didn't answer her. He turned and walked toward the brown stallion.

"It's Judd," I whispered. "He's dead."

A hot, stinging shower washed away the dirt, and clean clothes made me feel more presentable, but neither could erase the shock of what had happened. I walked down the somber hall, deeply conscious of the fact that Judd Bradford's body lay in his room nearby.

Ruth Tyler had a hot breakfast waiting but fatigue was laying heavy hands on me. I choked down some scrambled egg and half a cup of strong black coffee. Jay managed to eat a little more, but he ate almost mechanically, with little thought of what it was or how it tasted. The lines of worry and tension were gone from his face, but I read sorrow and a sense of loss in the shadows around his eyes.

Mrs. Tyler was clearing away the breakfast dishes when we heard the sound of a car approaching. I glanced at Jay and he said, "That'll be the sheriff and Walt Marlowe."

"Who's Walt Marlowe, a deputy?"

"No, the vet. But he also acts as coroner and mortician when the need arises."

I looked at Jay fearfully, dreading the questions that were sure to be asked.

He pressed my hand and got up from the table. "Tell them what you have to," he said.

Sheriff George Fossett was a big man with a thick chest and a bulky shoulder spread. He had a head of smooth, sandy hair and light blue eyes that were a startling contrast to his deeply tanned face. Walt Marlowe was slightly taller than the sheriff with a lean, sinewy frame. He had big, bony hands and small brown eyes.

I had prepared myself for a cold, impersonal greeting with brusque questions to follow. Instead, both men expressed their shock and sorrow to Jay in soft voices. Judd Bradford had been their friend and neighbor for years. I began to realize his death would be felt as a personal loss to the entire community.

After speaking with Jay, Walt Marlowe went directly upstairs to attend to the body. George Fossett turned to the rest of us.

"All right now, I've gotta ask everybody here a few questions and it's gonna have to be one at a time. I know we're all friends and neighbors, but when it comes to the law, I gotta follow a certain procedure. Jay, seein' as how you're the only relative, I'll start with you. By the way, where's John and Helen, and the rest of the family?"

"They're all down at the hospital in Rock Springs," Sam Tyler

223

answered. "The truck crashed down in the gulley yesterday and John was hurt real bad."

George Fossett ran a hand over his hair. "Why the hell wasn't I called about John's accident? I saw the truck in the creek on our way here, but I was too busy thinkin' about Judd to give it much thought." Before anyone could answer, he shushed all replies with, "Nevermind! Nevermind! Jay, you can fill me in on all this. The rest of you just stay put!"

The Tylers and Bert Tingey sat in silence around the big oval table and more than once I was tempted to put my head down and go to sleep. Finally, Jay appeared in the doorway of the dining room with the summons, "Angela, Sheriff Fossett would like to ask you a few questions now."

I pushed back my chair and got to my feet, feeling totally awake now and very nervous. Jay took my hand and I clung tightly to his strong brown fingers as we crossed through the dining room into the living room.

A few chairs and sofas were huddled against the walls, but the large room was still half empty from the party two nights before. The floor was bare and scuffed.

George Fossett looked up from his notebook and waved to an empty chair near his. "Sit down, Miss Stewart. This shouldn't take too long."

I moved forward and sat down with a stiff back and tightly set lips. Jay stood beside my chair.

"Would it be all right if I stayed?" he asked.

George Fossett glanced at him briefly then gave a shrug of his big shoulders. "I guess so. Just don't try to answer any questions for her."

The sheriff's manner was blunt and direct, but not unkind. I found I could answer his questions with complete honesty and candor until he said, "There's only one other thing I'd like to know. Why did you ride away from the ranch yesterday afternoon? It seems to me, it would have made a lot more sense to stay here and wait for Jay and Bert to get back from Tyler's. Especially with a bad storm blowin' in."

Jay didn't move and his face didn't disclose the slightest reaction to the sheriff's question, but I felt his tenseness as if it were my own. I knew then I could never reveal what had actually taken place, even though there was a bullet in the side of the barn to prove my story.

"Helen gave Judd a strong sedative before leaving for the hospital and he slept for several hours," I told the sheriff. "I was fixing some lunch for Jay and Bert when he came downstairs. He was still very upset by all that had happened. I tried to talk to him, to calm him down—but it didn't do any good. I was afraid—afraid he might harm himself and I knew I wasn't strong enough to handle him so I rode for help."

George Fossett continued to write in his notebook for a few moments, then he looked up at me. "That'll do, Miss Stewart. Thanks for your help."

I got to my feet and Jay's hand moved swiftly to cover mine. I saw the silent gratitude in his eyes.

After everyone had been questioned, Ruth Tyler made fresh coffee. The sheriff and Walt Marlowe were relaxing at the kitchen table when Janet and Thayne walked in.

Thayne glanced around the room with a perplexed frown. "What's going on? What's happened?"

"Has someone been hurt?" Janet asked fearfully.

George Fossett put down his coffee cup and looked into both their faces. "I'm real sorry to have to tell you this, and I don't know an easy way to do it. Your grandfather was killed this morning. He fell down a rockslide somewhere up the Right Fork."

Janet and Thayne were too stunned for tears or speech. Reed got up from the table and went to Janet's side, putting a strong arm about her shoulders.

Jay asked quietly, "How's John? Is he going to be all right?"

Thayne mumbled, "Yeah, he's going to make it. He's got a broken leg, a few cracked ribs, and a dislocated shoulder. But it could've been a lot worse. What the hell was Grandpa Judd doing up the Right Fork?"

"Sit down, boy. You, too, Janet," George Fossett directed. "I know it's an awful shock to come home after what happened to your dad and find out that your grandpa's dead. It's a shock to all of us. Jay was going to take me and Walt up there in a few minutes. Thayne, you can come along if you want to and I'll explain what happened on the way. Ruth, I think you'd better stick around here for a while and see to Janet."

Sam Tyler asked, "Do you want me and Reed to come with you? We'll be glad to do what we can."

The sheriff shook his head. "No, I don't think so. I know you've got your work to do. Maybe you could get somebody to take care of the chores around here tonight, though. Bert, do you think you could rustle some horses together? Jay says we can't make it up there in his jeep."

"Do you want me to go along?" I asked, trying not to sound as weary as I felt.

"No, I want you to hustle yourself upstairs for some shut-eye," he ordered in firm but kindly tones. "You're lookin' deadbeat, and we don't want anybody else in the hospital."

I slept solidly through the rest of the day and didn't stir until the evening breeze was blowing soft and cool through the window. I shivered and sat up, for a moment confused as to why I had been asleep so late in the day. Then I remembered. Judd was dead. I wanted to lie back down and sleep again, sleep until the horrible, dull ache had left me. Then I thought of Jay and the sheriff's investigation. He had probably returned long ago. Why was the house so still and silent?

I got off the bed and quickly ran a comb through my hair, then hurried out into the hall. The door to Judd's room was open and all that remained of his presence was the imprint his body had made upon the bed. I hurried past his room and down the stairs. Where was everyone? My steps slowed as I approached the kitchen. Here, lights were burning brightly and the smell of food warmed the air. Janet was just lifting a steaming casserole out of the oven and Thayne was sitting at the table.

I looked at their wan faces, not knowing what to say. But I had to know. "Where's Jay?"

Thayne said, "He left over an hour ago to tell Mom and Dad about Grandpa Judd. He asked us not to wake you."

"Come sit down with us and have something to eat," Janet said. "Mrs. Tyler sent this casserole over a little while ago and Mrs. Fossett came by with a cake. Everyone's been so nice—" Her voice broke and she glanced away from me.

I got a plate out of the cupboard and some utensils from a drawer and brought them to the table. "Janet, it's so hard to know what to say. I hope you know how sorry I am—how bad I feel about what happened this morning."

She nodded dully and spooned the casserole onto our plates.

Thayne was unusually silent throughout the meal. It was to be expected that the death of his grandfather would have a sobering influence on his usually raucous nature, but I had never before seen him this subdued.

Finally, after Janet had risen to take our dishes to the sink, I asked him, "How did the rest of the investigation go?"

"That's what I've been trying to get out of Thayne ever since he came back," Janet said with annoyance. "He hasn't told me a thing and neither would the sheriff. I didn't expect Jay to. He never says much about anything." She gave her brother a disgruntled look as she sat back down at the table. "Honestly, Thayne! I think I have just as much right as you do to know what went on!"

"I know you do, Sis. But it's hard for me to talk about it." Thayne glanced at me. "I don't know exactly how to say this—I'm lousy at apologies. I can't remember the last time I said I was sorry for anything, but—I am—sorry. Sorry for every rotten thing I've said and for the way I've treated you."

I met his serious blue eyes in surprise and embarrassment. An apology was the last thing I expected to hear from Thayne Bradford. I tried a faint smile and said, "I don't think that was such a lousy apology. With a little practice, you'll probably get real good at it."

Thayne flashed me one of his old grins. "Thanks, honey. The next person I plan to practice on is Jay. I guess you know he's quite a guy."

Janet stared at her brother. "Since when did you think Jay was so wonderful? You've certainly done a terrific job of disguising your admiration for him all these years."

Thayne fingered his mustache and gave his sister a sheepish grin. "I know. Believe me, little sister, I know. But after today . . ." His breath came in a long, slow sigh.

Janet leaned forward in her chair. "What happened up there?"

"Before I say anything, you've got to promise that you won't repeat any of this outside our own family. I know that's the way Dad will want it, and we owe that much to Jay for sparing Grandpa Judd."

Janet's eyes were growing wider and rounder with his every word. Now she shot me a sideglance of hesitation.

Thayne said, "Angela already knows most of what I'm going to tell you. She was with Jay when he found his father's grave."

"His father—his father's grave?" she repeated, totally astounded.

"Sis, Uncle Jason never ran off the way we all thought. He was killed—by Grandpa Judd."

"What are you saying? I don't believe it! Grandpa Judd would never hurt anybody! What sort of lies did Jay tell you up there?"

"They weren't lies. I saw the grave myself. And the marker Grandpa Judd put up." Thayne looked at the horror in his sister's eyes and said softly, "It wasn't murder—but what happened was his fault. It's a long story, and he's kept it a secret from everyone all these years. Grandpa Judd told Jay everything before he died."

Janet put a hand to her face and shut her eyes for a moment. "You said—you saw the grave?"

"It's in a small cave up in the hills. Jay took us there after the sheriff investigated the rockslide where Grandpa was killed." Thayne swallowed and said in a low voice. "Walt had to open up the grave. I don't know how Jay stood it, but Walt said it was necessary to make a positive identification of the body before Uncle Jason's death could be recorded officially. Lord, I thought I was going to get sick, but Jay never said a word. Walt found a gold wedding band with an inscription inside, so the grave wasn't disturbed too much."

"Will the body have to be moved?" I asked him.

"No. Walt said that Uncle Jason's death and gravesite will be recorded with the state and that's all that needs to be done. Jay's got guts, but he's Indian enough that I don't think he could take having his father's body moved. I could see how relieved he was. Before Marlowe and the sheriff covered the grave back up, Jay put something inside—I couldn't see too well, but it looked like a book."

"His father's diary," I said softly. "That book was all Jay had to remember his father by."

"Why would he want to put it in the grave?" Janet asked, puzzled. "I should think he'd want to keep it if that's all he had."

I didn't answer her and Thayne said, "Maybe it's an Indian custom or something. Anyway, I told Jay that as soon as Dad's well enough, we'll go back there and seal up the cave with rocks."

"I'm glad. That will mean a lot to Jay."

Thayne smiled a little at me.

"Well, Jay got everything he wanted, didn't he?" Janet said with bitterness in her voice. "His father's name will be cleared and now Grandpa Judd's memory and reputation will be ruined forever! Everyone in Dusk will be talking about it!"

"I wouldn't blame Jay if he did want to get back at us," Thayne said. "All these years we've treated him like dirt—admit it, Sis! A lot of people would say Jay had the right to some revenge. But he doesn't want it that way. Jay told Marlowe to record his father's death as accidental and then made both him and Sheriff Fossett swear they would never tell anyone about what Grandpa Judd did. He said he didn't want people making a lot of talk about Grandpa Judd the way they had his father. Man, that really got to me!"

"Then, no one but our family knows?" Janet said slowly.

"That's right. Not even the Tyler's know about the grave. Bert Tingey does, but he's not the type to go shooting off his mouth about it."

"Jay must have loved Grandpa Judd, after all," Janet said in amazement.

"He always has," I told her. "And Judd loved him, too," I added softly, remembering the look in Judd's blue eyes when they had rested on his grandson's face.

Thayne cleared his throat and shoved back his chair. "Well, if it's all the same to you girls, I think I'd better hit the hay early tonight. Tomorrow morning's going to come all too soon for me."

"I'm tired, too," Janet said in a subdued voice. "I think I'll just leave the dishes and go to bed. How about you, Angela?"

"You go ahead. I'd like to stay up a while and wait for Jay."

I wandered about the room, too restless to read, and too preoccupied with my own thoughts to get involved in a television show. I heard the sound of an engine and the crunch of tires on loose gravel and ran to the window. Two bright headlights were moving up the drive. I wondered if Jay would go directly to the bunkhouse or stop here first. I decided not to chance missing him and ran out of the house. I reached the driveway just as he pulled alongside the big cottonwoods and switched off the motor. The door of the Bronco opened and shut behind him. Even in the darkness I could see that his tall form was marked with fatigue—bent head, slumped shoulders, and slow footsteps.

I spoke his name and the dark head jerked up in surprise. Then his arms reached out for me and I rushed into his embrace.

"This is what I've been needing all day," he whispered, holding me so tightly I could hardly breathe. He kissed me roughly and said, "As soon as this is over we'll leave. We'll put it all behind us. I know I've put you through hell these past two weeks, but—"

"Jay, you mustn't worry about me! You're the one who's suffered! Please, let me try to help!"

He touched my face with his fingertips. "You have helped—don't you know, Angel?" He didn't go on. He didn't need to. Looking at the dark blur of his face, I was struck with the sudden awareness that Jay needed me as much as I needed him. The realization was strangely sweet and fulfilling.

He took my hand and we began walking toward the gray stone house which was brooding in the moonlight much the same as on the night of my arrival. Only now it didn't feel eerie or menacing, just old and sad.

"I've been alone a good deal of my life," Jay was saying, "and it's never bothered me. In fact, I liked it that way—or at least, I thought I did. But last week—being alone in that cabin with you down here—I've never felt so frustrated and alone in my life! Whenever I thought about you, the past didn't seem important anymore. Having you was all that mattered! I decided to give up the search and had my gear all packed to come back down here when Bert walked in with the diary. That changed everything. Now, I almost wish I didn't know what happened. Maybe he'd still be alive . . ."

"That first night, when we were walking out to the ranch, you told me that knowing what happened was important. That trying to live your life without the 'hows and the whys was plain hell.' "

"I did say that, didn't I."

We reached the back porch and I paused to gaze up at him. "You're tired. Don't try to think everything through right now. Give yourself some time."

"I know you're right, but how do you stop thinking about it? I keep wishing I'd never left him alone up there—or that I'd been faster. There's so much I should have done."

"You did all you could! Judd wouldn't want you to blame yourself for what happened. For him, dying was a blessing."

Jay sighed and pulled me close. "Maybe you're right. I'll never forget the look of peace on his face."

It seemed to me as if Dusk's entire population was in attendance at Judd Bradford's funeral. The old stone church was full to capacity with mourners wishing to pay their last respects and offer sympathy to the Bradford family. Afterwards, Judd Bradford was buried on his own land, in a grassy, tree-shaded cemetery. The little graveyard was enclosed by a wrought-iron fence.

Inside, markers were erected to Judd's parents, his younger brother John, and his wives, Nora and Lizzy. Judd was laid to rest between them and a simple prayer was offered by his son. Janet and Helen wept openly and a few tears slid down the sunburned cheeks of Tadd, David and Stuart. Thayne stood behind his father's wheelchair with head bowed low. And Jay—Jay stood erect with his face lifted to the hills. And I knew he was seeing a rocky mound with a roughly carved wooden marker.

That evening, Thayne built a fire in the fireplace and the family grouped themselves around it. Bert Tingey had been invited to join the Bradfords and was toasting his old bones as close to the fire as possible.

I listened to the lively snap of the pine logs and the hiss of resin being licked by the flames, and was reminded of another evening similar to this. So much had changed since that evening of "Do you remembers?" around the fire. Then, Judd's bulky frame had filled the big recliner. Now, John was sitting in the easy chair, his bad leg resting on a hassock before him. On that other evening, Jay had been in self-imposed exile, miles away in a cabin in the hills. Tonight, he sat close beside me, his lean brown fingers clasping mine.

"Everything went well today, didn't it?" Janet said with a sigh.

"I ain't never seen so many folks at a funeral before," Bert commented. "Judd would've been right proud to know how much the folks in Dusk thought of him."

"It's hard to believe he's gone—" Stuart said in a thin, tight voice and could trust himself to say no more.

"We have a lot to be grateful for," Helen said quietly. "Your father's alive and he's going to get well."

John straightened up in the chair with a grimace of pain. His blue eyes were focused on Jay's sober features. "I know we're all going to miss Grandpa Judd," he began. "And I know you all loved him. But tonight—tonight I want to tell you about someone you never knew—a man who was as much a part of the Triple J as any of us here. A man I loved very much but never really understood until the past few days—my brother Jason."

Jay's back stiffened against the sofa and his dark eyes flew to his uncle's face. John returned his nephew's startled look with a smile.

"I know I promised you I wouldn't repeat the things you told me the other night, but there are times when a man has to break a promise. I don't think my tellin' the truth is going to change anybody's feelings for Grandpa Judd. It isn't our place to judge him—just love him for what he was—or maybe, what he tried to be."

Jay bowed his head as John went on to tell the story of Jason's tragic death. When he finished, no one moved or spoke. John looked at the solemn faces around him, then said to Jay: "I don't know if I can put what

I've been feelin' into the right words, but—I don't want what happened over twenty-six years ago to put barriers between us, so to speak. There's been too much bitterness and hard feelings in this house. I know there've been plenty of times when you probably felt that none of us wanted you around—or even cared about you. But I want that to change. This ranch is as much your home as it is any of my children. You're part of us, son. And we love you. No matter where you go or what you do, I want you to remember that."

John stretched out his hand and Jay got up to take it firmly between his. Then he embraced Helen. When he turned around his face was young again. Years of bitterness and hurt were gone from his eyes.

"Will you stay with us?" Helen asked, her brown eyes brimming over with tears.

Thayne cleared his throat and mumbled, "I sure could use your help while Dad's laid up."

Jay looked at me with sudden concern. "What do you think, Angel? Would you mind too much if we waited a month or so?"

I smiled into his eyes. "That would be fine. I've been thinking maybe I should go home first, anyway."

"I know you haven't had much of a vacation," Janet said apologetically. "But I hate to see you go home so soon."

Helen chuckled and said to her daughter, "Janet, I'm surprised at you for being so dense! If Angela wants to go home, I suspect it's for a very good reason." She gave Jay a broad grin. "Am I right?"

"You're always right, Aunt Helen." Jay moved to the couch, took both my hands and pulled me up to stand beside him. "Maybe it's kind of a bad time for making announcements, but I think everybody might as well know. I've asked Angela to marry me and she's said yes."

Janet's mouth fell open and stayed that way.

Thayne gave a low whistle. "And folks say I move fast!"

"Where've I been while all this was happening?" John demanded and turned to his wife. "And how come you knew all about it?"

Helen gave him a smug, womanly smile and got up to hug Jay and me. "I had my suspicions the first night these two walked in here together. And I must say, I couldn't be happier!"

"That goes for me, too!" Bert Tingey put in with all the enthusiasm his gravelly voice could muster. "'Course you got the short end of the deal, Miss. This black-haired buck has really put me through—"

"Hold it right there, Bert!" Jay interrupted. "I don't want anybody talking her out of it!"

"What I'd like to know is how you talked her into it!" Thayne said and his family laughed.

I looked up at Jay with a little smile. "He didn't have to talk too hard, actually."

Jay bent his head to kiss me and I heard David say slyly, "What'd I tell you about the Indians beatin' out the cowboys and gettin' the girl?"

"I still don't understand how all this happened," John said, shaking his head. "But I can see it would be asking too much to expect anybody to calm down long enough to do a little explaining."

"What's to explain?" his wife said. "They're in love! Anybody with two eyes can see that!"

"Have you set a date?" Janet wanted to know, recovering from shock enough to speak.

"No, we haven't had much chance to talk about it," I told her as we sat back down on the couch.

"I suppose your mother will want a formal Eastern wedding," Janet said.

"Probably so, but I don't. I haven't much family back East, anyway. Just Mother and my Aunt Mildred. A small, simple wedding is all I want."

Jay relaxed against the couch cushions and took my hand firmly between his. When Janet had mentioned a formal Eastern wedding, his expression had been decidedly uncomfortable.

"What would you think about getting married right here?" Helen said suddenly. "Jay was born here, along with my children, and Lord knows there've been enough deaths, but as far as I know, there's never been a wedding. John and I were married in the old church in town, and Janet has her heart set on being married there too. But I've always thought this old ranchhouse would be a real nice place for a wedding."

Jay looked at me and I could see he was pleased with the idea. I gave him a little nod and smiled.

"That sounds wonderful, Aunt Helen."

But we don't want you to go to a lot of trouble," I told her. "With Janet getting married in September you'll have enough to do."

Janet let out a sudden little shriek and said, "Angela, if you marry Jay, you won't be able to be my maid of honor!"

Jay smiled at his cousin. "Angela Stewart won't, but if you ask her real nice, Angela Bradford might be your matron of honor."

Janet pulled a face, then laughed. "Oh, all right, but matron of honor sounds so old."

Thayne got up to shake both our hands and said almost wistfully, "Angela Bradford. That sure has a nice ring to it. Congratulations to both of you!"

232

Chapter 24

"Calms appear when storms are past;
Love will have his hour at last."

Philip Dryden

Mother and I arrived at Dusk in the afternoon; a hot, dusty, August afternoon. My emotions, as I turned the car onto the gravel road which ran alongside the railroad tracks, were a breathless mixture of relief, anticipation and dread. Relief, that I was actually here, anticipation to see Jay again after an interminable six-weeks apart, and dread of what Mother might say or do upon meeting the Bradfords. After the six week seige just past, I wasn't looking forward to any more battles.

Mother's reaction to my sudden return home had been one of unconcealed delight. She naturally assumed I would be traveling to Europe with Aunt Mildred. I explained immediately that I would not be going to Europe; that I had come home for another reason, much more important. Jay.

Mother listened politely all the while I told her about him, our meeting, his search to discover the truth about his father, and its results. I omitted much of what Judd had done, not wanting to frighten her over things now in the past. After I had finished speaking she smiled and said, "You were very wise to come home, Angela dear. It's understandable how you and this Jay person could be—well, drawn together by all that happened, but of course, what you feel for him isn't really love. Now that you're home again, I'm sure you'll see that, too."

Mother's philosophy over the whole affair was quite simple. Ignore something and it will go away; that is, if it ever existed at all. This tidy little attitude lasted about one week, during which time Jay telephoned twice and I methodically went through boxes of sentimental trivia I had been storing in the basement for umpteen years.

Mother's next tactical move was logic. During the next two weeks she presented articulate, well-meaning, and scrupulously sensible reasons why I should not marry "that Jay person." Her campaign was brilliant and made the fact that Jay and I were in love sound totally illogical and irrelevant. But, at the end of two weeks, even Mother had to admit defeat. And Mother has never taken kindly to failure in any sense of the word. She became alternately argumentative and bitterly silent. Whenever Jay telephoned, she would leave the room with a vengeance and when I tried to include her in my little shopping trips to purchase items for my trousseau, she made frigidly polite excuses. She refused to listen to anything I said if it had to do with Jay.

One night, in late July, Jay's telephone call interrupted a particularly bitter argument. I had been telling Mother that I wished I had never come back home; that she didn't care about my happiness. All she wanted was to run my life. She was close-minded and prejudiced.

Mother had been telling me that I'd regret the day I let myself get carried away by an uneducated savage. All Indians were potential if not actual alcoholics. Indians were lazy. How could that Jay person hope to provide a decent living for us by selling a few cheap paintings?

Jay knew something was wrong the moment I said hello, and insisted on knowing what had upset me. I poured out all my frustration in a torrent of emotional sentences and when we said goodbye, neither of us felt any better. He was angry and I was miserable.

The next day I purposely avoided Mother by remaining in my room until after she had left for work at the gift shop. Then I went on a shopping spree that lasted until the department stores locked their doors. When I returned home the hour was close to ten and Mother was in the living room waiting for me.

"It's about time you decided to come home!" she said by way of greeting. "Is your wedding gown in one of those packages?"

I said rather coldly, "No, I haven't found one yet."

"Well, tomorrow's Saturday. What do you say we go shopping first thing in the morning? I suppose I should buy a new dress myself, although heaven only knows what sort of clothing would be suitable for a wedding in a ranchhouse."

I stared at her.

Mother motioned to me with an impatient gesture. "Well, put your packages down and let's see what you've bought; a lot of sheer little nothings, I suppose."

"Mother—are you all right? What's happened?"

"Put your packages down, Angela! It makes me nervous to have you standing there staring at me that way! That's better. Now I'm not going to say that I approve of your marrying this Jay person, but I may have been a bit

234

hasty in judging him. Since you're so determined to go through with it, I've decided to make the best of the situation. Besides, I could hardly refuse when Mrs. Bradford invited me to be their guest for a week; especially when they have already invited some of their relatives to attend the ceremony. It would look very bad if the bride's mother weren't there."

I took this all in with a dazed shake of the head. "Helen called? Helen talked to you?"

"Well, of course. We had quite a nice little chat. She sounds like a decent person, so I suppose her nephew can't be all bad. Angela, will you get that silly grin off your face? If we're going to leave here by next weekend, I'm going to need your help getting the gift shop in order. And I suppose we'll have to think of some sort of announcement to send to our friends and family. Heaven only knows what your poor father would say about all this," she sighed.

"If he were here, Daddy would love Jay," I said softly.

Now we were here, driving along the winding dirt road which led to the Triple J. I noticed a few changes that summer had wrought in the surrounding country. The soft, tender green of June had ripened and dried into the gold of August. Tall fields of alfalfa were now shorn and bare with haystacks giving evidence of a successful crop. The rushing, muddy stream of early summer was now a mild-mannered brook, and the surrounding hills were a dusty brown.

"We're almost there," I told Mother, unable to keep the excitement out of my voice. "If I remember right, the gulley isn't too far from here and then it's only a mile further to the ranchhouse!"

"Thank goodness!" said Mother. "Imagine having to travel over this ghastly road every time you wanted to run into town for something."

I laughed. "The Bradfords do very little 'running into town.' "

"Well, I suppose that's understandable. From what I saw of Dusk, there probably isn't much there worth running in for. Angela, will you please drive more slowly? I still say they should have named this place 'Dust' instead of Dusk. I hope my asthma doesn't flare up." Mother sniffed and drew a dainty handkerchief out of her purse.

I pulled the sun visor down to shield my eyes from the glare of the late afternoon sun and took a quick glance in the rear-view mirror, hoping our long hot drive hadn't taken too great a toll on my appearance.

Mother didn't look the least bit wilted. Every wave of her light brown hair was perfectly controlled, her lime green knit dress was wrinkle free and in perfect taste. Everything about Mother was always in perfect taste. Mother would never have decided to walk along a winding gravel road at twilight. Mother would have been perfectly content to wait in town. Well, not content exactly, but she would have made the best of it. Mother

235

certainly wouldn't have been so clumsy as to fall in a stream and Mother most definitely would never have gotten involved with a Bannock-Shoshoni Indian by the name of Jayhawk.

My hands gripped the steering wheel more tightly and my stomach was in a turbulant state. What if Mother were totally obnoxious to the Bradfords? What if Jay had changed? What if he didn't love me?

"Angela, dear, there are some men working near that haystack over there. I believe they're waving at us."

I turned my head to look. Some forty yards off the road, Stuart, Tadd, and David were shouting and waving their cowboy hats wildly in the air. Then I saw a tall figure standing on top of the neatly squared haystack. Sunlight glinted off his black hair, gleamed brightly on bronze shoulders, chest and arms. I jammed my foot onto the brake pedal so hard the tires skidded in the loose gravel and Mother was thrown forward against the dashboard.

"Angela, for heaven's sake, compose yourself! There's no need to wreck the car!"

I switched off the motor and yanked the car door open.

"Angela! Where do you think you're going? Angela!"

"It's Jay!" I cried, as if that one word were explanation enough for anything I might say or do.

My carefully imagined plans for a cordial, casual encounter were joyfully abandoned as I ran out into the field to meet him. His arms reached out a strong welcome and his kiss smothered all my ridiculous doubts.

We walked slowly back to the road with the afternoon sun in our eyes and all its fire and warmth in our hearts. Mother lifted her head at our approach and a polite smile parted her lips. But there was something in her eyes that surprised me. She looked somehow unnerved, or touched, I wasn't sure which.

"Mother, this is Jay."

"So I gathered," she said dryly.

Jay leaned down and kissed her smooth cheek. "Thank you for coming," he said warmly.

Mother was too flustered to make a reply, but she didn't appear displeased.

"Would you mind if I rode back to the ranchhouse with you?" he asked. "The boys are nearly finished with their work here and I can send Thayne back for them in the truck."

"Why, no—I suppose not," Mother said faintly.

I ran around to the driver's side while Jay climbed in beside Mother. I noticed with a smile that her back arched into sudden rigidity as Jay's broad, bare shoulder nudged against her.

As the car took the steep grade down into the gulley, Mother said, "Angela told me that your uncle was injured in an accident near here. I hope he's recuperating."

"Uncle John's doing real well. His left leg is still in a cast, but he's determined to have that off before Janet's wedding next month. His biggest problem is that he wants to be up and around, taking charge of everything on the ranch, and the doctor says he needs to take it easy a while longer."

"It really has been a tragic summer for you, hasn't it?" Mother said with a sympathetic sigh. "First, your uncle's accident, then your grandfather's death . . ."

Jay stretched his arm along the back of the seat and gave me a meaningful look. "Oh, it hasn't been all bad."

The ranchhouse was a delightful surprise to Mother.

"Why, it's almost English!" she exclaimed as we drove up the tree-lined drive.

"My great-grandfather came over from England and settled here," Jay explained. "He built this house."

"It's very lovely."

I switched off the ignition and leaned back against the seat with a happy sigh. "It's so good to be back!"

Mother sniffed. "To hear you talk, anyone would think you'd been gone six months instead of six weeks."

"Funny, I thought it had been at least six years," Jay said with a smile and got out of the car. He held the door open and offered Mother his hand.

"Thank you, I can manage," she said stiffly, but allowed Jay to take her arm just the same.

I got out, stretched my legs, then heard a loud bang. It was only Janet, bursting out the back door like a minor explosion. Helen followed, wearing the same gray cotton dress I had first seen her in. Thayne sauntered out last, tucking his shirttails into his Levis.

Janet gave me a fierce hug, Helen bestowed a motherly kiss and Thayne looked at Jay with a twinkle in his blue eyes.

"Do you mind if I kiss the bride or will I get my face smashed in like the last time?"

Jay chuckled and Mother's eyebrows went up a notch.

"Go ahead," Jay said with a grin. "Just don't put too much into it."

Thayne planted a brotherly peck on my cheek to which Jay gave an approving nod. Then Jay took Mother's arm and led her into our circle.

"Mrs. Stewart, this is my aunt Helen, her daughter Janet and son Thayne."

After introductions, Helen immediately took Mother in tow saying, "You're probably half dead from the heat. Come on inside and I'll make you

237

something cold to drink. Supper won't be for over an hour, so you've got time for a nice nap."

Mother responded graciously, "Thank you, Mrs. Bradford. I think perhaps I will take a rest. But I never sleep in the afternoon."

Mother slept solidly until after six and was awakened only by my coming into our room to freshen up for dinner. Janet had insisted that Mother and I share her room for the week and had moved across the hall into Thayne's bedroom. When I asked where Thayne would sleep she replied, "Out in the bunkhouse with Jay and Bert." She smiled at my amazed expression and said, "I know what you're thinking, but Jay and Thayne have gotten really close since Dad's accident. Between the two of them, they've handled the ranch just beautifully."

Mother was rested and refreshed after her nap and ready to admit that the ranchhouse was charming and the Bradfords warm, delightful people.

I stood before the mirror brushing my hair and asked casually, "And Jay? What do you think of him?"

"Well, I'm not sure yet. He's not exactly what I expected. But just because he's reasonably attractive and has eyes that would melt an iceberg doesn't mean he'll be a good provider—or a good father." Mother looked at me and her lips curved into a smile. "Still, I'm beginning to understand why you were so strongly attracted to him. And the way he looks at you is almost embarrassing!"

"Mother!"

She laughed a little at my expression. "My dear, I'm not so old that I can't recognize a certain look in a man's eyes when I see it. In fact, if I were your age that young man would probably have a very unsettling effect on me. Very unsettling."

Mother was noticeably taken aback when Jay entered the house for supper. Dressed in his dark burgundy slacks and mauve shirt, with his thick black hair neatly brushed, he presented a startling contrast to the Jay she had met earlier in the afternoon, clad only in Levis and cowboy boots.

Helen served supper in the dining room that night in honor of our coming. It was an unforgettable experience watching Mother discover the delights of ranch cooking. I had to cover a smile with my napkin as Mother broke one on her cardinal rules by asking for another helping of roast beef. As for me, Helen could have served bread and water and I would have been perfectly content.

After dinner we gathered in the living room and Jay insisted that Helen and Janet join us and leave the supper dishes until later. I thought I noticed a significant glance pass between aunt and nephew as Helen obligingly put away her apron.

Mother was in extremely good humor. She laughed at the antics of the younger boys and chatted with John and Helen about our drive West. No mention was made of Jay or our marriage until Mother suddenly turned to him and asked pointedly, "What exactly are your plans for the future? Do you do anything else besides paint?"

I should have been expecting this. Mrs. Edward R. Stewart was a canny expert at laying a framework of innocent chatter before thrusting a question with the sharpness of a rapier.

John spoke up with surprising zeal. "Jay's paintings are doing real well, Mrs. Stewart. And if he has a mind to, we'd sure welcome his help here on the ranch this fall and winter. The Triple J is as much Jay's home as it is mine."

Mother took this in calmly with a slight lift of her brows.

Jay put an arm about my shoulder and smiled at Janet's father. "I appreciate the offer Uncle John, but I'm afraid I won't be able to stay on at the ranch after this month is out. Last spring I applied for a teaching position at several colleges and universities, and a few days ago I got word that I've been accepted by Colorado College in Colorado Springs to teach a course in fine arts."

My arms flew around his neck and after a fervent kiss I demanded, "Jay, why didn't you tell me? You never mentioned a thing about teaching at a college!"

He looked down at me, a pleased grin spreading across his face. "I didn't tell you before 'cause I hated to get your hopes up if it fell through. Then, when the college telephoned, I figured you were probably on the road so I decided to wait and surprise you."

Helen gave a delighted chuckle. "I was in the kitchen when the call came or I wouldn't have known about it myself. I've been sittin' on pins and needles all evenin' waiting for Jay to break the news."

"Those folks are mighty lucky to have you," John said proudly, giving Mother a look which completely passed her by. She was staring at the fireplace, a little smile playing around her lips and a shine to her eyes. I could almost hear her now, telling Aunt Mildred and all her friends about "my son-in-law the college professor, etc., etc."

Thayne and Janet were offering their congratulations to Jay when Tadd suddenly blurted out, "Hey, what'll your students call you? Professor Jayhawk?"

Mother spoke up then and said quite seriously, "His students will address him as Professor Bradford, of course."

Jay laughed and said, "Well, to start with, Mr. Bradford will do just fine. It'll take a while to work up to a full professorship. I would like to go on and get my doctorate though and Angela can continue her studies, too, if she wants to."

"Of course she'll want to!" Mother stated with absolute certainty.

Jay and I exchanged glances.

"Is that painting over the mantlepiece one of yours?" Mother inquired politely. "I don't believe I've had the pleasure of seeing any of your work."

Jay smiled and answered. "No, that's a print by Frederic Remington. It was a favorite of my grandfather's," he added softly. "I've just finished a painting though, that I'd like to show you. If you'll excuse me a minute, I'll go get it." He gave my hand a squeeze, stood up and walked out of the room.

I turned to Janet, "Jay didn't tell me he was working on another painting. What's it like?"

She answered with a shrug. "I don't know. I haven't seen it."

"I have," Thayne answered with a secretive smile and would say no more.

Mother, always the mercenary, said, "If you don't mind my asking, how much do Jay's paintings usually sell for?"

"The last one went for close to nine hundred," Thayne said.

"Dollars?" said Mother and coughed.

Thayne nodded and shot me a sly wink.

Jay returned carrying a large piece of canvas nailed to a board. "I haven't had time to get a good frame for it," he said, presenting it to Mother. "I hope you like it."

Mother looked at the painting in her hands and drew a startled breath. Her eyes grew soft as she studied the canvas. "Lovely," she murmured. "It's perfectly lovely! And it's good!" she declared with enough surprise in her voice to make Jay smile. "It's very good! Angela come over here and look at this!"

I rose and moved behind her chair to look over her shoulder. In Mother's lap was a grassy hilltop, a tender sunrise and a girl sitting on a smooth gray boulder. Sharing the sunrise with the girl was a furry, fat ground squirrel.

My eyes sought Jay's in surprise and pleasure.

"The likeness is extraordinary," Mother continued, looking up at Jay with wonder and new respect. "And to think you did it from memory! Remarkable!"

"I'm glad you like it because it's yours," he said.

Mother stared, then recovered herself. "Oh no, I couldn't. It's beautiful, but—" She looked lovingly at the painting then stood up and offered it back to Jay.

"I want you to have it," he said. "Besides, since I'm marrying the original, I thought it might be nice for you to have a copy around the house."

Mother smiled, then reached up and kissed him on the cheek. "Thank you, son," she whispered.

240

The week that followed was filled with choice pages that will live forever in my book of memories: Mother in Levis on a horse . . . A picnic in the hills with Reed and Janet . . . Bert Tingey squirting Mother squarely in the face with a stream of milk as she watched the milking . . . Horseback rides at dawn . . . Evenings around the piano with Helen playing and John and Mother singing duets . . . And Jay, most of all.

Always before, our moments together had carried a tense undercurrent of disapproval from the Bradfords and that horrible, nerve-strangling fear that something might happen to him. The past had hung over our relationship like a dark cloud. Now the sun was in our eyes. For years, Jay and I had traveled narrow, solitary roads, loneliness marking the way. Now, we had each other making life's joys all the greater and its sorrows lighter. All the dreams in the world belonged to us. We were almost giddy in our happiness.

In those few days before the wedding, neighbors and friends dropped by the ranch bringing gifts and good wishes. The calico lady presented me with a pair of beautifully embroidered pillowcases; the polka-dot lady came by with six months supply of chokecherry jelly because she knew it was Jay's favorite. Bert Tingey gave us a big, old-fashioned rocker that we both knew he couldn't really afford. Helen added a big cast-iron Dutch oven to our store of gifts, along with a recipe for stew which was guaranteed to keep any man's stomach happy. Their simple gifts made Aunt Milderd's huge, sterling silver tray seem gaudy and overdone in comparison.

Mother was frantic that we wouldn't have any flowers, but the day before the wedding the living room was a veritable bower of blossom and fragrance, thanks to many thoughtful neighbors in town who had searched through their own gardens for late-blooming flowers and sent them out to the ranch in big, old-fashioned vases. My own bouquet was to be a simple sheaf of white roses.

On a bright, wind-blown Wyoming morning, I awoke with the realization that today I would become Jayhawk's wife. On such an incredible day as this, it seemed grossly inappropriate that I should have to do anything so commonplace as go downstairs and eat breakfast. But Mother insisted with a firm look and the dire words, "You'll need your strength—for later!"

Tadd, Stuart and David gave me a rousing chorus of "Here Comes the Bride!" as I entered the kitchen and Bert Tingey stopped spooning hot mush into his mouth to say appreciatively, "Seein' that sparkle in yer eyes almost makes me feel young again. No wonder that poor boy's in such a lather."

John and Thayne chuckled at this and I asked, "Where is Jay?"

"Out milkin' the cows," Thayne answered with a grin.

"On his wedding day?" Mother cried, aghast.

"Well, we had to think of something to keep him occupied," John explained. "I sort of thought the cows might calm him down some."

Bert chuckled and said with a shake of his tousled gray head, "I ain't never seen that black-haired buck so stirred up! Jest lookin' at him makes me nervous!"

Even a simple wedding in a ranchhouse must have its traditions and Mother, Helen and Janet saw to it that I was appropriately dressed in "something old, something new, something borrowed, something blue." Mother had given me a strand of pearls which had belonged to her mother and Helen loaned me a white lace handkerchief which she had carried on her own wedding day. Janet supplied the "something blue" in the form of a frilly satin garter.

Jay was waiting for me at the foot of the stairs, looking handsome and distinguished in a dark suit and tie, but somehow unfamiliar—until he smiled and took my hand.

We repeated our vows before a small gathering of family and friends in the ranchhouse where Wenona had given birth to a small, black-haired son some twenty-six years before.

The Thompson's were there, and the Tyler's. Even Parley Evans and his wife drove in from Lander to be present.

Mother remained serene and composed throughout the short cere-mony. It wasn't until I turned around to embrace her as Mrs. Jason Bradford that the tears began to flow. Suddenly, everyone was encircling us and I was kissed and hugged until I felt dizzy. Marsha sidled up to offer her red-eyed congratulations and Jay planted a hearty kiss on her pink lips. For a moment, I thought the girl was going to swoon to the floor. Amid the cheers and laughter, Larry Thompson said: "You shouldn't have done that, Jay! Now Marsha won't wash her face for a month!"

Helen served us a delightful luncheon complete with homemade wed-ding cake. Afterwards, the guests lingered, telling jokes and stories that must have been told at hundreds of weddings before ours. When Jay took my hand with a meaningful look, I gave him an answering smile and went upstairs to change. Mother insisted on helping me as I exchanged my white wedding finery for the practicality of blouse and slacks, and packed some last minute items.

"It doesn't seem decent somehow, your not having a nice going away suit," she sighed.

"But Mother, you know we're driving straight up to Jackson."

"I know. But at least toss your bouquet to the girls. Keep up a few of the old traditions for your poor old Mother's sake."

I smiled and hugged her. Dear, sensible, practical Mother still loved the sentimental traditions in spite of herself.

Janet and Marsha were the only girls eligible to catch the bridal bouquet and when I tossed it over the stairs, Marsha made a frantic dive in front of her cousin. Somehow, she managed to trip over her own two feet and dump the roses right in Bert Tingey's arms.

"Bert's the next one to be married!" David and Tadd chanted as the old man stood with crimson cheeks, clutching the roses.

"Oh, no I ain't!" he retorted and presented the bouquet to Janet.

Jay made his way through the crowd and said, "Ready to go, Mrs. Bradford?"

I took his arm and floated out of the house, stopping only to kiss Mother and Helen goodbye.

We made our exit through torrents of rice tossed out an upstairs window by Marsha and Janet. I gave a startled gasp which ended in a laugh when I saw Jay's Bronco. Toothpaste garnished the windshield and windows in lavish curliques. Pink toilet paper bows were attached to the door handles and headlights. A noisy assortment of tin cans dangled from the back bumper and a pair of white jockey shorts was flying high in the breeze from the antenna.

Jay calmly helped me inside, made a gallant bow to the laughing throng assembled on the back porch and we drove away. We made a necessary stop down in the gulley to clean up the Bronco. The toilet paper came in handy to wipe off the toothpaste. The tin cans were easily discarded. Jay decorated a nearby bush with the shorts and we were off.

We made excellent time to Jackson. There was no standing in fields of wildflowers or stopping to look at antelope on this trip. In fact, I was scarcely aware of the scenery until Jay turned off the main highway a few miles out of Jackson and took a dirt road which zig-zagged in switch-back fashion up into high timber. Soon we were lost in the silent green of pine forests laced with aspen.

The cabin was located in a secluded clearing. It was small and built mostly of rough pine with a natural rock fireplace climbing up one side. Wildflowers bloomed around the doorway and the tawny gold of a late afternoon sun was reflected in the small windows.

"It looks as if it grew here rather than being built," I said, taking in every detail with delight.

"Except that it has a few modern conveniences that don't grow in forests—like indoor plumbing," Jay said with a teasing smile.

It didn't take long to unpack and put our nest in order as Jay had come up earlier in the week to clean and air out the cabin. I sat down on the bed. Jay was right. The bedsprings did squeak—and suddenly, I felt very much like a nervous bride.

Jay looked at me and smiled. "Why don't we take our supper ouside? I know just the place."

Behind the cabin was a dense grove of evergreens. As we entered, a golden shaft of light was streaming through the sweeping arch made by two pine trees. A pair of black and white butterflies pirhouetted through the amber haze. Forest birds sang their sweet, wild songs in branches high above and somewhere below us, a brook was laughing to itself.

Jay spread the blanket on the ground and lay down full-length upon it, locking his hands behind his head. I sat down on the edge of the blanket and rummaged through the picnic basket. Inside were soft rolls, cheese, hard-boiled eggs and some of our wedding cake. I picked up the hard-boiled eggs, seriously wondering if I would be able to eat a thing. Without noticeably turning my head, I let my eyes roam over my husband's long, muscular body and realized that most of my nervousness had gone. Anticipation, sweet and sensual, was surging through me now.

Jay looked at me and asked in a tone that was one shade too casual, "Are you very hungry?"

I moistened my lips and smiled at him. "No. Not very."

His earth-colored eyes reached deep into my soul and read every trembling thought. We both knew the time was now. I put the hard-boiled eggs back into the basket and Jay drew me down onto the blanket beside him.

The winds purred softly in the pines. The forest birds grew still, and the mountains bore silent witness to our love.